Date with Death

Julia Chapman

DATE WITH DEATH

Minotaur Books
New York

DATE WITH DEATH. Copyright © 2017 by Julia Chapman. All rights reserved. Printed in the United States of America. For information, address St. Martin's Press, 175 Fifth Avenue, New York, N.Y. 10010.

www.minotaurbooks.com

The Library of Congress Cataloging-in-Publication Data is available upon request.

ISBN 978-1-250-10936-1 (hardcover)
ISBN 978-1-250-10937-8 (e-book)

Our books may be purchased in bulk for promotional, educational, or business use. Please contact your local bookseller or the Macmillan Corporate and Premium Sales Department at 1-800-221-7945, extension 5442, or by e-mail at MacmillanSpecialMarkets@macmillan.com.

First published in Great Britain by Pan Books, an imprint of Pan Macmillan

First U.S. Edition: April 2017

10 9 8 7 6 5 4 3 2 1

For Isabel

In your 90th year, a slice of the Dales just for you.

Date with Death

Prologue

Mist. Fog. Or even brume. Dense cloud lapping at the muted glow of the station lamp; twin tracks emerging suddenly from the murk, the edge of the platform softening into nothing. It was too far inland to be a haar or a fret. But however it was labelled, it made the dark, early-morning hour redolent of death.

Richard Hargreaves, alone in this cold, shadowy world, stamped his feet, the sound smothered by the dampening shroud, and lamented the paucity of words to describe this recurrent feature of autumn in the Dales. Unlike the Inuit in the frozen north with their wealth of terminology for snow, the locals here had very few ways of representing these dark, damp, drizzly days.

Fog, then. It was too thick for mist, visibility almost zero, and gave no hint of being burned off, should the sun ever rise above the hills to penetrate the low-lying vapour mass. He pulled his scarf tighter against his chilled neck, thrust his hands in the pockets of his overcoat and smiled into the gloom.

Last day of the week. Two days without having to get up to catch the six-thirty train. And this evening with *her*. There was a lot to look forward to, despite the dreary weather.

He had no idea how wrong he was.

To his right, the flare of an approaching light bled into the blanket of grey. Richard Hargreaves, for the last time in his life, hunched his shoulders, shoved his hands further in his pockets, and stepped towards the edge of the platform.

When the blow struck him in the back, he had no means of defence. No means of stopping himself falling.

1

How was it possible to love somewhere and hate somewhere at the same time?

Not sure there was an answer, the motorcyclist pulled over at the top of Gunnerstang Brow, turned off his bike, took off his helmet and stared down at the slate roofs that cluttered the dale below. Mid-afternoon with the October sun hanging low, the sheer limestone cliff that formed the backdrop of the town was ablaze, casting its reflected light on the houses and streets of a place he hadn't been near in fourteen years.

Bruncliffe.

A squat collection of dwellings, cut through by a river and a train line and hemmed in by the abrupt rise of the fells on three sides, it nestled confidently on the valley floor as it had done for centuries, bookended by the tall chimneys of long-disused mills. Despite its isolation, its inhabitants believed themselves to be at the centre of the universe. Arrogant. Forthright. Quick to highlight faults. A lot slower to praise. And wary of offcumdens – outsiders. Like him. Born and raised there, but never local.

He pulled his gaze away from the buildings, let it rove over the green hills, the distinctive stone walls marching up and down their steep sides, the swell and fall of land that stretched into the distance. The indignant squawk of a pheasant scratched at the silence, followed by the pleading bleat of a sheep.

It was a long way from London and the life he'd been leading. Which was why he'd returned.

Refocusing on the town, he followed the route the river took, cascading from the north; and there, off to the south and a white blur against the green, he saw Ellershaw Farm, the Metcalfes' place. Sheltered by the hills, yet with an open prospect, it had always been well maintained. Pristine. But then it hadn't been run by a drunkard.

Instinctively, his attention swung back up the dale, past the jumble of housing, out the back of the town to the cleft of two hills where the sun no longer lingered. And the wry smile that had settled on his bruised face dissolved into a frown.

Home. The only one he had right now. Otherwise he wouldn't be here, up on this hill, filled with this feeling of aversion and longing.

Elaine Bullock could do many things. She could name every flower that flourished in Hawber Woods. All the trees, too. She could identify a bird from the first few notes of its song. She could also talk for hours about the clints and grikes that patterned the limestone pavement which defined the local landscape. What she couldn't do, however, was waitress.

'Bugger!' she muttered as the stack of plates she was carrying back to the kitchen gave a sudden wobble, sending a knife clattering to the stone-flagged floor. It was closely followed by its sibling, a fork.

'Are you planning on dropping the lot, Elaine?'

demanded the taller of the two elderly ladies standing by the counter, both of them dressed in black. She indicated her companion with her walking stick. 'It's just that my sister's heart's not what it was, and she might appreciate a bit of notice. Isn't that right, Clarissa?'

'Leave her be, Edith,' came a soft rebuke from her sister. 'She's learning, bless her.'

'I'm trying,' said Elaine, stooping to retrieve the way-ward cutlery, finger-smudged glasses slipping down her nose and dark plaits swinging against her cheeks.

'You can say that again! Two days in and you're trying my patience.' Arms folded and stretching a white apron across an impressive paunch, shoulders almost touching the sides of the kitchen doorway, Titch Harrison glared down at her. 'When you've finished scrabbling around on the floor, there's two plates as need serving. And be quick about it.'

He stood to one side, letting her slip past with a despairing shake of his head. Seconds later the loud crash of shattering crockery hailed from the kitchen, followed by muffled curses. Titch rolled his eyes.

'Just as well we're quiet,' he grumbled, glancing over at the table by the window, the couple of tourists seated at it his only customers. 'All the folk down at that funeral don't know what they're missing. Knife-throwing! Plate-smashing! That Bullock lass will be eating fire next! And she'd be a damn sight better at it than waiting tables because, heaven knows, she couldn't be worse.'

'Give her a chance, Douglas,' admonished Edith Hird, former headmistress of Bruncliffe Primary School and the only person in town who insisted on using the chef's given name, her reluctance to adopt his ridiculous nickname stemming from both her memory of him in her class-room and the fact that she'd known him since he'd been in nappies. Sizeable nappies they'd been, too. 'She's young and she's a hard worker.'

'She'll bloody need to be, with the amount of extra work she creates,' he muttered, a faint flush spilling up his cheeks from his ginger beard. Thirty years on from primary school, and still Miss Hird's sharp tongue could return him to his mumbling youth. Then the severity of her attire reminded him of the occasion. 'How'd it go?' he asked gently.

'As you'd expect,' said Edith. 'A full house and not a dry eye.'

'Such a shame,' murmured Clarissa. 'Such a young man.'

'Aye, a right shame. He was a good lad.' Titch stared at the floor, not given to eloquence at the best of times. In the present circumstances he was particularly struggling. 'Hope they'll do, anyhow,' he said, gesturing at the two trays of sandwiches on the counter. 'Tell Barbara it's all I could put together at short notice.'

Edith nodded. 'She'll be glad of them. She's panicking she's not got enough to feed all those that turned out. What do I owe you?'

'A tenner.'

'Don't be daft,' said Edith bluntly, opening her purse. 'You might not have been top of the class in maths, but even you knew your times tables. Now, what do I really owe you?'

Titch was saved from further castigation by the disbelieving tone of Miss Hird's sister as she raised a bony hand towards a figure visible through the window.

'Edith, is that . . . ? It can't be . . .'

Edith Hird turned to see what had captured Clarissa's attention, squinting across the road at the motorbike and the man sitting astride it. It should have been hard to tell, with the distance and her ageing eyesight. But she knew straight away, even with the mane of black hair that graced his shoulders. It was the defiant way he was staring down at the town, the familiar brooding intensity – which had grown into hostility as the years passed and he became branded as a renegade – accentuated by the livid bruising on his cheek. The motorbike was a giveaway, too. Everyone in Bruncliffe knew that bike.

As Titch and the two elderly sisters moved closer to the window to get a better view, Elaine Bullock was crossing the cafe to the only occupied table, her entire focus on the plates in her hands.

'Here you go. Home-made cottage pie and chips,' she announced cheerfully as she approached the waiting diners, relieved to have made it without any mishaps. Then she made the fatal mistake of glancing outside and her gaze was caught by the sight of the man on the motorbike. She only had time for a glimpse of his profile before he put his helmet on. It was enough.

'Oh my God!' she gasped, plates tilting in her hands to a precarious angle, everything sliding towards the edge. 'It's . . . that's . . .'

'Trouble,' said Titch, oblivious to the dripping plates. 'With a capital T.'

'I need to make a phone call,' said Elaine, hastily depositing the meals onto the now gravy-smeared table before hurrying over to the coat stand, grabbing her mobile from her jacket pocket and rushing towards the back door, leaving her customers bemused in her wake.

'Well,' said Edith, still transfixed by the man on the other side of the road, a smile growing on her face. 'Looks like life in Bruncliffe is about to get interesting.'

He slipped his helmet back on, turned the key in the ignition and, as the bike throbbed to life, cast a glance over his right shoulder to check the road. Instead he caught the hard stares of his audience.

'Damn!'

He'd been so focused on the town below, he hadn't registered the building that sat atop the hill. Or, rather, he'd registered it, but hadn't taken in the changes. Gunnersthwaite, the Harrisons' farm. A ramshackle place when he was growing up, a dumping ground for old cars and broken machinery, windows rotting in their frames. Clearly it had been renovated and put to a different use.

'Hill Top Cafe', proclaimed the sign, a blackboard by the door promising home-cooked food and locally sourced produce.

And in the window on the right he could see three faces, all of them staring back at him. Old Miss Hird, a smile dancing on her lips; her sister, Clarissa Ralph, hand across her mouth; and behind them, the broad features and ginger beard of Titch Harrison himself.

'Damn!' he reiterated, flipping his visor down with an

irritated flick. He should have known better. With all his training. All his years undercover. He should have been alert to the situation. To the presence of the enemy.

Now the whole town would know he was here before he'd even crossed the parish boundary.

He kicked the bike off its stand, revved the engine way more than was necessary and, in a roar of noise, tore down the hill towards his future. And his past.

At the bottom of the hill, near the heart of Bruncliffe, the throng that had been gathered in the sunlit churchyard was beginning to disperse. As it separated, some going to view the wreaths laid next to the newly dug grave, others approaching the bereaved family, a muted protest came from its midst.

'Can't even go to a funeral in peace!' muttered Delilah Metcalfe, trying to discreetly fish her vibrating mobile out of her trouser pocket. 'That's the third time in five minutes.'

'That's what you get for being a romance entrepreneur,' whispered the tall young man next to her.

He was rewarded with an elbow to his ribs, hard enough to make him wince and draw the attention of the elderly man standing the other side of him.

'Behave, Ash Metcalfe!' came a sharp hiss. 'And as for you, missy, don't even think of using that thing. Show some respect.' A gnarled finger pointed at the mobile now in Delilah's hand, and a pair of fierce eyes under bushy brows reproached her.

'I was just turning it off,' she murmured, face going pink as she slipped the phone back in her pocket. She did her best to ignore her brother, who was doing his best not to laugh.

Which was a nice change, as it hadn't been a laughter-filled day.

Delilah's morning had been spent dealing with a disgruntled client who, fresh from his farm, had stormed into the office of the Dales Dating Agency demanding his money back because he'd been on ten dates and still hadn't found a wife. As he'd stood there thumping her desk and ranting at her, making Tolpuddle growl quietly over in his basket on the floor, she'd found her diplomatic skills – and she wasn't blessed with an abundance – stretched until she could bite her lip no more.

'Have you ever thought, Mr Knowles,' she'd finally responded, when he started casting aspersions on her business and her ability to trade in romance, given her own hapless past, 'that your lack of success could be of your own making?'

'How do you mean?'

'I mean that your aversion to using a toothbrush and your insistence on wearing boots covered in cow-shit on a date are probably not helping your cause.'

He'd jerked back, glanced down at his offending boots, then his brows knitted together and a stern finger was thrust in her face. 'They'll take me as I am!' he'd declared. 'And be glad of it.'

Clearly, mused Delilah as she joined the long line of mourners beginning to walk towards the church gate, the women of the Dales felt differently. In the end, she'd offered the offended farmer a place on the next of the recently launched speed-dating nights – no charge, of course. The man had gone off with a broad smile, proud of his hard-driven bargain, leaving Delilah to only hope that he worked on his self-presentation skills before the next time she saw him.

That is, if she was still in business the next time she saw him. There was a stack of credit-card bills on her desk, her mortgage payments were due and her overdraft was already stretched beyond the agreed limits. Hardly surprising that the bank manager had called her in for a meeting. But she could have done without the funeral beforehand. Especially one which brought so many painful reminders.

She let her eyes steal across to the far corner of the churchyard where a granite headstone shone in the sunshine.

'You all right, sis?' Ash Metcalfe noted the direction of her gaze.

Delilah nodded, blinking rapidly. 'Fine. Just – you know – memories.'

'Humph!' came a sharp bark from beside her. 'Memories are highly overrated.' Seth Thistlethwaite, eyes fractionally less fierce than earlier, eyebrows just as bushy, took her elbow in a firm grip that belied his arthritis. Whether his hold was seeking support or offering it, Delilah didn't resist. 'I find the here and now to be far more enjoyable. But there's no denying this is a sad business. So young . . .' He shook his head in bemusement.

'Sad indeed,' replied Ash. 'I still can't believe that things had got that bad and no one knew.'

'Is it official then? Was it definitely suicide?' asked

Delilah as they paused at the church gate, the bright sunshine at odds with the melancholy topic of conversation.

Ash shrugged. 'The inquest won't take place for a while, but there seems to be no doubt.'

Mr Thistlethwaite gave another bark. 'Jumping in front of a train leaves little room for doubt.'

'But it still doesn't explain why, though,' said Delilah. 'I mean, he seemed to be finally getting his life back together after his divorce . . .' She faltered, struck, as she had been repeatedly since she heard the awful news, by her last impression of Richard Hargreaves. Having called into the office to renew his subscription after a three-month trial with the dating agency, he'd been full of talk about the future. He'd been like the Richard of old; the Richard before his life had unravelled.

When he'd moved back to Bruncliffe three years before, his cosmopolitan wife – far from finding the rural idyll she'd fantasised about – had quickly become isolated, exasperated by the realities of country living where everyone knew her business, and uncomfortable with the forthright opinions of the people her husband had been raised amongst. A place where, rather than having the status of a university lecturer's wife, she was viewed as the woman who'd married the butcher's son. An offcumden, to boot.

Within six months she'd filed for divorce. Within another few she was gone, back to Manchester, taking their two young children with her and leaving Richard shell-shocked in her wake.

The man who'd sat across the desk from Delilah several

weeks ago, happily rubbing Tolpuddle's head while catching up on local affairs, had been a different person. He'd reminded her of the young boy who'd spent many days at the Metcalfe farm, larking around with her brothers. There'd been no hint of depression. No sign of despair. And definitely no inkling that a week later he'd throw himself under a train.

Delilah shivered, her skin rippling cold as though the sun had dipped behind a cloud.

'Aye,' concluded Seth Thistlethwaite. 'A right sad state of affairs. There's something to be said for not letting things get on top of you, eh, Delilah?' He released her from his grip, eyes still holding her in place. 'There's more to life than business, you know.'

His words coaxed a laugh out of the young woman, lightening the atmosphere. 'Let's see if I agree with you once I've been to the bank.'

He nodded. 'You'll find me in the Fleece if you want to drown your sorrows. You joining me, Ash?'

Delilah's brother shrugged. 'Why not? The best part of the day is over, and it would be only fitting to toast Richard. I've just got to speak to Rick. I'll catch you up.'

With a quick kiss on the cheek for Delilah, Ash passed through the crowd of mourners gathered on the footpath, heading towards a group of men standing to one side. Seth Thistlethwaite watched him go.

'Surprised he's not bawling with grief, yon Rick Procter,' he muttered, eyes on the well-built man Ash was now talking to.

'Rick? I don't think he knew Richard that well,' said

Delilah. 'Not since school, and even then, Rick was a few years older.'

Seth gave another curt laugh. 'No doubt you're right,' he said. 'But he's just lost a sale on a new house. And that's about the only thing as would make that man cry.'

'A sale . . . ?'

'Richard Hargreaves. He was talking about buying one of them blasted boxes Procter's built down on the flood plain. Won't be going through now, though. Can't say as I'm upset for Procter.'

Delilah smiled at the gruff verdict. 'Honestly, you and your gossip. I don't know how you find all this out. As for Rick, he's a good man. Look at all he does for the town.'

The glare that fastened on her had none of the twinkle of moments before. 'Good deeds don't necessarily make for a good heart. Right, I'm off for a pint.' He turned to go and then twisted back to face her. 'You getting out running again, young lady?'

She shifted her gaze to the pavement. 'I gave it up, remember?'

Seth Thistlethwaite grinned. 'Of course you did. Stupid of me . . . Anyway, good luck with Woolly at the bank. Don't let him give you a hard time.'

With a wave of a hand, he walked off, leaving Delilah to cross the road. She needed a fortifying cup of coffee before she faced the worst. As she headed towards Peaks Patisserie, thoughts already on the meeting to come, she was ignorant of two things: her mobile phone, still switched off, now held five frantic messages; and there was a very distinctive motorbike coming under the railway bridge towards the church.

On the other side of the road, Seth Thistlethwaite, retired geography teacher and athletics coach, had paused to watch his former pupil. She was lying about the running. He'd seen her, up on the fells in the early hours. While his eyesight wasn't what it had once been, he'd know her distinctive style anywhere. It was impossible to forget the best athlete that had ever been through his hands. And that grey shadow of a dog striding alongside her.

It had to be a good thing. It must mean she was getting over the worst.

He was still watching her when he heard the motorbike approaching, the engine more of a purr than a roar. Coming along the main road, under the bridge, the rider in black leathers, dark visor. He knew it straight away. A Royal Enfield. Scarlet. There'd only ever been one of them round here and now it was back.

He was back.

The old man glanced across at Delilah as she headed towards the marketplace. Did she know? She would soon – the bush telegraph would see to that.

Returning his attention to the bike, Seth watched it pass the church, continue along the main road and then, as expected, it turned left before it reached the open square in the centre of town. He was heading home. Although what he'd find when he got there . . .

Seth Thistlethwaite started walking faster. Things in Bruncliffe had just taken an unexpected twist and, for a man of his advanced years, he had need of a pint to make sense of it before all hell broke loose.

'How was it?'

Sitting on a sofa by the window of Peaks Patisserie, looking out over the marketplace and wishing she was miles away, Delilah glanced up as her sister-in-law placed a coffee in front of her. 'Awful. Packed, as you'd expect.'

'Did you make my apologies? I've been flat out in here, and besides . . . I just couldn't face it.'

Delilah placed a hand on Lucy Metcalfe's arm, noting the strained expression beneath the dark-blonde hair, and gave a gentle squeeze. 'I spoke to the Hargreaveses. They understood.'

A smile flitted across the other woman's pale features. 'Thanks.' She looked down at the papers fanned out on the table. 'Rather you than me,' she said, gesturing at the spreadsheets and accounts. 'What time is your meeting?'

'In half an hour.' Delilah grimaced as she scooped a layer of froth off her coffee with a spoon. 'I'm not feeling confident.'

'Huh! You should be. Look . . .' Lucy took the copy of the *Craven Herald* from the rack of newspapers inside the door and began to flick through the pages, before folding the paper back and passing it to Delilah. 'Here. Take this with you and show old Woolly that you're famous.'

Staring up from the page was a far-from-flattering photo of Delilah, next to an article about the speed-dating events.

Delilah groaned.

'It's not that bad. Anyway, you can put me down for

the date night in November,' said Lucy with a shy grin. 'Can't believe how much I enjoyed the last one, considering . . .' She glanced over at the photo of a young man in military uniform hanging above the counter, a black ribbon decorating the edges of the frame, then back at her sister-in-law. 'Thanks, Dee, for pushing me to take part.'

Delilah shrugged off the gratitude in true Bruncliffe fashion. 'I was only making up numbers.'

'You won't need to for the next one,' said Lucy, laughing as she pointed at the paper. 'Good luck at the bank. Call in and let me know how it went if you have time.' She squeezed her sister-in-law's shoulder and then hurried back to the till where a queue of people had formed.

Delilah turned her attention to the article and the awful picture that made her look like a rabbit caught in the headlights. Still, as long as that didn't deter customers, it was all publicity and perhaps it would bring people to the website.

She let her eyes drift over the text once more. And then down to the small item below. She wasn't aware of dropping her spoon, white foam soaking into the print. She didn't notice her body tense, the sharp intake of breath that caused Lucy to glance over in concern. She noticed nothing but the two paragraphs.

A local hiker found dead in the depths of Gordale Scar, his body only discovered when his family alerted the emergency services about his disappearance. Knowing the treacherous terrain in that area, which saw countless accidents every year, the news of itself didn't shock Delilah. But the name of the hiker . . . Martin Foster. The very same name that had registered with the Dales Dating Agency a month ago.

Two of her clients dead in the space of a week. A co-incidence? Probably. Even so, it was with trembling fingers that she tore out the article and slipped it into her pocket.

2

While the afternoon sun shone down on Bruncliffe, lighting up the imposing Victorian town hall with its front-facing gables and mullioned windows, and turning the glass of the estate agent's, the bank and the newly refurbished bakery into a blinding brilliance, towards the back of the marketplace, on a narrow road that led up to the fells, the autumn light had already faded. Low-slung in the sky and unable to reach over the three-storey stone buildings that lined this tapering street, the sun had left long shadows in its place: shadows which reached across from one side to the other, casting into shade the hairdresser's with its sign bearing a sheep and a pair of clippers beneath the words 'Shear Good Looks'; and the slim building next door with 'To Let' plastered across the ground-floor window. Likewise, the stones of the pub opposite – the oldest pub in Bruncliffe and the smallest – were unlit by the warming sun. Hunkered down on this neglected byway that had once been the thoroughfare for the town, lacking hanging baskets of late blooms, windows bare and without a single advertising board outside, on that afternoon the ancient hostelry seemed as surly and ill-humoured as the man who ran it.

'How was it?' A pint of Black Sheep thumped onto the bar, a meaty hand held out as the question was posed.

'Grim. It's not right burying a young man like that.' Seth shook his head and fished in his pocket for coins, unwilling to give the landlord of the Fleece a penny more than was due. It wasn't solely on account of his pub's name that Roger Murgatroyd was surreptitiously known as Fleecer; the man's reputation for being slow to return change making the nickname more than apt. Being of wide girth and a short temper, however, he was unlikely ever to become acquainted with this epithet. Instead, he was more commonly hailed as Troy.

'Surprised there's not been more of it,' came the gloomy response from Troy, as his fat fist closed over the proffered money. 'With the way the economy's been going.' He nodded towards the windows on either side of the door, through which could be seen the premises next to the hairdresser's. 'From what I hear, it won't be long until that's closing up for good.'

Seth took a sip of beer, refusing to be drawn, and acknowledged to himself that, despite the truculent nature of its host, the Fleece always guaranteed a good pint.

'I mean, a dating agency, for Christ's sake. Thought Delilah would have known better, being raised in these parts.' Troy continued to glare at the building, the first floor of which housed the offending business. 'It's like that rabbit-food shop on the high street, or that fancy cafe the Metcalfe widow opened. It won't be long before they're closing their doors, too, because there's no place for the likes of them around here.'

Seth took another sip and declined to enlighten the man on the other side of the bar that, actually, the organic food store was in talks to move to a bigger place and Lucy

Metcalfe's Peaks Patisserie had just taken on two more members of staff. He simply drank his beer and allowed Troy the floor – the same tactics he'd deployed for decades to gather information.

'Dating agency! Pah!' Troy turned to the old man. 'Would you use one?'

'Nope.'

'Do you know anyone round here that would?'

'I can think of one or two that should,' Seth replied, with a cackle.

'Well, you wouldn't catch me setting foot in the place,' said Troy.

Seth raised his glass once more, because there was no reply to be made. After all, it was well known throughout the dale that the landlord of the Fleece was only married thanks to the freakishly hot summer of 1995.

With the sun shining down from clear blue skies that year, the residents of Bruncliffe had basked in the unnaturally good weather, none more so than confirmed bachelor Roger Murgatroyd, recently appointed landlord of the Fleece on his father's retirement and a man whose moods were closely tied to meteorological conditions – commonly agreed to be the reason he was still single. It was into these rare circumstances that the young Kay Hartley had unwittingly stepped.

Over from Skipton on a day out, she'd been in a party of girls who, finding themselves on the back road of Bruncliffe, had entered the Fleece. Being first through the door, Kay had been momentarily blinded in the sudden gloom and as her focus struggled to readjust, she'd become aware of the vibrant personality behind the bar. Troy's head was thrown back in laughter, a rich peal of enjoyment issuing forth. She hadn't stood a chance.

She'd come back the following weekend. The weekend after that, with the heatwave still holding firm, Troy – high on sunshine and something he presumed was love – had recklessly proposed. Kay had accepted. And a month later, on her wedding day, the skies clouded over, the rain arrived, and her groom retreated back into his normal sulk, his cheerful alter ego only emerging whenever the sun turned the Fleece golden and the mercury climbed the thermometer. Which, in Bruncliffe, was not as often as you might think.

Twenty years on, Kay Murgatroyd had never complained about how the Fates conspired against her. Instead, to the amazement of the locals, she'd stayed in the town and in her marriage, a regular feature behind the bar and a genius in the kitchen. And, if truth be told, it was her influence on the pub that kept the regulars coming, even when Troy refused to yield to pressure from competition and revamp the faded interior, its two rooms decorated with floral carpet and brass-laden walls.

The slam of a van door and the clatter of ladders caused Seth to turn from his contemplation of the pub's decor.

'What's he parked there for?' muttered Troy, scowling at the vehicle outside the window. 'He's blocking the light.'

They watched, with the curiosity common to people in small towns when witnessing something out of routine, as the driver carried his ladders across the road, propped them against the glass front of the building opposite and then returned to his van.

'Window cleaner?' suggested Troy.

Seth shook his head. Knowing the perilous state of Delilah Metcalfe's finances, he doubted she'd be spending good money on something she was able to do herself. Plus, if she was going to have the windows cleaned, she'd use her cousin's husband's brother, who had a thriving business nipping up and down ladders with a wet sponge. Although, having experienced the man's efforts, Seth rather suspected he'd done his training on a ship: nice clean circles and not one corner touched. So perhaps Delilah had called in an outsider after all. Because that's what the man leaning into the white van was.

'Afternoon!' Rick Procter's voice rang out from the doorway and a large group of sombrely clad people from the funeral followed him into the pub, Ash Metcalfe and his oldest brother Will amongst them, as well as the stocky figure of Harry Furness, the livestock auctioneer. 'First round's on me, in memory of Richard.'

A crowd of bodies made for the bar, blocking Seth's view out of the window. Pint in hand, he got up and wandered over to the door.

'What's up, Seth? Do we smell or something?' called out Rick.

'He's being nosy,' said Troy, tipping his head towards the activity outside as he started pulling pints. 'Know anything about it, Will?'

'New tenant,' came the succinct reply.

'What kind of business?' asked Rick, watching, along with everyone else, the man climbing the ladder across the road.

Will shrugged, the taciturn farmer never one to talk

much, especially about family concerns. 'Delilah didn't say.'

'I don't think she knows,' volunteered his younger brother. 'It's all been a bit rushed. Someone contacted Taylor's two days ago and agreed a lease for some kind of office set-up. Not sure what, though.'

'We're about to find out,' said Seth, as the man they were all staring at began fixing letters to the glass in front of him.

It didn't take long. Three simple initials in gold, neatly spaced across the window. Three simple initials which, as the sign-maker came down the ladder and gave the onlookers a clear view of his handiwork, set the pub abuzz.

'Christ!' muttered Ash, looking from the ground floor to the floor above and then back again.

'Wait till Delilah sees this,' said Rick over the raised voices filling the room.

Seth drank the last of his pint and headed back for another. Not because he was thirsty. But because this was turning out to be a day filled with trouble, and one beer simply wouldn't do.

It hadn't taken long to leave Bruncliffe behind, the houses giving way to fields and then to the steep valley sides. He'd followed the road as it turned between the hills, the sun sliding from his back as he entered the darker dale of Thorpdale where, before long, the tarmac ended, a rough track taking its place, making the Royal Enfield judder and bounce beneath him.

He slowed down, not wanting to wreck the bike as he negotiated around the holes pitting the lane, deep enough to cause damage, no attempt having been made to fill them. It was worse than he remembered. Either they'd had a run of hard winters or no one was taking care of it any more.

One look at the land alongside suggested it wasn't just the track that had been neglected. Fields unkempt, not a sheep to be seen. Gates hanging from broken hinges, the stone walls that criss-crossed the land crumbling in places. It didn't give the impression of a prosperous farm. But then it hadn't been doing well when he'd left, foot-and-mouth seeing to that. Even so, he hadn't expected this.

He eased to a halt, engine idling, and stared up the length of the dale, a small house visible in the distance on a spur of land, two streams running either side. Behind it, the towering mass of the fell looming over it all.

Twistleton Farm.

With a sense of foreboding, he turned the throttle and headed for home.

Back in Bruncliffe, in an austere room overlooking the marketplace as befitted a man of prudence, Delilah Metcalfe was equally apprehensive.

'Delilah, dear,' the man behind the desk said, twisting his computer screen to face her. 'The figures don't lie. You're badly overdrawn, you're trying to handle two mortgages, and the money simply isn't coming in. As your bank manager, and a friend of your father's, I'm deeply concerned. Something is going to have to give.'

'You don't seem to understand,' she said, trying to bridle her frustration as she pushed her carefully prepared documents across the desk towards him. 'It's an internet start-up. Of course it's not going to make money straight away. But these figures prove it's growing.'

'All they prove is that there are a lot of lonely people in the Dales,' he said with a sigh. 'However, I'm not convinced that providing a dating agency for them is a viable way to make a living. Or run a business. So far you don't seem to be reassuring me.' He tapped the papers in front of him. 'The Dales Dating Agency is entering its third year and you've yet to make a profit. In fact, it's swallowing what little money you manage to eke out of the website design business. If you keep going at this rate, neither enterprise will survive. Nor, young lady, will your house.'

Delilah lowered her gaze, a familiar panic clawing at her stomach. Debt. So much of it. It wasn't what she'd envisioned when, newly married and deeply in love, she'd established a business with her husband. They'd timed it well. The internet was expanding rapidly, broadband allowing for larger and more elaborate websites, which were becoming essential for commerce. And Delilah, with her talent for coding, her passion for IT and several years in the industry, was perfectly poised to make the most of it. Add in a partner with a background in graphic design, and the future looked bright for Bruncliffe's first website development company.

It had been. They'd built up a solid client base and a great reputation. Then things had begun to fall apart. In the short space of a couple of years her brother Ryan had been killed in action, the business had been run into the ground by her husband while she was caught in the grip of grief and, finally, her marriage had collapsed, ironically just as she was getting the dating agency off the ground.

Delilah had been stubborn at the end, refusing to accept that it was best to close the two companies she'd set up with her husband and walk away, just as he was doing from their relationship. But the thought of failing in both love and commerce had galled her. Equally, the idea of giving the town even more to talk about had filled her with horror. So she'd taken on the house with the mortgage and the business premises, requiring yet more outlay. She'd had the web design service and the Dales Dating Agency transferred to her name. And she'd been slowly heading for insolvency ever since.

She stood to lose it all if she didn't turn things around. Or, as the man across the desk was suggesting, cut her losses and focus on the venture that was more profitable. But something held her back. Some of it was pride – the fact that the dating agency had been her idea, established in the dark months before her marriage broke down, and her sole focus as her life fell apart. Yet underneath all that, she was convinced it would work, no matter what the locals said. Or the man opposite.

'I know it doesn't look good,' she said, indicating the spreadsheet, which depicted a failing business in brutal rows and columns. 'But some of it can be explained by the fact that I've introduced speed-dating sessions. It's taken a bit of outlay to get them off the ground, but they're becoming really popular and now I've even got people coming from as far as Reeth and Leyburn to take part. I've also got quite a few commissions for website designs coming in and I've rented out the ground-floor office, starting today. All I need is a little more time . . .'

Norman Woolerton ran a hand across his balding head and sat back to take in the words he'd heard on countless occasions in this small office, with its view across the heart of Bruncliffe. That's what they always thought, the failing entrepreneurs protesting that their product simply had to find the right niche; the farmers pinning everything on the next lambing season; the business start-ups willing to throw good money after bad. In his forty-plus years working in the only remaining bank in town, and even more so since the crash, he'd seen them all. And had to keep seeing them around the town for years afterwards, as they tried to reconstruct their lives post-bankruptcy. He was loath to let Ted Metcalfe's daughter follow the same path – not after what the family had suffered in the last few years. On a more personal note, his wife was Ted's cousin and he'd never hear the end of it if he let a relative slide into financial ruin.

But . . . recently there had been a lot of 'buts'. The blasted internet was the cause. While Norman could judge a traditional business by running an eye over the accounts, he'd found that his instincts, honed after years of living in the same place and understanding intricately the world of commerce in Bruncliffe and its surroundings, were less sure when it came to the internet. It opened up the world of trade beyond the fells and dales which he knew so well. And as for this business in particular . . .

A dating agency. The town had been alight with speculation when it was announced. The sceptics had dismissed it as another gimmick from a woman who couldn't settle down. The pragmatists had pointed to an internet already swollen with websites aimed at singles. While the more malicious had poked fun at the idea of Delilah Metcalfe being an advisor on love.

The least likely person to be accused of being a romantic, she had a head filled with computer code, an outspoken manner as a result of being the youngest child with five older brothers, a painful disregard for sentimentality, and a right-hook that her oldest brother, Will, had passed on from his short-lived boxing career. But maybe she also had a head for business.

The bank manager picked up the papers she'd produced for him and glanced at the numbers again. Sensing him wavering, Delilah leaned forward.

'I can do this, Uncle Woolly,' she said, her childhood name for the banker slipping out unchecked in her desperation to get his approval. 'The website was set up specifically for farmers, but word has got out and I'm getting people from all over the Dales. People who have lived here all their lives but haven't had a chance to meet someone. Or have, and it ended badly and now they want to try again. It's aimed at Dales folk. People like me. I know them. And this business is made for them. It will succeed. If you could just see to—'

He cut her off with a nod of his head. 'Six months. I'll allow you an extension on your overdraft for a further six months. But if in that time the business doesn't show considerable improvement, then I'm sorry, but I'll have to take the steps neither of us wants to happen.'

She was around the big oak desk, which had been his bulwark against the borrowers of Bruncliffe for almost half a century, and a kiss was planted on his whiskered cheek before he could protest.

'Thanks. You won't regret this, I promise!'

'Make sure I don't,' said the bank manager gruffly as he straightened his tie and fidgeted with the keyboard in front of him. 'Now get on with you. I've got another meeting to get to.'

Delilah gathered up her papers and was out of the door before he could change his mind. But her euphoria was short-lived. As she headed for home up the hill at the back of the town hall, she experienced a swell of trepidation for her future. She wasn't to know that trouble was about to arrive from the past.

Derelict and abandoned. Scraps of machinery littering the yard. Slates slipped on the roof, paint peeling off the windows, a couple of broken panes. The chicken coop they'd made the year before she died nothing more than a jumble of rotting planks. And, encroaching on it all, the steep sides of the fells, plunging the small farmhouse into early shadow.

He pulled off his helmet, dumped it next to his rucksack on the ground and approached the back porch, heart pounding in his chest. The last time he'd been here, things hadn't gone so well.

'Dad?' He knocked and pushed at the same time, the door squeaking open to his touch, and he stepped into the kitchen. 'Dad? You home?'

Stupid question. Where else would the old man be?

It took a few seconds for the smell to reach him. Mildew with a tinge of something else. Booze? A bark of laughter escaped his dry throat and he glanced around, taking in the bottles that covered the small worktop. The crushed empty cans on the table. And the sink. Full of pans and dishes, thick mould flourishing across them.

It was bad. Worse than he'd anticipated.

'Dad?' he called again, the word coming back to him in an echo typical of an empty house as he stuck his head into the front room.

Cobwebs and a thick layer of dust on every surface. His father's chair, sagging and worn, cigarette burns dotting the arms. The colourful rag rug, where she used to curl up with him next to the fire in the winter, the big book of bible stories a heavy weight across her lap. The rug was falling apart, the fabric frayed, bald patches where his father's feet had rested. He crossed to the dresser, pulled open the cupboards to reveal bare shelves where once the best china had been stacked. Likewise, the drawer which had been filled with Sheffield's finest cutlery was empty, the felt tatty and blotched with age and covered in a scattering of mouse droppings.

It was the same as when he'd left. Just dirtier.

He turned to go and noticed the space on the mantelpiece. Her photo. Gone.

'Dad? You here?' he asked with less certainty as he headed for the stairs. He took them two at a time, nervous of what he'd find.

Empty rooms. His own, smaller than he remembered. A musty duvet spread across the single bed, its faded pattern one he recognised. Nothing on the walls. He'd had no idols by then. Nothing to be proud of. A small collection of paperbacks. Crime mostly, which was ironic. And the rough-hewn desk he'd made in woodworking classes and had never used, academic study not fitting into his life on the farm.

Chest constricting as the past crowded in on him, he gave a cursory glance through the open door of the bathroom, recoiling at the smell of collapsed drains, and entered the front bedroom. Bed unmade, a tangle of sheets and bedspread on the bare mattress. The wardrobe hanging open, half of it empty, hangers strewn across the floor. The other half still filled with her clothes. A couple of dresses. Blouses. A hat on the top shelf he could never remember her wearing. He reached out to let his fingers trail across the fabrics, pulling them back hastily at the damp they encountered.

What the hell?

It had never been this bad.

A creak from below; the back door.

In two quick strides he was across the room and heading down the stairs, angry. As angry as the day he'd left fourteen years ago.

'Dad!' he shouted. 'What's going on—?'

A cold touch of metal on his chin pulled him up short on the bottom step. Just like the day he'd left, he was staring down the double barrel of a shotgun.

3

Four o'clock on the dot. Not a moment sooner. The tight bugger had made her hang around and fold napkins while the anxiety gnawed a hole in her stomach and Delilah's phone remained unanswered. If she hadn't needed the job, Elaine Bullock would have told Titch where to stuff it. But her part-time hours as a lecturer in geology weren't enough to cover her living expenses and the field trips so essential to her work. Iceland last year. The Vosges Mountains the year before. And, if she got the money together, Monument Valley next September. So she'd bitten her tongue, got on with her work, and kept an eye on the clock. When the little hand reached the four, she'd flung down her apron and fled.

Grabbing her bike from behind the cafe, she slipped her bag across her chest and started cycling. Downhill all the way to town and she wasn't going to touch the brakes once. This was an emergency, after all.

'Easy!' His hands rose into the air, the shotgun unwavering as it pressed against him. 'It's me.'

A middle-aged man, eyes focused with a strange intensity, George Capstick hadn't changed much. Although it was the first time he'd turned a gun on a neighbour.

'It's me, George.'

'You're back.' Not a question. A statement. No surprise, either, because George didn't like surprises.

'I'm back.' Still the gun remained prodding the soft underneath of his chin.

George blinked slowly. Processing, that's what Dad had called it. A lot of locals had a meaner way to describe it. 'That's your dad's motorbike out there.'

He nodded, no stranger to the odd slide of conversation. 'He gave it to me.'

A shake of the head. 'You stole it. 1960 Royal Enfield Bullet 500. It's your dad's.'

He didn't argue. Wasn't inclined to, when the weapon was still pointing at him. 'I brought it back. So do you think you could lower the gun?'

Another slow blink. 'Can't. You're trespassing.'

It was his turn to blink. 'Trespassing? This is my home, George. Remember? Me and Dad live here.'

George shook his head once more, the pressure on the gun intensifying. 'Not your home any more. It's Mr Procter's home. And he pays me to guard it.'

'Rick Procter? You mean . . . ?' He looked around. Empty. Not just for the day, but vacated. 'He owns the farm? Since when?'

George shrugged and stepped back, lowering the gun. 'Sorry. You need to talk to your dad.'

Anger shimmered through his veins. 'I intend to. Once you tell me where I can find him.'

Down past the church, whipping past a turning car and bunny-hopping up onto the pavement, provoking disgruntled responses from a couple of pedestrians. She left the bike against the handrail, ran up the three steps into the cafe and collided straight into something solid.

'Watch out!' The stonemason, Rob Harrison, no less well built than his brother Titch, caught hold of Elaine as she bounced back off what the geologist could only term a corundum-like chest – corundum having a hardness rating of nine and being one of her favourite minerals – leaving her glasses askew and her head reeling. 'Where's the fire?'

'Sorry, Rob. Emergency!' She twisted out of his grasp and hurried towards the counter. 'Lucy . . . Lucy!'

Her cries brought the owner of Peaks Patisserie rushing out of the kitchen, flour all over her hands. 'Elaine, whatever—?'

'Delilah – I need to talk to her and she's not answering her phone. Where is she?'

Lucy Metcalfe glanced at her watch. 'The bank, most likely. She had a meeting with—'

The door crashed shut. Elaine Bullock was already gone, tearing across the marketplace on her bike and leaving the cafe owner and the stonemason to wonder what on earth was going on.

Two cushions torn to shreds. Her old running shoes, which she'd stupidly left in the rear porch with him, chewed and mauled. And paw prints all over the glass.

A lot better than expected, thought Delilah, surveying the damage. Clipping a lead onto the culprit, she left the cottage by the back door, crossed the tiny yard that looked out from a height over the roofs of Bruncliffe, and turned right out of the gate onto Crag Lane to begin the walk back into town, Tolpuddle by her side.

Separation anxiety was how the experts described it. The minute Delilah was out of sight, her dog went berserk. Which, if he were a poodle or a dachshund, might not be such a problem. But for Tolpuddle . . .

She glanced down at the large grey dog walking happily next to her. He'd been fine at first, fitting into their lives without a problem. But when the arguments started, closely followed by the break-up and then the divorce, Tolpuddle had begun to show signs of stress whenever Delilah wasn't around. Which was why she'd nipped home to pick him up before going to meet her new tenant. It was either that or come home to bedlam.

She sighed. A small cottage heavily mortgaged, a business premises also mortgaged, a struggling website design business and a dating agency yet to find its legs. Plus a Weimaraner with anxiety issues – albeit the only good thing to come out of her divorce. No wonder Uncle Woolly had reservations about her future. No wonder she was finding it harder and harder to smile these days.

The dog leaned against her, as if sensing her unease.

'We'll sort it, eh, you daft dog.' She scratched his head and hoped she was right. At least, with someone renting the ground-floor office at long last, there would be a bit of guaranteed money coming in. It wouldn't cover the mortgage, but it would be a start.

With a lighter step, Delilah Metcalfe continued along the lane, the outcrop of rock which gave it its name looming over her on the left, a view out across the town on her right. She loved living up here, above it all. Even if the walk home was an effort sometimes, particularly after a visit to the pub. Not that she went out drinking much now – a lack of money and a sensitive dog being effective deterrents.

Feeling her thoughts sliding back into despair as she approached the steep drop down Crag Hill to the market-place, she decided to continue along the higher road a bit further before descending. It would give her more time in the last of the sunshine and she was glad of the warmth on her face.

'We'll sort it,' she said again. This time with more confidence.

'She's not here, love.' Mrs Pettiford gestured towards the empty office at the back of the bank, before turning to the flushed face that was breathing heavily all over the partition.

'What time did she leave?'

'Oh, it must have been at least thirty minutes ago. She was heading home,' added Mrs Pettiford, noting the hot hands now splayed on the glass.

'Thanks, Mrs P,' Elaine Bullock hurried back out of the door.

'I hope you catch her,' Mrs Pettiford called after the retreating figure, who was already out of the door and on her bike, cycling away. 'And I hope I'm not here when Ida Capstick sees what a mess you made of the glass,' she said to the empty space before her.

With that in mind, Mrs Pettiford started clearing her desk. It wouldn't be long before the formidable cleaner arrived.

*

Homeless. He raced faster than was sensible across the rough track, bike jerking and bucking beneath him as he headed for the road. How the hell was he homeless?

George Capstick had watched him carefully across the yard, the gun trained on him the entire time. Then he'd apologised once more, a hint of tears in his eyes as he'd stood aside to let him go.

He bore George no malice. The man had done more than enough for Twistleton Farm and its occupants in the last twenty-six years, working alongside a boy out with the sheep during the day and then helping put a drunken wastrel to bed every night. All for a pittance, often nothing more than a cobbled-together meal and a cheap beer – there'd always been plenty of beer.

George Capstick owed him nothing.

Tarmac sighed under his wheels. He revved the engine and roared back down Thorpdale. He'd been made homeless twice in one week. He had precious little money. And he was facing dismissal and criminal prosecution.

Feeling even more like the black sheep of Bruncliffe than he had when he left, he raced towards the town. He had an appointment to keep.

'Delilah?' Elaine Bullock hammered on the back door of the cottage perched on the hill above the town. But she knew she was out of luck. Tolpuddle's lead wasn't hanging on its hook in the porch. And if Tolpuddle was out, so was Delilah.

Muttering curses, Elaine hurried back to her bike, her bad temper momentarily alleviated by the sight of the low sun burnishing the rock face overhanging the narrow lane.

Limestone. Her favourite of all rock types. Although the red siltstone of Monument Valley had to be up there. Along with the glassy-black depths of obsidian. Which technically wasn't a rock, but was too beautiful to be argued over. Then of course there was bog iron, its name alone making it a contender. And serpentinite, she ought to consider that—

'Afternoon.' A passing jogger disturbed her geological daydreams.

'Afternoon.' Elaine raised a hand in greeting and, in doing so, saw her watch. She'd just spent several minutes with her head in the clouds. Or rather, the ground, given that she'd been thinking about rocks. She was never going to find Delilah in time at this rate.

With a tut of reproach for herself, Elaine Bullock cycled back the way she'd come, her mind still so full of minerals that she failed to register the flash of red as a motorbike roared past on the road below. Reaching the junction at the bottom of Crag Hill, she paused. Where next? She thought for a moment and then turned, unheedingly, in the wake of the motorbike towards Back Street.

There was only one place left that Delilah was likely to be.

'I've never seen owt like it.'

'Daft, is what it is.'

'Perhaps there's more to it than we know?'

'Don't see how that's likely.'

Soaking up the conversation from the large group that had gathered at the windows, Troy Murgatroyd pulled another pint, face as sombre as the decor of his bar. But on the inside he was smiling.

A funeral. And then something out of the ordinary, right outside the pub. There could be nothing better for business than this coming together of two such occurrences – the former bringing the people in to seek solace, the latter keeping them entertained and on-site, once the beer had helped restore their downcast spirits.

'What time's Delilah due down, Ash?' Seth Thistlethwaite asked the Metcalfe brother next to him, who was also keeping watch at the window.

'Any moment now. Here's the new bloke from Taylor's.' Ash nodded towards a bright-orange Mini which had pulled up outside, emblazoned with the slogan 'Taylor-Made Homes'. A young man in a crumpled suit, the cuffs and ankles some inches short of the end of his limbs, was getting out, a folder clutched business-like under his arm.

A buzz of anticipation went through the spectators as the estate agent crossed to the building that was under such scrutiny, selected a key from a large collection and let himself into the ground-floor office, unaware of the crowd opposite. Or the reason for their interest.

The throb of a motorcycle came next, cutting to silence as it parked behind the Mini.

'Oh, Christ!' muttered Seth, before taking a long drink from his pint.

'What?' Ash glanced at the old man and then back at the motorbike and the man getting off it. 'Do you know him?'

Seth didn't reply, just watched as the man strode

towards the open door where the estate agent was waiting. How they didn't recognise the bike, Seth didn't know. That flash of scarlet. The chrome. It was so distinctive.

But then they were too busy watching the man who was now easing off his helmet, rucksack slung over one arm, his back turning to the onlookers as he approached the estate agent in the doorway. A mass of black hair touching broad shoulders. Lean body. Still they didn't realise. Seth cast a sideways glance at Will Metcalfe, who was as oblivious as the others. There was going to be trouble. Once they cottoned on.

Perfect timing. Delilah had extended her walk by taking the furthest of the two sets of steep stone steps that led down from Crag Lane to Back Street and it had brought her out just beyond the antique shop, with a couple of minutes to spare. Turning right, back towards town, she could see Stuart from Taylor's already leading someone into the office. She picked up her pace. Things were going to be okay.

'. . . So I trust it's to your liking?' Stuart Lister smiled, trying to hide the nerves that his shaking hand betrayed as he rifled through his folder for the paperwork. He was also trying not to stare at the various shades of black and blue on his client's cheek.

This was the first step in his new life in this town, his first transaction for Taylor's, all conducted over the internet in the space of twenty-four hours with a client who had never seen the premises but was in a hurry. Hoping the deal wouldn't fall through now that the man could see the office in person, the trainee estate agent pulled out the relevant papers and reached in his pocket for a pen.

'It's fine,' said the man, propping his rucksack against the battered filing cabinet as he took in the red-flocked wallpaper, the coffee-stained desk, the two rickety chairs and the peeling lino flooring with a wry smile. 'Just what I need.'

'Wonderful, wonderful. And I organised the sign-writer as you requested—' Stuart came to a halt, hand held out to indicate the results of his efforts. Because opposite, in the twin windows of the pub, a host of faces were peering out, staring at . . . what were they staring at?

His attention was drawn to the arrival of a woman and a grey dog.

'Ah, your landlady is here. Shall we . . . ?'

He gestured for the man to precede him and they headed for the door.

Delilah was almost at her office when she noticed. She froze, jerking Tolpuddle to a halt as his lead tightened.

Was it a joke?

She stared at the ground-floor window, gold lettering splashed across the glass. It couldn't be right. There'd been a mistake.

She looked up at the floor above. Older lettering, faded and slightly tatty, there for a few years now – three letters to indicate her business.

D D A

Dales Dating Agency.

She lowered her gaze back down. Three letters, freshly affixed, to indicate goodness knows what.

DDA

Then she felt the eyes on the nape of her neck. The pub, full of people, all of them watching to see her reaction. She turned back to the offending window and felt her blood fizz. Two businesses with the same initials. It was bloody ridiculous. She'd throttle whoever had authorised this without her permission. Seeing a figure materialise in the open doorway, she began to cross the road.

Elaine spotted her quarry as soon as she turned down Back Street. She didn't notice the Mini or the motorbike or the crowd of faces peering out of the pub windows. Or even the windows with the duplicate signs. She simply raised a hand off the handlebars and waved frantically at the figure crossing the road.

'Delilah!' she shouted. 'Delilah! He's back!'

They heard the shout in the pub. The Bullock lass calling out something about someone being back. But they were too preoccupied with the drama unfolding in front of them. Delilah had seen the sign. And her fists had clenched and her shoulders had tensed in a way Bruncliffe locals recognised.

'Wouldn't want to be that young lad right now!'

'Or the new tenant . . .'

'You not watching, Seth?' asked Ash, as the old man eased to the back of the crowd.

A shake of the head was the only reply. Seth Thistlethwaite had no desire to watch. Because he knew what was coming. And he knew there was no way to stop it.

'Look, look – they're coming out,' said Harry Furness,

his auctioneer's voice carrying across the room. Then there was silence. Stunned.

'It's . . .'

'That's . . .'

'I'll bloody kill him!' Will Metcalfe dropped his pint and rushed for the door as mayhem erupted amongst the onlookers.

He'd noticed the faces in the pub. Deliberately kept his helmet on and his back to them as he walked up to the estate agent. But now there was no avoiding it. With an ironic smile for his audience, he stepped out onto the pavement and then he saw her. Delilah Metcalfe, no longer a scrawny teen but now a young woman, a large grey dog next to her. His smile became genuine as she stepped towards him. She was probably the only person in Bruncliffe he'd been looking forward to seeing.

His years of training should have alerted him. The furious expression that flickered into shock. The tension in her shoulders. The balled hands. But at that moment the pub door flew open and Will Metcalfe tumbled into the street, his brother Ash and chubby Harry Furness doing their best to restrain the much stronger man.

'I'll kill him!' he heard Will roaring, the pub dwellers spilling out raucously behind, the large grey dog beginning to bark, Elaine Bullock jumping off a bike and grabbing the arm of the enraged farmer . . .

He turned back to Delilah just in time to see the blur of a fist flying in his direction.

'You!' she yelled, as her famous Metcalfe right hook

connected with his chin and sent him sprawling into a heap on the ground.

'Welcome home, Samson, lad,' muttered Seth Thistlethwaite into his pint in the now-empty bar. 'Welcome home.'

4

The cold slobber of reality brought Samson O'Brien to. A tongue, rough, wet, rasping the length of his face. His eyes opened to a grey shadow looming over him.

'Tolpuddle, that's enough,' snapped a female voice.

Samson's focus swung onto the blurry figure of Delilah Metcalfe tugging at the dog's collar, trying to pull him away, the dog resisting.

'Yeah, Tolpuddle, cut it out. You don't know where he's been.'

The retort provoked laughter, its instigator slouched against the pub doorway, pint in hand. Rick Procter, a half-smile gracing his handsome features, stared at the man slumped on the pavement opposite.

'Tolpuddle, eh?' managed Samson, his hand coming up to the large grey head, fingers scratching behind the ears. The licking stopped, replaced by an ecstatic panting, bellows of hot dog breath fanning the last of the dizziness away. Resting lightly on the dog, the only sentient being showing him any kind of favourable reception, Samson got slowly to his feet as the hostile crowd watched on.

'I see you've still got the right hook, Delilah,' he muttered, concentrating solely on her as his blurred vision cleared.

'And you've still got a glass chin,' she spat back.

He grinned at the typical riposte, felt a twinge of pain shoot up his face from injuries old and new and let the grin subside. 'Didn't realise Bruncliffe had abandoned the handshake as a form of greeting.'

'We save that for those who are welcome round here,' said Rick.

'And you're not one of them, O'Brien,' growled Will Metcalfe, Elaine Bullock still holding onto his arm.

One eye on the burly farmer, Samson raised fingers to his tender chin. 'So I gather.'

'It's probably best if you just head home, Samson.' There was a hint of apology in Ash Metcalfe's suggestion as he stood to one side. 'Best for everyone.'

A grumble of consent came from the onlookers and Samson could almost feel the wave of belligerence that carried it. He was outnumbered. Not for the first time. If this was an undercover operation, he'd be considering his escape route, looking for a rapid exit and praying to get out in one piece. But these were Dales folk, his friends and neighbours. Former friends and neighbours, if the current mood was anything to go by. So how to deal with it?

As he had nowhere else to go, he didn't have an option.

'Problem is,' he said, arms folding across his chest, 'this is my home.'

'Since when?' Will took a step forward, dragging a pro-testing Elaine with him. 'You left this place over a decade ago and never looked back, leaving the rest of us to clear up after you. You can damn well do the same today.'

'Sorry. Not possible. I've moved back and I'm setting up business here.' Samson gestured towards the window behind him. The window with the bright new lettering.

'You mean . . . ?' Delilah looked from Samson to the young estate agent, Stuart, who was shuffling nervously in the doorway of her building. '*This* is my new tenant?'

Stuart gulped, his Adam's apple tracing a sharp line up and down his thin neck as Delilah's anger shifted in his direction. 'Mr O'Brien . . . yes . . . he's rented—'

'O'Brien! The clue's in the name, you halfwit! You should have known I would never rent to him.'

The young man gulped again. 'Sorry . . . I didn't comprehend . . . you didn't say . . .'

'Let him be, Delilah,' came an older, calmer voice from the pub doorway. Seth Thistlethwaite stood surveying the scene, a bit more grizzled than at the disastrous christening fourteen years ago when Samson had last seen him. The old man's head dipped in a muted greeting before his attention passed back to Delilah.

'How was the lad to know?' he continued. 'He's from Skipton.'

Samson's lips tweaked into a grin, despite his aching jaw. Only in Bruncliffe could a place a mere thirty minutes' drive away be considered an entire universe apart when it came to local politics. The lad was now nodding in terrified agreement, willing to sacrifice himself on the altar of ignorance if it meant deflecting the wrath of the woman before him.

'Yes, yes . . . precisely. Besides,' Stuart mumbled, fumbling at the folder he was holding, 'it was rented under a different name.'

'He's right.' Samson was openly smiling now as the hapless estate-agent-in-training held out a quivering piece of paper towards his seething client. 'I used the company name on the paperwork.'

'I don't care what you used,' snapped Delilah, 'we have no agreement.'

'But . . . but . . . you've signed the contract,' stuttered Stuart, that very document now in his trembling hand.

'Sod the contract!' Delilah snatched the offending piece of paper and tore it in two. 'I am not having this man renting my office.'

'Perhaps,' said Seth Thistlethwaite, with a nod towards the curious faces that were crowding the narrow backstreet, 'you would be better off finishing this discussion inside? Unless you want Bruncliffe to know all your business, Delilah?'

Delilah Metcalfe turned to see a host of people behind her, some with hair in rollers from the salon next door, others spilling out of the antique shop or drawn down the road from the hardware store by the noise. Neighbours. Friends. All of them known to her. And all watching with interest as she provided the headlines for the Bruncliffe news. Her cheeks went crimson.

'Inside,' she hissed to the estate agent, tipping her head towards the office before turning to Samson. 'And you! But don't expect to be staying long.'

And to the dismay of those gathered outside, Delilah Metcalfe ushered Samson O'Brien, the terrified young man from Skipton and her dog, Tolpuddle, into the disputed office space and firmly closed the door.

'If only she'd answered her phone, all this could have been avoided,' bemoaned Elaine Bullock, ensconced at the bar of the Fleece, where most of the onlookers had repaired once the drama outside had been concluded. Much to Troy Murgatroyd's delight.

'Avoided? Where'd be the fun in that? I was hoping she was going to hit him again,' laughed Harry Furness.

'She might have to join the queue,' said Ash. 'Did you see those bruises? Delilah wasn't the first to take a swing at him this week.'

Eyes on the office window across the road, beyond which three figures could be seen, Will Metcalfe grunted, anger still simmering on his ruddy features. 'Probably nothing less than he deserved.'

'Huh! All seemed a bit harsh, if you ask me.' Seth thumped his empty glass on the counter, eyebrows beetled into one harsh line of disapproval.

'Good job no one's asking then, eh, Seth?' responded Rick Procter. 'Because you're in the minority. Folk round here know exactly what O'Brien is. And they'll be slow to forgive the way he's treated people in this town. His own father, for Christ's sake!'

Ash nodded. 'It's true, Seth. He walked out on his dad, left the farm in a mess. And our Ryan would be turning in his grave if he knew how Samson had treated Lucy. He didn't even come back for the bloody funeral.'

Seth bit his tongue – not an easy task for a veteran Dalesman used to venting his opinions. But this was tricky. Whereas it could be argued that the young Samson had had no choice but to leave a failing farm caught in the ravages of foot-and-mouth, and with a drunkard at the helm boozing away whatever meagre profits came in, it had to be acknowledged that the Metcalfes had every right to feel aggrieved with him. Best man at his best friend's wedding, godfather to the same man's son, yet when Ryan Metcalfe, the friend in question, had been killed in action in Afghanistan two years ago, not a word had been heard from Samson O'Brien. Until now.

'I still think we ought to cut him some slack,' he muttered.

Rick Procter let out a disparaging snort. 'He's a reprobate, Seth, and you know it. He left here under a black cloud and, from what I hear, he's back under another.'

The property developer's words caught the attention of the pub. 'What do you mean?' asked Will, dragging his gaze from the window across the road.

'Rumour has it he's been suspended.'

'From the force?'

Rick nodded. 'Gross misconduct. There's likely to be a criminal investigation.'

'Come on, Rick, you're making this up,' said Elaine. 'Samson has his faults, but I can't see him as a bent copper.'

'I'm just reporting what I've heard.' He shrugged. 'Personally, I'd believe every word of it.'

'That's hardly an endorsement,' said Seth dryly. 'And as we've yet to hear his side of the story, I still maintain it's not right treating a man like that when he comes home.'

'You're forgetting, he doesn't have a home here any more.' Rick Procter stared down at the old man, a smug glint in his eye. 'Old Boozy sold it.'

Seth shot him a look of distaste. 'Aye, a nice piece of business that was, too. You should be proud of yourself. Negotiating such a good deal with an alcoholic.'

Rick bristled, broad shoulders pushed back as he leaned towards the retired teacher. 'I am proud of it. Old Boozy was rotting away on that crappy farm, not able to afford to get the help he needed. At least he's getting support now. Not that his son cares.'

'Easy, easy . . .' Harry Furness placed a hand on the tensed arm of the property developer. 'No point in us all falling out over this. How about another pint? Eh, Seth?'

Troy Murgatroyd moved over to the Black Sheep pump in anticipation, never knowing Seth Thistlethwaite turn down a free beer. But his hand stalled in mid-air as the old man stood up off his stool, his head shaking furiously.

'I'd rather take a sup with the devil,' he snarled as he brushed past the property developer and headed for the exit. 'Happen as he'd have more morals!'

The door slammed in his wake, leaving a hiccup of silence before Rick's booming voice smothered it. 'If that pint's still on offer, Harry . . .'

Laughter filled the bar as the auctioneer pulled a face and reached reluctantly into his pocket.

Elaine leaned towards Ash, her gaze on Rick who was now holding court, telling some ribald rugby tale. 'Do you think there's any truth in what he said?'

'About the dismissal?' Ash gave a soft laugh. 'You know Samson. He's capable of all sorts.'

'But corruption?'

Ash grimaced. 'Once upon a time I'd have said no way. Now . . . ? Who knows? He's been gone a long time.'

He stared across the road at the bright lettering covering the glass, and then at the fierce profile of his brother, who had maintained his position by the pub window, pint held in a tight grip. 'Either way, Samson's not welcome. I can't see this ending well.'

While Ash Metcalfe was making his dire predictions, in the ground-floor office of the Dales Dating Agency things were getting heated. And Stuart Lister was beginning to reassess his capability to be an estate agent. Or a peacemaker.

'Perhaps . . . perhaps we could try to resolve this without . . . without any further animosity . . . ?' he stuttered as his two clients faced each other, one like a cat about to strike, the other with a disdaining demeanour that poured more fuel on the fire, while the massive grey dog turned restless circles between them.

'How's the hand, Delilah?' The sardonic question from the man lounging on the window seat prompted a feral growl.

'Fine,' came the retort, the scarlet welt along her knuckles telling a different story. 'Better than your chin, I'll bet.'

'I wouldn't be so sure. I've taken harder shots. This week, in fact.' He pointed at his discoloured cheek.

'All merited, no doubt.'

He grinned. 'Probably. But none of them from someone as attractive.'

She growled again, the dog beginning to whimper in response.

'Here, Tolpuddle.' Samson held out a hand and the dog responded, settling by his side, large head leaning against Samson's thigh as mournful eyes regarded his mistress.

Delilah's lips thinned into a narrow line. 'I can't believe you had the audacity to come back. And to do it in such an underhand manner, not even using your real name on the contract.'

He shrugged, still fondling the dog's ears. 'I didn't think I'd be welcome. Not with the way I left.'

'Yes, not your finest hour. Fighting with your own father at Nathan's christening. It was low, even by your standards.'

'Is that why you hit me?'

'No,' snapped Delilah. 'I hit you so Will wouldn't!'

Samson laughed. 'You haven't changed a bit.'

'What the hell would you know? You haven't been here. You couldn't even be bothered to make it back for—' She faltered, then blinked furiously, face turned away.

'Make it back for what?' he asked, tone softer, sensing the change in her.

'You know bloody well for what!' She whipped back to confront him. 'Ryan's funeral.'

His hand froze on the dog's head and his eyes dropped to the floor.

'No answer? No futile excuse? How typically O'Brien,' she goaded. 'Your best friend dies in the line of duty in Afghanistan and you leave Lucy to cope alone – not a single bit of contact. Not even with your godson.'

He made no reply, just stared at the ground, face blank.

A heartbeat passed before Delilah wheeled on Stuart, standing in the corner, folder clutched to his chest like armour. 'The contract is cancelled,' she snapped. 'Do what you have to do to sort it out.'

Stuart Lister felt his spirits sink. He'd had an inkling

things weren't right when Miss Metcalfe had decked her prospective tenant. Though he hadn't been long in the business, he suspected it wasn't the norm – even in Bruncliffe. But now, with her eyes flashing and her fists clenching once more, he knew his first deal for Taylor's estate agents was about to amount to nothing.

'Of course . . .' he managed. 'I'll just need your signature to authorise the bank transfer.'

'What transfer?'

'The first month's rent. It was paid in today. Under the circumstances . . . it has to be returned . . .' Stuart stumbled to a halt under the ferocity of her gaze.

'You mean that money is already in my bank account?' Delilah asked.

He nodded. She turned away, bottom lip caught between her teeth, and he noted the pallor replacing the flush of anger. She paced over to the window, then back to the desk, the dog letting out soft sounds of anxiety as he tracked her restless movements. Then she crossed to the window once more, slapped her hands on the glass and stared at the vibrant letters spaced across it. Her shoulders lifted and she took a deep breath, as though coming to some momentous decision.

'What does DDA stand for anyway?' she asked, nodding at the lettering, her tone still clipped but the venom gone.

'Dales Detective Agency,' said Samson. 'Catchy, don't you think?'

'A detective agency? Here? You must be mad. Who needs a detective in this place?'

'You'd be surprised.'

'I would! But as a landlady, I don't want surprises. I want regular payment from a reliable tenant.'

'Would six months' payment up front be reliable enough?' Samson was watching her now, smiling again.

The estate agent held his breath, unsure what had caused the sea change, but sensing a breakthrough nevertheless.

She shrugged. 'Possibly. But there's still a problem.'

'Which is?'

'The initials. In case you haven't noticed, they're already taken.'

'By?'

'The Dales Dating Agency.'

A roar of laughter escaped from Samson's throat, making the dog jump. 'A dating agency? In Bruncliffe? Who the hell had that half-arsed—?'

'So,' said Stuart, leaping into the gulf that was about to rip his tentative deal apart. 'Perhaps I could get you both to sign a new contract to reflect this generous offer from Mr O'Brien? Six months' rental up front . . .'

He let it dangle there, a much wiser negotiator than he gave himself credit for as, unbeknownst to him, Miss Metcalfe struggled between pride and desperation.

'Yes,' she finally snapped. 'But one more condition. A six-month lease only. I doubt the Dales Detective Agency will still be in business after that.'

Stuart immediately had his folder open, rifling through the pages for a blank contract before either client changed their mind. Samson meanwhile was standing up, a grin across his face as he held out a hand.

'You won't regret it,' he said.

'I'm regretting it already,' retorted Delilah, ignoring the hand and grabbing hold of Tolpuddle's collar instead, pulling the disloyal dog over to her side. 'But I will take great delight in watching you fail. Because no one around here needs a detective.'

A doorbell sounded and Samson, closest to the door, headed into the hall. A soft murmur of voices and then he was guiding a statuesque woman dressed from head to toe in black into the room.

'Mrs Hargreaves!' Delilah crossed to the bereaved mother, anger instantly forgotten in the face of such blatant grief. 'What on earth are you doing here?'

The butcher's wife, fresh from burying her only son, held out the local paper and pointed a shaking finger at the classifieds. 'The detective agency . . . Is it open?'

'Yes,' said Samson. 'It is. And I'm at your service.'

She nodded, tears beginning to spill over her lower eyelids. 'Good. I need your help. I think our Richard was murdered.'

5

'*Tea?*' Delilah slammed the teapot back onto the counter and added milk to three mugs. 'Could I make *tea*? Who the hell does he think I am? His bloody secretary or something?'

She reached into the cupboard above the sink for the biscuit tin, still ranting.

'And that smile! As if that makes any difference to the fact that he's bossing me around. In my own building!'

Lips in a tight line, face thunderous, she opened the tin and shook a generous helping of chocolate digestives onto a plate. She would have used the stale ones that she'd left open by mistake, but her sympathy for the bereaved Mrs Hargreaves called upon her Bruncliffe hospitality. Placing the lot on a tray, she remembered the sugar.

'"Two spoons, please,"' she mimicked, hand stretching for the sugar bowl. Then she paused, a wicked smile replacing the glower.

Sod the sugar. He could take it as it came. Strong and milky.

Reaching into the cupboard one last time, she added a couple of treats for Tolpuddle. Not that the faithless hound deserved any spoiling. The way he'd carried on when they'd entered the office, sitting at Samson's feet, fawning on him . . .

A wave of annoyance washed over her again. What a bloody mess!

She crossed to the window of the kitchen up on the first floor. Looking out between the D and the A of the initials spanning the width of the glass – the same initials that were now ridiculously mirrored in the window below – she could see her brothers standing guard in the pub.

Her heart sank. They'd be so disappointed in her. In her utter capitulation. But what choice did she have?

Bloody mess was right. She wanted to be able to send Samson packing, his behaviour fourteen years ago at her nephew Nathan's christening reason enough. Even thinking about it made her grimace. Everyone trying to be upbeat for the sake of Ryan and Lucy, but in a rural gathering in May of 2001, the spectre of foot-and-mouth and financial ruin was hanging over them all. Not to mention the acrid stench of burning carcasses.

No wonder things had been tense. But there was no excuse for how Samson had behaved at the christening party; attacking his father in the marquee at the rugby club, knocking over a couple of tables and sending people flying. It was Ryan and Will who'd managed to separate the two men, Will taking a drunk and dazed Mr O'Brien home, while Samson stormed off.

Whatever the reason had been for his outburst, they'd never found out. Word came the following day that Samson was gone. As was his father's motorbike. Until today, they hadn't seen or heard from him since.

Although they'd heard *of* him, thanks to Seth Thistlethwaite. Seth's brother, a police officer in Leeds, had come across the Bruncliffe exile working in a pub and persuaded him to apply for a place with the West Yorkshire force. According to Seth's reports, delivered regularly in the Fleece, Samson had excelled in training – much to the surprise of almost everyone in Bruncliffe – and, after spending a couple of years as a constable in Leeds, had had a fast-track promotion to the Met down in London. Something to do with an undercover drugs operation. That was the last they'd heard, and that was more than a decade ago.

In the meantime, Samson's father had continued to drink, until the sight of Mr O'Brien staggering out of the Fleece became commonplace. When he'd finally lost his licence for drink-driving, he'd taken to drinking at home. It had been Ida Capstick, his only neighbour, who'd called the ambulance when she found him collapsed in the kitchen. He'd gone into hospital and Rick Procter stepped forward to help, offering to buy the derelict farm and set Mr O'Brien up elsewhere.

And where had Samson been all this time? Not in Bruncliffe, that was for sure. Add to that his lack of contact when Ryan was killed and it was no wonder people around here wanted nothing to do with him. Especially her brothers. The man was amoral and totally selfish; not traits the Metcalfes identified with. Or tolerated. But . . .

Her thoughts returned to her predicament. Those bills. The overdraft. The mortgages that needed to be paid. And the determining factor – the rent that had already been deposited in her account and which Woolly, the bank manager, would have taken into consideration when he made his damning assessment of her finances.

If she gave it back, he'd have her in his office in a flash

and would no doubt withdraw his reluctant offer of a six-month extension of her current banking arrangements. Which would mean the end of her business. Possibly even bankruptcy.

So here she was. Making tea for the man downstairs who was now her tenant, the young estate agent having proved remarkably efficient once it came to drawing up a new contract and making sure it was signed by both of them before he left.

She sighed, the window misting up before her. She really wasn't looking forward to breaking the news to her family over Sunday lunch in three days' time. Not that she'd have to break it. This being Bruncliffe, word would fly over the hills and up the dale, and the Metcalfe clan would know all about her treachery before nightfall. And as for Mrs Hargreaves' visit . . .

Delilah had been trying not to think about it. Richard's mother sitting in Samson's office and declaring that her son had been murdered. That particular snippet of information would be all over the place before Mrs Hargreaves even left the building. If it wasn't already. And how long until someone – Samson, most likely – connected the dots and discovered that Richard wasn't the only Dales Dating Agency client to have died recently?

The investigation could bring nothing but bad publicity for the business.

Feeling instantly ashamed of her selfish preoccupations when there was a grieving mother downstairs, Delilah reached for the tray and left the kitchen.

It would turn out to be a coincidence, she reassured herself as she walked along the landing. The link between the two deaths nothing more than bad timing, and Richard's demise nothing more than a cry for help that had come too late. After all, this was Bruncliffe. Murders never happened here. In the meantime, she would keep a close eye on Samson's investigations.

She halted at her office door, spying the notepad and pen lying on the desk.

If he was going to treat her like a secretary, she would behave like one. And get as much information as she could, in the process.

'And you've been to the police?'

Mrs Hargreaves nodded, a balled-up tissue pressed against her lips as though that could hold back the grief. She was sitting on a chair on the other side of the desk, head lowered, gaze on the floor. So far, she'd only answered in monosyllables.

Samson had never been more out of his depth. Crazed addicts. Enraged dealers. Ruthless drug barons – he'd faced them all during his time with the Met and in his subsequent years with the Serious Organised Crime Agency and the National Crime Agency. Yet he'd felt less nervous than he did now. Confronted with such heartbreak, he found himself floundering, lurching through the interview while feeling like a brute. This was Mrs Hargreaves. The imposing woman who manned the counter at the butcher's, starched apron girdling her generous frame. As able as her husband to handle a cleaver, and one of that rare breed of women who saved her words for when they were needed.

She'd never shown any overt affection for the young

Samson as he traipsed into the shop once a week, grubby hands clasping coins that never were enough. He'd mumble his order, ashamed to be buying the cheapest cuts, such small amounts. And she'd tell him to speak up, saying there was no shame in an honest pound. He'd been a good age before he realised: that gruff tone, the blunt admonishment which brought laughter from the other customers – it had been a cover. While he was busy staring at the floor and wishing it would swallow him, she was slipping extra meat into his order. When he was fifteen, a truculent teenager using attitude to conceal his vulnerability, he'd announced one day as she cut up strings of sausages and he saw two more than he'd asked for go in the bag, that he didn't want her charity. She stared at him, gave a loud laugh and promptly held her hand out and told him what he owed her for countless years of free produce.

He'd blushed, grabbed his shopping and left. He never raised the issue again. And she never added anything to his order. Apart from at Christmas, when a black pudding or a pork pie would find its way in amongst the offcuts and minced beef.

Now this Amazon of a woman was sitting across from him, tears on her cheeks and inches away from complete despair. His heart went out to her. But the questions had to be asked.

'So what did the police—?' He broke off as the door opened and Delilah returned, a tray in her hands. 'Thanks, Delilah.'

He stood, grateful for the interruption, and took the tray, surprised to see there were three mugs on it. He turned to say something about client confidentiality and realised Delilah had taken his chair. Literally. She'd lifted it out from behind the desk and had, instead, set it down next to the now sobbing butcher's wife. Taking Mrs Hargreaves' hands in hers, she leaned in and started talking quietly to the woman.

So Delilah was staying. Smothering a sigh of exasperation, Samson put the tray down and perched on a corner of the desk while his client cried onto the shoulder of his landlady. As beginnings of new enterprises went, it probably wasn't the best. But it was typical Bruncliffe.

'I'm so sorry,' the butcher's wife said some minutes later, sitting up straight and dabbing at her swollen eyes with her tissue. 'I didn't mean to make such a fuss . . .'

'Don't be daft, Barbara.' Delilah stretched for a mug of tea and placed it in the woman's hands. 'Here, get that down you while we get to the bottom of this.'

Barbara. Delilah's casual use of Mrs Hargreaves' name struck Samson. He'd left before he'd earned that right, before he'd really entered Bruncliffe's adult world. Yet here was Delilah, an awkward adolescent when he'd last seen her, now on first-name terms with one of the pillars of Bruncliffe society.

'I presume you've been to the police?' continued Delilah, flipping open the notepad on her lap, pen poised to write.

'We've already established that,' Samson said, before taking a sip of what passed for tea in these parts. He winced at the rugged flavour, the bitterness. 'Did you . . . is there sugar . . . ?'

Delilah nodded. 'Two spoons, as instructed.'

Christ! The tea was harsh enough to etch granite. Presuming his taste buds had refined over the years, he reached for a biscuit to help ease the ordeal, taking one of the ones that had fallen off the plate.

'That's—' Delilah paused, pointing at the digestive in his hand, and then smiled.

'That's what?' he asked, biting into the biscuit, a strong taste of yeast hitting his palate.

'Nothing. So, Barbara, what exactly did the police say?'

Samson coughed quietly, trying to concentrate on what was being said while attempting to swallow the disgusting foodstuff that Delilah was passing off as refreshments. He felt a nudge on this thigh. Tolpuddle.

'You saviour,' he murmured, passing the remainder of the digestive to the dog, who was far more appreciative of these strange delights. Taking another sip of tea to scour his mouth, he turned his attention back to Mrs Hargreaves.

'Not a lot,' she was saying. 'They implied I was being stupid.'

'So they don't suspect foul play?' asked Samson, before Delilah could take charge again.

'No. They have no evidence to suggest that.' The butcher's wife turned pleading eyes to Delilah. 'But surely that works the other way, too? I mean, there's no evidence to suggest he killed himself, either.'

'There was no note?' Samson asked gently. 'No behaviour leading up to the day that might have pointed to suicide?'

A robust shake of the head was followed by a steadier voice. 'Not a thing. He was happy. First time I'd seen him so happy in years . . .' She addressed Delilah again. 'You know how it's been for him. With that woman doing what she did.'

Delilah nodded and, seeing Samson's raised eyebrow, turned to him. 'Richard moved back here three years ago with his wife and two children. It didn't work out—'

'She wouldn't let it work out!' snapped Mrs Hargreaves. 'Didn't give it a chance. Didn't give any of us a chance before hightailing it back to the city.'

Samson, knowing the realities of living in the town under the claustrophobic attention of its citizens, felt a passing twinge of sympathy for the maligned ex-wife. 'And Richard had got over this?'

Delilah nodded again. 'Yes. He took it hard at first, but in the last year he'd really begun to move on.'

'I'll say!' added Mrs Hargreaves. 'He was all set to buy one of those lovely houses Rick Procter's built at the end of town. And he'd been on a couple of dates.'

Samson glanced at Delilah, looking for confirmation, but she just shrugged, offering no further details.

'What about his friends? Have you spoken to them?'

Mrs Hargreaves shook her head, hands now fidgeting in her lap. 'I haven't had the chance. And besides, Ken said not to bother them. He thinks . . . he thinks I'm being silly. But I know . . . knew my boy. He just wouldn't have done this. Not to me.'

She looked up at Samson for the first time, her eyes filled with pain. 'Can you help? Can you find the person who killed him?'

Samson O'Brien, home less than twenty-four hours,

found himself nodding. 'I'll do what I can, Mrs Hargreaves, I promise.'

'I think it's your round, Rick,' said Harry Furness, waggling an empty pint glass in his hand.

The pub had got even busier as the working day began to come to a close and curiosity drew locals down to the Fleece to hear about the return of Bruncliffe's black sheep. And possibly get a glimpse of round two of the punch-up that had been held earlier. The tables were all full, small groups were standing around and a low hum of conversation filled the room.

'Right you are,' said Rick, already reaching for his wallet. 'Same again?'

'Aye, why not.'

'Will? Ash? Either of you fancy another?' Rick asked the two Metcalfe brothers who were by the window, Will's dark face set in a scowl as he glared over at the newly christened detective agency. Like Delilah, he hadn't inherited the Metcalfe colouring or stature, measuring a good few inches shorter than his fair-haired younger brothers, but Will more than made up for his lack of height with his strength. And temper. He wasn't someone Rick Procter would care to take on.

'Not for me,' Ash said, collecting his jacket from the back of a chair. 'Might call it a day. Leave Delilah to sort out this mess.'

'Will?'

The oldest Metcalfe shook his head, his gaze firmly fixed on the shadowy shapes that could be just made out in the room opposite.

'Suit yourself,' said Rick. 'Just the two pints it is, then.' He turned to head for the bar and his mobile began to ring. 'Sorry, Harry,' he said, after a glance at the screen. 'I've got to take this. It's work. You get them in and I'll be right back.' He thrust a tenner at the auctioneer and made his way to the pub door before answering the call.

'Can you talk?' asked the voice on the other end.

'Just a moment.' Rick let the door close behind him, and turned right down Back Street. He paused in the archway that led down behind the antiques shop, casting a glance around to check he was alone. 'Go ahead.'

'I trust you've heard who's back?'

'I've heard.'

'And?' Irritation crackled down the line.

'And what?'

'For God's sake, Rick. I've got a lot at stake here. We need to be careful.'

'Don't worry. It's all in hand.'

'And the farm? Will that be a problem?'

'Let me deal with that. I've got someone keeping an eye on it for me.'

'Is he trustworthy?'

Rick gave a sharp laugh. 'Oh yes. Totally.'

There was a long pause and Rick could imagine stubby fingers tapping on a desk as anxiety took hold. Then, 'I still think we need to hang fire for a while. Just until we know what O'Brien's up to.'

'If that's what you think,' said Rick, trying to hide his impatience. There was no need for such caution. But he was a partner in this deal. He had to remember that. 'We'll give it until Christmas. From what I hear, O'Brien won't last that long anyway. He's in more trouble than we could ever give him.'

'Well make sure you're right. I can't afford to have this come back on me.'

The call ended abruptly. Rick pocketed his mobile and, deep in thought, headed back up the street. When he reached the door of the Fleece, he hesitated, the thought of a pint suddenly making his stomach sour.

Panic. That's what he'd sensed from the caller. And panic could cause everything he'd worked for to be lost in an instant.

No longer in the mood for alcohol, he glared over at the detective agency and then continued on his way towards the marketplace.

Bloody Samson O'Brien. That was all they needed.

'So, do you really think you'll be able to help her?'

Samson chose to ignore the scepticism coating Delilah's question as he re-entered the office, the hunched-over figure of Mrs Hargreaves passing by the window outside. 'I'll try. But I doubt I'll discover what she wants me to.'

'You mean you think he committed suicide?'

He nodded. 'This is Bruncliffe. Murders don't happen that frequently in places like this. Not out of the blue. Which means it's far more likely that the police are right and Richard did kill himself, even though it's hard for his mother to accept that.' He shrugged. 'All I can do is try and find some definitive proof as to the cause of his death. Then perhaps Mrs Hargreaves will be able to come to terms with it.'

'Where will you start?'

Samson smiled and gestured towards the notepad on her lap, Tolpuddle's head now lying across it. 'For someone who doesn't think there's a place for a detective agency in town, you suddenly seem very keen to be involved.'

'I thought you might need a hand!' snapped Delilah. 'And to be honest, given what little you know about Bruncliffe these days, I was right.'

'Sorry,' Samson raised both hands in apology. 'Yes, you're right. I did need your help. Seeing Mrs Hargreaves upset like that . . .' He dropped heavily onto the chair the bereaved woman had been sitting in, the legs creaking ominously under the sudden weight. 'Thank you. You helped break the ice.'

Delilah's lips parted as though on the verge of a retort. Instead she dipped her head in acceptance.

'As for what's next,' he continued, holding up a bunch of keys. 'Mrs Hargreaves gave me these, so I'll start with a quick search of Richard's house and then do some background investigations – talk to his friends, people he mixed with . . .'

'And they are?'

Samson grinned. 'I'm a detective, Delilah. I'll find out.'

'And waste days doing so. I'm a local. Just ask me!'

He laughed. 'Okay, okay. I'll ask you. But in the meantime, if you're going to intrude on my meetings, do you think you could provide better biscuits? Those things are revolting.' He pointed at the oatmeal digestive on the tray and Delilah smiled, the first time he'd seen her smile since he'd clapped eyes on her outside. Face alight with mischief, she reached for the offending biscuit and held it out to Tolpuddle.

'There's nothing wrong with my biscuits,' she said, as the dog gobbled down her offering. 'But as for these Dog-gestives . . . you'd have to ask Tolpuddle.'

Samson froze, eyes flicking between the last morsel disappearing into the dog's mouth and the biscuits left on the plate. Completely different. A plate of chocolate digestives and . . .

He felt bile rise up his throat. 'Dog-gestives? You let me eat a dog biscuit?'

She was laughing now, the sound rippling around the empty room as she stood to go, the dog following her. 'Serves you right,' she managed between bursts of laughter, 'for asking me to make tea.'

The door closed in her wake and Samson was left staring at the plate of digestives. And the notepad Delilah had forgotten to take with her.

He picked it up, eyes skimming across the page of notes she'd taken. Clear, concise, important elements underlined. She'd make an excellent assistant, he thought wryly, as long as she was never asked to make tea or allowed to give free rein to her temper. Within the space of an afternoon, she'd floored him with a right hook and then knowingly fed him dog food. It seemed like Delilah hadn't changed much in the years he'd been gone.

Although she'd developed an ability to hold a grudge, judging by the reserve she'd been treating him with so far. While Mrs Hargreaves had been in the room, Delilah had been like her old self – open, confident, and with a streak of generosity that knew no limits. But the minute the butcher's wife had left, the shutters had come back down. Until the revelation about the biscuit.

He grinned. That laugh of hers, the way she had of throwing her head back in abandonment when life was funny. Just like Ryan—

The thought jolted the smile off his face. Ryan, who was dead and buried. He'd been trying not to think about it ever since Delilah had dropped her bombshell. It was too much to deal with right now. Tonight, when everything was sorted, he would allow himself to mourn the loss of his best friend. And tomorrow he would have to visit Ryan's widow and try to explain why he'd never been in touch, why he hadn't even made it to the funeral. In the meantime . . .

He started flipping through the pages of Delilah's note-pad, the detective in him unable to resist, curious as to what type of business she ran from her office upstairs. Notes from that morning detailed a meeting with a client – something about smelly boots and bad breath scrawled in the margin, alongside a brilliantly drawn Cupid being sick. Intrigued, he turned back more pages.

A date for something she referred to as 'SpeedyD'. Next month. In the evening. Lucy's name written next to it and circled multiple times.

Skipping to the first page, he was back in September: a meeting with a Tom Alderson, who'd signed up for three months. Three months of what? Alderson . . . The only Tom Alderson he'd known had been the son of a farmer up Hawes way. If it was him, was Delilah some sort of agricultural supplier?

He was puzzling over this, all the while idly leafing through her notes, when he saw a name he recognised.

Richard Hargreaves. Delilah had had a meeting with

him a couple of weeks ago, according to the date. He'd renewed for a further three months and signed up for 'SpeedyD', whatever that was, in October. But Richard Hargreaves had been no farmer. As Mrs Hargreaves had announced with pride, he'd been a lecturer in linguistics.

So Delilah wasn't selling agricultural supplies. But what was she up to? Samson flipped the notepad closed and saw the answer decorating the front cover.

The Dales Dating Agency.

The business Delilah had referred to earlier – the one that shared the same initials as his own. It was hers.

He grinned, glancing at the window and the lettering that advertised his new enterprise. No wonder she'd been annoyed about it. They shared the same initials and the same building. Then the incongruity of it stuck him. A dating agency! Delilah Metcalfe, with her forthright opinions and lack of romance, was in charge of organising people's love lives. Only in Bruncliffe!

He started to laugh, but a sudden thought trapped the sound in his throat. Thumbing frantically back through her notes, he found the page he wanted.

Richard Hargreaves. He'd been a client at Delilah's dating agency. Yet when Mrs Hargreaves had mentioned that Richard was possibly seeing someone, Delilah had offered no confirmation. Nor had she revealed that he was one of her customers. Why not?

She didn't trust him. Or something more?

He dropped the notepad back onto the desk and lowered his head into his hands, wincing at the contact with his cheek and chin.

It had been a hell of a day. A brutal welcome back to

Bruncliffe, the realisation that he was homeless yet again, the shock news about Ryan and then that bit of sheer madness when he'd offered to pay six months' rent up front to secure this office. Money that he should have been using to find somewhere to live. But when he'd been faced with Delilah's reluctance to have him as a tenant, it had suddenly seemed imperative that he persuade her to change her mind. Even if that now meant he had no money in the bank.

He rubbed his hands gently over his face and on a long sigh, got to his feet. It had been a hard homecoming all right. And it was about to get harder. It was time he paid a visit to his father.

'Had any visitors, George?' Arms folded, Rick Procter leaned against his Range Rover outside the Capsticks' cottage. Situated at the start of Thorpdale, it was tucked into the hillside, offering a commanding view of the surrounding land – land which Rick now owned. But while the house was pristine, windows glinting, paintwork fresh, the yard was chaotic. Bits and pieces of farm machinery lay dumped in random piles, hens strutting around them pecking relentlessly at the ground, and in the corner stood a vintage David Brown tractor, tools and parts strewn around it. Rick's attention, however, was on the man standing rigid in the doorway of the old barn, shirtsleeves rolled up, spade-like hands covered in oil.

A slow blink and then the lips moved. 'No, Mr Procter.'

'Good.' Rick turned to stare up the dale at the property just visible in the distance. Twistleton Farm. No one could reach it without passing here. Which is why George Capstick made the perfect watchdog. That and his pliability. He returned his gaze to the man. 'You'll tell me if anyone does come calling?'

Another blink, measuring at least three heartbeats. 'Yes, Mr Procter.'

'Good man.' He took an envelope out of his pocket and laid it on an upturned water butt. 'I knew I could rely on you.'

This time Rick was sure George Capstick would never open his eyes again, so long was the hiatus. But then his eyelids popped up and he shuffled over to pick up the envelope, never coming within arm's reach of the property developer, like a wary hound.

'Thanks, George. Keep in touch.' Rick threw up a hand in parting and got in his car, the usual wave of relief washing over him at escaping from the awkwardness of interacting with the man he still referred to as 'Brains'. Struck, as always, by the brilliant irony of the nickname for a man distinctly lacking in grey matter – unless you counted his uncanny ability with anything mechanical – he pulled off, turning left onto the road to head back to Bruncliffe. Driving into the setting sun, he reached for his phone. His partner was worrying over nothing.

In the yard of his small cottage, George Capstick was staring at the envelope in his hand. Devil's money. That's what his sister Ida said. He walked slowly across to the house, slowly took off his shoes and entered the kitchen. Ida wasn't home. She worked most days. But he knew what to do. He pulled open the middle drawer of the dresser and threw the unopened envelope in on top of all the others.

Devil's money. Ida said they were saving it, for when the devil came and tried to take their house, like he had Mr O'Brien's. And now the devil was asking about visitors. George blinked. There'd been no visitors. Not here.

He closed the drawer and, with his head full of the delicious roar of a Royal Enfield engine, headed back to work.

Hills. He just wasn't used to them. Already he could feel the backs of his legs protesting as he walked up Fell Lane. He wasn't used to people, either. Or at least, not people who knew him. In the short distance from his new office, across the marketplace and onto Fell Lane, Samson O'Brien had never felt more exposed. For a man who was used to living his life incognito, it was disconcerting.

They stared. Openly. And then gave a nod of acknowledgement because it would be bad manners not to say hello. Even if the face of the person offering a greeting was puckered up in a frown of disapproval. He'd not lingered over the walk, uneasy with the attention, but had had time to note the changes in the town.

Two of the banks were gone from the square. In their places were an Indian restaurant and a cafe called Peaks Patisserie, which was doing good business despite the afternoon drawing to a close. He'd also noticed the organic food shop, the enlarged premises of Taylor's estate agents with its double frontage and, of course, Hargreaves' butcher's with its blinds drawn and a 'Closed' sign on the door.

Leaving the marketplace behind, he'd turned right onto Fell Lane and felt the strain on his calves. With his destination in sight, he began to feel the strain on his nerves, too.

It was a two-storey building, split into flats, each one having a small balcony overlooking the spacious front lawn. They were high enough up at the back of the town to offer great views and to catch the last bit of sunshine as the evening approached. But it was a far cry from the isolated splendour of Twistleton Farm.

What the hell had made him sell?

Anger mixing with apprehension, Samson took the path up to Fellside Court and entered the building. He was met with the sound of laughter. Bellowing down the hallway and bursting with life, it brushed aside any notion he'd had that the place might be full of old people waiting to shuffle off into the heavens. He followed the noise along a bright corridor, one side floor-to-ceiling glass looking out onto a courtyard and the fell rising at the back, the other a wall covered with dramatic photographs of local scenery: bluebells out in Hawber Woods; Bruncliffe Crag burnished gold in the setting sun; Pen-y-ghent looking resplendent under a covering of snow; Ribblehead Viaduct arching across the landscape; and there at the end, one that took his breath away. A panoramic shot of Thorpdale, its fields stretching up towards the curve of hills at the top, two streams bisecting the land and a small farmhouse nestled between them. Home. Or at least, it had been.

'Can I help you?'

He turned to see a young woman standing in the doorway of an office, blonde hair pulled back into a severe ponytail, the high cheekbones and hint of an Eastern European accent suggesting she was an offcumden, like him. Her eyes widened slightly as she took in the damage to his face.

'I'm here to see Joseph O'Brien,' he said.

'Apartment eighteen.' Her clipped reply was cut through by another burst of laughter, this time a woman's voice joining in, lightening the deeper tones. 'Or you could try the residents' lounge. Just along this corridor and around to the left. Please sign in first.' She pointed at the sideboard beneath the picture of Pen-y-ghent where a book was lying open and, with a curt nod of her head, retreated back into her office.

Samson dutifully entered his details in the visitors' book and then followed her directions, curious as to what was causing such amusement. He took in the well-tended plants, the immaculate carpets, the pristine walls as he went. The place was impressive. As was the lounge.

Running the entire length of the right-hand side of the U-shaped building, it too had a wall of glass looking out over the courtyard, armchairs and sofas scattered throughout the large space. But the residents weren't taking in the views of the stunning hillside and crags that rose above. Instead, they were gathered around a table at the far end.

'He's cheating!' exclaimed one old lady, leaning on a stick and peering over the head of the person in front of her. Even from the doorway, Samson recognised the sharp tones of Edith Hird, his former headmistress. 'He has to be.'

'How dare you insinuate that my man would cheat!' came an indignant response from the man opposite her. 'It's sheer brilliance, is what it is.'

'Only brilliance around here is your shiny bald head, Arty,' retorted the man next to him, the audience chortling in appreciation.

'Well, I don't care how he does it,' said a petite white-haired woman, staring down at the table in awe. 'I think it's wonderful. Do it again, please.'

Samson moved across the room towards the commotion, the familiar slap and shuffle of cards carrying over the top of the crowd of people.

'Time to place your bets,' urged the man called Arty, his deep tones suggesting it was him Samson had first heard laughing. 'You, sir, want to place a bet?'

Samson realised he was being addressed as the entire room turned towards him, Miss Hird's eyebrows lifting in recognition. He smiled. 'That would all depend on what I'm betting on.'

'A feat unparalleled. A talent untapped. A man who defies odds.' Arty was in his element, arms thrown wider with each exclamation, until he was in danger of knocking over the oxygen trolley of the frail gentleman standing beside him.

'Don't waste your money, son,' warned Miss Hird. 'He,' she said, pointing at Arty with her stick, 'is a retired bookmaker and would fleece you in a second. And he,' she gestured over the people in front of her to where Samson caught a glimpse of someone sitting, 'is cheating.'

'Edith, if you say that again, I'm going to have to sue you for defamation of character,' thundered Arty.

'Aye, only problem is, you'd have to have character in the first place,' quipped the old man with the oxygen cylinder, much to Edith's delight.

'So what's the trick?' asked Samson, closer now and able to see a grey head bent over the table, cards flashing between gnarled hands.

'I bet you,' said Arty, grinning at the prospect of a customer, 'my man here can shuffle through the cards and then name every one back to you in the exact order.'

'And the stakes?' asked Samson, his heart beginning to thump.

'Same as always. A bag of Jelly Babies.'

Samson took one more step, looked at the seated figure, the trembling hands holding the cards, and slowly shook his head. 'Bet's off,' he said, throat tightening.

The audience groaned.

'But why?' asked Arty, crestfallen. 'You didn't even give us a chance.'

'Because I've seen this trick before.'

Then the old man at the table looked up and the years fell away, leaving Samson feeling like he was staring down the barrel of a shotgun once again.

'Welcome home, son,' said Joseph O'Brien, a wary smile on his face. 'Welcome home.'

'Bloody tourists!'

Up out of Bruncliffe and over Fountains Fell, across the flattened top of Pen-y-ghent, into Wharfedale and up over the bleak expanse of Fleet Moss, in a field on the lower slopes of Wether Fell, Tom Alderson was cursing.

'What the heck do they know about farming?' he muttered, quad bike bucketing across the rough terrain as it climbed the hillside. 'Dead sheep in a field and they bloody panic.'

He reached the stone wall on the far edge of the field and stopped the bike at a closed gate. It was dusk, the lights in the farmhouse in the distance pinpricking the dying day. That was where he should be, sitting in the kitchen having a coffee with his father and discussing the highlights of their long day over at the Wharfedale auction, while his mother got tea ready. Instead, before he'd even had a chance to tell her that one of their shearling rams had fetched top price, his mother had sent him back out of the door. The Chairman of the Parish Council had been on the phone. Apparently a tourist had called several times to report that there was a dead sheep in the furthest field on Wether Fell Side.

Like that was a catastrophe – a dead animal lying in a field. But if the same do-gooder called the county council, then next thing Trading Standards would be out and the farm could be facing a hefty fine. So here he was, dog-tired and wishing he was at home, heading out to pick up a dead ewe.

'Bloody tourists!'

He opened the gate, the land on the other side rising steeply away from him. Up across this field and into the next and he'd be there. He turned back to the bike and failed to see the shadow peel away from the stone wall. Failed to see it tower over him. He heard the sound of the air rushing to part as something was brought down at pace. But it was too late.

6

'I heard you were back.' Joseph O'Brien held the door to his flat open and stood aside to let his son through, taking in the broad shoulders, the shoulder-length hair, the unforgiving blue gaze just like hers. He noticed the bruises, too. 'Wasn't sure if you'd come and see me.'

'Neither was I,' muttered Samson, entering the compact lounge. A two-seater sofa, an armchair, a TV and patio doors leading out onto a small balcony offering fantastic views of Bruncliffe and the hills beyond it. No cobwebs. No cigarette burns. And not a bottle in sight.

Joseph watched him appraise it all, then move into the kitchenette through the archway, opening cupboard doors, checking the fridge.

'You won't find any,' the older man said quietly. 'I'm sober.'

A harsh laugh was followed by a disbelieving look. 'I've heard that before.'

Joseph shrugged. 'It's true.'

'Since when?'

The older man's head snapped up to challenge his son's stare. 'Does it matter?'

Samson blinked, cheeks reddening slightly as he returned to the lounge. 'Sorry,' he muttered. 'Old habits . . .'

'I know a lot about old habits, son.' Joseph smiled and gestured at the sofa. 'Take a seat. I'll make us a cuppa.'

'No . . . no, it's fine. I don't have time . . .' Samson crossed to the balcony doors, tension radiating from him as he looked out. 'Seems like a nice enough place.'

'It's grand. Suits me down to the ground. The people are great, and the facilities – you saw the lounge, and there's even a gym where they hold yoga classes and the like. Nothing too strenuous, mind. Then there's a cafe where they do a delicious Sunday roast. You should come sometime—' Aware he was babbling like a desperate salesman, Joseph broke off, unnerved by his son's rigid back. The silence swelled around them and a familiar dryness seized his throat.

He coughed and tried again. 'I hear you brought the old bike with you. Good to know she's still running well.'

The glass doors reflected the hint of a smile which flickered across Samson's face. 'She's a beauty. Do you want her back?'

No apology. Not that Joseph expected one. Or wanted one. He'd driven his son out of their home. That the bike had been taken in the process seemed only fair. 'No, son,' he said, shaking his head. 'Me and your mother had our time with her. She's yours now.'

Samson's attention remained fixed on the balcony. Then he asked the question Joseph O'Brien had been expecting. And dreading.

'What happened to the farm?'

'I sold it.'

Samson turned to face his father, the telltale tightened jaw revealing the anger he was fighting to conceal. 'So I gather. Why?'

'Because . . . because I couldn't cope any more. God knows, Samson, I wasn't coping when you were there – how did you expect me to cope when you left?'

'When I left? Don't you mean when you kicked me out?'

Joseph thrust his hands in the pockets of his cardigan, his head dipping at the backlash. 'I was drunk—'

'You were always drunk. The only difference that time was that you were holding a shotgun. Pointed at me.'

Joseph swallowed hard, the urge to drink welling up out of nowhere. If he got through this without succumbing to temptation, he would be sober forever, he thought wryly.

'I'm sorry. It wasn't . . . I never meant to . . .' He shook his head, annoyed at his inability to articulate what he needed to say. To explain why he'd done the awful things he had. But none of it was explainable. Not to someone who wasn't in thrall to alcohol. The mess in his head. The emptiness in his heart. The misery that only drinking alleviated. Until it only made it worse.

'I'm sorry,' he said again, the word sinking into the gulf between them.

Samson waited a beat and then turned back to the view. 'So you sold the farm. To Rick Procter, of all people?'

'He offered me a good deal, son. A lifeline when no one else could. Or would.'

'I'm sure he did! Probably rubbing his hands at the prospect of dealing with an alcoholic.' He gestured at the flat around them. 'You bought this in return?'

'Kind of.'

'Kind of?' Samson was staring at his father now, frowning. 'What does that mean?'

'I rent it.'

'You *rent* it? I don't understand.'

It was Joseph's turn to look out of the window, unable to bear the weight of his son's judgemental stare any longer. 'I didn't quite have enough to buy anywhere—'

'Christ, Dad! You drank it all?'

Joseph grimaced, the pleasure of having Samson acknowledge his paternity diminished by the pain of the accusation. But the truth was harder to explain, so he let it pass with a shrug.

'Christ!' Samson muttered again, running a hand through his hair. 'What a mess.'

Disappointment. It was an emotion Joseph O'Brien had become used to seeing on his son's face. He fought the urge to close the distance between them, to put his arms around his son's strong shoulders and tell him not to worry. That things were different. But it was too early to tell. Two years dry. It was a mere drop in the stormy ocean of overcoming his addiction. So he wasn't about to make any promises.

'What brings you back?' he asked, shifting the focus.

'Work. Or lack of it.'

'You've quit the police?'

'Kind of.' Samson gave a half-smile, offering no more than his father had.

'So what are you going to do? And where are you staying?'

'I'm setting up a business here. A detective agency. It'll tide me over until things are sorted and then . . .'

'This isn't long-term?'

'I doubt it.' Samson turned once more to the window and then to the small bookcase in the corner, a photograph in a silver frame atop it. 'There's nothing much here for me.'

Joseph followed his son's gaze. She was beautiful. Would always be. Long, dark hair falling across part of her face, blue eyes full of laughter as she looked into the camera, mouth split into a wide smile. Twenty-six years dead, and still she filled him with longing.

'At least you brought Mum with you.' Samson was crossing the room now, heading for the door. 'Although I doubt she'd approve of you selling the farm.'

He stopped, hand on the doorknob, as though regretting his last retort. Then he shrugged. 'Look after yourself, Dad. I'll see you around.'

The door closed behind him and Joseph O'Brien's first action was to check the time. The Spar would still be open. He could get down there and back in the growing dark without anyone noticing. And he'd be set for the evening, a bottle in his hand. Something to take away the chill.

Then he lifted his gaze to the photograph, to her laughing face. *At least you brought Mum with you.* What a fool that boy could be. For next to the young mother in her best dress, standing so proudly over the prize-winning sheep at the Malham Show, was an equally proud child. Dark hair like hers. Eyes as blue as hers. And his face lit up with happiness.

'I brought you too, Samson,' he said bleakly, blinking away tears in the darkening room.

'Knock, knock!' The announcement and the door

opening coincided and Arty Robinson stood in the door-way, a posse of elderly people craning over him to see into the flat. 'We're off to the chippy. Look smart or we'll miss the early-bird special.'

'I don't want—'

'Not a matter of what you want, my lad. I need your help. How else am I going to get all these geriatrics down the hill?' He tipped his bald head at the crowd behind him, walking frames and an oxygen trolley making his point.

'Don't know who you're calling geriatric,' sniped Edith, tapping Arty sharply on the ankle with her stick. 'At least my heart is sound.'

'And so would mine be, if I didn't have to put up with you lot! Come on, Joseph, don't leave me at their mercy.' Arty's face was pulled into an expression of entreaty that would have weakened a man of stone.

'Okay, okay.' Joseph laughed despite himself. 'I'll be with you in a minute.'

Arty grinned and then shooed the rest of the group out into the corridor, the door closing on a resumption of their good-natured bickering.

It was what he needed – a distraction. No doubt Arty and the others were well aware of that, being no strangers to the O'Brien saga that had been entertaining Bruncliffe for almost two decades.

Feeling the flicker of desire for drink fading, Joseph crossed to the bookcase, picked up his wallet, ran his finger over the two laughing faces, and headed for the door. He would make it through today. And tomorrow morning he would wake up sober, knowing his son was back in town.

It was only as he caught up with the others at the far end of the corridor that he realised Samson hadn't said where he was staying.

The body was a dead weight. Lifting it, slumping it over the quad bike, the dark coming down fast. Soon it would be total, pierced only by the headlights pointing into the hillside. It would provide the perfect cover.

A push of the throttle and the bike began moving, heading up the steep fell, carrying its inert load on a final journey.

'He's *staying*?' Towards the back of the now-closed Peaks Patisserie, Elaine Bullock was sprawled on a sofa, staring across the coffee table, a muffin suspended halfway to her mouth. 'Blimey, Delilah. I can't see that going down well in town.'

Delilah collapsed into an armchair, dropped her head into her hands and groaned. 'I know. I'm going to be a pariah when people find out. And when Will hears . . . I won't be allowed to set foot on the farm.'

A hand stretched out to grasp the despairing young woman's arm. 'It won't be that bad. I'm sure you have your reasons, and people will understand.'

Delilah looked up at the serene face of Lucy Metcalfe. 'No they won't. Because my life is such a mess, I've had to give in and allow that man a base to build a business, here where he's not welcome. In Bruncliffe terms, I've sold out.'

Lucy laughed and passed the plate of muffins over to her upset friend before her other friend ate them all.

'There's plenty would have done the same, Delilah – Will amongst them. Don't tell me he wouldn't abandon his high morals if it meant saving Ellershaw. He lives and breathes for that place.'

'How little you know him,' mumbled Delilah, gazing disconsolately at the pile of blueberry muffins before her. 'He's made of granite when it comes to forgiveness.'

'Actually, granite isn't as hard as you think,' Elaine interjected through a mouthful of cake. 'Topaz is tougher. And prettier. And then there's—'

'Either way,' said Lucy, cutting off Elaine's mineral-based digression, which wasn't helping Delilah's mood. 'I don't see how it's Will's place to be doing the forgiving. It was Nathan's christening that Samson interrupted and it was Ryan's funeral he didn't attend, so if anyone has a right to hold a grudge, it's me.'

'And you don't?' Elaine asked, stretching for another muffin.

Lucy shook her head. 'No. And neither did Ryan.' She glanced over at the photo of her young husband above the counter, her face a mixture of pride and sorrow. 'He didn't have a bad word to say about Samson, despite that ruckus at the christening. All he regretted was that he lost touch with him . . .' She shrugged. 'Makes me think that if Ryan was here now, he'd be welcoming Samson back with open arms.'

'He'd be the only one,' muttered Delilah.

'Not if I can help it!' Lucy tilted her chin, face uncharacteristically defiant. 'I think he'll be a breath of fresh air for the town and I, for one, am happy he's come home. And if that sets me at odds with my brothers-in-law . . .'

She shrugged again and reached out for a muffin, as though in a further act of rebellion.

Elaine grinned with blue-stained lips. 'She's right, Delilah. Will has no right to be getting indignant. And as for the rest of folk in Bruncliffe, perhaps they'll all benefit from a bit of O'Brien charisma around the place.'

'Charisma?' spluttered Delilah. 'Sheer bloody-mindedness more like. I don't know how I'm going to survive the next six months.'

Lucy patted her on the arm. 'Easy,' she said, beginning to smile. 'Sign him up for the dating agency. When word gets out, you'll have a flock of women wanting to join. You might as well make money out of all this.'

'Lucy Metcalfe!' exclaimed Delilah through a grin, as Elaine collapsed in laughter. 'Just when did you get to be such a capitalist?'

'When you two started coming round here and eating all my profits,' replied Lucy, as her friends continued to laugh. 'Joking aside, though, I don't feel any resentment towards Samson over the christening or the funeral. As for that business with his dad – that's their concern.'

'Might be Rick Procter's concern, too,' said Elaine, face serious once more. 'I wouldn't like to be him when Samson confronts him over the sale of Twistleton Farm.'

'But Rick was doing Mr O'Brien a favour,' protested Delilah. 'How can Samson possibly object, when he wasn't even here and his dad didn't know how to get in touch with him?'

'Even so, you know how Samson felt about the farm. The connection to his mother . . .'

'Such a connection that he buggered off and left it!'

'Talking of the farm being sold,' said Lucy, refilling their coffee cups. 'Where's Samson staying? Do you know?'

Delilah shook her head. 'No. He could be sleeping rough for all I care.' And with that, she finally reached out to take a muffin.

'Tom's taking his time.' Lynn Alderson cast the words over her shoulder as she drained the potatoes, plumes of steam curling around her arms.

'He is that,' agreed her husband, rising from his chair to stand at the long window which looked up the darkened dale towards Wether Fell. Twin points of light in the distance located his son. 'He's not on his way back yet, either, by the looks of things. Must have met a problem.'

'Or been on his phone while his tea spoils!'

Bill Alderson laughed. 'Don't be too hard on him, love. He's a good lad—' He paused, leaning closer to the glass. 'That's odd . . .'

'What?'

'The lights. They just went out.'

'Probably a sheep standing in front of the bike.'

But Bill Alderson wasn't convinced. Partly because he knew just how powerful those lights were. And partly because a sense of unease had assailed him at seeing them extinguished.

'I'll go check on him,' he said, reaching for his jacket hanging on the back door. 'Won't be long.'

'Tell him his tea is ruined,' said Lynn with a smile. 'And yours too, if you don't get back soon.'

The door had already closed on her departing husband

and he was jogging to the Land Rover. In a scatter of gravel he pulled out of the drive.

Where to stay? The evening was upon Bruncliffe, shops shuttered, street lights fighting a battle against the growing dark.

At least he should be safe here. Despite the reception he'd received. The punch from Delilah had been nothing compared to the assault he'd sustained at the beginning of the week. Samson touched his cheek, the flesh still tender, the bone bruised. He had more bruises under his clothes. His ribs. His back. There'd been three of them in bala-clavas, waiting for him as he returned home late at night. The attack had been vicious and only interrupted by a passing Good Samaritan who'd chased the men off and helped Samson into his flat. He'd tried his best to get the police involved, but Samson wouldn't hear of it.

He was the police. And he was more than involved.

Taking the advice of the one person he could trust, he'd decided to leave town, put distance between himself and the trouble he was caught up in. He'd thought only of Bruncliffe. With everything that was brewing – the sus-pension, the accusations – it had seemed like the best option. A quick search on the internet and he'd found the vacant office space that would provide him with an income. He'd presumed he'd have a place to stay. Maybe even a welcome of sorts.

How wrong he'd been. He was stranded up here in a hostile environment, waiting for a call to tell him things had blown over and he could head back to London. He'd been warned it could take months.

Basically he was in exile in his own home town.

Samson walked wearily back to his office. He'd stopped at the Spar off the marketplace to pick up a couple of sandwiches, shunning the idea of eating out, both on economic and social grounds. He wasn't in the mood for anyone else to try picking a fight. Not tonight. Not after that meeting with his father.

It hadn't gone how he'd planned it – his shock at seeing Joseph O'Brien bringing a surge of guilt and regret to the surface, which he'd then masked with anger. Typical O'Brien reaction. Bury the real emotion with aggression.

He hadn't intended to be so curt. But then he hadn't been expecting his father to look so old. A good ten years younger than some of the folk who'd been in the lounge at Fellside Court, yet Joseph O'Brien could have passed as their contemporary, the decades of hard drinking having taken their toll. Hollow-cheeked, nose patterned with broken capillaries and a shake that accompanied his move-ments – even his voice, that soft Irish accent which had wooed his wife with its ability to break into beautiful song, was cracked and strained. He was a shadow of the vibrant man Samson remembered from his early child-hood. Before his mother died and the drinking began.

At least he was sober. That was one thing Samson hadn't been banking on, having learned the hard way not to hold out hope when it came to his father's ability to abstain from alcohol. How long would it last, though?

Samson turned down Back Street, the hardware shop on the corner closed, likewise Plastic Fantastic next to it, the collection of colourful buckets and basins that decor-ated its exterior during opening hours removed for the night. And there, looking forlorn underneath a street light, his scarlet motorbike.

Damn! He'd forgotten all about it. He couldn't leave it out here on the road. While he doubted crime had rocketed since he'd been away, he didn't trust the members of his welcoming committee not to tamper with it out of malice.

Throwing his leg over the bike, he switched it on, the engine's throaty rumble loud in the confines of the small street. It was enough to bring a couple of faces to the window of the Fleece. Ignoring them, he turned the Royal Enfield around, turned right at the hardware store and then took a sharp right, down the narrow ginnel that ran at the back of the shops. A high wall marked one side, holding back the gardens of the houses perched above on Crag Lane. On the other side were a series of gates. He stopped outside the third one, got off the bike and let himself into a small yard with a key from the bunch Delilah had reluctantly given him.

He'd leave the bike here for now. Then he'd go round to the Coach and Horses on High Street and get a room. If he could afford it. He wheeled the bike inside onto the concrete paving and was about to close the gate when he remembered his rucksack, propped next to the desk in his new office.

Might as well go in through the back door, now he was here. It would avoid the attention of the drinkers in the pub.

Gate locked behind him, he walked up the path through deep shadows, with barely enough light for him to locate the lock. Country-dark. And this was in Bruncliffe. By now, Twistleton would be isolated in a world of black, the moon and the stars on a clear night the only illumination. God, how he missed that. The thought blind-sided him.

Opening the back door, he felt for a light switch and let the bare bulb of what seemed to be a boot-room chase away his nostalgia. Walking boots. Muddy trainers. Wellingtons. Discarded around the floor, barely space to step without tripping over footwear. And that damp, musty smell of soil. He picked up the nearest shoe, a size twelve. Yeti-feet! Unless he'd missed something earlier, some of these weren't Delilah's.

Curiosity aroused, he threw it back on the floor. So, Miss Metcalfe had her love life sorted without need of her own dating agency. Hopefully the lucky man had a strong chin. He'd need it, thought Samson ruefully, rubbing a hand over his own tender face.

Glad to leave the odour of feet, he entered the small kitchen which, with the cloakroom next to it, was all part of his rental package, according to his new landlady. He looked longingly at the kettle. A coffee would be perfect with his sad meal for one. In hope rather than expectation, he opened the fridge.

Empty. Nothing in the cupboards, either. But there was a second kitchen upstairs. There must be, as Delilah had made that awful tea up there earlier.

He opened the door onto the hallway. Afterwards, he couldn't give an explanation for his behaviour, but for some reason he didn't put the light on. Perhaps it was the fact that the fanlight above the door was allowing ample illumination from the street lamp outside. Or perhaps he knew, even then, what he was intending to do.

He headed upstairs, to be greeted by a locked door. Delilah's office, spanning the back of the property. Along the landing, at the front, he found another kitchen, larger than the one downstairs and, more importantly, with coffee and milk. And Dog-gestives, should his Spar sandwich prove insufficient. He filled the kettle – again using only the light from the street, which was filtering past the three initials decorating the window – and while it was boiling, decided to investigate the second floor. He was a detective after all.

Stairs creaking, he climbed up to arrive at a narrow landing, three rooms giving off it. The first door yielded a small bathroom in which he could just about discern the outlines of a shower, toilet and sink. Being at the back of the building and with a skylight above, he risked pulling the light cord to reveal a line of soaps and shampoos on the inset shelf in the shower cabinet, a faint smell of coconut perfuming the air. Only one towel on the radiator. One toothbrush in the mug above the sink.

Intrigued, he returned to the landing and went to the next door, which opened halfway before being blocked by something. Thick curtains pulled over the window, again overlooking the backyard; he flicked on the light. Junk. Piled high. A dining table. A sofa. Two easy chairs. Lots of boxes. Even a bed, which was what was stopping the door from opening fully. Looking more closely, he saw the quality. This wasn't junk. So what, then? The contents of someone's house, stored up here. For what?

He turned off the light, pulled the door to and crossed to the final room. This door opened wide, looking out onto the pub opposite through an unadorned window.

And in between was a mountain of boxes, all labelled in a clear hand. He squatted down next to the closest stack, squinting to make out the words in the weak light. *N's LP collection. N's books. N's maps. N's kitchenware.*

Storage. Delilah was storing furniture and belongings for the mysterious *N*. Samson closed the door, his mind already ticking over.

She wouldn't notice. Not if it was for a few nights. Just while he got on his feet.

He returned to the room next to the bathroom. A bed. It'd be a sin not to use it. Especially when he had his sleeping bag in his rucksack. And she'd never know. He'd set the alarm on his mobile to go off early, grab a shower and be down in the office before she even got here.

Where was the harm in that?

None, he told himself, choosing to ignore the fact that he'd been skulking around in half-light to avoid alerting the neighbours to his presence. With a clear conscience, he descended to the ground floor to collect his rucksack. Might as well get settled in.

Sheep. In the middle of the road. The headlights picked out the startled flash of eyes as the animals scattered before the approaching vehicle. How the hell had they got loose?

Concerned, Bill Alderson pulled up at the gate into the lower field. It yawned widely onto an expanse of black, supplying the answer to his question. The bloody gate was open. Cursing roundly, he turned the Land Rover off the road and got out, the closing door loud in the darkness. Torch providing a narrow path of light, he started up the sloping pasture towards the top field. He was halfway across the grass when he realised what was missing.

The quad bike. He couldn't hear it. Or see it.

'Tom?' he called out, worried now. 'Tom, lad? Can you hear me?'

An owl hooted sharply in response, triggering the bleat of a sheep somewhere ahead of him. Nothing else other than the wind swirling mournfully around the dale. Then the beam of the torch plucked a gatepost from the night. Bill flicked the light to the left, expecting wooden rails and the solid brace that he'd repaired numerous times. But the gate wasn't closed, two sheep standing nervously in the space it should be occupying.

'What the hell—?' No wonder the animals were out – both gates left open. It wasn't like Tom to be so careless.

Anxiety growing, Bill Alderson entered the top field, the land rising sharply under his boots. Directing the light along the wall next to him, he began to work it slowly across the dark. There. About a hundred yards away, the unmistakable shape of the quad bike, overturned, wheels silhouetted against the night sky. Bill was already fumbling for his mobile. When his torch caught the contrasting pallor of an arm protruding from beneath the dark mass of bike, he started running.

'Ambulance,' he screamed into the phone. 'There's been an accident . . .'

Across the black fields and the stone walls, within the cosy confines of the farmhouse, Lynn Alderson watched the bobbing torchlight and wondered just how much longer her menfolk would be.

7

Early – way too early for a body that had been denied caffeine. Samson watched the dark surrendering gradually, the fells taking shape, edges sharpening as the light increased.

Once dawn broke, it was going to be a stunning day. Cold, though, the bite of the wind blowing across the open space telling him it was late October in the Dales. He shivered inside his jacket, chilled from his walk down, and wondered how long it would take his southern-softened constitution to re-acclimatise.

Lowering his eyes from the shadowy expanse of the hills, he concentrated on the platform in front of him. Bruncliffe Old Station wasn't much of a place. Built in the heady days of rail expansion to serve the Leeds-to-Morecambe line, it had been the first station in the area, situated a lonely mile south-west of the town centre. But when the Midland Railway company got approval some years later to run a train line through the middle of Bruncliffe en route to the north, a new station was built in the town and this outpost became somewhat neglected.

Samson had always liked travelling from here. He had good memories of the place: a rare outing to the seaside, his mother's excitement almost as keen as his own; a trip to Leeds to watch cricket, even though it was something his father, as an adopted Englishman, struggled to appreciate.

In all those years the station hadn't changed much and it retained a certain simplicity, an old-world charm. A small hut offering shelter on either side of the tracks, a level crossing for passengers rather than the safety of a bridge. And the views. When the sun rose, there would be a clear panorama of the rising fells, Bruncliffe a mere huddle of slate and stone below them.

But if Mrs Hargreaves was right, what had happened here was far from quaint.

Murder. Could it have been?

With the sky beginning to be stretched with light, peeling the night slowly back from the beautiful scenery, it was difficult to imagine something so heinous. But Samson knew from experience that death was no respecter of environment; there was no sentimentality when it came to killing. And this was the perfect place to commit a crime. The platform was set back from the road, a thick line of trees shielding it from view. Around it, fields unfolded emptily, stone walls criss-crossing them, not a house in sight. Add to that the murky conditions on the morning in question, and there had been ample opportunity for someone to give Richard Hargreaves a helping hand towards his early destiny and not be seen.

Not even on CCTV, apparently.

Above him to his right, a lone camera stared across the platform. Despite a week of trying, Samson had been unable to gain access to the footage, the train company and the police both refusing to part with it. It was frustrating.

In his previous role he'd have had his hands on it

immediately. Seconded from the Metropolitan Police, he'd spent the last six years working within the highest law enforcement agencies in the land: the Serious Organised Crime Agency and its replacement, the National Crime Agency. He'd been part of an elite group of detectives leading investigations into drug cartels and criminal gangs. Nothing had been beyond their powers.

Now he was a mere private detective and couldn't even get permission to see a bloody CCTV video.

He kept telling himself this reduced status was temporary. One phone call from London and he'd be back in the high-octane world of real detective work. After seven days in Bruncliffe, that phone call couldn't come quickly enough.

In the meantime, however, given that Richard Hargreaves had died in mid-October, before the clocks went back, it was debatable how much would have been captured by the camera anyway. Almost a fortnight later, at six-twenty in the morning the station wasn't exactly ablaze with light, even with the benefit of that extra hour. Throw a thick mist into the equation . . .

All the same, Samson would have preferred to have seen the footage for himself so he could rule it out. Instead, he'd opted to drop by the station at the exact time Richard would have been there. But now he was on the platform, cold and desperate for a coffee, he wasn't entirely sure why he'd come.

On the off-chance that he'd uncover a vital clue that would prove Mrs Hargreaves right?

Only trouble was . . . there was no motive for murder. In the week since she'd asked for his help, Samson had discovered nothing that would imply the death of her son was anything other than suicide. His visit to Bruncliffe's oversized Victorian police station opposite the library on Fell Lane had been a waste of time, producing only bad memories. The minute he'd entered the small reception area, he'd been ambushed by the past – his dishevelled father sitting on the wooden bench, watching with blood-shot eyes as his son was led out from the cells. The father was still drunk; the son battered and bruised from a fight in the Fleece the night before. But through his befuddled, sleep-deprived state, the teenage Samson had seen how they appeared – these O'Briens – to the desk sergeant. The shame had hit him hard and he'd dragged his mumbling father out onto the street, where George Capstick was waiting to drive them home.

He'd not told his father what the fight was about – what were they ever about? A defence of someone who was never sober long enough to worry about the names people called him. Samson had arrived at the Fleece at last orders, intending to take his father home. He'd found him in a belligerent mood, determined to drink more. They'd argued and Samson had turned to go, when a well-built man at the other end of the bar made a quip about Boozy O'Brien. Without even taking a moment to consider the differences in size, Samson lunged, grabbing the opportunity to vent his frustration with both fists. When the police arrived, he'd have gone for them too, if Ryan Metcalfe hadn't caught hold of his arm.

He was seventeen. Working long hours on the farm. Trying to care for an alcoholic. He'd been a tinder box

waiting for the spark. Perhaps the old sergeant had understood, for he'd let Samson off with a verbal warning.
Nothing on the record. Although, when he found out that
the unlicensed Samson had driven into town in his dad's
car, he'd insisted the lad spent the night in the cells.

Wiser now, with the benefit of his years in the police
force behind him, Samson could appreciate the actions of
the officer – even if at the time he'd been furious. A night
alone in a cell being sufficient to cool any temper, it had
been a more subdued teenager who'd walked into the
reception area the next morning. It was the first and last
time he'd been in police custody.

When he'd returned to the forbidding building the
week before, Samson could see that nothing much had
changed. The high counter with its sliding glass partitions
still ran parallel to the back wall, a low wooden bench
opposite beneath the window. To the left of the entrance,
a notice board carried a list of missing persons alongside
an invitation to meet the Police and Crime Commissioner;
to the right, a locked door led to the rest of the station.
And to the overnight lock-up, which Samson could attest
was far from five-star accommodation.

He'd approached the young constable behind the desk
and introduced himself. Uniform almost dwarfing his thin
frame, the lad had started stuttering and stammering
before disappearing into the back office. He'd re-emerged
with a heavyset man; someone Samson recognised straight
away.

'So, the rumours are true.' The sergeant rested thick
forearms on the counter. 'Unfortunately.'

'Good to see you too, Gavin.'

'You in trouble already?' The sergeant gestured at the bruises which were fading, but still visible.

Samson repressed a smart retort. A couple of years older, Gavin Clayton was a born policeman – even though it had taken him multiple attempts to persuade the police authority of that – and had never quite believed trouble-maker Samson O'Brien's conversion to the right side of the law. Which, to be fair, was understandable. While Samson's change of heart had happened on the road to Leeds, rather than to Damascus, it had been just as incredible for those who knew him.

But then they didn't know the reason why he'd left Bruncliffe so quickly. Samson wasn't about to enlighten them.

He forced himself to smile. 'Not yet. I'll let you know when I am.'

'So how can I help you?'

Pulling a business card out of his pocket, Samson slid it towards the officer.

'The Dales Detective Agency?' A snort of laughter followed. 'Bit of a comedown for the Met's finest, isn't it? Seems like you're fast-tracking the wrong way these days.'

Another bite of the tongue, resisting the urge to comment on backwater coppers. Or the substantial girth that rested above the waistline of the officer's trousers, suggesting more time raiding the biscuit tin than offenders' houses. Nor did Samson correct the assumption that his last posting was with the Met. If the inhabitants of Bruncliffe were largely ignorant of the work he had been doing for SOCA and the NCA, now wasn't the time to tell them.

It would only make his fall from grace even more dramatic.

'Felt like a change,' he lied, wondering how long it would be before the truth followed him home. Hopefully he'd be long gone by then. 'I'm doing some work for Mrs Hargreaves.'

'Richard's mother?' Sergeant Clayton looked up. 'Has she hired you?'

Samson nodded, eliciting a curse from the man on the other side of the desk.

'Damn! I told her she was on a hiding to nothing. Daft woman is throwing good money away on a fool's errand.'

'I'll try not to take that personally.'

'Take it how the hell you like. There's nothing suspicious about Richard's death. It was suicide.'

'You found a note?'

'Didn't need one. He threw himself in front of a train. What more notification do you need?'

'And the CCTV?'

'Nothing on it.'

'Can I see it?'

The sergeant had bristled. 'Think you might spot something us rural coppers didn't? Listen, O'Brien, it was suicide. Plain and simple. And on your way out of here, it's worth noting that Bruncliffe folk don't take kindly to those who swindle money out of grieving mothers.'

Samson had left empty-handed.

If the police station had proved fruitless in the detective's search for something suspicious about Richard Hargreaves' demise, the dead man's home hadn't been any better. The semi-detached house across the road from the school, with its carpets in need of a vacuum, dust thick on the bookcases, and telling blank spaces where furniture and pictures had once rested, had suggested a divorced man with little appetite for domestic duties, but not much else.

However, if there wasn't a motive for murder, there didn't seem to be much reason for suicide, either.

Samson ran a hand over his weary face and regretted once again that he hadn't made time for a coffee before coming to stand on this bleak platform. For the last six days he'd been rising before dawn, grabbing a quick shower and hustling down to his office, so that when the back door crashed open at seven, he was already at his desk.

He hadn't banked on Delilah having a cleaner when he'd made the decision to sleep in the spare room on the top floor. The first morning had almost been a disaster. He'd been coming out of the shower when he heard the door slam two floors below and had dressed hastily, no time for drying. Or underwear. He'd made it as far as the first-floor kitchen and was looking nonchalant – as non-chalant as someone wearing jeans over a damp backside could – when Ida Capstick marched in.

Another aspect of Bruncliffe that hadn't changed. The same whippet-like frame, face all angles. And a sour expression, which, in all the years he'd lived at Twistleton Farm with the Capstick siblings his nearest neighbours, he'd never seen graced with anything resembling a smile. Friday morning had been no exception.

'George said tha were back,' had been her greeting.

Closely followed by 'What's tha doing up here? Haven't tha got a kitchen of tha own downstairs?'

He'd gestured at the stocked cupboards, given her his best roguish grin, and offered to make her a cup of tea. It was the latter that deflected her suspicion and she'd gone about her business, vacuuming and dusting, with no further questions. That night he'd set his alarm for an hour earlier.

It wasn't ideal, the way he was living at the moment. Having to sneak around, careful not to leave any signs that the office was more than just the place where he worked. His sleeping bag was stuffed into the top of one of the boxes in his makeshift bedroom every morning and the box resealed before he had a shower, one ear permanently cocked in case Ida changed her routine. When he'd meticulously wiped away all traces of moisture from the shower tray, breakfast was an apple and a banana. And coffee, of course. In the evening, the charade of being seen to leave by the front door was followed by an aimless ride around the area, until he could be sure Delilah had gone home. Then he drove down the ginnel at the back, parked the motorbike in the yard and let himself into the building. His tea was eaten in the first-floor kitchen in the dark, the light of the street lamp the only illumination. After a liberal spray of air-freshener to remove the smell of curry, Chinese or fish and chips, he retired to bed where, with the thick curtains pulled across the back window, he would read one of the books from the box next to the bed before going to sleep.

He really needed to find better accommodation, if only

for the sake of his waistline. Plus he hated the deceit, telling anyone who asked where he was staying that he was renting a place in Hellifield, six miles down the road. It was far enough from Bruncliffe that it justified the presence of his motorbike in the backyard of the office every day, and far enough that no one in town would detect his lie.

But for now, his morals and his weight were going to have to be sacrificed, as his unauthorised use of Delilah's spare room was the only way he could afford to stay around. While his current dishonourable status – suspended, pending investigation – came with full pay, he was reluctant to spend a penny of his salary, aware that he might have to cover his legal costs if things in London went badly. With six months' worth of rent already gone from his savings, however, he had precious little left to live on. Which was why he needed to wrap up the Hargreaves case quickly.

Suicide, then. He sighed, not looking forward to telling Mrs Hargreaves the news. But there was no other answer. Casting a last sour glance at the useless CCTV camera, Samson began walking towards the path back to town. Two steps later, he stopped.

Something was nagging at him.

He looked over his shoulder at the camera once more. There was something odd about it. The way the lens was pointing . . .

On the platform opposite, the watchful eye of an identical camera was ignoring him, its focus on the length of concrete where passengers would stand. But the one on this side . . .

It was tilted so that the lens was watching the track. Not the platform.

He walked over to the post supporting the camera, turned his back on it and moved forward, following its line of sight. A short distance and he was at the edge of the platform. To his left, the station light. To his right, the tracks.

Even allowing for a wide angle of coverage, the camera wasn't in the best position for providing surveillance. Either the people who'd installed it were idiots or . . . it had been moved.

Wind perhaps? Or something more malicious?

Samson hunched his shoulders, a familiar feeling of suspicion in his gut. Then a loud horn blared from behind and set his heart thumping.

The six-thirty train, pulling into the station so close to him that the air rushed against his jacket. He jumped away from the platform edge, breath ragged, and threw an arm of apology up for the scowling guard.

He desperately needed a coffee.

It was a puzzle, all right. A puzzle indeed.

Water in the shower tray when Miss Delilah wasn't in yet. It was the second time this week. And it was strange. The young lady must have arrived early and gone out again, leaving the tray wet and liable to mould. Tutting her disapproval, Ida Capstick ran a cloth around the porcelain. If it happened again, she'd have to remind Miss Delilah of the merits of wiping down. Might have to tell her about the odd smell in the room next door, too.

Ida gave the mirror a quick clean, gathered together the

tools of her trade and placed them in her bucket, before going back into the spare room.

That was better! She took a deep breath, fresh October air from the window she'd left open filling her lungs. The odour was less noticeable now, merely a faint trace of something – a deep, woody scent with a hint of lemon. Like an expensive floor polish. Probably something spilling in one of the many boxes. She negotiated her way between the stacks of cardboard and furniture and reached over to shut the window.

She'd keep an eye on it, she decided, picking her way back to the door. Even though officially she was only contracted to clean the main areas – the downstairs office, kitchen and cloakroom, the first-floor office and kitchen and the bathroom up here – she'd got into the habit of popping into the two unused rooms on the top floor once a week to give them a vacuum. As much as she could, considering the amount of stuff piled up in here.

Ida cast a critical glance over the contents of the room. Miss Delilah holding out hope, was what it was. Foolish child. That husband of hers had been nothing but a flash smile and quick patter, just like his father. Bruncliffe was well shot of him – even if Miss Delilah didn't seem to think so, storing all his belongings when she should be selling them and using the money to support her business. She even had his shoes still cluttering up the back porch, as if he was due home any day . . .

Ah well, it wasn't her problem. She was done here. Next up was Taylor's. Hopefully the tight-fisted old bugger wouldn't be in. Then she could sneak a cuppa to keep her going, seeing as young Mr O'Brien hadn't been around this morning to offer her one, like he had done every day for the last week.

At the thought of the new tenant, Ida gave an instinctive nod of approval. He was an early riser, that one. And a hard worker. There was folk around town who'd do well to take a leaf out of his book. Despite all that was being said about him.

Bucket clanking, Ida Capstick made her way down the two flights of stairs to the ground floor. Returning the bucket to the cloakroom, she let herself out of the back door and into the morning as fingers of light streaked the sky.

It was going to be a clear one. Cold, too. All the more need for that cuppa.

Delilah Metcalfe was gasping for a cup of tea. She ran down the hillside towards Crag Lane, Tolpuddle bounding ahead of her, the dog still full of energy despite a good run across the fells. She loved this part of the day as the heavens grew light and, if you were lucky, the sun rose over the Crag to shine down on Bruncliffe.

Given that it was the last Wednesday in October, it would be a while before the sun got up on this particular morning. But then the darker starts suited Delilah, too. She could go for a run without being seen. Apart from by Seth Thistlethwaite, of course, the sharp-eyed old man having somehow spotted her. After he'd mentioned it at the funeral the week before, she'd been half-expecting her former coach to air his views on her return to the hills, but he hadn't. Which was unusual, as Seth rarely held back from expressing an opinion. Perhaps he sensed she wasn't ready to be pressured into competition . . . yet.

Two months she'd been back running and it had made her wonder why she'd ever stopped. That feeling of freedom as you crested a fell and saw the expanse of moor laid out before you. How could she have turned her back on that?

Love – that was how. Or what she'd thought was love.

It had been just after her twentieth birthday when Bernard Taylor, Bruncliffe's ambitious estate agent, had decided it was time to embrace the opportunities being presented by the internet. But typically, he'd been reluctant to pay the going rate. So he'd approached Delilah, who by then had been working for an IT company in Skipton for a couple of years, gaining hands-on experience in an industry that was changing by the minute. Having heard good reports about the help she'd already given to some of Bruncliffe's businesses, Bernard offered to be her first official client. He was also the catalyst that changed her life.

Or rather, his son Neil was. Charismatic, urbane, sophisticated, the graphic design graduate was a far cry from the lads she met at Young Farmers get-togethers. He didn't talk incessantly about sheep, for a start. It hadn't taken long for her treacherous heart to fall for his charms; and Delilah never questioned why, if he was such a creative talent, Neil was back in Bruncliffe selling houses for his father. She was too in love to question anything. Within weeks they were dating. Within six months she'd given up running. And before the year was out, she'd moved in with him and he'd left his job in order to pursue a career in design.

It was only looking back that she was able to see the flaws. The months Neil had spent not working, bemoaning the cultural desert that was the Dales and refusing to sacrifice his artistic beliefs in order to find clients. When she'd mooted the idea of going freelance herself, he'd been quick to support her, turning her solo project into a joint venture. She'd been flattered. His expertise would make their company stand out. By the time she was twenty-five, they were married and co-owners of a website development company. They bought a small cottage, high up at the back of town, and an office premises off the marketplace. For Delilah, life was like a dream.

Then Neil had had an affair.

Delilah had found out the way everyone in Bruncliffe found things out – from someone letting something slip after a pint or two. It transpired that the whole town had known about the florist in Grassington who'd needed a new website, and got more besides. It also transpired that Delilah had more of a forgiving heart than she'd thought. She'd accepted Neil's apologies. She'd buried her pride. She'd tried to forget. And she'd wished for the first time in years that she was still running so she could escape the town, the sympathetic looks and the pointed comments.

But if she'd thought her world had fallen apart when Neil's attention strayed, she realised how much more she was capable of being hurt the day Ryan was killed. On the outside, she stayed strong for Lucy and Nathan, but inside she went to pieces. She let the business slide and turned to Neil for solace. Which is when she'd seen her husband in a new light: the light her brother Will had always viewed him in. While the debonair designer embraced the role of supportive husband for the first couple of months, he soon tired of the commitment. He began to moan about the hours he was having to work. He began to complain about the fact that she was always sad. And finally, he came home with a puppy, his remedy for Delilah's grieving.

She doubted he had any idea how perfect that gift had been.

Tolpuddle burst into Delilah's life in a blur of paws, ungainly legs and love. So much love. He adored the pair of them, but especially Delilah. When she found it hard to get up in the morning, he was there on the bed, gambolling around, begging her to come and play. In the face of such enthusiasm, she found it impossible to stay depressed and before long, returned to work, Tolpuddle establishing his place in the office by her side.

Her return to her desk, however, brought bad news. The company was struggling, partly due to the recession, which had really taken hold, but mainly because Neil hadn't been doing his job. Or rather, he'd been concerned with the design part of the business, neglecting the more prosaic aspects such as securing new clients and chasing slow payments. He'd always claimed he was the style in their company while she was the substance. She realised now that, as a graphic designer, he hadn't meant that to be a compliment.

As she struggled to get things back under control, Delilah had come up with the idea of the Dales Dating Agency. Neil hadn't been enthusiastic. So she'd worked in the evenings, staying late at the office with Tolpuddle while she developed a concept she was sure would be successful. The irony of it all was that as she was trying to build a business based around love, Neil was having another affair.

This time Will told her about it. Told her she was an idiot as well. Given the Metcalfe propensity for stubbornness, that should have been enough to see Delilah forgive Neil a second time. Perhaps it would have been, if her husband hadn't blamed *her* for his wandering affections. She was never home. She never had time for him. She gave all her attention to Tolpuddle.

Then he'd announced that he was leaving her for this latest flame, a student from Leeds who was young enough to believe in his dreams – dreams Delilah had once believed in herself. They'd sorted out the finances, Neil wanting nothing to do with either company, or the properties they had mortgages on, as he was moving to London to pursue his career. Will had advised her to cut her losses too, but Delilah had refused to give up on everything. Her marriage was dead; she would fight to the death to keep her businesses alive. And so she'd ended up saddled with debt, running two companies, and with a Weimaraner who came out of the divorce with anxiety issues.

All in all, thought Delilah, jilted wife and dog were both doing well. Her broken heart had healed and she'd moved on, holding no bitterness for a relationship that had been too hasty, its participants too young. She heard from Neil occasionally, had his furniture stored on the top floor of the office building and had no doubt that she'd still find him charming, if she were to bump into him in town.

But she'd never forgiven him – or herself – for the running.

How had she allowed Neil to persuade her to give it up? Although, to be fair, she'd been coerced. He'd been so persistent. The training had got in the way. He hadn't liked her heading off for races at the weekends. He'd always had something planned in advance that would clash with the major events. Until it all became too much of an effort for a young woman who was head over heels.

Plus, she'd felt the pressure. Not from Seth, but certainly from the other locals. Always asking how she was doing. Always boasting to outsiders about Bruncliffe's fell-running prodigy. Club junior champion, national junior champion . . . only a matter of time, everyone said, before Delilah Metcalfe, Bruncliffe's finest, was English National Fell Running Champion.

So many capital letters; such a heavy weight to bear.

She'd quit on a wet Tuesday night in March when Seth had been shouting at her, pushing her to run faster, accusing her of slacking, of carrying winter weight. Something inside her had just snapped. She'd walked off the playing fields and never went back. And Seth being Seth, he'd never asked her to. While everyone else was busy telling her what a mistake she was making, what talent she was wasting, Seth Thistlethwaite simply let her be, concentrating his coaching skills on those who wanted to benefit from them.

Bloody idiot! She shook her head in despair at her younger self, took the final bit of grassy slope in one bound to land on the tarmac and sprinted with Tolpuddle down the lane to the house. With the prospect of a lovely day ahead – lunch with Ash and then a family get-together in the evening to celebrate her parents' wedding anniversary – she swung through the gate in a fine mood. It was only when her hand automatically reached round to the small pocket on the back of her running top that she realised.

She'd brought the office key by mistake.

Damn! She was locked out of the house.

She checked her watch. Eight-fifteen. She could be at the office in minutes, where both a spare key and a spare set of clothing were kept. She glanced down at her shorts and mud-splattered legs. If he was there, it would be game up. Samson O'Brien, her old running partner and inspiration, would know she'd been running.

What choice did she have?

'Come on,' she called to Tolpuddle, who was already at the porch, panting, ready for breakfast.

She started running, the dog quick to follow, down Crag Lane to the steps that dropped steeply to the ginnel which ran at the back of her building. Taking them in bounds, she arrived in the narrow passage and sprinted towards the back gate. And almost collided with Ida Capstick, who was just coming out of the yard, pushing her bicycle.

'Morning,' said Delilah, doubled-over to catch her breath. She wasn't worried about being seen post-run by Ida, as the cleaner's discretion could be relied on. Getting two words consecutively out of the woman was a marvel.

'Tha's headed for another shower!' The statement was delivered as Ida's disapproving eyes took in the muddied legs below Delilah's shorts. 'One a day's enough for most folks.'

'Yes . . . no . . .' Delilah faltered, confused, while Ida nodded brusquely and headed on her way, wheeling her bike. Delilah and Tolpuddle were left staring after her.

'What was that about?' muttered Delilah, watching the cleaner disappear around the corner – the cleaner she couldn't afford, but was too scared to sack.

That wasn't strictly true. She'd tried on a couple of occasions. She'd first broached the subject a year ago; Ida had stared her down into a gibbering wreck, and nothing had changed. The next time, Delilah had tentatively suggested that Ida cut her hours to two days a week, thinking that would at least be a start. Ida had nodded, lips in a thin line of condemnation, and had turned up the next day as usual. And the next. And the day after that. But when Delilah had gone to pay her at the end of the week, Ida had opened the envelope and put three days' worth of her wages back on Delilah's desk.

'Tha can keep that,' she'd said, pushing the money away from her.

'But you're still working five days,' Delilah had protested, pushing the money back again.

'And tha's not paying for it,' Ida said with a sniff. 'Mr Taylor is.'

Delilah had blinked, not understanding a word of this communication, but her cleaner had left the room before she could ask for an explanation. That explanation came a few days later, not from the lips of the cleaner but when Delilah overheard the estate agent, Bernard Taylor – her former father-in-law and the mayor of Bruncliffe – moaning in the Fleece that Ida Capstick had demanded a wage increase. And from then on, Ida had continued to clean the

Dales Dating Agency offices five mornings a week, but took pay for only two of those days. Bernard Taylor, it seemed, unbeknownst to him, was subsidising the rest.

'She's an enigma, that woman,' said Delilah with a shrug of incomprehension.

Tolpuddle panted back at her and then let out a sharp bark, reminding the whole neighbourhood that he hadn't been fed yet.

'Talking of cutbacks . . .' threatened Delilah, smiling down at the dog. 'How about you go on a diet?'

Tolpuddle looked up with the martyred expression which had earned him his name, making Delilah laugh as she entered the yard. That laugh was quickly smothered by a curse.

A scarlet motorbike stood resplendent on the concrete paving.

'Damn!' she muttered for the second time that morning. Samson was already in the office.

She glanced down at her running kit. There was no way he wouldn't notice it. And for some reason, she didn't want the attention. Her running was private – until such time as she chose to make it otherwise. Plus, he might offer to come with her, like he used to do when Seth wanted someone to stretch her. The pair of them – her in her teens, Samson almost adult – striding out across the fells in the evening light. It used to be the highlight of her week, and she sometimes wondered if her lack of enthusiasm for the sport hadn't arisen as a result of Samson's abrupt departure from town. With no one else to challenge her, she'd become bored, making it easier for Neil to discourage her. Now that she had regenerated her love of running, perversely she didn't want Samson sharing it. Nor did she want to contemplate what Will would have to say, if word got around that Delilah had been seen out on the hills with the man he considered the devil incarnate.

So, there was only one thing for it. She was going to have to sneak into her office unobserved.

8

Standing at the bedroom window, Samson watched the trail of children heading for the school, their shrieks and laughter filling the silent room, chasing away the stillness of an empty house. How must it have felt living here, he wondered, when your own kids had been taken away from you? Would that daily reminder be enough to make you kill yourself?

He turned his attention back to the cheap MDF desk that took up one wall of the smallest bedroom in what had been Richard Hargreaves' home. Papers and folders were strewn across its surface: articles on language acquisition, students' assignments, bills . . . Samson had been through it twice already and there was nothing to indicate that the man who'd lived here had been in danger.

Sitting amidst all the paperwork, Richard's laptop had offered up its contents with no resistance the first time Samson had visited the house, the lecturer clearly not having felt that he had anything to hide. Anything that might have got him killed. Nevertheless, Samson sat down and skimmed through the emails again. They were mostly work-related matters, apart from those sent by the Dales Dating Agency – an acknowledgement that Richard had renewed his membership for a further three months, and confirmation that he'd signed up for the next Speedy Date night.

Speedy Date night. Samson laughed, the sound abrupt in the quiet. It sounded so . . . tacky. So unlike Delilah. He couldn't imagine her playing Cupid. For the last week she'd stomped past his open door every morning with a grunted greeting, stopping only once to enter his office and slap a piece of paper on his desk – a list of Richard Hargreaves' friends. Other than that, she had made no effort to interact with him. In fact, if he'd been a sensitive soul, he might have been upset by her obvious resentment of his presence.

But he wasn't sensitive. His last twelve years in Bruncliffe had seen to that. You didn't get to be the son of Boozy O'Brien and survive without developing a thick skin.

He pulled his mind back to his work. No enemies that were apparent. Nothing to suggest Richard had got mixed up in anything shady. And as for his finances . . .

A jumble of bank and credit-card statements in the top drawer of his desk showed that Richard Hargreaves was just about managing – regular payments to his ex-wife and a hefty mortgage eating into his monthly salary. But there was no record of loans, official or otherwise, which might have pointed to trouble. Nor was there enough to justify throwing himself under a train. Especially when the second drawer contained brochures for a new housing development down by Low Mill, and pages of detailed financial reckoning in what Samson presumed was Richard's hand.

The lecturer had been planning to sell his house to buy

one of the smaller properties, which, judging by the figures he'd written down, would have left him with a tidy sum. Sufficient to clear the minor debts that he did have.

Samson got to his feet. He was wasting his time here. There was nothing to imply, either in this room or any of the others, that Richard Hargreaves had been murdered. He had one more appointment to keep and then he'd write up his report. Suicide. It was the only explanation, even if Mrs Hargreaves couldn't accept it.

He walked slowly down the stairs, heart heavy at the thought of breaking the news the grieving mother didn't want to hear.

Delilah slipped off her running shoes and turned the key quietly in the lock. One hand on Tolpuddle's collar, she crept into the building, easing the door shut behind her, and crossed the small kitchen silently on sock-clad feet.

'Stay!' she whispered to the dog as she began inching along the hallway towards the open office door.

Tolpuddle completely ignored her. With a sharp cry of delight, he bounded into the office, punctuating his arrival with loud barks.

'Bloody hell!' muttered Delilah. There would be no sneaking past now. Instead, she would have to adopt what had become her morning routine of late – getting by Samson's door without having to speak. While she might have acquiesced and accepted his tenancy, it didn't mean she had to go out of her way to be friendly. Not after the ear-bashing she'd taken from Will over Sunday lunch, when he'd let her know how he felt about Samson O'Brien being under her roof.

He'd been scathing. She'd tried to defend her corner, but it was difficult without revealing the true extent of her debts, something she'd so far succeeded in shielding from her family. It was bad enough that Will's disparaging opinion of her choice of husband had been proven well founded the day Neil Taylor ran off with another woman, leaving Delilah to hide her heartache for fear of her brother's caustic comments. Admitting that she'd been left almost destitute as a result would simply be giving Will something more to crow about.

Which is why Delilah had taken the latest brotherly reprimand on the chin, even when her mother – not normally one for holding a grudge – failed to support her. As far as the Metcalfes were concerned, Delilah had let the side down. So for the last week she'd been taking out her frustration at this injustice by snubbing her tenant, in a trail of logic that made perfect sense. To her.

Tolpuddle re-emerged in the hallway and she reached down to grab his collar, the dumb dog not quite on board with the decision to shun the new occupant. Every morning he ran into the office and showered affection on Samson, much to Delilah's disgust. And no doubt, to Samson's twisted delight. Today, however, Tolpuddle was looking forlorn.

'Decided to be loyal, for once, eh?' Delilah murmured as the dog let out a low whine. Then she couldn't resist. She turned, stiff-necked, and glanced into the room.

Empty. No dark shape at the desk. No cheeky smile cast her way as she stalked past. No suggestion that they go running together. Her face fell into a frown and, despite having successfully negotiated her way into the building undetected, she felt a sense of deflation. Which, being a Metcalfe, was closely followed by annoyance.

'Coming and going at all hours,' she muttered as she thumped up the stairs, Tolpuddle following without the usual fuss. 'Treating the place like a hotel.'

She was still muttering some time later when she emerged from the shower. She wasn't so disgruntled, however, that she neglected to wipe down the tiles and the tray. Being annoyed was one thing. Running the risk of Ida Capstick's wrath was another.

By ten o'clock, Samson still hadn't returned to the office. And he still hadn't managed to get a cup of coffee. But he was rather hopeful the latter was about to be rectified.

In a room overlooking the marketplace, he was comparing his surroundings with his memories. He looked around the refurbished office at what was now a contemporary space: the beautiful paintings of local scenery complementing the light furnishings; the heavy desk replaced by a glass table; the tasteful ash shelving that seemed to float on the walls . . .

The solicitor's office wasn't how he remembered it. It had been all wood panelling and plush carpet the day he'd walked in behind his father, both of them in their only suits, which had seen a lot of use that week. They'd sat stiffly on one side of the oak desk while, on the other, Mr Turpin had frowned over his glasses at the pair of them, the closest the lawyer had come to showing sympathy to any client.

Samson had been eight years old. The legalese meant nothing to him. The dry words which his father soaked up without comment were wasted on the young lad. He'd been there for one reason only: he'd begged his father to take him, convinced that the solicitor was some long-lost relation to the famous highwayman, and eager to see his mask.

Unsurprisingly, with expectations set so high, the day had been a disappointment. His comprehension of just what he'd lost not having sunk in; an awareness of all he would lose over the next few years something no one could have had. It had simply been a day wasted inside when he could have been scrambling over the hills or picking blackberries, or anything rather than listening to this old man mumble on.

Somehow, Samson thought twenty-six years later, today's meeting might be just as much of a waste of time. Having come away from Bruncliffe Old Station with his mind full of speculation, his return visit to Richard Hargreaves' house had left him unconvinced that foul play had been involved in the lecturer's death. Neither was he convinced it wasn't. He didn't hold out much hope that the next thirty minutes would help him make up his mind.

'Ah, Mr O'Brien . . . Samson, sorry to have kept you waiting.'

Samson turned, and felt time shift as he took in the smart-suited young man with outstretched hand in the doorway. 'Matty?'

Matthew Thistlethwaite beamed. 'To my friends!'

'I thought you were in Manchester?' Samson crossed the room to greet the man with a handshake and a slap on the back.

'I was. I did my training over there and then got home-sick.' He grinned and Samson could see the skinny youth of years ago, head stuck in a book as he walked home-wards, ignoring the teasing of the bigger lads. 'This place came up for sale when old Turpin retired, so I took a chance.'

'You kept the name, I see.'

Matty laughed. 'Despite what you think, it's good for business. No one forgets a lawyer called Turpin. Plus, they can't complain if my fees are highway robbery.' He gestured at the armchairs in the corner of the room. 'Tea? Coffee?'

'Coffee,' said Samson. 'My stomach isn't robust enough yet for Bruncliffe tea.'

'Two coffees, please,' the solicitor called through to the outer office 'And not too strong. We've got a southerner present.'

He closed the door on the burst of laughter in the adjoining room and took a seat opposite Samson. 'I heard you were back,' he said, eyes twinkling with mischief.

'I'm sure you did. Your uncle Seth was one of many witnesses to my homecoming.' Samson rubbed his chin, which a week later still felt tender to the touch. 'I'm also sure you've heard that not everyone's happy about it?'

Matty raised both shoulders, hands palm up. 'You always used to tell me not to bother about what people thought of you. Why start now?'

Samson gave a dry laugh at his own youthful wisdom being handed back to him, decades on. 'Perhaps because I've grown up?'

'Shame the same doesn't apply to everyone in town,' Matty replied with an equally dry tone.

A young man entered carrying a tray. 'Thanks,' said Matty, standing to take the drinks and place them on the low table between the chairs. He waited for the door to click closed, before resuming his seat and concentrating on his guest once more. 'But I doubt you called in to discuss local politics. So what can I help you with?'

'Richard Hargreaves,' said Samson, reverting to the directness of his birthplace. 'His will, to be precise.'

The solicitor looked surprised. 'That's not what I was expecting.' A raised eyebrow of enquiry prompted the solicitor to expand on his comment. 'Well, I thought . . . I was expecting you to ask me about the sale of the farm.'

'Twistleton Farm?' Samson went still. 'Were you involved?'

'No. Rick Procter never uses me for his property sales. In this case he used two firms based in Skipton to oversee the purchase.' Matty pulled a face. 'He was kind enough to take care of the legal side of things for your dad, too.'

'Are you suggesting it wasn't legitimate?' asked Samson, a dangerous quiet to his voice.

A firm shake of the head met his question. 'I'm sure it was legitimate. Just not that sure it was moral. You know how your dad was . . .'

'Drunk. He was easy prey. And then he drank all the proceeds.'

'There wasn't much to drink,' said Matty. He shifted in his seat, uncomfortable delivering this bad news. 'Rick paid him well below market value, even considering the condition of the place.'

Samson turned away, letting his gaze rest on the busy marketplace below as a knot of anger and guilt clenched his stomach. He was ashamed at how quickly he'd jumped to conclusions. More ashamed that his father hadn't felt it worth his while to correct his son's wild accusations about where the money for the farm had gone.

'There was nothing I could do,' explained Matty. 'It was all cut and dried before I got wind of it. Rick arranged for your dad to get a place in Fellside Court—'

'Where he has to pay rent to live in a shoebox!'

'A shoebox owned by Procter Properties.'

The blue gaze snapped back onto the solicitor. 'Rick owns that place?'

Matty nodded. 'Like I said, it was all cut and dried before I knew. And the way most folk around here see it, Rick Procter is an angel. He took a tumbledown property off the hands of an alcoholic and rehoused him in newly built sheltered accommodation. It hasn't harmed his reputation, either, that your dad subsequently sobered up.'

'Is there anything I can do?'

'Legally speaking, I'm not sure there is.'

'And illegally?'

A wry smile came in response. 'Given how he treated me at school, I'd be the last to put you off. But seriously, Samson, watch your back when dealing with Rick Procter. He's become a very powerful man since you left here. You don't want him as an enemy.'

'I'll bear that in mind,' said Samson. 'As for the real reason I'm here . . . Richard Hargreaves' will?'

Matty grimaced. 'Sorry, but I can't be of much use

there either. The contents of a will remain confidential even when the client is deceased.'

'I understand. But I just need you to enlighten me on one or two things.'

The solicitor looked out of the window at the butcher's shop across the marketplace, the bulky figure of Ken Hargreaves visible behind his counter, his wife alongside him. 'So it's true that Mrs Hargreaves has asked you to look into Richard's death?'

'How the hell do you know that?'

Matty chuckled. 'You *have* been away too long.' He reached for his coffee and took a sip, contemplating Samson over the rim. 'Richard was a good man. One with poor taste in women – with a single exception – but a good man nevertheless.'

'A man that would have contemplated suicide?'

'No. Not now.' He placed the cup back on the table.

'You think he might have done in the past?'

The solicitor steepled his fingers and leaned his chin on the apex. 'It's no secret that I handled his side of the divorce. Neither is it a secret that it was bitter. Annette was after her pound of flesh, eager to make Richard pay for bringing her to this backwater.'

'I thought she was the one who wanted to move here?'

A bushy eyebrow that marked Matthew Thistlethwaite out as the nephew of Seth rose in an ironic arch. 'Funny how people reshape the past when it comes to divorce. Yes, it was Annette who brought Richard back to Bruncliffe. But when the red carpet wasn't rolled out for them, she took the huff.'

Samson grinned. 'So I'm not the only one to get short shrift?'

'You know what it's like,' said Matty. 'A prophet is not without honour . . .'

'. . . save in his own country,' Samson added, suddenly taken back to Sunday school in the Wesleyan chapel, his mother reading bible stories to the children sitting on the floor, Matty and Samson amongst them.

'Exactly. And Annette felt that loss of honour keenly. I did what I could to make it a balanced settlement but Richard was determined she should be looked after, that the children shouldn't be penalised.' He shrugged. 'He was low for some time after that. Who wouldn't be? But suicide . . . ?'

'You knew him well, then?'

Matty nodded. 'We were both professionals in a small town so we'd get thrown together at social occasions. Plus, I knew him a bit from school. We were in the chess club together.' A lopsided grin accompanied this confession, making the solicitor look all of twelve again. 'We were slow to discover the wilder side of life in Bruncliffe.'

'You mean there is one?' laughed Samson.

A shadow crossed Matty's face. 'It's getting that way. Drugs. Not in Bruncliffe yet, but around the edges, in the towns further south. Seems the chess club doesn't hold the same attraction for young teens any more.' He drained his cup of coffee and then gave a small smile. 'You'd know more about that than the rest of us, I suppose, given your line of work.'

Samson's head jerked up, trying to gauge whether the comment referred to more than just his career. But Matty's expression was guileless. If news of Samson's disgrace had followed him home, Matthew Thistlethwaite had yet to hear it.

Relieved, the detective returned to the reason for his visit. 'So if Richard didn't commit suicide . . .'

He let the thought hang between them, knowing Matty was smart enough to get the gist of the unasked question. After a few seconds contemplating his hands, now spread across his knees, the solicitor spoke.

'Murder. A grim thought for such a lovely day. But while I can't disclose the contents of my client's will, I can say with a clear conscience that it didn't provide any motive for foul deeds.'

Samson leaned forward in his chair. 'Annette didn't benefit?'

Matty fixed him with a wry look. 'You know, Mrs Hargreaves would be able to tell you all this. Why don't you ask her?' He glanced across the cobbled square once more and then back at Samson. 'Or perhaps you already have?'

Samson let out a bark of a laugh. 'Guilty as charged!'

'And what did Mrs Hargreaves say?'

'That Richard didn't leave a will. Can you explain how that would work? In general, of course . . .'

Matty's eyes lit up at Samson's cunning. 'Of course. "Intestate" is the legal definition. An awful word and, in most cases, an awful condition to be in. But in a case following divorce . . .' He spread his hands, face innocent. 'No spouse to claim prior rights. The entire estate goes to the children.'

Samson gave a resigned nod.

'Sorry. Not what you wanted to hear?'

'No . . . yes . . . Christ, I don't know.' He stood, Matty standing with him. 'But thanks for your time. And if you want to catch up in more relaxed circumstances . . .' He passed Matty a business card.

'Dales Detective Agency, eh?' Matty looked up from the card. 'I might have need of your services now and again.'

'You're the first one around here to think so.'

'Yeah, well, that's Bruncliffe for you. You're useless until they need you. How are your rates?'

'Not highway robbery, that's for sure,' said Samson with a laugh as they shook hands. 'Great to see you, Matty, and thanks.'

'Not sure I was of any help,' confessed the solicitor as he escorted Samson to the door.

Samson didn't refute him. In fact, it would be some time before the detective realised just how helpful Matthew Thistlethwaite had been. Right now, his mind was on his next appointment, which he'd been putting off for a week but could forestall no longer. He was dreading it. Even if it did include the promise of a delicious lunch.

9

Given that the sun was shining outside, Troy Murgatroyd should have been in a good mood. But the low temperatures, the bitter wind and a busy lunchtime pub had conspired to rub much of the shine off his disposition. As a result, his normal surly and sullen features were gracing the bar of the Fleece as Delilah entered, Tolpuddle by her side.

'Coffee please, Troy,' she said as she approached the counter where Seth Thistlethwaite was already in residence.

'*Coffee?*' spluttered the landlord. 'This is a bloody pub, you know. Not a fancy cafe. What's the point of me getting these in, if everyone just orders bloody coffee?' He cast an aggrieved hand over the gleaming beer taps in front of him.

'And a pie and chips,' added Delilah with a smile, trying to soothe the irate host. Her day had been going well so far, thanks to the continued absence of Samson O'Brien from the offices, and she wasn't about to let the sour humour of the man who ran the Fleece spoil it.

The man in question stalked towards the kitchen to pass on the order, leaving a trail of grumblings in his wake. 'What is it with food and hot beverages? Why can't folk just order a beer and be done with it? Bloody cafe culture, that's what I blame . . .'

'Nice to see Troy's full of sweetness and light, as usual,' remarked Seth Thistlethwaite, once the swinging kitchen door had cut off the landlord's gripes. His observation elicited a peal of laughter from Delilah as Ash, her lunchtime date, entered the pub. He crossed the room and leaned down to kiss her cheek.

'Someone's in a good mood,' he said. 'Considering you're officially the black sheep of the Metcalfe family.'

Delilah's smile slipped to a grimace. 'Did you have to spoil the moment?'

'You getting grief over young Samson?' asked Seth, eyebrows pulling together.

'What do you think?' Ash replied. 'She's harbouring a fugitive, as far as Will's concerned.'

'Idiot!' muttered Seth. 'Just you ignore them, lass. That lad's done nothing to deserve the cold shoulder. You're doing the right thing.'

A blush of shame spread across Delilah's cheeks. The only right thing she was doing was keeping her business afloat. But she didn't rush to correct the old man.

A coffee was slapped onto the bar in front of her. 'Anything else?' grunted Troy.

Ash was quick to answer for her. 'I'll have a pint, and a pie and chips. I'll pay,' he added, a hand out to stall Delilah's protests.

But she wasn't about to protest. With the way her finances were, lunch at the pub was an extravagance she couldn't really afford, so she was happy to let him foot the bill. Even more so when he'd recently been granted the contract to fit the kitchens in the development Rick Procter was building at Low Mill. Her brother's fortunes had been going in the opposite direction to her own of late.

'Thanks, Ash.' Delilah stretched up to peck him on the cheek. 'Good to know at least one of my brothers still loves me.'

'I wouldn't count on it,' said Ash with a grin. 'I'm just keeping you sweet so I can get the inside gossip and pass it on to Will.'

'Inside gossip you're after, is it?' Seth Thistlethwaite twisted round on his bar stool as brother, sister and dog settled at a nearby table, his eyes dancing with devilment. 'Won't be long before the Three Peaks comes round.'

Ash looked confused at this incongruous mention of the famous fell race, which was still six months away. 'That's hardly headline news, Seth. It happens every year.' He gestured at the back wall of the pub, photos of lean men and women hurtling down the sides of Pen-y-ghent, Whernside and Ingleborough adorning it. 'What makes this next one so special? You thinking of entering again?'

Seth shot the young man a look of contempt. 'My running days are long over, lad, as well you know.' He turned his fierce gaze on Delilah. 'But some of you young 'uns are just reaching your prime. And April won't be long coming.'

Delilah busied herself straightening the beer mats on the table, face neutral, refusing to give her old coach the satisfaction of even a flicker of interest. But it was there – a flare of excitement at the thought; closely followed by that familiar clench of the stomach muscles.

Nerves. It was a race that deserved nerves. And respect. Just short of a full marathon, but run up and down the sides of three of the biggest peaks in the Yorkshire Dales, it was tough. How long since she'd last run it? Years. Too long.

'Haring over hills is more Delilah's game,' said Ash, slapping his sister on the back. 'Those of us with brains concentrate our physical efforts on rugby. Isn't that right, Troy?'

The landlord, former celebrated hooker of the Bruncliffe team – which had flown as high as the top of Yorkshire Division One under his guidance, but now languished near the bottom – grunted as he thrust two plates on the table. 'Shame you haven't been showing them brains on the pitch a bit more, Ash Metcalfe. Might not be looking relegation in the face this early in the season, if you had.'

Delilah let out a yelp of laughter as Ash's jaw dropped at the accurate rebuke.

'Touché,' she crowed, picking up her knife and fork and feeling her stomach rumble appreciatively as the delicious scent of steak and ale wafted up from the golden pastry before her. She'd just cut into the pie, Tolpuddle lifting his head from his paws in anticipation, when the door opened and Will Metcalfe and Harry Furness, both wearing suits, walked in.

'Oh God,' she muttered, appetite fading as she eyed her oldest brother warily. 'I'm not in the mood for another lecture.'

'What's with the fancy dress, lads?' called out Ash.

'Funeral,' said Harry, coming over to take a seat, his eyes lighting up at the sight of their meals. 'That smells divine. Order me a pie and chips as well, Will,' he called out over his shoulder, ignoring the dark grumbling of the landlord at his request.

'Another funeral?' Seth shook his head. 'This dying lark is getting contagious.'

'Another young man, too,' said Will from the bar. 'Farmer over towards Gayle.'

'You knew him, I take it?' asked Ash, knowing his brother didn't forsake a day's work lightly.

Will nodded. 'From the auction, mostly. Bought sheep off him a few times. He was a decent lad.'

'His parents are distraught,' said Harry soberly, as Will placed two beers on the table and sat down next to Delilah, greeting her with something between a smile and a frown.

'How did he die?' she asked.

'Rolled his quad bike.' Will's reply had the matter-of-fact tone of a farmer who knew all about the risks involved in his occupation; knew that fatalities happened in a business increasingly pushed to make profits out of smaller and smaller margins. 'His father found him trapped under it. Poor sod was dead by the time the paramedics arrived.'

'And it was definitely an accident?'

Will whipped round to face Delilah, who was already regretting her question and wondering where it had come from. 'Of course it was a bloody accident,' he snapped. 'Why? You trying to find more cases for your pet detective? Not enough that he's barging around town harassing people over Richard Hargreaves' demise?'

'For God's sake!' Delilah slapped her cutlery down on her plate, the noise silencing the busy conversation of the pub. 'You just can't leave it, can you, Will?'

'And nor should I, when O'Brien is wringing money out of a grieving mother under false pretences. Giving her false hope and lining his pockets into the bargain. All thanks to you, of course. You should have sent him packing like we said—'

A hiss from Delilah was enough to make Ash intervene.

'Now, now, you two . . .' He put out a hand to calm the siblings, so alike when annoyed, with shoulders thrust back and chins jutting forward, fists clenched. 'There's just been a funeral. Show some respect.'

'Respect?' spat Delilah. 'He wouldn't know the meaning of the word.'

'That's fine, coming from you,' retorted Will. 'Not like you're besmirching your dead brother's memory or anything—'

The glass was in her hands and the contents over her brother's head before the rational part of her had a chance to intervene.

'Hey,' protested Harry Furness with genuine indignation as Will dripped beer over the floor beside him. 'That was my pint!'

'I'll buy you another,' snapped Delilah, thrusting her half-eaten meal aside and standing to glare down at her sodden brother, who was trying to mop himself dry with a handkerchief, Tolpuddle helping out by lapping at the wet carpet. Any remorse Delilah felt was matched by an urge to tip her meal over Will, too, and so, in an attempt to quell the surge of anger and frustration, she walked to the bar.

'Pint of Black Sheep, Troy, please.' The irony of the

order wasn't lost on her in the hushed atmosphere of the bar, all the customers staring as Will strode off to the toilets. She laid her shaking hands on the counter.

Were families supposed to be so complicated? Or was it only the arrival of Samson O'Brien that had made everything go pear-shaped? Her shoulders drooped and she felt the backwash of misery that always followed her flashes of temper.

'Good day for a run,' murmured Seth Thistlethwaite as he leaned over from his bar stool to place his hand over hers, a wink accompanying the rare show of affection. 'That'd clear your head.'

She nodded, braving a smile.

'Anything else?' Troy had his hand out, waiting for her to pay.

'No,' she mumbled. 'And sorry about the mess . . .' She glanced over her shoulder to where Will was resuming his seat, a damp patch marking the worn carpet despite Tolpuddle's best efforts.

Troy shrugged, lips tugging at the corners in the closest he ever came to a smile. 'It'll clean up and I sold another pint. Nothing to apologise for.'

Delilah took the glass, carrying it carefully in her unsteady hand, and turned back to the table where conversation, thanks to Ash's peacemaking efforts, had reverted to the topic of the funeral.

'Just outside Gayle,' Harry was saying. 'That farmhouse on the left, before you get to the steep drop into the village.'

'The Alderson place?' asked Ash, eyebrows raised, fork halfway to his mouth.

'That's the one. You knew him?'

'He was scrum-half for Wensleydale, but was too good for them. Had a try-out with us but . . .' He paused and shook his head. 'Tom Alderson.'

'That's him. Crying shame—' A sharp intake of breath from behind made Harry turn as Delilah, face ashen, dropped the full pint of beer onto the floor.

'Jesus, Delilah!' Will Metcalfe shot to his feet, trousers now soaked to match his shirt. 'What the hell—?'

But he was speaking to thin air. Delilah had rushed out of the pub, Tolpuddle on her heels, leaving the place in silence yet again. A silence broken by Harry Furness's plaintive cry.

'That was my pint!'

Behind the bar, Troy Murgatroyd was reaching towards the beer taps. Today was turning out all right after all.

Samson O'Brien crested the hill and pulled over, the motorbike throbbing as he twisted round to appreciate the landscape behind. Rolling green fields fell away from him, walls scrambling up and down their edges before giving way to the houses in the dale below.

On the opposite side of the town from where he'd arrived the week before, from here the view was more benign. Instead of the abrupt rise of the fells and limestone crags at the back of Bruncliffe, the grey of the houses nestled softly against undulating land, a pastoral patchwork of grass and stone. Behind it, a blue sky skimmed with thin cloud rested atop the far-off fells of the Lake District.

Ryan Metcalfe had chosen a wonderful place to live. Such a shame he hadn't got to spend long in it.

Heart heavy with regret and apprehension, Samson turned the bike down the small track to his right that led to High Laithe. He could see the static caravan, a long, green mobile home mounted on a concrete base, steps leading up to it. Next to it was Lucy's car and a white van. And across the gravelled yard, the barn that Ryan had been renovating.

He'd been putting off this moment all week. Finally, after worrying every time he set foot outside the office that he would bump into her at an inopportune moment, Samson had plucked up the courage to call Lucy Metcalfe. Typical Lucy, she'd laughed away his worries and invited him over for lunch on her day off. Knowing he could avoid her no longer, Samson had accepted.

Not that he'd be able to eat anything. His stomach was tied up in knots.

He parked the bike next to the van, taking in the name on the side. *Rob Harrison – Stonemason & Builder*.

'Heard you were back.' The rough voice came from a large figure emerging from the high arch of the barn door. Broad shoulders, massive chest and arms like thighs. Samson recognised the family traits immediately. Titch's brother. He had to be.

'You heard right.' Samson walked over, trying to assess the warmth of his reception. He was mere feet away when Rob Harrison cleared his throat and spat resoundingly.

'Took your time,' he muttered, staring at Samson through narrowed eyes.

Not wanting to risk a reception like the one from Delilah, but delivered with the bulging biceps of a man-mountain, Samson halted. Out of arm's reach.

'Been busy,' he said. 'Seems like you are, too.' He nodded towards the barn towering over both of them. Now he was close up, he could see that it was far from finished. Fresh render covered some of the outside walls and, through the great arch of glass behind the builder, piles of sand and cement, shovels, and a cement mixer covered the floor of what should be a lounge.

Rob twisted, glanced over his shoulder at the building site behind him, then grunted. 'Doing what I can. Lucy needs all the help she can get.'

For a man of few words, Rob Harrison sure knew how to use them and Samson felt the accusation strike home. He'd been away too long and had left his best friend's widow to pick up the pieces.

'Ryan would be grateful,' he said, meaning every word. 'And I'm sure Lucy is.'

Rob nodded, wiped a hand on his trousers and crossed the distance between them to grab Samson in a crushing handshake, his muscles flexing under the rampant lion tattooed on his upper arm. 'Welcome home,' he said gruffly.

'You found us, then!' called out a voice from behind.

Hand throbbing, Samson resisted the urge to shake it free from pain as he turned to greet Lucy, who was walking across the yard with a mug of tea.

'Glad to see you two getting along,' she said as Rob took the mug and, with a mock salute, headed back into the barn.

'You're not the only one,' Samson muttered with a wry smile. 'What do they feed him on? Raw meat?'

Lucy laughed, the sound light and fresh after the builder's gravelly conversation. 'Whatever it is, it's a lot. Ryan always used to tease Rob that he didn't choose to leave the army, but was begged to leave because he was costing so much to keep.'

'Did he serve with Ryan?'

'They were out in Basra together. Rob already had a few years' service in when Ryan joined. He looked out for him. And now he's looking out for me.' She smiled fondly in the direction of the barn where the builder was busy loading the cement mixer.

Then she reached out both arms and gathered Samson into a hug. She was thinner than he remembered, her cheekbones sharp under her pale skin, her wedding ring loose on her finger.

'It's good to have you home,' she said, kissing his cheek and slipping an arm around his waist. 'Come on, we've got a lot to catch up on.'

And before he could utter a word of the apology he had planned, she was leading him up the caravan steps, peppering him with questions about his life and reminding him of just what a wonderful woman his best friend had married.

Delilah Metcalfe stared at the computer screen and felt a cold snake of fear twine around her intestines.

In the past week she'd somehow managed to convince herself there was nothing in it, that there was no basis for her unease over the deaths of two of her clients. She'd even allowed her initial trepidation at the investigation into

Richard Hargreaves' death to be allayed by Samson's exasperation over the passing days – the curses as he slammed down the phone, the long face as he entered the office after another wasted morning.

Bruncliffe's only private detective was getting nowhere – because there was nowhere to get. Richard Hargreaves had committed suicide, Martin Foster had died in an accident, and if anyone did happen to make the connection between the two men and the Dales Dating Agency, so what? There'd be a bit of bad publicity, but that was it. Delilah and her business had nothing to fear.

But the minute she'd heard that name in the pub, she had realised she'd been deluding herself. She'd fled, leaving her meal uneaten in her desperation to make sure. And now she knew.

Tom Alderson. Thirty years old. A smiling face under short brown hair, eyes full of life, a smattering of freckles across his nose. He'd joined the Dales Dating Agency in the last week of September. He'd joined the growing list of her deceased clients as of today.

Richard Hargreaves. Martin Foster. Tom Alderson.

Three men. All dead. All with a connection to her business.

Could it still be just an awful coincidence? Simply three men who happened to join her dating agency and, unfortunately, die prematurely? Or was something more sinister going on?

Trying to stem the leap of panic in her chest, she made herself focus. Even if there was nothing untoward about the deaths, once the connection between them was made, the ensuing exposure would only be detrimental for her.

It would be enough to ensure the Dales Dating Agency started losing living customers. And she couldn't afford that.

So she needed to make sure. To start looking for an alternative link between the dead men before someone else came up with the most obvious one. Perhaps they all knew each other? Or were members of some other organisation? If she could find something external to the agency, she could help deflect the negative attention away from her struggling enterprise.

Fingers trembling, she pulled up her customer records for the men in question. As the printer began to whir in the corner, she stood up, crossed the room and closed the door. After a slight pause, she locked it.

This was sensitive information. The last person Delilah Metcalfe wanted poking around was the detective she shared the building with.

'I was undercover . . .' Samson knew how preposterous it sounded here in the caravan, as they ate lunch against a backdrop of green fields and a soft blue sky. 'I'm sorry. It's hardly an excuse.'

'Delilah wrote to you.'

'She did?' He shook his head. 'I didn't get it. I was off the radar for the best part of a year.'

'I know.' Lucy touched his arm. 'Really, I do. If you'd heard, you'd have been here.'

Her faith in his reliability made him feel even worse. Because he wasn't sure he would have come. Not if it meant breaking off an investigation. And as for Delilah's letter, how could she have got in touch? He'd moved house several times, adopting the nomadic lifestyle of an undercover operative, never updating his father or anyone else with the new address. Once he'd left Bruncliffe, he'd left for good.

Had Ryan understood that? Would he have been as forgiving as his widow, now that Samson was back?

'He knew you well,' said Lucy, her eyes flicking up to the photo on the small shelf that ran above the window as she read Samson's mind. 'He always said the two of you had ended up in the same jobs, just with different uniforms. And he got better weather.' A smile danced across her face. 'I suppose that's true enough.'

'Hardly! Think I'd rather be on a drugs bust than on patrol in Iraq or Afghanistan. I don't know how he did it.'

'Neither do I.' For the first time since she'd crossed the yard to greet him, Lucy's face fell. 'He never talked about it when he came home. Said he didn't want to dwell on it. Instead he'd bury himself in whatever work Will needed doing down on the farm. And then we bought this place . . .'

'It's a stunning spot.'

'Yes. He brought me up here one day while Nathan was at school. He had a picnic and everything. But just as we got here it started to rain. We ended up sheltering in the barn while the worst passed and when we came out, the view . . . It was breathtaking. Like someone had taken a giant can of Pledge to the dale. Everything was sparkling, the air was so fresh. And down below we could see Ellershaw Farm.' She laughed. 'Typical Ryan. He pointed at the farmhouse and said he liked it here because he could keep an eye on Will and his parents from above. Never mind the view! Then he told me the barn was for sale with planning permission. We got back to Bruncliffe and put an offer in and were living in the caravan just in time for the winter.'

'Was Ryan planning to renovate the barn himself?'

'That was the plan. Fate decided otherwise.' She sighed. 'Four years we've been living up here and while I don't mind it so much, it's getting hard for Nathan. He's four-teen now. That sense of adventure he had as a ten-year-old has gone. He wants a proper bedroom. Somewhere he can bring friends back to, without having to hear his mother singing through a thin partition while she irons!'

'It must be tough?'

Lucy shook her head. 'No. Tough is not having family or friends around you. This . . .' she waved a hand at the building site across the yard, 'this is just life.'

Not knowing how to respond to such a magnanimous attitude, Samson took another bite of the chicken-and-leek pie Lucy had served and tried to will his appetite to do justice to her culinary abilities. For there was no doubt about it, she was an amazing chef. But, unusually for him, he was having to force the food down. He was too tied up in grief, regret and shame to really enjoy it.

'Do you miss him?' The words were out of his mouth before he could retract them. He looked over at Lucy with contrition. 'Sorry . . . stupid question.'

'Maybe. But it's one no one around here dares ask.' Lucy grimaced. 'It's hard in ways I never thought it would be. I'm always so careful not to upset other people, like his parents, his family or even his friends, that I don't talk about Ryan so much any more.' She sighed again, brushing her hair back over her shoulder. 'Delilah took it really badly. As did Will. But it's Peggy and Ted I'm worried about.'

'Ryan's mum and dad?' Samson had a sudden image of Mr and Mrs Metcalfe in the doorway of the farmhouse at Ellershaw, a couple of dogs at their feet as they watched Samson and Ryan taking turns on Ryan's new motocross bike; Delilah – always Delilah close by her beloved brother's side – laughing as they tried ineffectually to do doughnuts. He felt a surge of nostalgia. And surprise. He'd forgotten so much that was good about his childhood. 'They're not doing so well?'

'On the surface, they seem fine. Peggy has thrown herself into all sorts. She's Bruncliffe's most willing volunteer. But Ted . . . He handed over the running of the farm to Will six months before Ryan was killed and so, when we all involved ourselves with work to get over the initial grief, Ted had nothing to do. Still doesn't. And he's drinking more than he should.' She gave him a sidelong glance, her head dipping as she acknowledged Samson's own experience of that affliction.

'And you?'

'I have Nathan. And the cafe.' She smiled. 'Not sure how much Ryan would have appreciated being replaced by croissants and strawberry tarts!'

Samson grinned. 'No. He wasn't one for tarts.'

Lucy let out a loud peal of laughter. It was enough to bring Rob Harrison out of the barn, his dark stare trained on the caravan. He caught Samson's eye before turning back into the building.

'That's a compliment, I take it,' Lucy continued, oblivious to the builder.

'What passes for one in Bruncliffe, anyhow.' Samson ate another piece of pie, this time his stomach growling in appreciation as he began to relax.

'So what about you?' she asked. 'How are things?'

'You probably know better than I do. No doubt you heard about my welcome party?'

'Yes. Idiots – Delilah included. Acting like children. Honestly!' Her indignation on his behalf drew a smile from Samson. 'Sometimes I'm ashamed to be a Metcalfe. A more stubborn bunch of people I have never met.'

'They had a point, though,' Samson said quietly. 'I should have come home sooner.'

'And done what? Held my hand by the graveside? I had plenty of people offering to do that, but the only one I wanted by my side was being buried in the ground.' She stabbed a piece of broccoli with her fork. 'And I can't imagine you're much use in a kitchen making cakes so really you were better off staying where you were, ensuring our streets are free of drugs.'

Samson watched her cut the broccoli with a sharp slice and pop it in her mouth, eyes flashing. 'There's the situation with my dad, too,' he said.

Her umbrage at his treatment by her in-laws dispelled in an instant. 'Ah, yes. Your dad. I hear you've been in to see him?'

'How . . . ?' He let the question lapse. He knew how. It was going to take a while to get used to the Bruncliffe grapevine again.

'My mother-in-law,' explained Lucy with an apologetic grin. 'Peggy does a couple of voluntary sessions down at Fellside Court every week. In-chair aerobics and the like.

She got talking to Edith Hird after her last one and some-how your name popped up.'

'As it would,' Samson said wryly.

Lucy spread her hands and lifted her shoulders. 'You know how it is. Small place. Not much going on. Although I hear there might be more going on than we think.' Her face became sombre. 'Is it true Mrs Hargreaves has asked you to investigate Richard's death?'

'Yes.' Samson deliberately took a forkful of pie, leaving silence for Lucy to fill. Which she dutifully did.

'It was such a shock. To think both he and Ryan . . . so young.'

'Do you think he killed himself?'

'No . . . I mean . . . why would he? Why now?'

'You think he might have done before?'

Lucy frowned. 'If you'd met his ex-wife, you might wonder why he hadn't jumped in front of a train a lot earlier.'

'Sounds like she wasn't popular. Did she earn that or was it typical Bruncliffe suspicion of outsiders?'

'Huh! No, this time the judgement of Bruncliffe was fair. Annette was such a bitter woman. She hated life here and made sure her husband wasn't much happier. Ryan had no time for her and neither did I, so we didn't see much of Richard after he came back. From what I gather, not many of his old friends did either. It was a real shame, especially considering how close Ryan and Richard were as kids.'

'And after the divorce?'

'Richard was depressed. Who wouldn't be? Annette took his boys back to Manchester, took their savings in lieu of the house. She even took the car. But it was the kids being gone that really upset him.'

'What about recently? Was he getting his life back on track?'

'He most certainly was. I bumped into him at one of Delilah's dating nights—'

'You went to a Speedy Date night?'

Misunderstanding the sharpness of the question, Lucy blushed. 'Yes, I did. Widow goes out once in a while. Shock-horror! You're as bad as the rest of Bruncliffe.'

'That's not . . . I didn't mean . . .'

'It's okay.' Lucy took a deep breath, waving away his stumbling apology. 'It's a touchy subject. Delilah asked me to go to make up numbers, so I agreed. Didn't think it would create such headlines.'

'So how was it?'

The familiar smile returned. 'Why? Are you tempted?'

'Christ, no!' The vehemence of his reply triggered another laugh from Lucy.

'It wasn't that bad,' she said. 'Actually, it was really good fun. Richard was there. A few other blokes I know from round here. And Elaine came too. Safety in numbers.'

'And how did Richard seem?'

Lucy regarded Samson, eyebrow raised. 'Is this in a professional capacity, Detective O'Brien? Should I be careful what I say?'

He shrugged. 'Possibly. Seeing as I can't get any of his friends to talk.'

'Who have you tried?'

'All of them. Delilah drew up a list for me and I called each and every one. Not one of them agreed to meet.'

'Not even Harry Furness?'

Samson shook his head. 'I left a message but he never got back to me.'

'That interfering Will Metcalfe!' Lucy muttered. 'He's put the word around, no doubt. Well, I'm not sure how much of an authority I am on the subject, but Richard didn't seem depressed that night.'

'He was having fun?'

'Yes.'

'Did he . . . you know . . . pull?'

'Pull?' she laughed again. 'Samson O'Brien, where have you been all these years? In a cave?'

'I'm a bit out of practice,' he conceded, grinning sheepishly. 'Did he get a date?'

'I don't know. That's not really how it works. You spend the evening talking to all the potential dates, no more than four minutes per date—'

'Four minutes? Is that long enough in Bruncliffe?'

'Long enough to hear all about the latest sheep auction or how the rugby team would fare better with a decent scrum-half,' replied Lucy with wry humour. 'Then at the end of the evening you go home and log on to your account and flag up anyone you would like to see again. The computer takes care of the rest.'

'You mean it notifies you when people want to date you?'

Lucy nodded. 'Then you decide whether to accept or reject or – and this is Delilah's own invention – leave it for now. It's a nicer way of letting people down without an outright rejection.'

Samson scratched his head. 'Do you think it works?'

'Yes. I think she has really hit on something. At the moment she's using her other business to prop it up, but soon it should be viable in its own right.'

'What other business?'

'The website development company.' Lucy laughed at his surprised expression. 'Yeah, Ryan could never get his head around it, either. His little sister capable of doing things with computers that he couldn't begin to understand. Delilah's a whizz when it comes to IT. All she needs now is for the bank to hold out a bit longer and she'll have two thriving businesses on her hands.'

'She's got financial problems?'

Lucy bit her lip. 'I shouldn't have said that. Not to . . .'

'Not to me. I understand.' And he did. It made sense now. That sudden change of heart when he'd offered six months' rent up front. Delilah needed the money to keep her dating agency alive. He felt a pang of sympathy. Twistleton Farm had always been in debt, the bank manager constantly chasing them for payments they couldn't make. Then foot-and-mouth had hit and everything had exploded. 'Don't worry – I won't say a word. Wouldn't want to give her an excuse to kick me out.'

'She wouldn't. She's softer than she makes out. And she's had a hellish couple of years, so don't take everything she says or does to heart.'

'Not even a right hook to the chin?'

'Not even that!' Lucy smiled. 'But getting back to your

day job. If you want to know more about Richard Hargreaves, go and see Edith Hird.'

'Miss Hird? Our old headmistress?'

'The same. She'll tell you all about Richard.' Seeing the puzzlement on Samson's face, Lucy added, 'She's his great-aunt. Didn't you know?'

Samson shook his head, stunned – not for the first time – at how these original Bruncliffians knew the lineage of everyone around them. And judged them accordingly. Including himself, with his Irish father and a mother from a distant dale. But when he'd complained about his lack of approved bloodline many years ago, his father had laughingly claimed that the locals were the ones at a disadvantage, tied to the land as much as their famous 'hefted' sheep. Just as the animals had become accustomed to the open spaces of the fells through generations of breeding and so never strayed, so the inhabitants of Bruncliffe were unable to break out for pastures new, thanks to the weight of the generations they carried with them.

While he could appreciate his father's wisdom now, it hadn't helped the young Samson feel any less of an outsider.

'Edith's at Fellside Court, as you're aware,' continued Lucy 'She shares a two-bedroomed apartment there with her sister, Clarissa. You should drop in on your way back and have a chat with them. They'll be delighted to see you again.'

'And see my father at the same time?' muttered Samson, sensing an ulterior motive in Lucy's suggestion. Her guilty expression confirmed his suspicion.

'It wouldn't hurt, would it? Two birds and all that—'

The squeal of brakes and the scrunch of gravel grabbed her attention. 'Nathan!' she said, rising to her feet as a figure came to a halt on a mountain bike outside the caravan. 'I bet he's come back for his phone.' She reached over to a shelf and picked up a mobile, the reverse decorated with a rampant lion – identical to the tattoo on Rob Harrison's arm – and a white rose. 'The Yorkshire Regiment symbol,' she explained, noticing Samson looking at it. 'In honour of his dad.'

Moments later, the door swung open and Samson felt his heart lurch as a replica of Ryan stood there in the small kitchen. Tall and broad, his muscles already developing and his limbs outgrowing his school uniform, the lad was Metcalfe through and through, fair hair falling across his face as he entered.

'Hi, Mum, is my mobile—?' The boy's gaze settled on the man sitting in the corner and the smile fell from his lips.

'Hi,' said Samson, standing to hold out his hand to this godson he had all but deserted. 'I'm Samson. One of your dad's friends.'

Nathan stared at him. Glared at his mother. And with a look inherited from his father's side of the family, snatched the phone, turned around and left, slamming the door behind him, his hunched figure crossing the yard in angry strides.

Lucy hurried to the door. 'Nathan,' she shouted. 'Come back here.'

But the lad didn't acknowledge her. He entered the barn, where the shadowy form of Rob Harrison could be seen approaching him.

'Sorry . . .' Lucy ran a distracted hand through her hair as her forehead creased in concern. 'He's not normally this rude. I didn't tell him you were coming as I didn't know how he'd . . . he's very protective of me.'

Samson put an arm around Lucy's tense shoulders. 'Don't. It's okay. The lad has every reason to be annoyed. Not everyone has your generosity of spirit.'

'Or the Metcalfe ability to hold a grudge.'

'Or that, thank God!' Samson was pleased to see her smile. He reached for his jacket. 'It's time I was off. Thanks for lunch. And for being so forgiving.'

Lucy put her arms around him and pulled him into a hug. 'You're part of Ryan,' she said. 'How could I not welcome you home?'

They walked out of the caravan, Lucy's arm resting through his, and as she reached up to kiss him goodbye, Samson felt the heavy weight of Rob Harrison's stare upon him. Standing next to the stonemason in the opening of the barn was Nathan Metcalfe, flushed face full of resentment.

'There's a storm coming,' said Lucy, pointing out over the dale at the dark clouds brewing above Gunnerstang Brow. 'You'd best get going.'

As he started the bike and pulled away, Samson wondered whether he'd be better off heeding her words and getting as far away from Bruncliffe and its belligerent inhabitants as he could.

10

By the time Delilah looked up from the printouts that covered her desk, the world outside had grown dark and rain was spattering against the window, driven by the wind.

'Nothing!' she muttered, throwing her pencil onto the papers in annoyance. 'Not a thing.'

Tolpuddle stirred in his bed in the corner, a stale smell of recycled beer wafting Delilah's way. It was enough to force her to her feet and across to the door to let in some fresh air. Switching on the landing light, she continued to the kitchen and filled the kettle, all the while her mind churning over the personal details of the three dead men. Her three dead clients.

All of them had gone to local schools, all three different ones.

Their occupations were varied – farmer, lecturer and electrician.

Two had been married previously and were recently divorced, Richard the only one to have had children.

Outside of work and family, Tom had been a keen rugby player; Richard had played chess competitively; Martin Foster had preferred potholing. And there was no record anywhere on the internet that they were on local councils together, affiliates of the same political parties or even churchgoers in the same parish.

In other words, there was nothing to suggest a link between them. Not a link that would overshadow the one she already knew about – their membership of the Dales Dating Agency.

She tipped boiling water into her mug, stirred the teabag vigorously, and tried to quash the flutter of fear in her stomach. Even if she kept her imagination under control and accepted that the deaths were coincidental, if word got out about the thread that bound the dead men together, her business would be given publicity it really didn't need.

How many clients would she lose? Enough to plunge her into bankruptcy?

She leaned back against the worktop, mug in hand, and watched the rain lash against the window.

Let it go. It was nothing. Just a twist of fate no one but her would notice.

But she couldn't. It wasn't in her nature. And besides, with Samson digging into the background of Richard Hargreaves, it was highly likely he'd stumble across the dead man's association with her agency. If he hadn't already. Her tenant had been out all day asking questions around town – and further afield, judging by the fact that his motorbike hadn't been parked in the yard when she returned from her disastrous lunch. Perhaps he had a lead? So she needed to do more digging of her own. That way, at least she would be forewarned if anything unsavoury was uncovered.

The thought of becoming an investigator brought an

ironic smile to her face. Having watched Samson O'Brien all week, how hard could it be?

She glanced at the clock on the wall. An hour before she had to leave for the farm for her parents' wedding anniversary celebrations – and what could be an interesting evening, given her behaviour in the pub at lunchtime. But before she had to think about facing Will, she would go back to her desk and comb through her records once more, using the internet again to widen the search. There had to be something she'd missed.

With a sigh she headed into her office, greeted by a low whine from Tolpuddle.

'It's all right,' she said, bending to stroke the grey head that lifted to her hand. 'It's just rain on the window. Be grateful we're not out in it.'

The dog relaxed, releasing more stale beer and forcing Delilah back to her desk.

'Honestly, Tolpuddle,' she moaned, fingers pegging her nose. 'That's the last time I take you to the pub.'

The dog raised an eyebrow, gave a glance at the inclement weather outside, and propped his head on his paws. In seconds he was asleep, dreaming of sunnier climes.

'Jesus!' Samson got off the motorbike and shook himself like a dog, a fine arc of water shedding itself from his jacket, and wished he was somewhere sunnier. He was soaked through.

The storm had hit as he was halfway back to town, the black clouds swooping over him at speed, unleashing rain as only the Yorkshire Dales could. Big, fat drops falling in rapid succession, his visor streaming, the road slick in minutes. If it wasn't for the temperatures, it could almost be considered tropical.

Boots squelching, jeans chafing his legs, he jogged across the courtyard to the rear entrance of Fellside Court.

'Come in, come in, or you'll catch your death of cold!' Clarissa Ralph, sister of the woman he'd come to see, was holding open one of the glass doors and ushering him in. 'Oh, look at you!' she said, hands flying to her mouth. 'You're wet through.'

'Well don't leave him out there,' called a voice from the far end of the corridor. Samson recognised the rotund shape and bald head of Arty, the retired bookmaker. 'Bring him down here where there's a fire on.'

Clarissa did as she was told, fluttering along beside Samson, her frail hand on his arm, her head barely up to his shoulder, making him feel elephantine.

'Oh, your dad will be pleased to see you,' she chirped. 'He's talked about you a lot.'

'I bet he has,' murmured Samson.

'And you're just in time, too,' she continued, smiling up at him, her white hair framing a sweet face.

'Just in time?'

Clarissa nodded, tightening her grip on his arm. 'It's the highlight of our day.'

'Come on,' bellowed Arty, now at the door of the communal lounge. 'It's about to start.'

'What's about to start?' asked Samson, entering the room. As before, a large group of residents were gathered, but this time they were all seated in armchairs facing the TV, his father amongst them. 'What's about to start?' he said again.

A group of heads turned to face him and replied in unison. '*Flog It!*'

'It's like *Antiques Roadshow*, but with more thrills,' explained Clarissa.

Arty laughed. 'That's one way of putting it. We like to guess how much the tat will go for.'

'And Arty always gets it wrong,' chipped in Edith Hird, gesturing to an empty chair. 'Come and have a seat.' Then she noticed the sodden clothing and the trail of wet footprints. 'Why, you're soaked through, young man! Joseph, he'll need to change or he'll catch his death of cold.'

Joseph O'Brien, who'd been looking on with bemusement as his son was gathered into the flock of Fellside Court, knew when he'd been given a command. He got to his feet and walked towards Samson, a twinkle in his eye.

'Come on, son,' he said, putting a hand on Samson's arm and leading him back out of the room, ignoring his protests. 'You know better than to argue with Miss Hird. Let's get you into some dry clothes.'

'And be quick,' added Edith, 'because it's about to start.'

Different addresses. Different jobs. Different lives. To all appearances, Richard Hargreaves, Martin Foster and Tom Alderson had nothing in common. Apart from dying. And one other thing . . .

All three men had been on the last Speedy Date night.

'Damn it!' Delilah sat back in her chair and stared at the screen where the records of her demised clients confronted her. Suspicion, disquieting and insistent, uncoiled within her, pushing aside all the rational arguments she'd been using to suppress it.

Three men dying suddenly. All members of the same dating agency. All participants in the last dating event.

How much coincidence did you need before starting to pay attention?

She reached for her mug. Empty. She didn't have time to make a fresh one. For a moment she was tempted to forgo the evening ahead, to call home and make an excuse so she could stay in the office and keep picking away at the threads of this problem that had the potential to sink her business. But she couldn't. Not after her behaviour in the pub earlier. Will would presume she was avoiding him, while the rest of the family would take her absence as yet further justification for her newly acquired black-sheep status.

Another half an hour, then. She'd go back over her records once more and tomorrow she'd start early, looking at the dating history of the men in question. And praying she didn't find any more parallels. Because this time she would be searching for a darker reason behind the demise of the three men, and hoping to God it had nothing to do with Mrs Hargreaves' suspicion of murder.

'Eight thousand pounds? For a cup made of rhino's horn? That so-called expert wants his head looking at!'

'And it's chipped.'

'It's bloody ugly, too.'

'Arthur! Language!'

'Well it is,' declared Arty, unabashed by the reprimand

from the former headmistress. 'And as for it being a cup – you wouldn't get a decent brew in that piece of rubbish.'

Samson stood in the doorway as the pensioners bantered back and forth, the TV holding their attention. He felt awkward in his new attire. When they'd entered the flat, his father had handed him some clothes and left him to change. Now he was dressed in cords that had a permanent crease down the front, a soft flannel shirt and a baggy, ribbed cardigan that could house two. Thanks to the difference in height between the O'Briens, the hem of the trousers was high enough to clear the puddles gathering outside and Samson's wrists protruded from his sleeves. But at least he wasn't wet any more.

'Samson, what do you think?' Arty was pointing at the screen where a brown cup-like object was on a pedestal. 'Would you pay eight grand for that?'

'No,' said Samson, crossing the room to take the empty chair next to his father. 'But I'd be happy to have some idiot pay me that for it.'

A wave of laughter greeted his reply.

'"Idiot" is right,' muttered the frail man with the oxygen cylinder Samson remembered from his visit the week before. 'Fools are soon parted from their money.'

'That must make you the wisest amongst us then, Eric,' quipped Arty with a wink.

Another outburst of laughter caused Clarissa to lean over and pat Samson's hand. 'Take no notice of them,' she said. 'They're always teasing each other. But it's so good of you to call in and see your father.'

'Actually, I came to speak to Edith,' replied Samson, rueing his blunt acknowledgement of the truth the moment it was voiced. But if his father took offence, he made no show of it, still laughing at Arty's last sally.

'Edith!' Clarissa was already calling across the room, her shrill tones cutting through the chat. 'Edith, he says he's come to talk to you.'

'What about?' Edith turned from the TV to face Samson.

'It's . . . er . . . perhaps we could talk somewhere . . . ?'

A stout wave of a hand dismissed the idea. 'Spit it out, lad. They're about to start the auction.'

Samson looked around at the elderly faces, all now concentrating on him.

'Well?' demanded Edith.

'It's . . . I'm kind of here in an official capacity.'

'You mean something to do with you being a private detective?' asked Arty. And just like that, the TV was forgotten and a clamour of voices beset Samson.

'Oh! How exciting,' exclaimed Clarissa. 'Has someone gone missing?'

'Or died in mysterious circumstances?' asked Eric hopefully.

'Or he's trying to find someone mentioned in a will,' added another man.

'Maybe he wants Edith to go undercover?' a plump lady suggested.

'Quiet!' Joseph O'Brien stood, raising a hand to subdue the growing noise. 'Give the lad a chance to tell us.' He turned to his son, shaking his head. 'Sorry. We lead sheltered lives here and tend to get a bit excited about anything out of the ordinary. Go ahead, Samson. Ask Edith what you want to know.'

'It's about Richard Hargreaves.'

Silence filled the room and all heads swivelled towards the former headmistress, whose eyes were narrowed, lips pursed.

'I wondered if that's why you'd come,' she said. 'Barbara mentioned she'd asked you to investigate.'

'Mrs Hargreaves? She's hired Samson?' Arty looked from the old lady to the detective and back again. 'Doesn't she think it was suicide?'

'Apparently not.'

'And what do you think?' asked Samson gently.

Faded blue eyes focused on him, still sharp despite Miss Hird's age. 'I'm puzzled, I must confess. He didn't seem to be particularly depressed when I last saw him.'

'When was that?'

'A week to the day before he killed himself. He called in every month or so. To check how we were.'

'He was a good boy,' murmured Clarissa, her hands trembling. 'Such a good boy.'

'I'm sure he was,' said Samson, laying his hand across hers.

'A good boy, but a soft one,' muttered Edith.

'Aye, that wife of his . . .' Arty let the sentence hang, heads nodding all around the room.

'She was something, all right. "Wicked" is the word that springs to mind. Taking his boys like that.' Eric coughed, his indignation taking its toll.

'So does Mrs Hargreaves suspect foul play, then?' Arty addressed his question to Samson.

'Sorry, I can't discuss—'

'Of course she does,' Edith Hird cut across Samson's

reply. 'What mother wouldn't? Surely it's preferable to have your son be killed than have him die by his own hand?'

Again the room fell quiet as they contemplated the suffering of the butcher's wife.

'Or in an accident,' said Arty. 'Like that lad they buried today.'

'What lad?' asked Eric.

'Some young farmer over towards Hawes. Got killed when his quad bike turned over on him. I met Will Metcalfe and Harry Furness coming back from the funeral.'

'How sad,' exclaimed Clarissa. 'Another young man.'

'What was his name?' asked Joseph O'Brien.

'Alderson,' said Arty. 'Can't remember what they said his first name was.'

'Alderson?' Joseph frowned. 'That rings a bell—'

'Oh, my goodness!' Edith was pointing at the TV, where the auction of the 'ugly' cup was reaching its conclusion. 'Forty thousand pounds, Arty! Shows what you know!'

'Forty thousand . . . ?'

'Madness . . .'

'Who on earth paid that much . . . ?'

In a flash the sombre atmosphere was replaced with excitement, the pensioners enthralled by the unexpected climax of their TV programme. Samson listened with half an ear. *Alderson . . . Alderson . . .* Where had he heard that name?

'Imagine! Forty thousand . . .'

'More money than sense . . .'

'Best episode ever . . .'

'You should have been an auctioneer, Samson. Think

of the cut . . . Samson?' Joseph O'Brien was talking to an empty chair.

'What got into him?' asked Arty as the residents of Fellside Court turned their attention to the young man running across the courtyard towards his motorbike.

'Not sure,' said Joseph.

The roar of the engine carried over the television as Samson sped away.

'Maybe he's just remembered he's got a cup made of rhino's horn in the cupboard at home,' said Arty and the room dissolved into laughter once more.

Alderson! Tom Alderson – the name in Delilah's note-pad. Another client of the Dales Dating Agency who had turned up dead.

Samson tore through the town, not even noticing that the rain had stopped, and took the sharp right down the ginnel to pull up outside the yard.

Logic suggested it had to be a coincidence. But Samson had been a policeman long enough to know that logic wasn't always right. Sometimes that tug deep in your belly, the crawl of nerves along your spine, the tingle of instinct that made you pause – sometimes you had to let that override all logic.

Which was what Samson was doing now.

Bike parked for the night, he hurried along the path to the back door, noting the light spilling out of Delilah's office window.

She was still here. He'd just have to work round her.

*

The downstairs door opening sent a draught of air up the stairs to pull Delilah from her morbid investigations and Tolpuddle from his dreams. Both dog and owner lifted their heads, Tolpuddle letting out a sharp bark and jumping from his bed to trot out onto the landing.

Samson was here. Damn!

'Hello,' he called out, his footsteps on the stairs already, forestalled by a flurry of barking as Tolpuddle gave him an enthusiastic greeting.

Delilah hurriedly closed the documents on her computer and gathered all the loose papers off her desk, shoving them in a drawer. When he appeared seconds later, there was no evidence of her dark suspicions. Apart from the sting of heat across her cheekbones.

'Evening! You're working late. Everything all right?' He was in the doorway, a hand on Tolpuddle's head, his gaze going straight to her flushed face.

Somehow she managed a smooth reply. 'Fine. Just getting things sorted for the next Speedy Date night.'

He smiled. 'Ah! Lucy was telling me all about it today.'

'She was?' Delilah felt her heartrate pick up. She tidied the pens on her desk to distract herself. 'And what did she say? Only good things, I hope?'

'All good. She really enjoyed it. I'd say you did her a favour asking her to go.'

'Not everyone thought so.'

'Let me guess – Will?' A dark eyebrow lifted with the question.

'Yes, Will. Dad thought it was too soon as well, and Nathan wasn't overly happy. He had a row with Lucy over it, accused her of being disrespectful. One or two others made comments . . .' Delilah shrugged. 'That's Bruncliffe for you.'

Samson's smile transformed into a grin. 'And people wonder why I left!'

'No. Actually they don't. They're more puzzled as to why you bothered to come back.' She lifted her focus from the desk to study the man before her. 'Why did you come back?'

'I'm looking for a wife.' The grin became even more roguish. 'And I heard there was a great dating agency in town.'

Delilah felt her lips surge into a smile despite herself. 'Well, as the owner of said dating agency, I have to suggest that you might want to rethink your outfit for your profile picture.' She pointed at the dark-brown cords that were floating a good few inches off the floor. 'Short-legged flares are *so* last year!'

Samson laughed. 'They're Dad's. I got caught in the rain on the way to see him, and Miss Hird was afraid I'd die of pneumonia.'

'Now you're just a casualty of fashion instead.' Delilah stood, shutting down her computer as she did so. 'Right. Time I went home.'

'Really? I was just going to get some takeaway. I can't persuade you to join me and pass on some more dating tips over crispy fried duck?'

'Not tonight. But thanks for the offer. It's Mum and Dad's wedding anniversary, so family calls.'

'Give them my best – if you think it's appropriate.'

'I'll wait until Will's out of earshot,' she said with a wry look. She picked up her bag and moved past him in the doorway, Tolpuddle padding along beside her. Hand on the bannister rail, she paused. 'Are you leaving now or will you lock up?'

'I've got a couple of things to do yet.'

'For the Hargreaves case?'

He nodded.

'How's it going?' Her pulse started racing again as she strove to sound nonchalant. 'Still think it's suicide or have you unearthed some deranged killer?'

'No deranged killers. Yet!' He flashed her a smile.

'Let me know if you do find any,' she said with an equally bright smile. 'Goodnight.'

Then she was down the stairs and through the kitchen, heading for the exit. It was only as the door closed behind her that she let her breath ease out between clenched teeth.

Why had that felt like an interrogation? Was it just her suspicions tainting everything around her? But she hadn't imagined Samson's reaction when she asked him about Richard Hargreaves. All that banter, the jovial demeanour, had been suddenly underlain by a stillness – like a hawk spotting prey halfway down a mountainside.

Had she given anything away? She didn't think so.

She was outside her cottage, spare key in the door, when she realised she'd made a mistake. She'd been so knocked back by his offer to get a takeaway together – and equally wrong-footed by her own inclination to accept – that she'd forgotten to lock her office. Should she go back?

The thought of having to face Samson again deterred her.

Leave it, she told herself as she let Tolpuddle into the

dark cottage ahead of her. It's not as if he suspected anything anyway.

Samson O'Brien stood in the doorway of Delilah's office
and looked around. She was hiding something. First the
failure to mention Richard Hargreaves had been a client.
Now the news of this second death was all over town,
via none other than Delilah's brother, and yet she hadn't
admitted the connection between the man buried today
and her dating agency.

Two of her customers dead. No wonder she'd looked
rattled when he walked in. Part of him would like to think
it was his male charisma that had brought the tinge of
rose to her cheeks. But he knew better. Especially when he
was dressed like something out of a clowns' cast-offs
catalogue.

No, she'd clearly been ruffled to see him. And then
she'd actually held a conversation with him. No scowls.
No snapping. She'd been human. She was definitely hiding
something.

He'd waited ten minutes, the length of time it would
take her to get home, before returning to her office. The
handle had turned without resistance, proof of how easy
it was to distract people. By playing on her discomfort and
standing in the doorway as she left, he'd managed to derail
her from her normal routine and she'd forgotten to lock
her office.

Closing the door after him to cut out the light from the
landing, he crossed to the desk and switched the computer
on – more in hope than expectation. The screen glowed
bright in the dark room. He glanced over his shoulder at

the curtainless window, outside a black canvas, the Crag looming unseen somewhere out there. He'd have to take the risk.

The computer hummed into life and presented Samson with a photo of Delilah laughing, her arms wrapped around a happy Tolpuddle, and a password request.

He cursed. Of course she'd have it protected. He tried a few long shots – date of birth, her dog's name, the name of her pet rabbit when she was a kid.

No good. Delilah and Tolpuddle grinned back at him. He opened the desk drawer instead, the screen providing enough light to see the contents. A jumble of papers, looking like they'd been hastily thrust in there. He pulled them out and his lips formed a silent whistle.

Bingo! The Dales Dating Agency client records for Richard Hargreaves, Tom Alderson and another man, Martin Foster.

Martin Foster? A third man. Was he dead as well? Entering the name into his mobile, he quickly got the answer.

'Jesus!' Samson stared at the newspaper report – another accident. Another of Delilah's customers who would go dating no more.

Three men, all connected to the agency and all dead in seemingly innocuous circumstances. Yet Delilah had been concerned enough to pull their records, proving that she was at least aware of the grim connection between her clients and a sudden spate of untimely deaths.

Perhaps even more than aware of it . . . ?

He let the thought settle in a corner of his mind, too much of a policeman to discount anything simply because of the past. Then he took photographs of the records before pushing them back in the drawer.

'Crikey, Dee,' he muttered, reaching a finger out to touch the photo on the screen as he stood to go. 'What have you got yourself into?'

He shut down the computer and when he left the room, it was exactly as it had been. Apart from one thing. The little red light blinking under the desk.

Her phone buzzed within minutes of her arriving home. Her security system had been activated. She knew what to expect before she logged on but even so, it was still a blow.

Samson O'Brien in his old-fashioned clothes, sitting in her office and trying to access her computer, unaware he was being videoed by a camera inside the monitor.

The swine! All that chit-chat before she left the building, the offer to have dinner together – it had all been a smokescreen. He'd simply wanted her out of the way so he could go snooping.

Cross with herself for not having seen through his charm, she watched him check the window behind him, ever wary. Then he tried to enter a password.

Her date of birth. What did he take her for? An idiot? He tried again. Tolpuddle. She laughed, the dog in question nudging her leg. Then, his last attempt, Carrots. The name of the rabbit she'd got for her sixth birthday. How the hell did he remember that? A flash of affection cut through her anger, but soon evaporated as Samson reached for the desk drawer.

She'd forgotten about the printouts of the client records she'd hastily hidden away.

He pulled them out. She heard him murmur Martin Foster's name, a frown forming as he stared at the last piece of paper, his mobile already in his hand, fingers typing. Then the soft curse.

He knew. He reached out and touched the screen, the microphone catching his words and transporting Delilah back to an idyllic childhood. *Dee*. That was what Samson and Ryan had always called her when she was a kid tagging along after them.

It was what she felt like right now. A child out of her depth.

The screen on her mobile went black and Delilah knew she was going to spend the rest of the night wondering what to do next. Wondering whether it was time to ask Samson to help her.

'It's me. Samson O'Brien.'

Standing in the first-floor kitchen, he waited a moment, knowing there would be panic at the other end of the phone in a house where no one ever called. When the rapid breathing had eased a bit, he continued.

'I need your help. Can you come with me tomorrow morning?'

Silence while a mental calendar was consulted. All those things to reorder in a mind that didn't like reordering.

'It won't take long,' he coaxed. 'And we'll be going on the Royal Enfield . . .'

Immoral, probably. To tempt like that. But he needed this expert help. He counted to five and then heard the stuttering reply.

'Eight o'clock? Sure. I can pick you up at eight. See you tomorrow.'

There was no goodbye. Just the relieved click of a receiver being replaced in the cradle. Samson O'Brien continued to stare out past the initials covering the window to the town below.

Whatever he'd been expecting when he made the difficult decision to come home, it hadn't been this. To be wondering what his best friend's sister was doing up to her neck in murder.

11

At eight o'clock, with the fells dark and sombre in the cold, grey morning, the streak of scarlet as the motorbike turned into the yard was like a flash of autumn in the middle of winter. Samson pulled up by the barn and before he had even got the stand down, George Capstick was hurrying towards him, a mixture of apprehension and excitement twisting his face.

'Ida says I have to have a helmet,' he blurted out, ignoring Samson's outstretched hand.

'Here.' Samson passed him his spare. 'Did Ida say anything else?'

'I have to be home by lunchtime. And no speeding.'

Samson nodded, keeping his smile in check as George swung his leg over and settled on the seat. When Samson revved the engine and rode out onto the road, the high-pitched, delighted laugh of his passenger mingled with the roar of the bike as it tore away out of Thorpdale.

Eight o'clock and Delilah was only just getting to work. So much for an early start. She let herself into the quiet building, the smell of air freshener and floor polish wafting down the hallway, helping to clear the fug in her head.

Not enough sleep. Too much family.

The evening before had been awful. Gathered around

the large kitchen table at Ellershaw Farm, the Metcalfes had presented a model picture of familial bliss for anyone peering in the window. Delilah's parents, Peggy and Ted, had been seated at opposite ends; Will, his wife, Alison, and their two children were down one side; Delilah, Ash, Nathan and Lucy down the other. Only the two middle brothers, Craig and Chris, had been missing, Craig in London and Chris in Leeds. Both were too busy to make it home on a weeknight, something Will couldn't help commenting on.

Ryan, too, of course. He'd been missing. That middle peg which had kept the family tethered. Since his death it felt like all of them had been left flapping in the wind.

Not that outsiders would notice anything. The table piled high with food. The surface chatter, which touched on nothing substantial. But beneath that, to an experienced observer, the signs were there.

Peggy Metcalfe was unable to sit still, keeping herself busy loading plates or clearing dishes while her husband sat at the furthest distance from her, a benign smile on his face hiding a heart that was broken. And a gaze that kept wandering to the door, as though expecting his middle son to walk in at any moment.

As for Will, expression thunderous, he snapped and snarled at his sister and was barely gracious with his wife. Sensing the tension like wild animals, the kids had vacated the table as soon as possible, taking an equally brooding Nathan with them. For once, Delilah had been glad to see the back of her nephew, the teenager having spent the entire meal either sniping at his mother or with his attention glued to his mobile. Although no one could blame the lad for being morose. He was still coming to terms with the magnitude of losing his father.

Delilah, for her part, had been too preoccupied to rise to any of Will's loaded comments, which was probably just as well after her loss of temper at lunchtime. But it meant she was poor company. Meanwhile Ash, in that maddening laid-back way of his, ate heartily and passed witty remarks like a man dining at his London club.

So it fell to Alison and Lucy to make conversation and cover the cracks, in the way that in-laws do when confronted by their spouse's feuding relatives. Delilah wondered if they returned home from these family gatherings of late to inspect their offspring like a mother looking for lice, hoping not to find any signs of those stubborn Metcalfe characteristics.

When Ash offered Delilah a lift home, she'd been grateful to get away. An hour later, she was lying in bed and unable to sleep, her thoughts skittering, anxious adrenalin coursing through her from the day's investigations. She'd finally drifted off in the early hours only to fall into fractious dreams, none of which she could remember, and had stayed in their thrall while the alarm beeped fruitlessly on the bedside table. It had taken the sudden weight of Tolpuddle on her legs to rouse her. And she'd woken with murder on her mind.

Gritty-eyed and crotchety, she made her way up the stairs to her office. A cup of tea. Then she would feel a bit more like facing the world and trying to discover why her clients kept dying.

*

The motorbike sped north, away from Bruncliffe, the fells lining the route as it snaked further into the Dales. Easing up as they passed through villages, increasing the speed once back on the open road, before long they saw the multi-arched span of Ribblehead Viaduct scything through the landscape ahead of them in an expanse of grey stone.

London had little to compare with this, thought Samson, taking in the structure which fitted so snugly into the hills. He turned right for Hawes and the road began to climb, open land stretching around them, dark and brooding in the reluctant morning. Greys and subdued greens, the occasional patches of conifers almost black, and the walls . . . always the walls dancing over the fields, cutting up into the fells. God, how he'd missed this.

Then the road was dipping again, dropping down towards Hawes and their turn-off, a narrow lane winding towards the village of Gayle, the engine noise bouncing off the stone walls hemming them in. Twisting and turning, cutting through the cluster of houses and across the river and then up the sharp hill at the back. He remembered this. Remembered coming here with his father.

Over the crest of the hill and the dale extended, Wether Fell looming above them on the left. A tap on his shoulder and George's arm was pointing at a collection of buildings down on the right.

The farm.

'Let's just hope someone's home and willing to talk,' Samson muttered into his helmet. He turned the Royal Enfield onto the track and headed for their destination.

*

By nine o'clock, Delilah was looking for patterns. Something in the way the three men had behaved, either at the Speedy Date night or on the website, that might have some relevance to their untimely passing. Something that might have triggered their deaths.

Murder. That's what she was presuming. No more time for coincidences.

It sounded so preposterous in the cold light of a Bruncliffe morning as she bent over her desk, Tolpuddle snoring lightly in the corner. But she needed to rule it out; needed to be certain that Mrs Hargreaves was wrong. Because if it transpired that the butcher's wife was right, then it opened the door to the awful possibility that Tom and Martin had also been killed. And perhaps that more Dales Dating Agency customers were in danger.

Skimming through her paperwork, Delilah pulled out the seating plan from the last dating event. She'd hired the upstairs function room at the Coach and Horses, the pub's location on the high street and cosy decor making it more suitable than the outdated Fleece – not to mention the friendlier staff. With the twelve tables laid out in a horseshoe, the women had been given the outside seats, and therefore a view of the entire room, and the men the inside, changing tables every four minutes. So the seating plan in her hand was only an initial one. But it showed that the three men she was focusing on had been placed apart: Richard at the second table, Tom at the fourth and Martin at the ninth. As they hadn't followed each other directly along the conveyor belt of dates, hopefully that meant the idea of someone simply killing all the male participants in order could be ruled out. And as far as Delilah could tell, the irregular spacing of the three unfortunate clients at second, fourth and ninth didn't lend itself to any mathematical basis for their deaths, either.

Not sure whether to be relieved at her deductions or appalled that she was considering such dire scenarios, she moved on to open the client files on the computer. Martin and Tom had been attending their first Speedy Date night; Richard had been on his second. No connection there then. So what about the night itself?

When she'd set up the Dales Dating Agency two years before, it had always been her intention to introduce live events, knowing that for some of her clients, real-life interaction would be more of a draw than the virtual sort. But with plenty of farmers amongst her clientele, she'd been determined that the evenings wouldn't become like Skipton auction mart, with men bidding on the best-looking beast or vice versa – particularly as many of her customers would be from the same area and would possibly know each other already. The last thing she wanted to do was make things awkward for people bumping into each other at Bruncliffe market on a Thursday.

So she'd kept it simple. An even number of guests, a low-key setting, a relaxed atmosphere . . . and a way of tracking your 'dates' that didn't reduce them to a score out of ten.

In a twist on the traditional score card used by most speed-dating companies, she'd come up with the idea of date cards: a set of small cards prepared for each participant with their name, age and key interests typed on the back, which, at the end of a four-minute segment, they simply swapped with their date. Then, when the evening was over, the participants returned home, logged on to their account on the agency website and, on the basis of the cards they'd collected, decided on their next step.

Again, Delilah had tweaked the standard formula. Rather than the sterile ticking of 'yes' or 'no' boxes to signify an interest in someone, which seemed so clinical after such a short amount of time, there were three straightforward choices. If you wanted to follow up your brief liaison with a particular person, you clicked on a box entitled 'I'd like to see you again'. If you were unsure, you simply chose 'Looking forward to catching up at the next date night'. And if you were certain you never wanted to see the person ever again, you clicked 'Thanks for a lovely evening'.

Polite. Friendly. And as most people plumped for the more affable middle option when lacking in interest, not only did the agency benefit from repeat business, but no one was left feeling rejected. At least that was the plan. Although, thought Delilah, if someone was bumping off the participants, it was possible she might have to revise that!

Knowing that nothing untoward had occurred on the evening in question – no heated disagreements between dates, no cross words exchanged during the hour of min-gling at the bar afterwards – Delilah focused on the online accounts for the three dead men. If there was anything to signal a potential link between them, it would be in there.

A whine from the dog basket drew her attention away from the screen, and Tolpuddle, heavy head on paws, eyes looking mournfully up at her, whimpered again.

'What's the matter?' she asked.

The dog's eyes flickered to the stairs and back to her, followed by another sound that was almost a snivel.

Samson. The bloody hound was missing Samson.

She stood and crossed to the window, staring down into the backyard where an empty expanse of oil-stained concrete told her the office downstairs wasn't occupied. Nine-thirty and he wasn't in. Had he discovered something? Found enough in his brief incursion of her office to set him off on a trail?

She returned to her desk with even more urgency, still hoping that the Dales Dating Agency wasn't embroiled in what could be Bruncliffe's first serial killing.

That would kill her business stone dead, for sure.

Samson had no idea how to play this. Turning up out of the blue to a farm he hadn't visited since he was a nipper, and in the wake of such tragedy. There was every chance they would chase him out of the place once they realised why he was here.

He rode slowly up to the farmhouse, a well-kept home in a courtyard of barns and outbuildings, and parked the bike next to a Land Rover. As he waited for George to get off, he saw the door of the rear porch open, a large man staring out at them.

'Get lost!' the man shouted, flapping his arms as though they were crows on newly sown fields. 'We're not willing to speak to you.'

George Capstick, helmet in hand, began to rock sideways, a soft mewing sound issuing from his tight lips.

'Mr Alderson?' Samson swung his leg over the bike and took his helmet off, a hand stretched towards the irate farmer in the hope of calming both him and George, all the while thinking that this had been a massive mistake.

The man clenched his fists and began to cross the yard. George rocked even faster, head held unnaturally still atop his swaying body.

'I said get lost,' snarled the farmer. 'We've had our fill of reporters. Now go, or I'll let the dogs out.'

'We're not—' Samson broke off as George began scurrying towards the nearest barn and disappeared inside.

'Where the hell's he going? Oi! Get back here!'

'George? It's okay, George, he won't harm us.' Samson ran after his old neighbour, not sure of the validity of his promises, given the angry shouts behind him. Or what had possessed him to bring George Capstick along on a mission so delicate. 'George—?'

He stopped abruptly in the doorway, the farmer slamming into the back of him and knocking his breath out in a sudden burst. He fell forward onto a hay bale, leaving a clear view for the man behind.

'What the—?'

'A Little Grey! You've got a Little Grey!' George Capstick, face alight, was sitting atop an ancient tractor, running his hands over the steering wheel, his eyes caressing the squat grey machine. 'TE20 Standard wet-liner inline-four engine can I start it?'

Mr Alderson stood, mouth open, the artless enthusiasm of the man on the tractor deflating his anger. 'It doesn't work . . . it was a project – my son . . .' His lip quivered.

'2088cc three-point linkage four-speed gearbox . . .'

'We're not reporters,' Samson said gently, while George

continued to rattle off unpunctuated statistics in the background.

'So I gather,' said the man next to him, a small smile appearing as George now wriggled under the tractor, an enthusiastic stream issuing forth from his new position on the ground. 'What are you then?'

Samson took a deep breath. 'I'm here . . . I want to talk to you about your son's death.'

The smile disappeared, replaced by wariness. And a visible struggle to control emotion. 'What about Tom?'

'It's complicated. Perhaps there's somewhere better we could talk? Privately?' Samson gestured at the figure leaning in under the raised bonnet and muttering away.

The farmer stared at George, then back to Samson. 'You'd best come inside then.'

'I'll be back in a minute, George,' said Samson, happy to see his former neighbour too engrossed in the old tractor to reply as the farmer led the way out of the barn. The conversation that was about to take place wasn't something the unique mind of George Capstick needed to hear.

Three men. One evening. And a mountain of data to comb through.

Even though Delilah had kept the system simple when she designed it, both for the users and the administrator, it was still going to take a while. By mid-morning, though, she felt she was getting somewhere.

Deciding to stick with the chronology of deaths, she'd started with Richard Hargreaves. On the night in question, he'd logged on to his Dales Dating Agency account almost as soon as the date event ended, which was unusual for a man. Normally it was the ladies who recorded their verdicts straight away, the men either playing it cool or, more likely, heading down to the pub and leaving it until they got home. Not Richard.

Out of the twelve ladies, he'd let seven of them down gently. Drawing a line down the page of her notepad, Delilah listed the names of all the women who'd been on the Speedy Date night, separating them across the two columns according to whether they'd been rejected by Richard or not. Then she turned to Martin Foster.

Clearly the electrician's first dating event hadn't left him cautious, as he'd gone onto the website the following morning and asked all twelve women if he could see them again. Which made him either desperate, or easy to please! On a fresh page, Delilah drew two more columns, although thanks to Martin's impartiality, she only had need of one.

Finally, Tom Alderson. He'd been the most reticent, waiting almost a full day before marking out only three women to follow up. Delilah entered the information on a third page and then sat back and looked at the notepad in front of her.

Two pages that offered her a glimmer of hope, and then a third – with its single column containing all twelve names – that totally skewed her burgeoning theory.

Damn! Thinking along the lines that hell hath no fury like a woman scorned, she'd been convinced she would find a correlation between the three men and the women they'd declined to get to know better after the date night. And while she couldn't believe that anyone would resort to murder simply on the basis of being rebuffed, it was at least a place to start.

Instead, there was nothing. Because all twelve women had been chosen by Martin Foster. Yet he was dead. So if the men had been killed, it wasn't on the basis of rejection.

What *was* the motive, then?

Wishing for the first time in her life that she had the mind of a murderer, Delilah Metcalfe turned back to her computer screen. The answer was in there somewhere. She just had to find it.

12

'The quad bike? Whatever do you want to look at that for?'

Bill Alderson was sitting across the kitchen table from Samson, the detective's business card tiny in his large hand, while his wife, Lynn, was pouring tea, good and strong judging by the odour rising from the three mugs.

'I just wondered—'

'You think it might have had something to do with the accident?' Mrs Alderson cut across Samson, eyes sharp in a face haggard with grief.

'Possibly . . .'

She turned to her husband. 'What harm could there be, Bill?'

'None, I suppose. But I don't understand why someone's come all the way out from Bruncliffe for this.'

Samson reached for his mug while searching for the right words, unsure how to put it. 'I'm investigating another accident,' he said finally.

'Like Tom's?' asked the farmer.

'Kind of.'

'How kind of?'

'A suicide.'

Fresh pain showed on the face of Lynn Alderson, the teapot still held before her like a shield. 'How could that be connected to Tom? You're not suggesting he turned that bike deliberately, are you?'

'No, no, nothing like that.' Samson cursed inwardly at his own clumsiness. A life lived undercover hadn't prepared him for interviews with grieving parents and, bizarrely, he caught himself wishing that Delilah was by his side. She'd know how to handle these people and their sadness without hurting them further. 'I just thought . . . if I could have a quick look at the bike?'

But the keen eyes of Mrs Alderson were on him again, scrutinising him. 'Was it the other mother who hired you?'

'Sorry?'

'The mother of the person who committed suicide. Did she hire you?'

'I'm sorry, I can't say—'

But Mrs Alderson's hand was already covering her mouth. 'You think it wasn't an accident?'

Samson froze, unsure which way to leap.

'You think someone killed our Tom?' Her voice rose high and hung above the table, shimmering like a blade.

Bill Alderson reeled back. 'Tom? You think someone killed him?'

'I can't be sure. It's just . . . a hunch. But I might be able to rule it out,' said Samson.

'But why?' Mrs Alderson asked, hand shaking as she replaced the teapot on its stand. 'Why on earth would anyone want to harm Tom?'

'I don't know.'

Husband and wife looked at each other and then Bill got to his feet.

'Come on then,' he said, heading for the door. 'It's in the small barn.'

There. Staring out at her from her computer screen. A pattern of behaviour shared by the three men.

Having drawn a blank with her initial theory – that the women who had been rejected would yield a common link – Delilah had returned to the data accumulated after the Speedy Date night, this time focusing on the women who had been chosen.

According to her records, Richard Hargreaves had sent five follow-up requests, two of which had been turned down. That left him with three interested ladies. Martin Foster, after his staggering decision to invite all twelve women to meet him again, had been rewarded with six acceptances. While two of Tom Alderson's three offers of a date had been favourably received.

So three women had wanted to date Richard; six had said yes to Martin; two had agreed to meet Tom. But only two names appeared in all three columns – two women who had accepted date requests from all three of the men who had subsequently died.

Finally Delilah had something to tie the deceased men together – even if it didn't seem a credible catalyst for the deaths that had followed. However tenuous though, it was a definite line connecting her dead clients and right now, that was all she had.

Delilah stared at the two names in front of her and wondered if she was looking at the name of a murderer.

'It's fine.'

'Nothing wrong with it at all? The brakes? The throttle?'

George Capstick was already shaking his head, eyes darting back to the large barn where the much more interesting grey tractor was waiting. 'It's fine.'

Samson covered his disappointment by stroking a hand across his face. He'd been so sure. So confident they would find something here; that there would be some evidence of foul play which would tie at least two of Delilah's dead clients together.

He'd crossed the farmyard in the company of both Lynn and Bill Alderson, noting the pristine conditions once more as they paused to collect George from his loving admiration of the Ferguson tractor. The doors of the larger barn were painted green, the paintwork bright in the morning light and the woodwork solid. The yard had been swept, a couple of hens scratching futilely at the barren surface. The drystone wall that ran around the perimeter of the property looked newly repaired in places. And when they arrived at the smaller, stone-built barn, it too was organised to perfection: a workshop with everything in its place. It had made Samson ashamed to think of the ramshackle outbuildings of Twistleton Farm.

'Tom kept the place in good nick,' Bill Alderson had explained, noting Samson's approving glances. 'He could turn his hand to anything. Apart from walling. We had to get someone in for that as neither me nor Tom are . . . were . . . much cop at it. Everything else though . . .'

He'd tailed off, his anguish clear to see, and Samson,

uncomfortable at the torment he was putting the Aldersons through, had been relieved when George had begun giving the quad bike a thorough inspection.

Now George was delivering his verdict. Apart from a few scratches and a couple of dents following the accident, the bike was in full working order.

Samson knew better than to question the judgement of his mechanic, George Capstick being more knowledgeable about anything with a motor than anyone Samson had ever met. But still, it wasn't what he'd been expecting. Or hoping for.

He'd convinced himself that the quad bike had been tampered with. That Tom Alderson's accident had been anything but. If he was on the trail of a murderer, however, the person he was chasing was covering their tracks impeccably.

A long exhalation next to him reminded him that not everyone in the barn was a detached observer.

'I'm sorry,' he said to the distraught parents, Lynn Alderson's face drawn, hands clasped to her chest. 'I thought . . . maybe the bike . . .'

Bill Alderson placed a solid arm across his wife's shoulders. 'No need to apologise, son.' He sighed heavily. 'It was a bit far-fetched anyway. Who'd want to hurt our Tom? And as for the bike . . .' He gestured at the surrounding workshop, everything tidied away, surfaces clear. 'Tom was particular about his tools. He wouldn't have been riding a quad that was defective.'

Samson nodded. It had been a long shot, but one the gnawing in his stomach wouldn't let him ignore. 'Thanks for allowing us to look at it,' he said. 'And I'm sorry to have intruded on your grief.' He turned to George, who was still gazing longingly over at the far barn. 'We're leaving, George.'

His mechanic gave his characteristic slow blink, shuffling his feet on the concrete floor. Then, after what seemed an age, he spoke.

'You need to tell them not to tape,' he said.

'Not to tape?'

George pointed at the handlebars of the bike, his eyelids closing for several seconds before reopening. 'It's dangerous,' he said.

'What's he talking about?' asked Bill Alderson.

'I'm not sure.' Samson watched his mechanic as he began to fidget, hands twitching, legs jiggling. 'What do you mean, George?'

'It's bad for the engine,' came the blurted reply. 'Too many revs.'

Nonplussed, Samson turned to the quad bike. Too many revs – so something to do with the throttle. He reached across to the right and rested his hand on the metal lever under the handlebar. Sticky. A tacky substance pulling at his fingertips.

Heart beginning to thump, he stretched his fingers up onto the handlebar. More traces of what felt like adhesive. A loop of tape had been wrapped around the throttle and onto the handlebar above. Jamming the throttle open. Making the bike rev . . .

'Can you think of any reason Tom would have had for keeping the bike running when he wasn't on it?' he asked.

Lynn Alderson looked up at Bill, who was already shaking his head. 'No. I know folk who keep the quad trundling through when they get off to open and close gates. But only an idiot would do that round here. The bike would be off up a hill and back on you before . . .' He paused, eyes darting to the handlebars where Samson's hand was still resting and then to George. 'Tape? My God. Someone taped the throttle open?'

'But that could kill someone—' Lynn Alderson's words sliced through the cold air of the open barn. Then she let out a small moan, her hands flying to her mouth. 'Tom! It wasn't an accident!'

Samson made no move to disagree.

The sharp ping of an email arriving startled Delilah back to her surroundings. How long had she been sitting there staring at the two names? Long enough for her tea to go cold and her computer screen to go blank.

Hannah Wilson and Sarah Mitchell. Such unremarkable names. As for the women themselves, Hannah was local, a year older than Delilah, and a librarian who bred Shire horses in her spare time. She'd joined the Dales Dating Agency six months before but hadn't really made much of the online options. But when Delilah had introduced the live events, Hannah had signed up for the first one and every one since. She was bubbly, cheerful, the perfect person for Speedy Date night.

A quietly spoken ecologist, Sarah Mitchell was almost the polar opposite of Hannah. Hailing from Leeds, she'd arrived in the Yorkshire Dales eighteen months ago to carry out research into otter populations and had stayed on to work for an ecology consultancy service based in

Hawes. She'd only joined the dating agency in September; October's dating event had been her first.

Neither woman struck Delilah as being capable of murder.

She slumped back in her chair and checked her emails. Two more requests to join the Speedy Date night the following week. It was almost fully booked now, demand such that Delilah had increased the number of participants to fifteen couples. The article in the local paper had proved to be great publicity.

It wouldn't be so great when word got out about the link between the dating nights and the recent deaths.

The thought sent a shot of anxiety through her, propelling her to her feet to pace the floor. What was she going to do? She only had a few days before the next event. And she could really do without anyone dying after that one.

From the corner of the room a soft sigh alerted her to the presence of Tolpuddle, head on paws, eyes watching her forlornly.

'Yeah, I know,' she muttered. 'You're waiting for him.'

She gazed out of the window into the empty courtyard below, and inspiration struck.

Suspicion. Unfurling itself, snaking through his mind. Turning the normal into the suspect. Casting scepticism on every coincidence.

After the discovery of the tape residue on the bike, Samson had accompanied Bill Alderson to the scene of the accident, George opting to stay behind and continue his inspection of the old tractor. They'd taken the Land

Rover, Bill pulling up inside the first gate where they got out.

'This was open,' he'd said, eyes filling with sadness as he recalled the night of his son's death. 'I should have known then there was something up. Tom never was one for being careless.'

'So it was in this field that you found him?' Samson looked up at the looming sides of Wether Fell, the autumn already turning the green to brown, and thought about how dark it would be here once the sun went down. And isolated, the only house visible being the Alderson farm in the distance.

'No, the next one.' Bill led the way up the field to the top gate. He paused, as though gathering his courage, and then passed through.

Samson's first impression was the steepness, grass rising sharply up to the far wall. It was similar to the fields at the outer edges of Twistleton Farm – tricky to negotiate even on a quad bike. No one who worked this fellside regularly would be stupid enough to ride directly up it.

'He was over there.' The farmer pointed to his left, where the ground was gouged and stained. He made no move to follow as Samson crossed to inspect the scene.

Crouching down, Samson ran his eyes up along the land, taking in the contours, the bumps and indents. A well-worn track snaked across the hillside, weaving lazily up to a gate set high in the left-hand wall. The route for the quad bike. A safe traverse across this tricky terrain. So why on earth hadn't Tom stuck to it? Because, judging by where the quad had ended up, something had urged Tom to take the more direct route to the top gate. Unless Tom hadn't been in a state to make that decision . . . ?

He looked back at the gate where he'd entered the field with Bill.

They'd been here, lying in wait, whoever had fixed the tape onto the bike. Tom would have stopped at the top of the first field, walked over in the headlights of the quad bike to the gate, and opened it. And out of the dark, rising up from behind the wall, his death had come to him.

How? Tom had been beneath the quad when his father found him, some distance from the gate. From what the Aldersons had said, his injuries – smashed pelvis, fractured limbs, broken vertebrae, extensive damage to the abdomen – were consistent with being trapped under a heavy four-wheeled motorbike. So if it hadn't been an accident, how had he got there?

There was only one way. A blow to the head. Then slump the body on the bike, start the engine, tape the throttle open and let go. The quad bike would have carried its cargo up the treacherous incline, until it could keep traction no longer. Then it would have cartwheeled back-wards and onto its inert passenger, leaving Tom Alderson dead in what would look to all intents and purposes like one more farming accident, the initial wound easily over-looked by a coroner as part of the overall trauma.

Callous. And calculated. For whoever had placed tape on the throttle had been composed enough to remove it. Which meant they'd approached the upended quad bike. No doubt checked the young man beneath it was dead, too, leaving nothing to chance.

Samson straightened up and walked back to the farmer,

who seemed to have diminished in stature since they'd entered the field.

'Well?' asked Bill. 'Do you still think it could have been deliberate?'

'My instinct says it was. But I don't understand how someone could have known Tom would be here that night. What brought him out here?'

'Why, the dead sheep, of course.'

'What dead sheep?'

'The one we got the call about. Some tourist came across a dead ewe on the right of way beyond.' Bill pointed towards the far gate up the hillside. 'They called the Chairman of the Parish Council. He called Lynn and when Tom and I got back from the auction, Tom went straight out to deal with it. That's where he was heading when . . .' His gaze rested on the site of the crash. 'If it hadn't been for that blasted ewe breaking her neck!' he muttered bitterly.

A ewe breaking her neck. That's what had triggered this. A sheep carcass on a public path. A concerned tourist calling the Parish Council. And Tom Alderson had ridden out in the dark to his death.

A death that could have been even more calculated than Samson had first thought.

'Is that the only access into the field where the sheep was?' he asked, pointing at the gate up above them.

Bill nodded.

'So Tom had to come through here to get to it?'

'Yes. Why?'

Samson was looking from the road to the first gate, and

then up to the far gate. It had been well planned. Some-where to hide. Terrain that would provide the perfect explanation for an accident. And now, with this informa-tion about the sheep, a certainty that the victim would arrive in this precise spot. But for the residual trace of tape on the handlebars, there was nothing to arouse suspicion.

'I don't suppose the Chairman of the Parish Council got the contact details for that tourist?' he asked casually.

Bill frowned. 'I doubt it. Why, is it important?' He paled as he grasped the implication of what Samson was asking. 'You think . . . it might have been a trap?'

'I can't say for sure. But someone put tape on that throttle. Someone who knew Tom would be out here that night. And it seems to me a dead sheep is a pretty good way to guarantee getting a farmer out to a specific field.'

'Christ! We have to call the police.'

A vivid recollection of Sergeant Gavin Clayton's cyni-cism as he discussed Mrs Hargreaves and her suspicions must have been enough to place doubt on Samson's face. Doubt which Bill Alderson read easily. His shoulders sagged.

'They'd think we were mad, wouldn't they? Nothing but a bit of stickiness on a throttle as evidence.'

Samson gave a small nod.

'So what then? We do nothing and let the bastard—' The farmer broke off and twisted away, putting his face into the wind, and once again Samson wished Delilah was with him to handle this man and his raw emotions.

The two men stood there in the vast field, dwarfed by the rising fell before them, the half-hearted trill of a lark way above sharp against their silence.

'Do you think it's connected?' Bill Alderson turned, eyes red-rimmed, expression bleak.

'Sorry?'

'To the suicide you're investigating. Do you think Tom's death might be connected?'

'Possibly.'

The farmer stared back over the landscape that he'd known all his life, as though assessing it anew in the wake of the last week. He shook his head in bewilderment. 'Why?' he asked.

'That's what I'm hoping to find out.'

'You mean you're going to look into this?' Bill Alderson pointed at the scarred ground beyond them with its ominous dark colouring.

'I'm going to try. I can't promise anything, though.'

'We can pay. I know it's what Lynn would want.'

Samson was already shaking his head. 'Let's talk about that if I manage to find whoever did this. In the meantime, I'll let you know if I discover anything that the police might be interested in.'

Bill Alderson held out his hand, a flicker of hope replacing the despair in his eyes. 'Thank you,' he said, grasping Samson in a firm handshake.

It was carrying the weight of that hope that Samson had left the Aldersons and dropped George back at his house. When she'd seen the excited state her brother had arrived home in, Ida Capstick shook her head in disapproval, shooting daggers of reproach at Samson while George babbled on about the Little Grey. So Samson hadn't lingered, turning the bike back onto the road and accelerating towards Bruncliffe.

The police station. That was going to be his first port of call. Not to report a suspected crime – as Bill Alderson had realised, that would be pointless. If their reluctance to probe into Richard Hargreaves' death was anything to go by, it would take something more substantial than a sticky substance on a throttle to make the local force sit up and take notice of this latest case. But although there was no point in involving the police at this stage, they did have something he was keen to see, now that his hunch about Delilah's dead clients was beginning to appear valid.

Slowing up as he entered the town, he passed Fellside Court on his left, a group of elderly people sitting on the benches on the front lawn. He recognised his father and Arty amongst them, both men raising their hands as the scarlet motorbike went past. Then he was pulling onto the forecourt outside the station. Praying that someone other than Sergeant Clayton would be on duty – preferably some outsider who'd never heard of the O'Brien family and their colourful history, and who possessed an ounce of investigative talent – Samson jogged up the steps.

'Afternoon, Mr O'Brien.' The young constable who'd been in reception on his previous visit greeted him from the desk, a shy smile on his face as he snapped upright, his uniform sagging over his thin chest.

'Afternoon . . .' Samson let his eyes slip discreetly to the kid's name badge, 'Constable Bradley.'

The lad's face reddened and his smile widened into a grin and Samson crossed his fingers.

'I need to see the CCTV footage taken the day of Richard Hargreaves' death.' He said it nonchalantly, as if it was his inalienable right. But Constable Bradley wasn't fooled. A frown replaced the grin.

'I'm sorry, Mr O'Brien, but . . . Sergeant Clayton said . . . we can't let you . . .' The lad shrugged, his bony shoulders almost piercing his shirt.

Damn. Foiled at the first hurdle. The same hunch that he'd had about Tom Alderson's quad bike was nagging at him about the camera at the old railway station. He really needed to see the video taken before and after Richard's fall onto the tracks. But how?

'That's okay,' said Samson, turning to go, already deep in thought. He was at the door before he realised the lad was calling him back.

'Mr O'Brien,' the young man was saying. 'Is it true you were one of an elite group of undercover officers for the Met in London?' There was no disguising the eagerness in the lad's voice.

Samson paused, wondering where such a rose-tinted view of his career had come from. 'I worked on some undercover drug operations, yes,' he said, his answer deliberately vague.

'What's it like? Working for the Met, I mean? Is it exciting?'

A flash of memory – a drug deal in a backstreet, adrenalin soaring as he tried to negotiate the dealer into a trap.

'That's one word for it,' he replied dryly.

'Did you make a lot of arrests?' The lad was leaning over the counter now, eager to catch every word.

'As a team, yes, we did. But a lot got away, too. And

it's not all glamour.' Another image from the past – holed up in an empty warehouse on a stakeout for two weeks, tracking the coming and goings of a drugs gang. He'd needed a long shower after that one.

But the lad seemed undeterred. 'That's so cool!' he breathed, eyes shining. 'It's what I want to do. I've got six more months of probation and then I'll be applying for the first job that comes up.'

'You want to join the Met?'

Constable Bradley nodded.

'What's wrong with the force up here?' asked Samson.

The constable rolled his eyes. 'It's boring. Nothing ever happens.' He leaned even closer over the desk, voice lowering. 'And you end up fat and dull like Sergeant Clayton!'

Samson laughed. 'Possibly. But as for nothing happening around here, there's more going on than you'd think.'

'That's what my grandfather says.'

'Your grandfather?'

'Eric Bradley.' The lad nodded in the direction of the open door and the road beyond it. 'He's in Fellside Court with your dad. The old man with the oxygen cylinder?'

'Ah, Eric,' said Samson, recalling the frail pensioner with the sharp tongue. He was also putting two and two together and working out where young Bradley had obtained his forgiving version of Samson's past. It wouldn't be long, though, before even Joseph O'Brien would struggle to put a gloss on his son's time with the police. Once recent events in London came to light . . .

'Grandfather says you think Richard Hargreaves was murdered.'

Samson took a deep breath and cursed silently. Bloody Bruncliffe. It bred rumour like weeds in a neglected allotment.

'Is that why you want the CCTV footage?' the lad continued, almost whispering now. There was something in the way he said it, head angled to one side like an oversized fledgling.

'Yes. I think it could be crucial.'

Constable Bradley glanced over his shoulder at the door cutting him off from the rest of the station, long fingers drumming nervously on the desk. Then he gave a sharp nod of his head as though coming to a difficult decision.

'You're not allowed to have access to it,' he repeated, a gleam in his eyes. 'But there's nothing stopping me having a peek. What exactly are you looking for?'

Samson grinned. The lad would go far. He leaned across the desk and gave Constable Bradley the details.

By lunchtime both Delilah and Tolpuddle were going out of their minds. Samson wasn't in yet.

Delilah broke off the relentless pacing of her office to stare down into the empty yard at the space where the Royal Enfield should be, the dog leaning heavily against her leg.

Today, of all days, he was running late.

She was toying with the idea of calling him, when she heard the back door open and the sound of heavy footsteps along the hall.

'Samson?' she called out, crossing to the landing. But it was the fair hair of her nephew that was coming up the stairs. 'Oh . . . hi, Nathan.' She covered her disappointment with a smile but Nathan simply grunted, the language of a typical teen, and passed her a paper bag.

'Mum sent these over for you to try. It's a new recipe.'

Delilah peered inside the bag, the contents still warm. Four fat rascals lay within, the rising aroma of cinnamon and nutmeg enough to make Tolpuddle lift his nose and give a speculative bark.

'They're not for you, mister!' said Delilah. 'They're for me and Samson. Isn't that right, Nathan?'

'Whatever,' muttered Nathan, face clouding over beneath his long fringe at the mention of his godfather. He turned away and entered her office.

'Let me just put these out of Tolpuddle's reach,' she said, deliberately not reacting to his change in mood. She'd learned over the last few months that the best way to treat her nephew when he was in this frame of mind was to ignore whatever was bothering him. Especially when she was too tense herself to be treading on eggshells.

With an ever-hopeful Tolpuddle at her heels, she walked the length of the landing to the kitchen and placed the cakes in the cupboard above the kettle, the dog opting to stay and guard them. She was gone for no more than a minute. But when she re-entered the office, it was to see an even more sullen young man slouched in her chair, staring at her monitor.

'Everything all right?' she asked.

He looked up, expression dark. Then he stood and pushed past her, racing down the stairs two at a time.

'Nathan!' she called out. The only response she got was the slamming of the back door.

Puzzled, she moved round behind her desk to see a document open on her computer, Lucy's name in the middle of the screen. The list of entrants for the next Speedy Date night. If Nathan hadn't known before about his mother's planned participation, he knew now.

'Damn it!' She should have known better than to leave her nephew in her office unattended, especially when he was so vulnerable. He'd be hurt. Enough to go and challenge Lucy?

Cursing her own stupidity and rueing her increasingly dysfunctional family, she phoned Nathan. Getting no reply, she left a short message asking if he was okay, before returning to her vigil at the window, her fears for her clients soon overriding any other concerns. She stood there for some time, hoping to see a motorbike being pushed through the gate. But nothing appeared.

'Come on, Samson,' she murmured, forehead pressed against the glass.

Perhaps she should call him? But no, she couldn't do this over the phone. It was too important. Besides, with what she was going to ask of Samson, this conversation needed to be face-to-face. Because it was going to take every last bit of her persuasive powers to get him to agree to what she wanted – the only way she could think of to save her business, and probably other lives.

Where the hell was he?

God, he was starving. He'd skipped breakfast in his rush to pick up George and had been on the go ever since. Carrying his hastily bought lunch, Samson left the motorbike in the yard and let himself in the back door.

He checked his watch as he walked through the kitchen. One o'clock already. Constable Bradley had promised to be in touch within the hour, planning to use his sergeant's lunch break to view the CCTV. Hopefully he would find—

Samson's train of thought was interrupted by instinct. That age-old alarm system was prickling his skin, sharpening his senses. What had triggered it?

He inched out of the kitchen, back against the wall, eyes scanning the hallway. Then he froze.

His door. It was closed. He always left it open.

A creak from inside the room, in the region of his desk. A careless footstep on lino-covered floorboards. Not very professional. Had it arrived already? The mess he had fled from? And if so, in what form? More men in balaclavas?

A weapon. He needed a weapon. No point going back to his kitchen with its empty cupboards and drawers. And trapping himself by going upstairs would be plain suicide. Far better to force the confrontation here where he had the advantage, blocking both exits.

He glanced down at the carrier bag in his hand. It would have to do.

Taking a silent step forward, he reached for the door handle. Shifting his weight onto the balls of his feet, in one swift motion he flung the door open, fired the carrier bag at the figure sitting at his desk and rolled across the floor. He was up on his feet in seconds, hands outstretched, ready to lunge before his assailant had time to react, when he was hit from behind by a second attacker. A large weight slammed into his back, knocking him to the ground. Twisting sideways as he fell, he landed heavily on his hip, his head inches from the edge of the desk. But before he could recover, the weight was on top of him. And licking him.

Big, long licks from chin to forehead.

'Tolpuddle?'

The dog barked and then resumed licking Samson's face, while from the chair behind the desk came a dry comment from the other would-be attacker.

'You sure know how to welcome a prospective client!'

He struggled to get out from under the dog and saw Delilah Metcalfe, face stunned, staring at him. Behind her, a dark trickle of coffee was running down the wall.

13

'What the hell was all that about?' asked Delilah as she picked up the carrier bag, now leaking coffee and containing two soggy sandwiches. She dumped it in the metal bin next to the desk, wiping her hands on a tissue.

Samson suppressed a groan as his anticipated meal was summarily dismissed.

'Well?' Delilah was looking at him.

He shrugged. 'I tripped as I came in the door.'

'And just happened to throw your lunch at me with uncanny accuracy?'

'It didn't hit you.'

'Only because I ducked! Who on earth did you think I was?'

'No one,' he snapped, hunger and spent adrenalin making him irritable. Plus she was touching on a subject he didn't want to talk about, the shadow of his suspension looming over them. 'What were you doing in here with the door closed anyway?'

Two hands slapped onto indignant hips. 'I was waiting for you and he' – Delilah glared at the hound nudging Samson's legs – 'closed the door while chasing after a ball of paper.'

Tolpuddle gave a bark of verification, a tight wad of crushed-up paper bag between his paws which Samson recognised as the wrapper off his prawn crackers from the night before. After he'd finished his meal, he'd lobbed it at the bin and missed. And had forgotten to pick it up.

'Besides,' she continued, voice decidedly waspish, 'you're a fine one to talk. Perhaps you'd like to tell me what *you* were doing in *my* office with the door closed last night?'

Samson did his best to prevent his jaw from dropping. How did she know? What had given him away? A delightfully triumphant smile traced itself across Delilah's lips and suddenly, stomach rumbling at the thought of food, his appetite for argument waned. He held up both hands in surrender and gave a tired smile.

'Okay, I'm sorry. But before we discuss that, I need to eat. Have you had lunch?'

'Not unless you count two fat rascals which I shared with Tolpuddle. I've been too busy.'

'So how about you risk the wrath of Bruncliffe society and accompany me?'

'To the Fleece?'

Samson looked over his shoulder at the facade of the pub across the road. It wasn't a place he'd graced with his custom when he'd lived here. Not when it was his father's favourite haunt and the landlord had no scruples about taking money from an alcoholic who was already drunk.

'Would you rather go elsewhere?' Delilah's tone had lost its sting. She was no doubt aware of the reasons for his hesitation.

'No,' he decided. 'Let's go there. As long as it won't get you blacklisted. Being seen with me, I mean.'

She laughed, the sound clearing the lingering antagonism from the room. 'I think I'll take the risk.'

Which was exactly how Samson felt about it. He'd take the risk of entering the one establishment in Bruncliffe he'd vowed never to support. Because he was investigating a murder. Possibly more than one. And if he was to get any information, the Fleece, with its cast of diehard locals, was the best place to start.

Fixing a neutral smile on his face, he followed Delilah and Tolpuddle across the road.

She waited until their food was served and then she hit him with it.

'I want to hire you,' she said, eyes studiously fixed on the ham sandwich in her hand.

Nostrils already twitching at the delicious aroma coming from his plate, Samson paused, a forkful of steak-and-ale pie tantalisingly close to his lips. 'Sorry?'

'You heard,' she hissed, shooting him a black look.

He couldn't resist. Despite his hunger. He laid the fork back on his plate and grinned.

'You want to hire me? A detective? I thought you said Bruncliffe had no need of detectives?'

Delilah bit into her sandwich, chewing slowly, and he could see the effort it was taking for her not to retort. Or storm out. He could also see something else. Fine lines of worry on her forehead, and apprehension in her eyes.

'Sorry,' he said, lifting up his fork once more. Given what he already knew, he shouldn't be making fun of her. No matter how tempting it was. 'I'm all ears.'

'And eyes, judging by last night. Did you find anything interesting in my desk?'

His head snapped up, food still not in his mouth.

'I work in IT, remember,' she said, 'which means I know a thing or two about cybersecurity. As a result, your uninvited visit to my office was captured on video, including you reading the papers you took from my drawer. So tell me, did you find anything interesting?'

One look at her face and he knew he wasn't going to be able to brazen it out. Slowly he closed his lips around the pie, sent a prayer of thanks to the god of food that had inspired such a divine morsel, and thought about his answer.

The truth. It was time.

'Yes,' he finally said. 'You think your clients are being murdered. I think you're right.'

If he'd thought it would shock her, he was disappointed. Instead her mouth tightened, the lines on her forehead deepening and the colour draining from her face.

'You have proof?' she asked, leaning in across the table.

He glanced around. It wasn't the best venue for such a conversation, but then, given that it was market day and the pub was packed with lunchtime customers, there was a steady thrum of noise beneath which they could talk openly.

That hum of voices had gone quiet when they walked in, Delilah first, Samson following, the large grey dog shadowing him as though offering protection from what could be a hostile crowd. How well Tolpuddle knew his home town.

'Sorry,' Delilah had muttered. 'I forgot it's market day. Everyone will be in here.'

'Should I go back and get my boxing gloves then?'

He was pleased to see her laugh, a reaction that triggered even more curious looks.

They'd made it as far as the bar unaccosted, receiving the odd nod of recognition from the older men, wary glances from the younger ones. But with no Will Metcalfe or Rick Procter in their midst, Samson began to relax. When they'd placed their order with Troy Murgatroyd – the landlord as morose as Samson remembered – Delilah steered them towards a table in the far corner of the smaller room in the rear of the pub, which provided some privacy.

'They'll forget about you soon and carry on with their gossiping,' she'd said as they sat down, both of them choosing to put their backs to the wall, offering a clear view of the room.

'Only now they'll be talking about me,' said Samson.

'And me. They'll be saying that you're leading me astray!'

She'd been right on both counts. The volume had gradually increased, the looks cast in their direction abated, and every so often they caught their own names in the current of conversation. Samson had to restrain a smile as he wondered what the pub clientele would make of it if they knew the young Metcalfe lass and Boozy O'Brien's boy were discussing murder.

'Proof?' he said, resuming their conversation. 'Nothing that would stand up in court.'

'But you've found something?'

He nodded. 'George Capstick found it over in Gayle this morning.'

'You've involved George Capstick in this?' Delilah's voice rose dangerously high, bringing heads swinging in their direction once more before she resumed in a more muted, but equally acidic tone. 'Who else have you broadcast it to?'

'No one.' He thought about Constable Bradley and the pensioners of Fellside Court. And Matty Thistlethwaite. All of them aware of his investigations. He concluded that now wasn't the time to tell Delilah that.

'So what did George uncover – you were at the Aldersons' farm, I presume?'

'Yes. We went to look at the quad bike.'

'And?' Her fingers were digging into the soft bread of her sandwich.

'George spotted that someone had taped the throttle open.' He didn't need to explain what that meant to her – someone who'd grown up around dirt bikes and quad bikes and farm machinery. She blinked, glanced down at the table and frowned.

'But how would that have killed Tom? Surely he'd have spotted the tape?'

'Precisely. Which means that when Tom Alderson got on the quad bike in the farmyard and prepared to ride up onto Wether Fell Side, there was no tape on the throttle.'

'So when . . . ?'

He let her think about it, her grip on her sandwich still vice-like. Then she looked up at him, mouth forming a silent O.

'The killer was waiting for him!'

Samson nodded again. 'Worse than that. Bill Alderson said Tom went out to collect a dead sheep that someone had called in to complain about.'

'You mean someone . . . set a trap? They lured him onto the hillside with a dead sheep?'

'Exactly. They waited in the dark, attacked him as he came through the gate on foot or on the bike—'

'And then taped the throttle open, with the quad pointing up the hill and him astride it.' She grimaced and placed her sandwich back on the plate, paler than he'd ever seen her. 'Poor bloke didn't stand a chance.'

He gave her a moment, watching her digest the news that one of her clients had been murdered. She took a deep breath, pulled her shoulders back and looked up, face determined.

'And the other two? Richard Hargreaves and Martin Foster? Have you uncovered anything that might suggest they were killed, too?'

'Not for Martin Foster.' He shrugged. 'The man died in a fall at Gordale Scar. You know yourself that it's not uncommon for accidents to happen there.'

It was true. A limestone ravine north-east of Malham, Gordale Scar featured towering cliffs and a deep gorge, creating a sinister atmosphere even on the sunniest of days. One slip on the walk to the top and a rocky reception lay below.

'So you're suggesting that he might have died naturally?'

'Not at all. I'm just saying that proving otherwise would be difficult. Whereas with Richard Hargreaves . . .'

Samson lowered his voice even more. 'I've got a feeling the CCTV at the station might yield something.'

'You mean there could be footage of the murderer?' Delilah's question was edged with tension.

But Samson, while taking another mouthful of pie, was already shaking his head. Delilah pushed her plate away, waiting for him to speak. If she noticed him cast an avaricious eye over her abandoned sandwich, she never commented.

'I doubt we'll be that lucky,' Samson finally said. 'Whoever is involved in this has been very careful throughout. They removed the tape from the bike. If I'm right about the CCTV, they covered their tracks there, too. And if it wasn't for Mrs Hargreaves, I probably wouldn't be investigating any of these so-called accidents. So I don't have any expectation that they'll have been so sloppy as to appear on video. But it might yield something. I'll find out later today.' He mopped up the last of his gravy with a chip and shrugged his shoulders. 'That's all I have. Not enough to go on. And no motive. What about you? What's made you eager to hire me all of a sudden?'

Delilah rested her elbows on the table and leaned in. 'I think I might have a connection between the men. Something other than just being members of the dating agency.'

'Like what?'

'They were all on the last Speedy Date night.'

Samson looked unimpressed. In fact, his attention had wandered to the ham sandwich sitting forlornly on Delilah's plate, an expression not unlike Tolpuddle's on his face as he contemplated the food going spare.

'Have it,' she said on a sigh, pushing it towards him. A

whine from next to her revealed that he hadn't been the only one eyeing it. She gave the dog a consolation pat on the head and resumed her tale. 'As I said, they all attended the last dating event.'

'And?'

'And that's more than we knew this time yesterday!' she snapped. 'Plus, I've been through their records. There are no patterns amongst the women they rejected. But they all chose the same two women for potential future dates.'

She had his attention now, even though he was still eating.

'Only those two women?'

'No. Martin Foster chose all twelve—'

Samson choked on the sandwich, eyes wide. 'All twelve?' he gasped. 'Was he mad?'

Delilah resisted a retort, knowing what she was about to ask of him. 'Whereas Richard,' she continued, 'chose five and Tom three.'

'And out of those, the men had two choices in common?'

She nodded.

'Did anyone else list either of the women in their preferences?'

'No. More than coincidence, don't you think?'

'I'd say so. I presume you have the names of these particular ladies?'

'Names, addresses, likes, dislikes. Even a bit of past history.'

'So when are we going to see them?'

'Next Tuesday evening at seven-thirty.'

Samson, finishing off the last of the sandwich, glanced sideways at Delilah's precision, an eyebrow arched.

'I told you I want to hire you,' Delilah said. 'Well, I want you to go undercover.'

Puzzlement replaced curiosity on Samson's face. 'I don't understand . . .'

'The next Speedy Date night – it's on Tuesday. I want you to join my dating agency and be one of the dates.'

He reacted exactly as she'd known he would. Hands up, jerking away from her as though she'd lobbed something toxic on the table between them.

'No way!' he was saying. 'Absolutely no way.'

'You have to,' she said, pressing forward. 'What other choice do we have? We have no concrete evidence. The police won't want to know. And if we go public with this, all we'll succeed in doing is ruining my business. But if we do nothing . . .'

She let the threat of more deaths hang in the air over the empty plates. He snapped his gaze away from hers, looking out across the crowd of people, and she knew he was trapped.

'There has to be something else we could do,' he said.

She folded her arms and tried to stop her lips from settling into a smug smile. Her idea was brilliant and he knew it. An undercover date stalking the potential murderer. And thanks to Delilah, they could manipulate the outcome of the event so that only Samson chose the two suspects, thus reducing the risk to her other clients.

Quite how she was going to be able to pay him for his

services, she hadn't yet worked out. But she'd think of something.

Samson turned back to face her and she couldn't hold in the laughter. His expression was one of pure terror.

'It won't be that bad. Fifteen lovely ladies to talk to. Most men would give their right arm for such a chance.'

'I'm not most men,' he muttered. He dropped his head in his hands. 'But this is the best way to find out what's going on.'

'So I take it that's a yes? You'll go undercover?'

He nodded wearily. 'How many people have already signed up?'

'It's fully booked for the women and with you on board, there's only one more space available for the men. If I don't have any takers by tomorrow evening, I'll have to ask someone to help out—'

'Delilah! Where's that useless brother of yours? He's supposed to—' Harry Furness, emerging from the press of people at the bar, spotted Delilah's companion only at the last moment. 'Oh. Sorry, I didn't realise . . .'

Samson stood, holding out a hand. 'Good to see you in less threatening circumstances, Harry.'

The auctioneer grinned, making a show of checking Samson's chin for bruises. 'Yeah. You're just lucky I had a good hold of Will that day. He'd have left you with a more permanent reminder.'

'He's not here with you, is he?' asked Delilah, eyes nervously scanning the room as the two men sat down.

'Nope. It's Ash I'm looking for. I want to kick his backside.'

'What's he done now?'

Harry grimaced. 'He's sprained his bloody wrist fitting a kitchen sink, so I'm a man down for the darts competition next Wednesday.'

Delilah laughed. 'No point asking me. I'm hopeless.'

The auctioneer was already looking terrified at the thought. On Delilah's one and only trial for the Fleece darts team even loyal Tolpuddle had deserted her side, the random nature of her throws ensuring that no one in a wide radius had been safe.

'Wouldn't dream of it. Ash is meant to be finding a replacement, only they need to be good as we're at home to the Mason's Arms . . .' Harry Furness let his words drift off as he stared at the man opposite him. Samson O'Brien. His prowess with the arrows was legendary. As was his stubborn refusal to ever play for the Fleece team. Or any other pub team, for that matter. All the years Harry had known him, he'd never seen Boozy's lad set foot in the pub apart from to bring his dad home. Yet here he was having lunch with Delilah Metcalfe, in full view . . .

Not one to miss an opportunity, Harry decided that this new approach to life on the part of Samson O'Brien was worth further investigation. Especially if it meant solving a problem of his own.

'Fancy playing, Samson?' he asked with studied nonchalance.

But the detective had been watching the auctioneer's face as it ranged from despair to hope to excitement, and he'd been anticipating the question. Long enough that he'd even had time to consider it. And surprise himself with the answer. Because Harry Furness wasn't the only one capable of turning a situation to his advantage.

'What's it worth?'

The question caught both Harry and Delilah off guard. A point-blank refusal. A polite demurral. That's what they'd been expecting. But this . . .

'Anything!' said the auctioneer, making a reckless offer in his haste to secure this unforeseen deal that could bring about a famous victory for the Fleece darts team.

Delilah noticed the gleam in Samson's eyes, the grin already beginning to form.

'Consider yourself signed up with me for the next Speedy Date night, then,' said Samson, flashing a smile at Delilah and clapping a spluttering Harry Furness on the back. 'Don't worry, I'm sure there'll be someone there to your taste.'

And with that, Samson and Delilah stood to go, leaving a stunned Harry Furness staring into his pint. Wondering how a man of his business acumen had just been so out-manoeuvred – and how he was ever going to live it down, once word got out that he'd been to a dating event – the auctioneer tried to think about the glory that would come when they won the darts a night later with his secret weapon in their team.

It took a few seconds for the real impact of the conversation to sink in. Samson O'Brien had joined the Dales Dating Agency.

When Will Metcalfe found out, feathers were really going to fly.

Delilah was still laughing about the duped auctioneer when she entered the office building, Tolpuddle and Samson a step behind.

'I can't believe you did that. Poor Harry!'

'What about poor me?' exclaimed Samson with a wounded look that was belied by the teasing glint in his eyes. 'At least this way I'll have some moral support. And we get to limit the number of potential victims. I can't see Harry electing to take things further with anyone.'

Delilah turned to reply, when the sound of a fist hammering on the back door startled her. 'Who on earth—?'

Her question was rudely interrupted as Samson flung her to the side of the hallway, shielding her from the doorway through to the kitchen with his body.

'Are you expecting anyone?' he whispered.

'No,' she said, puzzled by his overreaction, tension emanating from him. It had been the same earlier when he'd charged into his office and thrown his coffee at her. As though he'd been anticipating trouble. He turned to stare down the hall, his face close to hers, and she could see the merging yellow and green of the faded bruise on his cheek.

Was it connected? And if so, what exactly was this man caught up in?

A second burst of pounding rattled the glass in the frame.

'Wait here!' Samson eased away, creeping down the hallway and into the kitchen.

Delilah and Tolpuddle, neither excelling in the art of obedience, followed. And when more clattering came from the back door, Tolpuddle let out a loud bark of warning, making Samson jump. He turned round, raining down curses on both dog and owner.

'I thought I told you to wait in the hall,' he snapped.

'And I thought a detective would know that someone with criminal intentions doesn't normally come calling wearing a high-visibility jacket!' Delilah pointed at the yellow silhouette that could be made out on the other side of the opaque glass of the back door. 'For God's sake, open up and let whoever it is in before they break something.'

Accepting the wisdom of her observation, Samson strode across the room, unlocked the door, and a tall young man in a police uniform that was way too big for him stumbled into the porch, fist raised in anticipation of another bout of knocking.

'Mr O'Brien!' he exclaimed, as he tripped over the pile of trainers and wellies before righting himself. 'You need to see this. Now!'

In his hand, the lad was holding a USB drive.

'There! Look!'

Delilah leaned closer to the computer screen, eyes screwed up in concentration as she stared over the bony shoulders of the young man sitting at her desk. 'What?'

'That!' Constable Daniel Bradley pointed at the image. 'Do you see?'

Delilah shook her head, but a sharp intake of breath next to her suggested Samson had seen something she hadn't.

'I knew it!' he said, patting Danny on the back. 'Excellent work.'

Danny beamed. Delilah scowled.

'Show me again,' she said, ignoring the look shared between the two men as Danny pressed Play once more.

When the young policeman had made his dramatic entrance – his appearance at the back door apparently an attempt to remain undetected, given the clandestine nature of the evidence he was carrying – Samson had offered Delilah a brief explanation as he'd ushered all of them up the stairs to her office.

'You mean you paid him to get the CCTV footage the police refused to show you?' she'd asked when he finished.

'Not exactly. He offered.'

'Is that legal?'

Samson shrugged. 'I can't see there's any harm in him looking at it. This, however . . .' He'd grinned as he gestured at the constable sitting in front of Delilah's computer and pulling up a video file from the USB.

Now, on her second viewing, Delilah was hoping to see something that might make risking a spell in prison worthwhile.

The screen flickered to life, showing a black-and-white image of Bruncliffe Old Station from a camera above the platform. The two lamps either side of the passenger shelter were on, spilling light into the dark of an October morning, and in the middle of the picture stood a man, overcoat and scarf giving tell to the chilly temperatures, the satchel slung across his chest suggesting a daily commute.

Richard Hargreaves. The date and time at the top of the image revealed it was the morning before he died. His last journey from Bruncliffe Old Station. The train arrived to the right of the screen, Richard boarded and the carriages rolled away, leaving the station deserted.

Danny scrolled quickly through the rest of the day's footage, small figures moving in and out of view, but mostly the camera showing only the empty concrete platform, typical of such a rural station. Then, as the blur of darkness gave way to the teasing grey of dawn, he let the film roll again.

Another morning. Just before six-thirty the next day, according to the on-screen clock. But this time a thick mist makes it almost impossible to discern anything more than light and shade. In the left-hand corner a smeared brightness denotes the station lamp, then a dark shape lurches forward – the lens too fogged to give greater definition – as a blur of motion slices through the footage. The train.

Richard's death was reduced to nothing more than a fatal smudge of movement.

Danny froze the video and turned round in his chair to look at Delilah.

'Well?' he asked.

She stared at the screen and then back at the young man sitting in her chair. 'I'm sorry, I just don't—'

'Look at the positioning, Delilah.' Samson leaned over and clicked the mouse, starting the morbid film all over again. 'Here,' he said, pointing at the two lights and then at the lone figure of Richard Hargreaves on the day before he died. 'See where these are in relation to the camera? Now watch.'

He fast-forwarded and then paused. In the gloom of the following morning, Delilah could see the hazy aurora of the lamp and then . . .

She squinted at the screen and then jerked back. 'The light . . .'

Samson nodded. 'Go on.'

'There's only one visible.'

'What else?'

She looked again as the film rolled once more. The dark shape, the train . . .

'Oh! Richard. He's only visible at the very end.'

Samson nodded again, Danny smiling at her from the chair as she considered explanations for this new information. There was only one she could think of.

'The camera was moved!' she said. 'It's not focused on the same spot as it was the morning before.'

'Correct,' said Danny. 'You can only see one light, and you can't see Mr Hargreaves until he begins falling onto the track.'

'And the train is in the centre of the screen, not on the edge like a day earlier!' Delilah exclaimed.

'I don't suppose you've checked the overnight footage, too?' Samson addressed his question to the constable, who was already rewinding through the film. When the clock at the top of the image revealed it was just gone one-thirty in the morning, he let the video play. The screen consisted of two bright lights, a slice of platform between them and beyond that, nothing but the darkness of a country night.

'Here,' said Danny. 'Watch.'

Even Delilah saw it first time. The shift in perspective. Suddenly the lens was no longer centred on the platform. It had swung round so that the track, just about discernible, cut through the middle of the screen and the lamplight was thrown to the left-hand side.

'Could it have been the wind?' Delilah asked. But Danny Bradley was shaking his head.

'That's what the train company claimed when I called them. They said it's not uncommon for cameras to shift in high winds. But then I checked the Met Office for the night of October the fifteenth, the night before Mr Hargreaves died. It was still. Nothing strong enough to budge a camera, at any rate.'

'So you're saying someone moved it?' Delilah turned to Samson, who was still staring intently at the frozen video. 'What do you think? Was this a deliberate act by someone who didn't want the events of the next morning recorded?'

'I think this might give you the answer,' he said.

He leaned in over the keyboard to play the overnight footage once again, and for the second time they saw the change of focus as the camera was repositioned, the view now of the darkened track. Then Samson pointed at the screen where, in the left-hand corner, a long shadow shifted briefly across the edge of the picture.

'What's that?' asked Delilah, as Danny looked up at Samson in awe.

'That,' said Samson, expression grave, 'is the person we're searching for.'

'You mean . . .'

'They parked behind the camera. On its blind side. They moved it undetected and then drove off. Only, thanks to its new angle, the lens picked up the elongated shadow of the vehicle as it passed in front of the far light in the car park.'

He tapped the blurred image on the computer screen. 'That,' he said, 'is our killer.'

Delilah felt her excitement distil into a bone-chilling fear.

14

Samson had never been so afraid. He surveyed the small upstairs bar area of the Coach and Horses, his blood running cold at the scene before him.

Give him an alleyway full of thugs; a confrontation with an armed dealer; a derelict warehouse on a moonless night, every corner filled with terror. None of that had made him feel as out of his depth as the evening which lay ahead.

Women. Lots of them. Dresses cut to weaken his knees, jewellery that trapped his eyes, smells so intoxicating his senses reeled, and smiles that promised dangers of a delicious nature.

His instinct was to run. Go back down the stairs and out into the sharp air of a Bruncliffe November, to clear his head and return his faculties to normal. But this was work. And Delilah was relying on him.

'Samson!' A desperate voice called from the bar across the room where a pallid Harry Furness was already fortifying himself with alcohol.

Heart thumping, Samson began to make his way through the throng of sirens to the auctioneer.

Four days. Four of the longest days of her life, the hours stretching into infinity.

Delilah had taken to checking the local paper's Twitter feed, listening to local radio and watching the regional TV news, all the time dreading that she'd hear of another death. Another client murdered while they sat around and did nothing.

But what could they do?

They had no definitive lead as to the perpetrator. They had no way of narrowing down the identity of the next victim, beyond it possibly being a participant in the speed-dating event.

Samson had argued the case for patience, pointing out the less-than-flimsy nature of their evidence, but it didn't make it any easier. Thinking that someone might be targeting another Dales Dating Agency customer, while the owner waited for Tuesday evening to arrive.

Not that she hadn't been busy. Word had got out, thanks to Harry Furness and his loquacious nature, that Samson O'Brien had joined the dating agency and was taking part in the next Speedy Date night. And Delilah had been inundated with new membership applications.

Women. Lots of them. All wanting to join and take part in an event which Delilah had had to explain was already fully booked.

'What is it about black sheep and their appeal to the female sex?' she muttered as she stood, hands on hips, casting a critical gaze over the upstairs function room of the Coach and Horses. The night she'd been waiting for was finally upon her.

The lamps on the wall cast a suitably romantic glow; the furniture was cosy, positioned to afford privacy; soft music gave a background for small talk while preventing embarrassing silences; and the heavy curtains blocked out the November squall beyond the windows. For the rest, she'd kept it simple. No flowers on the tables that could be knocked over by awkward farmers; no tablecloths that would ruck and rumple under the broad forearms of rugby players; and sturdy chairs. Everything else was up to the crowd of people outside, an excited babble of female voices audible through the double doors that led to the bar area.

Thirty clients. Fifteen tables. And only an hour for the hopeful singles to find the person of their dreams. Or, in Samson's case, to identify the killer who was targeting the lonely hearts of the Dales.

She reached for her bag, a tremor besetting her hand as she pulled out the seating plan and fifteen sets of date cards, each set tied with a red ribbon. Samson had suggested that the two women he was most interested in – Hannah Wilson and Sarah Mitchell – be seated in the middle. Tables seven and nine. That way Samson, starting at table one, would have time to warm to his task before seeing the two suspects only minutes apart, giving him a chance to assess them against each other. Then, when the evening was over, he would go online to ask to see them again. Delilah's job was to make sure he would be the only man to do so.

On paper, the idea was sound. By altering the dating software, Delilah had created a snare to catch a murderer, a digital trap with Samson O'Brien as the bait. Here, in the last few minutes before the plan was put into action, the reality was making her tense.

Hands still shaking, she distributed the women's date

cards, placing Lucy Metcalfe and Elaine Bullock either side of Hannah Wilson, Elaine an unwitting breather for Samson before he moved on to the second suspect. When she'd placed the final set of cards on table fifteen, she stood back and looked at the evidence of her success.

Thirty people wanting to be part of the Dales Dating Agency event, and more queuing up in the wings for the next one. It was testimony to her hard work. Proof for any doubters that her dating agency was going to prosper. She should have been celebrating such an achievement. Instead, she was thinking about Samson O'Brien and the possible danger she was putting him in. Him and all the other male clients who were about to walk through the door.

She took a deep breath, checked her appearance quickly in the mirror which ran down one wall, and tried to tell herself that her unease sprang from the unfamiliar restrictions wearing a dress and high heels placed upon her. As she opened the double doors and prepared to greet her customers, she said a silent prayer that none of them would die.

'I can't believe you talked me into this!' Harry Furness was clutching his pint like an amulet, pale face staring into the mass of women arrayed before him.

'Makes two of us,' muttered Samson, assuming a similar pose but with only a bottle of ginger beer to protect him. He was tempted to break his lifelong abstention from alcohol. There was no doubting that it would make what was to follow a lot less painful. 'Did Delilah give you the pep talk?'

'Aye,' Harry grunted. 'Four minutes and no longer.

And no discussing politics, religion or sport. Or farming.'
He gave a baleful look. 'I'm a livestock auctioneer who
plays rugby and darts, so that's me buggered!'

'You could always talk about the weather,' offered
Samson with a grin.

'That's not going to be much of a conversation seeing
as we're in bloody Yorkshire!'

'Hello, lads.' Elaine Bullock was crossing the room
towards them, long hair released from its usual plaits and
now tumbling over her shoulders, an emerald-green dress
falling to mid-thigh, from where thick tights led to patent-
leather Dr Martens. She grasped a small book in one hand,
a pint of beer in the other, and as she grinned at Samson,
he noticed she had even cleaned her glasses. 'So the
rumours are true,' she declared, nudging Samson gently
with an elbow. 'You've come back to Bruncliffe to find a
wife.'

Samson laughed, glad to have a bit of normality in-
jected into what was so far a surreal evening. 'Something
like that.'

'And you as well, Harry?'

The auctioneer shook his head. 'I'm doing this as a
favour. That's all.' He glowered at Samson, as though the
cost of the favour already outweighed any possible
rewards.

'Ditto,' said Elaine, looking over her shoulder to where
Lucy Metcalfe was approaching. 'The things we do for
friends, eh?'

'And I'm forever grateful,' said Lucy with a smile,
hugging Elaine before greeting both men with a warm
embrace. As she kissed Samson's cheek he caught the scent

of wild flowers, like the meadows around Twistleton Farm in summer. 'You've both made an effort,' she said, leaning back to take in the smart attire of the two men.

'Likewise!' said Harry Furness, eyebrows still raised at the sight of the women he was accustomed to meeting in jeans. He grinned at Lucy. 'Do you have a licence for that outfit?'

The cafe owner immediately looked down at her dress, casting a hand over the black fabric that clung to her body, showing off her curves. 'Is it too much?' she asked, worried. 'I mean, I haven't worn it since Ryan . . . Do you think I should go home and change? I don't want to give the wrong impression.'

'It's fine,' exclaimed Elaine while simultaneously stepping hard on the auctioneer's toe, her words covering Harry's yelp of pain. 'Don't you think, Samson?'

'More than fine,' said Samson. 'Just ignore Harry. He's used to looking at farmers and livestock all day. He doesn't know class when it hits him.'

Elaine gave him a grateful glance.

'Goodness,' said Lucy with a self-conscious smile as she tugged once more at the hem of her dress. 'I feel fifteen and awkward all over again.'

'Well, you certainly don't look fifteen!' announced Harry, hoping to make up for his earlier mistake. A dark look from Elaine told him he wasn't doing so well, so he moved to one side before she could demonstrate her disapproval with another well-placed boot. He was relieved when the doors to the function room opened and Delilah appeared, ready to start the evening's event.

He wasn't the only one feeling relief. For Samson

O'Brien, the night could never be over quickly enough. As an expectant hush descended, he watched Delilah welcoming everyone, taking in the burgundy dress, the high heels, a woman he almost didn't recognise. Then she caught his eye and he saw the familiar tension.

She had a lot on the line. Her businesses. Her home, if Lucy's comments about her debts were true. And she was trusting him to be able to help.

He looked again at the people before him, most of the women gathered to one side. Was the murderer in their midst? The next victim too? If so, he needed to find out tonight. Because none of them – Delilah, himself, the other men here – could afford for him to fail.

'You haven't changed a bit!'

'You have, but only for the better.' Samson grinned at the woman opposite, owner of Shear Good Looks, the salon next to the dating agency, and a lady whose figure was somewhat more substantial than when they'd been in the last year of school together.

Jo Whitfield laughed, a delightful, deep sound, and Samson realised that, almost twenty minutes and five tables in, he was actually enjoying himself.

'Still got your dad's charm,' she said, acknowledging his flattery. 'How is he, by the way?'

There was genuine concern in the question. Just as there had been genuine interest shown by her friend, Lorraine, on the previous table – another woman he'd been at school with, but whom he couldn't recollect at all. Lorraine had taken great delight in teasing him about his poor memory and had proceeded to regale him with tales of Sunday school and how much his mother had been adored.

Whatever he'd been expecting, Samson hadn't expected this. A warm welcome from the ladies of Bruncliffe. And just as much fun with the three other women he'd talked to, who had been from further up the dale.

Sharp humour. Candid opinions. That wry take on life unique to the Dales. Samson had felt at ease from the first hello, which had been delivered with a cheeky smile and a firm handshake. Fourteen years away, but within minutes he'd been totally at home.

'Dad's doing well. He's got a good crowd of people in there with him.'

Jo pulled a face of terror. 'Miss Hird will be keeping them all in check.'

They both burst out laughing as a bell rang loudly from the other side of the room and, with reluctance, Samson stood to go.

'Don't be afraid to pop round for a coffee now and then,' said Jo, passing him one of her cards and taking one of his as he prepared to move on. 'A handsome man like you calling into my salon can only be good for business.'

She gave him a wink as he leaned down to kiss her goodbye and by the time he approached table six, where Lucy Metcalfe was waiting, he'd almost forgotten his true purpose. But beyond his friend, he could see the first of his suspects, Hannah Wilson, already talking animatedly to her next date. When Samson sat down, Lucy was surprised to see him frowning.

*

Five down. One more to go and then he'd be with Hannah Wilson. Delilah had been watching Samson's progress keenly. If he'd been nervous, it hadn't shown. He'd had the women warming to him with no effort at all. She'd kept a close eye on each of his dates and hadn't been surprised when she'd seen them pressing him to take their cards as he prepared to move on. One woman had even written something on hers – a phone number, no doubt.

He was popular, that was for sure. Laughter was following him around the room, along with quite a few adoring gazes. The part of Delilah that had known him for years was rolling her eyes at such pathetic behaviour over Samson O'Brien. The part of her that ran a business was wondering whether she'd be able to persuade him to come to the Christmas Speedy Date night.

But the biggest part of her, the one that woke in the night in panic at the threat to her business and her customers, was on tenterhooks. Two more minutes and then Samson would be placing himself in possible danger.

Delilah glanced at her watch, unsure whether she wanted to stop time or speed it up.

Harry Furness didn't know where the time had gone. For an evening he'd been dreading, it had passed quickly and he was already at table nine sitting opposite a quietly spoken young woman called Sarah Mitchell. She'd barely made eye contact when he sat down and he'd had to ask her name twice, so whispered had been the reply.

But there wasn't much that could throw the auctioneer. With a big smile, he leaned across the table.

'So,' he said, 'shall we talk rugby or the price that Texel tup went for at the last market?'

Her head snapped up, but when she saw the twinkle in his eyes, a smile dimpled her cheeks.

'Or perhaps,' he said gently, 'you could tell me something about yourself?'

Hands clenched together on the table before her, she glanced at him sideways like a Swaledale lamb threatening to skitter off up the fellside.

'I like otters,' she said, gaze dropping back to the table.

Whatever Harry had been expecting, that wasn't it. He leaned forward a bit more. 'Otters? Them buggers with the big teeth that can fell trees with a single bite?'

Sarah laughed, a bubble of sound which delighted Harry and made him glad he'd played the fool. 'No,' she said. 'You're thinking of beavers. Otters are much more interesting . . .'

When the bell went minutes later, Harry Furness found he was cursing Delilah. And wanting to stay where he was.

Table seven. Aware of Delilah's scrutiny, Samson took his seat.

'Hello!' Hannah Wilson was smiling at him, vibrant red hair – Samson didn't have the expertise to tell if it was natural or chemically assisted – falling to toned shoulders, long lashes over brown eyes, her chin resting on a manicured hand. She was the kind of woman that would eat him for breakfast and he found it hard to believe she ran the town's library, as Delilah had assured him she did. 'I was a few years below you at school,' she said. 'Hannah Wilson?'

He kept his eyes on hers, aware of the perilously low-cut neckline opposite, and was pretty sure she hadn't looked anything like this at Bruncliffe High School or he might have spent more time there.

'Hi. Samson O'Brien.' He offered his hand and it was grasped in a powerful grip. His surprise must have shown.

'I run a stable,' she said, shrugging. 'You need strong arms for mucking out. As for riding – well, you should see my inner thighs!' Her eyes flashed up at him, voice purring.

Samson reached for his drink, wishing not for the first time that night that it was a bit stronger than mere ginger beer. He had no idea how to get a hold on this conversation. Or the woman before him. But he was painfully aware he only had minutes left to do so.

She laughed, mistaking his silence for discomfort. 'Don't worry,' she said, touching his arm and giving a conspiratorial wink. 'I'm only joking. I'm a timid librarian at heart. And I have to say, I love your dad's taste in books.'

The conversation had tilted again, leaving Samson unbalanced as Hannah began extolling the brilliance of Lee Child. From vamp to bookworm in less than thirty seconds. This was a woman who would never leave you sure-footed, her personality shifting like the sands at Morecambe beach. But was she capable of murder?

'Enough about dusty books,' she finally said, her demeanour flirtatious once more. 'What about you? What brings you back to Bruncliffe? Apart from its gorgeous women, of course.'

'The weather,' he said, making her laugh. 'Seriously, it

was time to come home. But I've been away a while, as you probably know. So I thought I'd give this a go.' He cast a hand around the room. 'Try and meet some new people. How about you? Is it your first time here?'

Hannah shook her head. 'Oh no, I'm a veteran. Delilah really knows how to put on a good event.'

'So you're not here looking for love?' He risked a grin and was relieved to see it returned.

'Not at all! I just treat it as a fun night out.'

'So have you had many offers . . . any dates?'

She threw him a coy glance. 'That's as bad as asking a girl's weight,' she said. Then she smiled. 'A few.'

'Any worth mentioning?' He kept the grin in place.

'Not really – apart from . . .' She blinked, a sober veil falling over her features. 'Richard. Poor Richard. He was sweet.'

Samson had to restrain himself from leaning across the table. 'You dated Richard Hargreaves?'

She nodded. 'We were supposed to be going on a second date the day he . . . you know.' She pulled a face. 'I keep wondering if I could have done something. Spotted something, maybe.'

There was no doubting the concern, the twist of anxiety in her voice.

'He didn't seem depressed to you?'

'Not at all.' A soft sigh escaped her. 'Sorry, can we talk about something else?'

Suppressing his guilt at manipulating her, Samson tried another angle, his tone playful. 'I read online that hobbies are a safe topic for these events.'

Hannah's teasing smile slipped back into place. 'I like a

man who does his research. So, what do you like to do in your spare time?'

'Hiking. Being outdoors.' He paused and then cast the bait. 'I'm also thinking about taking up potholing, now I'm back.'

'Ugh! Crawling around under the surface of the earth. I can think of better forms of entertainment.'

Trying to ignore the scorching look she sent him, he gave a light laugh. 'A friend of mine got me interested,' he said. 'Martin Foster. He was at the last of these events, so you might know him.'

Well-shaped eyebrows drawing together, she frowned. 'Yeah, I know him. Sort of. He was supposed to call me to arrange a night out after last time, but I never heard from him.' She shrugged an elegant shoulder. 'That happens sometimes. People lose their nerve.'

'Maybe he got stuck in a pothole,' Samson joked, saying a silent prayer of apology for making light of the dead.

Hannah let out a peal of laughter, the clouds of moments before chased away by bright sunshine as the bell rang to end their time together. She lifted one of her date cards with a flash of painted nails and passed it to him.

'Perhaps you'd best steer clear of potholes then,' she said, voice seductive. 'It would be a massive loss for the women of Bruncliffe if you were to follow Martin's example.'

'I'll bear your advice in mind,' said Samson, taking his leave of her with a smile which he hoped concealed the unease besetting him.

One down. One to go.

*

Delilah was biting her nails. She'd been biting them for some time, almost four minutes, before she became conscious that it wasn't the best of images for the host of Speedy Date night to be portraying.

With an effort, she folded her arms, then decided that wasn't exactly welcoming, either. So she placed them by her sides and allowed her gaze to wander back to Samson O'Brien.

He seemed so relaxed, chatting with Elaine Bullock – who thankfully had put away the book she dipped into between dates. And sometimes during dates, if she perceived the four minutes to be a waste of her time. Samson was holding her attention though, laughing and joking as if this was just another night down the pub. When he'd stood to leave Hannah Wilson's table, he'd turned in such a way that Delilah had been unable to see his face and so she had no idea whether he thought the librarian a credible suspect.

Not that he would have revealed anything, if the rest of the evening had been anything to go by. Having watched him move from table to table, she'd been impressed by his ability to play the role of the single man at a dating event. No wonder he'd excelled undercover with the police. She could only hope he excelled at finding out who was murdering her clients.

Aware that her fingers had crept back to her mouth, Delilah pulled her attention back to her job in an attempt to calm herself. Watch the room. Make sure everyone is having a good time. Make sure no one is feeling neglected.

It had all gone well so far. Lots of excited chatter. Plenty of laughter. Even Mr Knowles, the disgruntled farmer she'd given the free date night to, seemed to be enjoying himself – although from this distance she couldn't tell if he'd taken her personal hygiene advice on board. But most importantly, no one had got drunk, which was always a worry when nervous men were in the vicinity of alcohol. And there were plenty of nervous men in the room. Her glance fell on the estate agent, Stuart Lister, perhaps the most nervous of all those here tonight – apart from Delilah herself, but her tension wasn't caused by affairs of the heart.

Stuart had called her the week before and had stammered his way around a variety of subjects, before she realised that he wasn't calling her in his professional capacity, but instead was hoping to join the dating night. She'd soothed his fears and told him it was an excellent way for someone new to the town to meet people. Privately, she was relieved that he was willing to give the women of Bruncliffe a second chance after her boxing display outside the pub the day Samson arrived.

If anyone could convince him that Delilah was an aberration amongst the women of the town, it was the person he was with now. Lucy Metcalfe, sensing a highly strung male, was leaning forward slightly, a smile on her face as she encouraged the estate agent to talk. She was gentleness personified and, once again, Delilah cursed the fate that had dealt her sister-in-law such a bad hand.

A beep from her stopwatch told her the four minutes were up. Delilah rang the bell and tried not to bite her nails as Samson took a seat opposite the second suspect.

*

'Sarah Mitchell.'

If Samson hadn't known her name beforehand, he would have struggled to make sense of the murmured words as he shook her hand. A small hand, brown from the outdoors but slender, fine bones visible under the skin.

'Nice to meet you, Sarah. You're not from Bruncliffe?'

She shook her head. 'Leeds originally. I live in Hawes now.'

Her gaze didn't lift from the table and Samson wondered why she was putting herself through an ordeal that was clearly agony for her. Where Hannah had been vibrant, her personality carrying across the room, Sarah was timid, almost jumping every time he spoke.

'It must seem quiet after Leeds?'

She shrugged. 'It's a nice place to live. Easy access to the fells.'

'You like the fells?'

Her face lifted and he saw a flash of life there for the first time.

'What's not to like?' she asked with a small smile.

'The rain?' he grinned.

Her focus returned to the glass in front of her, a small white wine which didn't look like it had been touched.

'This isn't your idea of a good night, is it?' he asked, gently.

She shook her head, a blush tracing along her throat.

'Mine neither,' he confessed. 'I'd rather be out on the fells in the rain.'

That made her smile again, her head tilting sideways as she glanced at him.

'So why are you here?' she asked.

He gestured in the direction of Harry Furness and told a blatant lie. 'Helping out a friend who was too timid to come on his own. You?'

She bit her lip, eyes flitting around the room. 'I thought someone might be here . . .'

'Someone you met at one of these events before?'

A slight nod was his answer.

'I take it he's not turned up?'

'No.' It was more a sigh than a word.

'Perhaps he's been waylaid. What does he do?'

'He's a farmer.'

'Well, that probably explains it,' said Samson, feeling despicable for the second time in ten minutes as he pretended not to know whom she was talking about. Or that the man in question was dead. 'He's most likely got caught up looking for a lost sheep or something.'

Sarah smiled. 'Thanks.'

'For what?' he asked, genuinely surprised.

'For trying to make me feel better.' She looked straight at him this time. 'But you don't have to. I'm used to being stood up.'

Samson felt his heart twist inside him. While he was long accustomed to playing roles undercover, he wasn't accustomed to upsetting women in the process. He had a fierce longing for the four minutes, and the entire night, to be over.

'What do you mean you don't know?' Delilah hissed, aware that they were surrounded by people.

The formal part of the evening had come to a close and the Dales Dating Agency members were mingling in the bar, the conversation a lot more animated than it had been an hour before. Samson and Delilah were standing to one side and she was demanding an update.

'I don't know,' repeated Samson, weariness in his voice. 'I'm pretty sure we can rule out Sarah Mitchell right away. She can't be much more than five foot—'

'She's five foot three, the same size as me,' Delilah corrected him with the acerbity of someone who'd spent her life defending her reduced stature in a family of giants.

'Like I said, not much more than five foot and, unlike you, she'd blow over in a good north-easterly.' It was the pursed lips that alerted Samson to his unintended insult. 'I mean, she's not built like you . . .' he backtracked. 'She's not . . .' He looked desperately at the strong shoulders before him, skimmed quickly over the contours that hadn't been there when he left Bruncliffe and let his gaze fall to the toned legs, the fell-runner's calves accentuated by high-heeled shoes.

He lifted his eyes back to Delilah's and saw the laughter she was containing at his clumsy attempts to rectify a situation he'd stumbled into.

'For goodness' sake,' he finally blurted, knowing this conversation had developed so many pitfalls, he was doomed to come a cropper either way. 'Just look at her.' He tipped his head at the petite woman standing closest to the stairs, as though ready to bolt at the slightest provocation. 'She's frail. There's no way she'd manage to haul someone of Tom Alderson's size back onto his quad bike. Plus . . .'

'What?'

'I think she really liked him.' He shrugged apologetically. 'Gut instinct says it's not her.'

'And Hannah?'

'Superficially, yes, she fits the profile. She's got the strength. I'd also say she's not the most stable of people. But . . .' He looked across the room to where the librarian was laughing, her hand on the arm of the man with her, eyelashes fluttering. 'She's fairly easy to read and I'd swear she didn't know Martin Foster was dead.'

'Could she be faking it? Not knowing, I mean?'

'Of course. But it didn't come across like that.'

Delilah let out a sigh, unsure whether it was in exasperation or relief. She'd known Hannah Wilson all her life and couldn't imagine the woman killing someone. Driving them to madness, perhaps. But not murdering them.

And as for Sarah Mitchell, the delicate young woman had won a place in Delilah's heart when she'd come to her first dating night and forced herself to participate, despite the obvious torture it was for her. On top of that, how could someone who loved otters with such a passion be capable of taking the life of another?

Knowing her logic would make the man next to her laugh out loud, Delilah kept it to herself. But what she couldn't keep to herself was her frustration. And her panic. After a tense evening, they knew little more about the identity of the killer than they had at the outset.

'So what now?' she asked.

Samson looked down at her. 'You've set the program to block any requests to or from the two women?'

'Apart from requests from you, yes.'

He nodded and reached for his phone. 'Then we stick

to the plan we formulated. I'll single out Hannah and Sarah for follow-up dates and we'll see what happens. After all,' he added with a wry smile, 'I've been known to be wrong when it comes to deciphering women. And right now, those two ladies are all we've got to go on.'

She watched him pull up the app for the dating agency and enter his choices and she felt a swirl of nausea curdle her stomach.

If he was right and the two women were innocent, then the remainder of Delilah's clients were in danger. If he was wrong, then he was placing himself in the firing line.

He slipped his phone back in his pocket and gave her a grin.

'What?' he said, eyes twinkling. 'You wanted rid of me a couple of weeks ago. Just think how happy it'll make Will when I get bumped off.'

She kicked him in the shin, aware that it wasn't behaviour befitting a dating agency hostess, but it was preferable to hugging him, which was all she wanted to do.

Harry Furness didn't believe in wasting time. He was an auctioneer. Once you got passions running, you acted. Throw in the next lot while the bidders were still grieving at missing the last one. Thump down the hammer before minds could be changed by the slow hand of caution. He lived his life the same way.

So when he saw Sarah Mitchell standing alone at the top of the stairs, fingers clenched around her untasted wine, he took his mobile out of his jacket pocket. A couple of quick swipes and the deed was done. With a deliberately measured stride he crossed the room, approaching her like he would a wary heifer. He was relieved to see the reappearance of her dimpled smile at his arrival.

What a night! Stuart Lister was walking home in the damp of a dark November evening, happier than he'd been since he arrived in Bruncliffe. Passing the deserted marketplace, he veered down Church Street and then crossed the road to the garish yellow facade of the Chinese takeaway. Inside, a queue of customers waited, figures blurred through the steamy windows. 'Happy House' – normally the sign was a trigger for despair for the estate agent as he approached a small door to the side of the shop front; a door which led to anything but a happy house. Tonight, however, as he entered the hallway of his awful flat, he was still smiling.

Trailed by the ever-present smell of prawn crackers, he climbed the steep stairs and let himself into his cramped living quarters. A bedroom too small to house more than a bed; a lounge that strained to contain a two-seater sofa and a TV; a kitchenette in one corner; and a bathroom that had long ago lost the battle against mould. All of it pervaded by the sweet-and-sour odours from the takeaway below.

It was all he could afford. For now. But if he kept working, kept finding tenants to rent from Taylor's, then the future would be bright. After tonight, he believed that bright horizon might be closer than he'd thought.

He reached for his mobile and pulled up the app for the Dales Dating Agency. And in the gloom of his shabby accommodation, he made his choice.

*

A ping, loud enough to cut through the whistle of the wind, and then the harsh glow of a mobile screen slicing through the dark. A broad thumb brushed across the phone and there, stark against the night, was the name of the next person to die.

15

'Bullseye!'

The raucous shout from darts captain Harry Furness made Delilah leap in her seat, her mobile falling from her hand and her sudden movement triggering a loud bark from Tolpuddle.

'It's okay,' said Samson, putting a soothing hand on the dog's head as Delilah glanced wildly around the crowded pub. 'Nothing to panic about.'

He'd have liked to have calmed Delilah in the same way, her nerves at breaking point twenty-four hours after Speedy Date night. But with Will Metcalfe and Rick Procter over by the bar casting dark glances his way, the last thing he wanted to do was start another brawl. If he was going to be attacked by the phantom murderer anytime soon, he'd prefer to be in a state to fight back.

'I don't know how much longer I can stand this,' muttered Delilah, picking her phone up from the floor.

'What, Harry's relentless crowing?' asked Samson with a grin, as the auctioneer did a jig on the oche to boisterous cheering from the partisan spectators.

She glowered at him. 'You know what I mean.' She placed her mobile on the table and folded her hands on her lap, so no one in the Fleece could see them trembling.

The pub was packed. Word had travelled fast through

Bruncliffe and the outlying villages – helped undoubtedly by the posters which had appeared overnight on community noticeboards up and down the dale – that Harry Furness had persuaded the legendary Samson O'Brien to play darts for the Fleece. Against none other than the Mason's Arms.

Only Seth Thistlethwaite and his contemporaries could recall the last time the smallest pub in Bruncliffe had beaten the team from Gargrave, Troy Murgatroyd never having had the honour of victory in his lifetime as landlord. Tonight, after a blazing start by the home side with Will, Harry and Rick Procter winning their games, it looked like history could be rewritten. The locals had already secured a lead of three games to love, and Samson had yet to play. And for the first time since Troy took over the pub, no one had heard him grumbling about the money he wasted paying the league fees for the darts team every year. He was too busy serving pints to be complaining.

Delilah Metcalfe, however, wasn't feeling the joy.

She'd spent the day in her office, checking and rechecking the dating agency systems, making sure the net she'd created had no holes in it. So far, it seemed to be working. Only Samson's date requests had made their way to Hannah Wilson and Sarah Mitchell, all others having been blocked by the modifications she'd made to the program. Likewise, any moves by Hannah or Sarah to take things further with any of the men they'd met had been intercepted. As a result, Hannah had four would-be suitors she didn't know about; Sarah, despite her timidity, had captured the attention of two. Delilah had made sure these unlucky admirers received the softest of rejections – *Leave it for now* – and had even gone so far as to delay the replies, hoping to console the men with the thought that the two ladies had at least deliberated over their decisions.

Her role as Cupid's evil twin hadn't made her mood any better. But it had to be done. Until Hannah Wilson and Sarah Mitchell could be ruled out of any involvement in the suspicious deaths besetting the Dales Dating Agency clients, Delilah had to protect not just the hearts of her male customers, but their lives too.

Not knowing whether her attempts to safeguard them had been effective, however, was unbearable.

'One-hundred-and-eighty!' Harry bellowed, his voice trained from years in the auction ring to travel greater distances than the two rooms of the Fleece, and consequently deafening at close quarters.

Delilah sat on her hands and forced herself to relax. If someone was going to try and bump Samson off, they would hardly choose darts night in the Fleece to do so. Unless, of course, you counted her brother Will in that number. Currently standing at the bar, pint in hand, his black stare hadn't strayed from the detective for the duration of the evening.

If looks could kill, Samson would already be dead. At least, thought Delilah with a wry smile, her dating agency couldn't be blamed for that one.

Eight-thirty in the evening. Who in their right mind would arrange a viewing for that time?

And what letting agency in their right mind would agree to go through with it?

Unfortunately for Stuart Lister, an agency desperate to

rent out a property that had been on their books for over two months would. And had.

The estate agent stood in the porch of the empty farmhouse, staring out into the dark. Total dark. Unlike Skipton, where he was from, where street lights kept the night at bay, here there was nothing. Not even the moon or the stars as the clouds smothered the sky, making it as black as the desolate moorland below it.

No headlights dipping over the horizon, either. He'd wait another ten minutes and then he was heading back to Bruncliffe and the vibrant facade of Happy House. It would be a welcome beacon after this.

The request had come mid-morning. Julie, the receptionist, had received an email from a Dr Howson wanting to look at a property on Henside Road that evening. As head of the rentals department – which was not as impressive as it sounded as Stuart was the only member of said department, although Mr Taylor assured him they would be taking on more staff soon – it fell to Stuart to deal with it. So he'd got out the files and looked it up.

It was a remote former farmhouse that was up for sale, the owners having relocated back down to London after their dream life of working from home in the countryside had turned sour – turned into divorce, if Julie was to be believed. And no wonder. All this space with no one in it, just the two of them rattling around. It was enough to test the strongest of relationships. With no sign of a sale in over twelve months, they'd decided to rent it out in the interim. But that hadn't produced many takers either. If Stuart could land a tenant tonight, it wouldn't hurt his long-term prospects with Taylor's.

He checked the time on his mobile. Dr Howson was twenty minutes late already and Stuart had no way of making contact, the screen on his phone indicating that not only was there a lack of lighting in the area, but there was a lack of mobile signal, too.

It was looking like this was going to be a no-show. Stuart sighed, thinking about the tricky drive over from Bruncliffe, the innocuous-sounding Henside Road turning out to be a single-track road that wound up onto bleak moors near Fountains Fell. Hemmed in by the Dales-defining stone walls on either side and with several steep hills thrown in, it hadn't made for a pleasant journey. He hated to think it might have been for nothing.

Willing twin beams to appear at the end of the lane that led to the house, or the sound of an engine to drift across on the wind, Stuart shifted his weight against the door frame and wished that he smoked. It would help pass the time. Maybe make him look a bit older, too. Because he could do with looking older. Twenty-eight and still people mistook him for some fresh-faced lad straight out of college and damp behind the ears. His mother was always telling him it was a blessing. That when he was fifty he'd be glad to lose a few years. But right now, it felt like a curse.

If he looked older, perhaps the blunt rejection he'd got after the Speedy Date event would have been different.

Staring wistfully into the dark, Stuart Lister made the decision to wait five minutes more. It was a decision that would change his life.

Three all. Three games left to play. A tense captain of the Fleece darts team was pacing around by the bar as the players took a break to savour the delicious spread laid on by Kay Murgatroyd, despite her husband's objections.

'I don't understand it,' muttered a disconcerted Harry Furness, his swagger of the previous hour replaced by a nervous hunch of the shoulders. 'Total collapse!'

'Maybe you should have broken for food earlier,' said Samson, winking at Lucy Metcalfe and Elaine Bullock who were standing next to him, both of them enjoying a slice of cheese-and-onion tart. 'These athletes need to keep their stamina up.'

Elaine spluttered on a laugh, looking pointedly at the crowd of men bustling around the trays of sandwiches and tarts, pints in hand, the average shape of the participants a long way from athletic. Even young Danny Bradley, who was at the opposite end of the scale from the majority of his teammates, was hardly a model of vigour, his skinny arms sticking out of a flapping T-shirt. But Harry Furness was desperate enough to grasp at straws.

'Do you think that was it?' he asked, with a worried frown. 'Perhaps I should have brought some energy bars along? I mean, it's a total collapse. Three games on the trot . . . They're coming back at us and they still have their strongest player to throw. Two more games – that's all we need. But it's not as if we have a lot of quality left on our side. No Rob Harrison for a start, and it's not like Danny Bradley's much of a substitute . . . so it could all come down to you, Samson—'

The witterings of the panicking captain came to an abrupt halt as a mini-Yorkshire pudding filled with beef and garnished with horseradish sauce was thrust at him.

'Try one of these,' said Samson, hoping the food would

serve two purposes – take Harry's mind off the match and shut him up at the same time. The approach of Ash Metcalfe helped his cause.

'Thanks for stepping in tonight,' said Ash, shaking hands gingerly, his wrist heavily bandaged. 'Don't know what we'd have done without you.'

'I'm sure you'd have managed,' Samson replied, aware of the unrelenting scrutiny of Ash's older brother from the other end of the bar, as yet another Metcalfe dared to fraternise with the devil.

'Any chance of Rob making a last-minute appearance?' demanded Harry through a mouthful of Yorkshire pudding.

Ash shook his head. 'He's torn a muscle in his shoulder repairing a wall. He's in a bad way apparently.'

Harry groaned, casting a despairing glance at Danny Bradley, the slight figure of the constable a mere shadow of the stonemason, both in physique and ability with the darts.

'Have faith,' Ash counselled his captain. 'Samson and Danny will save the day.'

'Don't speak too soon,' said Samson. 'We've got to win our games yet.'

'Speaking of winning,' continued Ash with a grin. 'How did everyone get on last night? Are your dance cards filled?'

'Not mine,' muttered Harry, a second Yorkshire pudding gone and a third in his hand. 'I got knocked back for the only date request I sent.'

'You sent a date request?' Ash asked, eyebrows raised. 'Who to?'

Harry shook his head and tapped a finger against his nose. 'Not telling.'

'What about you two lovely ladies?'

Elaine grinned, reaching for a second slice of tart. 'I didn't send out any, but I did get one response.'

'And?' Lucy nudged her. 'Are you going to accept?'

'Not on your life. It was some farmer with bad breath who didn't even take the hint when I started reading before the four minutes were up.'

'You read? During the dating event?' asked Samson, suddenly recalling the book she'd been carrying the night before.

Elaine nodded, licking her fingers and reaching for her pint. 'Yes. Why not? I'd rather be immersed in the world of rocks I'm interested in than in some bloke with rocks for brains.'

Lucy laughed, while the men regarded the geologist with something between awe and terror, none of them wanting to be on the receiving end of such a snub.

'And you, Samson?' asked Elaine. 'Have you been inundated with requests?'

'A few.'

'How many's a few?'

A snort from behind made her turn to where Delilah was standing, a plate of food in her hand and a glint in her eye. 'Try ten,' she said, bestowing a disbelieving look on Samson as she spoke. 'There is no accounting for taste.'

'Ten?' Harry almost dropped the sandwich he was holding, head flicking between Delilah and Samson. 'You had ten women send you a date request?'

Samson gave a boyish grin. 'What can I say? The ladies

of Bruncliffe appreciate me, even if their male counterparts don't.'

His response prompted a groan from Ash and a loud laugh from Elaine, while Delilah shook her head and wandered off to talk to Seth and Matty Thistlethwaite.

'I'm pleased for you, Samson,' said Lucy, patting him on the arm. 'Even though I didn't get any.'

'Not one?' asked Harry, still eating.

'Nope. I didn't get any after the October event, either.'

'Don't let Delilah hear you say that,' warned Samson with a grin. 'She'll tell you it simply means you need to sign up for the next one.'

'I don't know about that. I think Tuesday night was my last foray into the speed-dating world. It's too difficult . . . with Nathan. I didn't tell him about this last one and I've felt guilty all week.'

'There's nothing to be guilty about,' said Ash, putting an arm around his conscience-stricken sister-in-law. 'Ryan wouldn't have wanted you to stay at home for the rest of your life. Isn't that right, Elaine?'

'Totally,' concurred the geologist through another slice of tart. 'Although I think he'd have been happy for you to stay at home and bake us all a bunch of these. You need to get the recipe off Kay Murgatroyd.'

'I already have,' said Lucy. 'Swaledale cheese. That's the secret.'

'So can I expect some next time I pop in to Peaks Patisserie?'

'Only if you're paying,' quipped Lucy.

'Paying? Huh! Seems like Troy isn't the only one willing to fleece his friends . . .'

Samson turned from the banter between the two women to see Ash and Harry huddled together over Harry's phone.

'He's sending Lucy a date request,' whispered Ash with a wink.

'Can't have her feeling left out.' Harry Furness slipped his phone back in his pocket. 'And at the very least, she might make me one of those cheese tarts!'

Samson laughed and slapped him on the back. 'Enough about cheese tarts. We've got a darts match to win. You'd best call the lads to order before they eat too much to play.'

The captain of the Fleece team pushed back his shoulders, stuck out his chest and then bellowed for the players to resume the match. There was no possibility of anyone not hearing.

A no-show. All the way out here for a no-show. Stuart Lister turned the orange company Mini out of the lane that led to the farmhouse, glad to be back on the properly surfaced Henside Road, and tried not to be too annoyed.

What would he have done with his evening anyway?

Gone and watched the darts at the Fleece probably. From the way everyone had been talking in the office this morning, it sounded like a big deal. Samson O'Brien – the man whose arrival had caused such a commotion a couple of weeks ago – was now being touted as the saviour of Bruncliffe darts.

It might have been good to see the match. Better than standing around in the dark waiting for Dr Howson to make an appearance and jumping every time there was a noise. For despite what people thought, the countryside was far from quiet. The sudden low of a cow as he'd been locking up the house had nearly frightened him to death.

Headlights travelling ahead of him and picking out the stones that walled in the narrow road, Stuart drove carefully back towards the town. He made better time than he had on the way out, being more prepared for a road that rose and fell as it twined itself around the contours of the fellside, and he was beginning to think it might be worth stopping by the pub after all. It was only just gone nine. The match wouldn't have finished yet. But first he had to negotiate the steep descent and climb that led up to the turning for Goat Lane.

With his headlights pointing out into dark nothingness, Stuart paused at the top of the hill, the road plummeting away beneath him in a gradient that would be dizzying in daylight. At night, it was a step into the unknown. He eased the Mini into a low gear and, foot firmly on the brake, guided it cautiously down the twisting drop. By the time he reached the cattle grid at the bottom, his heart was in his mouth and his hands were sweating on the steering wheel.

Now to get up the other side. He looked at the two precipitous lines of stone wall rising above him into the inky sky, a slender strip of tarmac between them.

Slow and steady. And pray nothing came down the hill towards him.

Switching brake for accelerator, he began to climb. He was halfway up the sharp incline when they came over the crest – two dazzling beams of white light glaring down at the orange Mini.

He stamped on the brake, waiting for the lights to stop. But they didn't. They were rolling towards him at tremendous speed. And from such a height.

A tractor. It had to be. He flashed his lights. No response. Hadn't they seen his car? How couldn't they have? He flashed again and sounded the horn. Still the lights bore down on him.

Panicking now, he shifted the car into reverse.

Was there space down below at the cattle grid? Could he pull in there and let the maniac past? He couldn't tell, the road behind bending away from the reversing lights. He'd have to try it or this idiot would hit him.

Easing off the brake, he let the car roll gently backwards, hand on the horn at the same time. He turned to look out of the rear window, but there was little to see, the stone walls disappearing into the blackness of night. Then he twisted forward and knew it was all futile. The massive tyres of the tractor were there, right in front of him. And in a screech of metal, the Mini and its passenger were pushed backwards down the road.

'Stop!' screamed Stuart, foot pumping the useless brake. 'Stop!'

He was still screaming when the car was slammed into a wall.

'Double top!' yelled Harry Furness, throwing his arms around Danny Bradley, who had just secured a vital point for the Fleece. The constable, appearing even younger out of his uniform, was grinning widely, elated at his part in this spectacular match.

'Four all,' said the opposition captain, shaking his head

in disbelief. Normally the Fleece was known as a team of non-starters. A team that the Mason's Arms looked forward to trouncing on a twice-yearly basis. But tonight . . .

Something had got into them. They'd led at the outset, which was unheard of. And now they were pulling themselves back from the dead, the latest contender a stringbean of a young man whose arms didn't look strong enough to hold a dart, let alone throw it, somehow beating one of the best players the Arms had.

'Must've been summat in that tart,' his teammate next to him muttered as he picked up his darts.

'Aye. Well see as you have a slice of it before you play their last lad then,' grumbled the captain, as the final Fleece player stepped up to the oche.

'Go on, Samson,' shouted Elaine. 'Beat the buggers!'

'Go on, lad,' echoed Seth Thistlethwaite, his nephew Matty standing next to him.

'Make sure I finally get something back for the blasted league fee,' grumbled Troy Murgatroyd.

The tension rose. Silence fell. Four all, with one game left to play. Samson tried not to think about the weight that was resting on his shoulders.

There was a weight. On his chest. Pinning him down. And his legs. Trapped. He couldn't move. He could hear a scream, thin and sharp, coming from somewhere beyond him. Or from him. He couldn't tell.

He opened his eyes, something wet on his face, stinging, and through the cracked windscreen, beyond the shadow of the tractor that was so close – too close – he saw a blurred shape.

A person. Coming towards him.

'Help!' he cried. 'Help!'

But the only help Stuart Lister was about to get was not the kind he wanted. He was about to be helped out of this life and into the next.

'Three more darts, lad. That'll do it!'

Samson closed his eyes and tried to ignore the well-meaning advice from the crowd.

It had been a closely contested game, both players starting well. But the man from the Mason's Arms, a burly, red-faced butcher, had started pulling away, capitalising on Samson's rustiness. So when the man had stepped forward with a score of one hundred and sixty left to achieve, it had seemed the dreams of the home crowd were about to be crushed.

But the butcher had crumpled under the pressure, his final dart clipping a wire and landing on the floor to give him a total of one hundred and twenty. Only forty left to get. He wouldn't miss next time. Which meant Samson had this one opportunity to win the match for the Fleece.

Trouble was, he had to score one hundred and seventy, the highest score that could be achieved while meeting the criteria of finishing on a double or the bull.

Treble twenty, treble twenty and the bull. That would do it.

No pressure then.

He took a deep breath, opened his eyes and settled himself, letting the creaking seats, the muffled coughs, the tense breathing around him fade into the background. Focus on the circle in front of him, he raised his arm and let the first dart fly.

'Treble twenty!' shouted Harry and the room sucked in its breath.

Two more to go. He lifted his arm again, concentrating on that wedge of red towards the top of the board, which looked smaller now, a dart already stuck in it. With a sharp flick of his wrist, he released his second throw.

'Treble twenty!' Harry's shout was met with a roar from the pub, people jumping to their feet, a couple of pints spilled.

'Quiet, please; quiet, please,' called the captain of the Fleece team, flapping his arms in an effort to curb the excitement. 'Give him a chance, folks.'

The crowd hushed, their expectation making the air thick, bodies craning forward waiting for the last throw . . . which had to land in the bullseye.

Samson stared down at the gaudy carpet, threadbare at his feet, and forced himself to relax. And an image of his mother came to him, standing in her stockings in the kitchen, aiming at the dartboard on the back door. Hair pulled back, a smile lighting her face, and to her side, his father, laughing.

On that beautiful memory, he looked up, bent his arm and, without hesitation, sent his dart winging towards the red circle at the centre of the board.

'*Bullseye!*' screamed Harry Furness, sending the pub into wild celebrations. Lucy and Elaine were jumping up and down, Seth Thistlethwaite was slapping his nephew on the back, and Delilah was grinning, Ash's arm around her shoulders. Even Troy Murgatroyd was allowing himself a satisfied smile.

Samson wished with all his soul that his father was there to see it.

'Help!' The sound faded to a whimper as Stuart Lister's body began to shut down. Blood poured from his forehead, his crushed ribs hampered his breathing, and his legs . . . his legs – he couldn't feel his legs.

Blackness encroaching at the edges of his vision, he struggled to see the blurred figure. Next to the car now. Reaching in through the broken window.

'Help . . .'

He tried to turn his head but his neck wouldn't cooperate. Tried to welcome his saviour.

'Please . . .' A gurgle of air, blood trickling over his bottom lip. 'Please . . .'

Then a broad hand, placing something across his nose and mouth, pushing his head back into the headrest. He couldn't breathe. He couldn't struggle. He was about to die.

Lights flickering at the periphery of his consciousness, Stuart Lister began to lose the tenuous grip he had on his life.

'From zero to hero in two easy weeks!' Delilah was grinning up at him, punching him on the arm, all her fears of earlier forgotten for now.

Samson grinned back. 'I wouldn't say I've won over everyone.' He threw a glance at Will Metcalfe and Rick Procter at the bar, neither of them looking like they were in a joyous mood, despite the jubilation around them and having been part of a winning team.

'Oh, those two!' Delilah tossed her head. 'They'll come round.'

'Only when they hear I'm leaving.'

'Who's leaving?' demanded an exuberant Harry Furness, bouncing up with a slice of cheese-and-onion tart in one hand and a pint in the other. 'You can't leave yet, Samson, lad! The night's still early. Get yourself a real drink and celebrate properly.'

'This'll do me fine,' Samson replied, raising his bottle of ginger beer. 'I can get drunk on the victory.'

'And what a victory!' Harry crowed. 'We're the stuff of legend now. The team that beat the Mason's Arms!'

Delilah rolled her eyes. 'If you don't mind, I'll leave you two to revel in your own glory. But don't praise him too much, Harry.' She pointed towards the window and the Dales Detective Agency across the road. 'That office isn't very large. I'd hate to lose a tenant because his head was too big to fit inside.' And with a laugh cast over her shoulder, she walked over to Lucy and Elaine.

'So,' said Harry, cutting straight to the point. 'Can I sign you up as a permanent member of the team?'

Samson lifted both hands. 'Whoa! Steady on. I stood in as a substitute for Ash. I'm not sure I'm ready to make any long-term commitments.'

The auctioneer regarded him through narrowed eyes. 'Aye. I can understand that. It's not as like folk round here welcomed you with open arms, myself included. But this has changed things. You must see that?'

Looking across the room at the glowering countenance

of the oldest Metcalfe, Samson didn't see anything of the kind. Plus, his own plans didn't include being around long enough to complete the darts season. When that phone call came, he'd be leaving.

'We'll see,' he said.

'Well, if I can't sign you up for the team, can I sign you up for tomorrow?'

'Tomorrow?'

'Bonfire Night. The rugby club is holding its annual celebrations. I could do with a hand in the morning setting the fireworks out. You up for it?'

But Samson wasn't listening. He was revisiting the past, hoisted on his father's shoulders, watching rockets scream into the dark sky, his mother's hand in the small of his back offering security. The rugby club's annual party on November the fifth had been legendary. Huge fire. Lots of fireworks. Baked potatoes and toffee apples. It had been a highlight of his childhood. Until he was eight.

It was just after his mother died. His father was already struggling to control his drinking by then, but had yielded to Samson's relentless pleading and taken him to see the bonfire. Once at the rugby club, however, memories had overcome the recently widowed father and he'd got blind drunk, staggering around, causing a nuisance and getting in the way. It had been towards the end of the evening, the fireworks finished but the fire still blazing, when Joseph O'Brien tripped over and fell into the flames.

Two quick-thinking men had dragged him out of the fire before any real damage had been done. His hair and eyebrows were singed and he'd had burns on both hands. But the main talking point as the story made its way around town over the next few days was that Boozy O'Brien – as he would forever be known – had kept a tight hold of his can of beer the whole time. Mortified, his son had never asked to be taken to the Bonfire Night celebrations again.

'Come on,' cajoled Harry, taking Samson's lack of response for reluctance. 'You owe me. I went through the torture of that date night and got two kicks in the teeth for my trouble. So the least you could do is help me out.'

'Two kicks in the teeth?' asked Samson, dragging his attention back to the present.

'The Patisserie Queen gave me the cold shoulder. An outright no, not even the offer of leaving it until later.' The auctioneer's show of being indignant was belied by the twinkle in his eyes as he looked over at Lucy Metcalfe.

Samson laughed. 'Serves you right! Teasing her like that. She's giving you a taste of your own medicine.'

'That's as maybe, but it doesn't change the statistics. Two blows to the heart. The least you could do is help me out tomorrow.'

'Okay, okay,' Samson grinned. 'But then we're quits.'

'Ten o'clock in the clubhouse, then. See you there.'

Harry Furness swaggered off, accepting a hail of congratulations as he made his way to the bar, where he started hassling Rick Procter to buy a round of drinks for the successful darts team. Samson was watching the shark-toothed smile of the property developer as he faced Harry's persuasive powers, when there was a tentative tug at his sleeve.

'Mr O'Brien?' Danny Bradley was standing next to him.

'After your performance tonight, Danny, I think it's time you started calling me Samson.'

A flush stole up the lad's skinny neck, settling in the hollows of his cheeks. 'Yeah, that was fun. Worth giving up a run out with the Harriers at any rate.'

'They still run on a Thursday evening?' asked Samson with a pang of nostalgia for his weekly outings with the Bruncliffe Harriers.

'Every week. You should come with us, now you're back. Persuade Miss Metcalfe . . . Delilah . . . to come too.'

'She doesn't run with you any more?' Samson glanced over to where Delilah was talking to Will and Rick Procter.

Danny shook his head, eyes also settling on Delilah, but with a look of adoration. 'Not for a long time. Wish she did. She's a legend in fell-running circles and I reckon I could learn a lot from her.'

Samson didn't disagree, partly because it was true, but also because he was puzzling over what could have made Delilah give up something she'd been so passionate about. And something she'd been so naturally good at.

'But Mr—Samson,' Danny continued, 'I wanted to ask if you'd discovered anything else. You know, about . . . Mr Hargreaves.'

'Not exactly,' Samson said, keeping his reply vague, aware that there was a lot the constable didn't know. The connection with the two other dead men, for a start.

'It's just that . . . I feel bad not telling Sergeant Clayton what we saw on the CCTV footage.'

'I understand. But I don't think it's time to be telling him anything just yet. It's not as if we have anything concrete to offer him.'

Danny bit his lip, clearly in a quandary.

'Look,' said Samson, feeling for the lad he'd placed in such an awkward position. 'How about you call in at the office tomorrow after lunch? I'll bring you up to speed with everything I've got on the case.'

The clouds cleared from the constable's face. 'Thanks, Mr—Samson. I'd really appreciate that.'

Knowing that Delilah wouldn't be as appreciative when she heard the dating agency's problems were going to be divulged to an outsider, Samson was left wondering how he would tell her what he was planning to do.

Lights. Bobbing over the dark slope of the fellside. Close now. Voices shouting. It was time to go.

Like a shadow slipping back into the night, a dark figure peeled away from the orange Mini, leaving the inert figure of the estate agent pinned in the bright beams of the tractor.

When a tipsy Harry Furness started begging Troy Murgatroyd to get out the karaoke machine, Samson knew it was time to go. He scanned the noisy crowd for Delilah, needing to make sure she wasn't going back to the office before he settled in for the night. After all the excitement of the last couple of days, the last thing he wanted was his landlady discovering that he was sleeping in her spare room on the quiet.

He pushed his way through the mass of people still celebrating, to the small room at the back of the pub. There, in a corner, Delilah was sharing an intimate conversation with Rick Procter. The property developer was bent over her, his blond head close to hers, a large arm draped over her shoulders as he whispered in her ear.

The running shoes in the back porch. The yeti-boots that he'd tripped over the first day. It made sense to Samson now. Delilah was dating Rick Procter.

Feeling like he'd been punched in the stomach, he turned away. Rick Procter, of all people. The man was a snake. A bully who hadn't left his schoolyard habits behind when he grew up. Delilah could do so much better—

'Samson?' She was at his elbow. 'Do you want another drink?'

He shook his head. 'I'm heading home. Say goodnight to Lucy and Elaine for me and thank them for their support.'

'Lucy's already left. She's got the caravan to herself tonight, so she's gone back to watch *Dirty Dancing*.'

Samson laughed and made to go, but Delilah held his arm.

'Be careful,' she murmured, concern on her face.

'Weren't you leaving, O'Brien?' Rick Procter had moved to join them and Delilah let her hand fall. Samson chose to ignore him.

'Well . . . erm . . . I'll see you tomorrow,' Delilah stammered. Then she nodded towards Tolpuddle, who had crept out from under a table and was now leaning against Samson's thigh. 'Take him with you, if you want,' she said with a light laugh, her gaze much more serious.

Samson fondled the dog's ears, aware of what she was offering. Security. A guard dog. But he shook his head. 'Think I'll leave you the pleasure of recycled beer,' he said as a sour, hoppy odour crept up from the region of the dog. 'I'll see you tomorrow. Sometime late morning, as I'm helping Harry at the rugby club first thing.'

She reached out to squeeze his arm and then headed for the bar, leaving Samson face-to-face with Rick Procter. Tolpuddle issued a low growl and Samson's affection for the dog increased at their shared distaste of the man opposite. Even so, he gently curled his fingers under the collar around the Weimaraner's neck. Just in case. Oblivious to the danger, Rick Procter leaned in, his voice dropping, the tone hostile.

'I don't get you.' He held Samson with his glare. 'You've had ample chance to bugger off for good yet you're still here, hanging around like a bad smell. Are you thick or something?'

Samson lowered his gaze, eyes resting on the huge hands of the property developer, which were flexing, the tendons thick across the broad backs. Those hands were itching to hit something. And Samson had no desire to offer up his face as target practice.

He shrugged. 'Guess it must be the latter.'

'Well just so you know, Mr Detective, I'm digging into your past. Looking for whatever it was that made you come scampering home.' Rick Procter pointed in the direction of Delilah, who was chatting to Seth Thistlethwaite at the bar. 'And when I find out, we'll see how welcome you are with the lovely Miss Metcalfe. So don't go getting too cosy in Bruncliffe, because you won't be in town for long.'

Samson willed himself to stay calm, fighting the tide of anger that was threatening to breach his self-control. 'I'll bear that in mind,' he said, teeth gritted.

'Good lad.' Rick Procter stepped back. Out of arm's reach. His final words were delivered with a taunting smile. 'Your dad took my advice, and look how well that turned out.'

Furious, as blinded by rage as he had been in his teens, Samson stepped forward, fists ready to fly despite the consequences. But Tolpuddle beat him to it. Tearing out of Samson's grip, the large dog leaped up, thumped both front paws onto the chest of the property developer and knocked him back into a group of men from the Mason's Arms, drinks spilling everywhere as Rick Procter fell to the ground.

'Watch out!'

'Clumsy oaf!'

'Think you owe us all another round, mate.'

'What happened?' asked Delilah, returning from the bar just as Rick Procter was picking himself up from the floral carpet, cursing, the men around him cursing too.

Samson smothered a smile, Tolpuddle back at his side and looking as innocent as a puppy. 'Not sure. Maybe he's had one too many, eh, Rick?'

The property developer shot him a look that Samson recognised. A look he'd seen countless times in his work undercover. It was the look of a ruthless man.

Turning his back on the menace contained in that stare, Samson patted Tolpuddle one last time. 'I'm off,' he said.

'I mean it, be careful,' Delilah said again.

Samson acknowledged her with a nod of the head and, with the blood still pounding behind his temples, made his way out into the night.

Danger. Delilah was worried that he was in danger. But

he knew his biggest threat didn't come from external factors. It came from within himself. It was what had got him in trouble down in London. And if tonight was anything to go by, it would get him in trouble back here in Bruncliffe, too. If it hadn't been for Tolpuddle . . .

He grinned ruefully at the thought of planting a fist in Rick Procter's face. The man deserved it. But he knew that if he was going to confront the property developer over Twistleton Farm and the way his father had been treated, fighting wasn't the solution. He needed to think it through. Get his facts sorted. Use the time he was here to try and get the farm back.

Calmer now, he started walking, heading up Back Street towards the marketplace and then turning right down the dark ginnel towards what was now his home. Although how long he'd be calling it that, once Rick Procter uncovered his past, was debatable.

From the bar, Rick Procter watched him go. That confident stride he'd had even as a child. The easy way he had with people as they patted him on the back and congratulated him. The man was becoming a problem – joining the dating agency, playing for the darts team, helping out at the rugby club. And cosying up to Delilah.

So much for him being gone by Christmas. O'Brien was settling in and becoming part of the town. It wasn't what was needed. It wasn't part of the plan.

Six months. He'd give O'Brien six months to move on. And if he was still here after that, he would just have to be dealt with. In whatever way was necessary.

'You ready to order or are you going to stand there

dreaming all night?' Troy Murgatroyd stood before him, expression surly as always.

'A round of drinks for my friends over there,' said Rick with a large smile, pointing at the group of players from the Mason's Arms who were still grumbling. 'And one for yourself too, my friend.'

He could afford to be generous. With what the future had in store, he could afford to be very generous indeed.

'Bloody hell—'

'There's a man in there—'

'It's one of Taylor's cars—'

'Call an ambulance—'

Away from the cosy interior of the Fleece and up over Bruncliffe Crag, across Bruncliffe Scar and a deserted landscape scattered with limestone, the dark fellside above Henside Road was now lit up by the bobbing headlights of twelve fell runners from the Bruncliffe Harriers. Soon it would be welcoming the strobing lights of the emergency services, too.

16

Samson was standing in the congregation, watching Delilah walk up the aisle, Tolpuddle by her side. At the altar, her bridegroom waited. Samson craned his neck to see who it was. But Mrs Hargreaves was in front of him, a huge hat with feathers on her head blocking his view. He leaned to the side and saw the groom's profile. The blond hair. The handsome face. Morning suit stretched across broad shoulders.

'No!' he shouted, trying to leap into the aisle. 'No, Delilah!'

Then the stairs creaked, his eyes flew open and Samson O'Brien was instantly awake in the dark of his makeshift bedroom on the second floor, and sensing danger.

Pushing his sleeping bag aside, he eased to his feet, picking up the golf club he'd dug out of one of Delilah's many boxes the night before. Silently, he stepped the short distance to the door.

There. He could hear someone on the landing. Moving this way.

Holding the club in both hands, he shifted his weight onto the balls of his toes and watched the door handle begin to turn.

Now! As the door swung open against the bed, he leaped forward into the light and prepared to wield the club. Instead, he was met with a sharp blow to his midriff and a yelp of surprise, the golf club clattering to the floor.

'Ida,' he gasped, doubled over as he tried to draw breath into his lungs. 'What are you doing here at this hour?'

The cleaning lady, brandishing her mop and face rigid with shock, glared down at him. 'Tha's got the question all wrong, Mr O'Brien. More like tha tells me why tha's sleeping in Miss Delilah's bed!'

Ida Capstick might have lived her entire life in Bruncliffe, but still, she liked to think she was a woman of the world. But what she'd seen that morning had fair shocked her. Reaching for her tea, her hand trembled and she had to grasp the mug in both hands to stop the liquid from spilling all over her newly mopped floor.

She'd arrived at Miss Delilah's place no earlier than normal and had noticed nothing out of the ordinary as she let herself in by the back door. The motorbike – that contraption that had her George in raptures – was parked in the yard, so she'd expected to see young Mr O'Brien at his desk as usual. But his office had been empty.

He was out then, she'd surmised, listening to the silence of the three-storey building. So she'd set about her work. By the time she reached the top floor, she'd been in a world of her own, thinking about the win she'd had at bingo the night before and the two steaks she was planning on buying for tea as a celebration. Bingo was her only vice. She didn't drink. Had never been tempted by smoking. But once a week she went to Bruncliffe Social Club and tried to get a full house.

It'd been quieter than normal last night, given the darts match in the Fleece. Perhaps that had helped send the win her way? She'd been musing on this when she'd approached the spare room at the back of the building and opened the door.

He'd come at her out of the dark like the last of the Mohicans, black hair swinging around his shoulders, chest bare, golf club high above his head, and as naked as the day he was born.

She'd felt her heart stutter in fear and admiration at this attack from such a prime specimen of a male, and had reacted with the only weapon she had to hand. Her mop. Straight in his gut. Lucky for him she hadn't aimed lower. Then he'd really have been in pain.

'Sorry, Ida,' he said as he placed a plate of biscuits in front of her. The good ones, she noted. Not those cheap, plain things Delilah kept for clients she didn't like, but the chocolate-coated special ones which cost a fortune. As young Mr O'Brien wasn't paying, happen he wouldn't care.

Ida took two, immediately dunking one of them in her tea.

'I'm really sorry,' he repeated, running a hand through his hair, which was a bit tamer now, his body thankfully clad in T-shirt and jeans so at least she was spared the sight of all that flesh. That amazing chest. Those biceps.

She heard the splosh as half of the over-dunked biscuit in her hand fell into her tea in a sodden lump.

'Damnation,' she muttered, wiping up the spilled liquid with the sleeve of her overalls. Then she stared at the young man opposite. 'How long has this been going on?' she demanded.

He looked at the floor. 'Since I arrived. George met me at the farm the day I got here and told me it was sold. I was homeless. And I don't have a lot of money. So . . .'

'So tha's been camping out here?'

'Yes.'

She pursed her lips, making sense of the times the upstairs shower had been damp first thing in the morning. That strange musky scent in the spare room, too – deodorant or aftershave, or some such thing. 'Does Miss Delilah know?'

He shook his head. 'No. I wasn't expecting to still be here. Thought it would only be a night or two and that it wouldn't harm anyone. But I'll have to tell her now. And find somewhere else to stay.'

Ida Capstick took a long sip of tea, watching the man she'd seen grow from a child on the farm next door. He'd always been good to George, him and his father both. And his mother . . . she'd been a saint. She took another sip of tea, even though it was rather on the weak side for her, young Mr O'Brien having lost the art of making a true Yorkshire brew in the years he was down south, and came to her conclusion.

'No concern of mine where tha stops. Just don't go scaring the life out of me like tha did this morning.'

A beaming smile split his face. 'Thanks, Ida. I'll get sorted soon and move out before Delilah knows anything about it.'

'And another thing,' she said, extracting her pound of flesh. 'I've taken to these biscuits. Happen as they'd be nice with that morning cuppa tha makes me most days.'

'Anything else?'

'Underpants.' She busied herself with clearing the cups off the table as heat rose up her face. 'Make sure tha wears underpants at all times!'

'Consider it a deal,' he said, face crimson.

'Aye, well, that deal will be off if I find as much as a drop of water in that shower up there of a morning. Understand?'

He nodded and stood up, offering her his hand to shake. Ida Capstick took it solemnly, doing her very best not to smile.

Harry Furness was in a muddle. Head thick from the night before, he'd left the house twice and had had to return, first to get the keys for the rugby club and the second time to get the keys to his car.

It wasn't a good omen for the day to come, he thought as he pulled up outside the clubhouse, nine-thirty already showing on his watch on this bright November morning. He let himself into the small building, leaving the door unlocked for Samson, and made his way through the main function room and bar to the kitchen. A coffee – that would help. Then he could start the delicate work of sorting out the fireworks.

He didn't hear the front door creak. And if he had, he would have blamed the wind, which was whipping along the dale in its usual autumnal fashion. He'd have been wrong.

Bloody Delilah! She'd been the cause of him attacking Ida Capstick – and whilst in the nude!

By quarter to ten, Samson was still cringing at the

thought of his early-morning surprise, the cleaning lady's shocked face something that would haunt his dreams for a long time. Luckily he'd not had his underwear drip-drying in the shower when she arrived, or she might have been less than forgiving. Although, given that she'd just been set upon by a naked man wielding a golf club, the laundry dripping all over her clean bathroom might have escaped her notice.

He groaned, head in his hands.

It served him right for being a fool. Instead of having an early night when he got in last night, he'd had the bright idea of staking out the pub from the spare room at the front of the house. Huddled down between two piles of boxes, he'd sat by the window watching the locals drift homewards, waiting for Delilah to appear. Why? He couldn't really answer that, but it was something to do with Rick Procter. He hadn't wanted to see her leaving with him.

He'd finally been rewarded gone midnight, when Delilah and Tolpuddle emerged from the Fleece. She'd stood there for a second or two, concentrating on her mobile with the dog by her side, before the pub door opened again, emitting a wave of noise and the golden-haired property developer. He leaned down to say something to her and she'd laughed, his arm around her shoulders.

From his hiding place above, Samson felt bitter disappointment wash over him. His best friend's little sister was dating a man Ryan would never have respected. And Samson had no right to intervene.

Then the pub door had swung open one more time,

Elaine Bullock appearing on the pavement with Ash Metcalfe behind her. The four of them had walked up the street and into the night, leaving Samson staring after them.

Blood fizzing, it had taken him an age to get to sleep and he'd forgotten to set his alarm. The next thing he knew, Ida Capstick was coming up the stairs, tearing him out of some stupid dream about a wedding.

So Miss Delilah, as Ida called her, was entirely to blame.

'Morning!'

Samson looked up from his desk as Delilah and Tolpuddle entered the room.

'We're running late this morning, aren't we Tolpuddle?' She leaned down and fondled the dog's ears, a smile of delight on her face.

'You're not the only one,' he muttered.

'Well, it's not often we have a guest stay over. It's a perfect excuse for a leisurely breakfast.' She grinned at him and his dark mood got darker.

'None of my business,' he said, stacking the files he'd been reading and preparing to leave.

'Have you got time for a coffee? Before you go?'

'No.'

'Oh.' She seemed surprised by his churlish tone. 'It's just there's some things I need to talk about.'

He made a point of looking at his watch. 'Best make it quick.'

'Okay then. You've got two dates tonight.' She turned on her heel and walked out, the dog looking from the door to Samson in confusion, unsure of whom to follow.

'What do you mean?' he shouted after her as she walked up the stairs, the thump of her feet telling him he'd triggered her temper. Her voice floated back down to him.

'Hannah Wilson and Sarah Mitchell. They both accepted your date request, so I booked dates for you tonight.'

'But . . .'

She'd stopped and was leaning over the bannister rail, looking down. 'What? Is there a problem? Because I thought this was what we agreed when I *hired* you.'

'Yes, it was, but—'

'Are two in one night too much for you to handle?' she asked, sarcasm barely veiled.

'No . . . no it's . . . nothing. Don't worry about it. Just tell me where and when.'

'Six-thirty in the Coach and Horses for Sarah. She's agreed to come over here. I thought that was safer than you going all the way over to Hawes, considering that you might be in danger. And then eight o'clock for Hannah.'

He nodded. 'Where am I meeting Hannah?'

'The Crown.' Delilah named the pub on the outskirts of town. 'Sarah will probably head home straight after your date, but in case she doesn't, I thought it best to have two different venues. They both know it's just for a drink. Sort of a preliminary date, so you should be able to make your excuses with Sarah when it's time. I can't imagine she's the type to keep you talking.'

Six-thirty and eight o'clock – the whole evening taken up with it.

'Samson . . . ?' He looked up at her face, which had softened slightly. 'You will take care, won't you?'

'I promise,' he said.

She gave a sharp nod and entered her office, leaving him to set off for the rugby club and wondering about two things.

Why was he so upset that he would be missing the Bonfire Night celebrations? And why had Ida Capstick mentioned that he was sleeping in Delilah's bed? If that was Delilah's bed, then what the hell was it doing in the spare room upstairs? He was out of the door before he remembered Delilah's mystery guest and his mood turned even darker.

When they'd designed the clubhouse twenty years ago, as well as an office, changing rooms, a kitchen and the all-important bar, the men in charge of the rugby club had had the foresight to build a storeroom, too. Situated at the end of the hallway that led from the front door, it was normally the realm of the caretaker, filled with such mundane items as cleaning utensils and supplies. But for the week leading up to Bonfire Night, for Harry Furness it became a veritable treasure trove.

Unlocking the door, he flicked on the light and crossed to the metal cabinet that he'd had installed a few years before. It was secured with a standard lock and two padlocks. Because you could never be too sure. Working quickly, he opened them all and turned the handle, feeling a burst of excitement as he looked inside.

Fireworks!

The cabinet was filled with them. Rockets . . . Catherine wheels . . . fountains . . . Roman candles . . . sparklers for the kids . . . and this year, a surprise. He'd treated the club, and himself, to a display-standard firework called The Godfather. After seeing a demo online, he'd been unable to resist, and was confident it was going to provide a spectacular finale. One that Bruncliffe would be talking about for years to come.

Anticipating a great evening, Harry started stacking the fireworks in neat piles on the floor, ready for transporting outside. He was nearly finished when he realised that the diagram he'd drawn up for the display was still in the car. Muttering about his inability to concentrate and thinking that the excess of alcohol the night before might not have been the wisest of ideas, he went back out into the hallway. When he saw a figure silhouetted against the light coming through the front door, naturally he presumed it was Samson.

'You made it!' he said, squinting at the brightness in his hungover state as he stepped towards the shadowy shape. Then Harry realised his mistake. 'Oh, sorry, I was expecting someone else. But it's good to see you anyway—'

The silhouette raised an arm, strangely misshapen in the illumination from behind, and the auctioneer felt something strike him hard on the side of the head. In a crumple of limbs, he fell to the floor.

'Mr O'Brien . . . Samson!'

With his dark mood having ensured a brisk walking pace, Samson was almost at the rugby club when the police car pulled up alongside him, Constable Bradley leaning across from the driver's seat.

'Morning Danny. How's the head?'

Danny grinned sheepishly. 'A bit sore. But it was worth it. We beat the Mason's Arms!'

Samson laughed, the young man's joy infectious. With the sun shining, the wind whipping leaves along the road, and a great darts victory to dwell on, it was hard not to celebrate this wonderful morning. Despite his earlier bad humour.

'Is that what you stopped to tell me?' he asked with a smile.

The constable's face became serious. 'Not quite. I wanted to let you know that I might be a bit late for our appointment after lunch. I'm on my way to the hospital to interview someone who was in a car crash last night.'

'On your own?' Samson could tell the lad wasn't relishing the task.

'Hopefully not. Sergeant Clayton is supposed to be meeting me there. But seeing as I was passing, I thought I'd mention it . . .'

Samson nodded. With Airedale hospital a good forty minutes' drive away, Danny would be pushing it to get there and back before lunch was over. 'I'll see you when you get back then. No rush. And drive carefully.'

'Will do.'

The police car pulled away from the kerb and Samson continued on his way, the grounds of the rugby club visible ahead. Harry's car was parked outside the clubhouse. Hoping the auctioneer had a cup of coffee waiting for him and possibly some cake, Samson walked unwittingly towards the beginning of what would be a black day for Bruncliffe.

*

287

Petrol. Poured out in a wide arc around the floor.

The body wasn't where it was supposed to be. But there was no time to change it. The auctioneer had been expecting someone. And afterwards, who would be able to tell where he'd been when it all went up?

With a flick of a wrist, a match was lit and thrown to the ground. The thin line of liquid flared, snaking brightly out of the kitchen and into the main room, flames leaping at the curtains and curling over the bar. By the time the back door out of the kitchen closed, the fire was already taking hold, encircling the prostrate auctioneer in the hallway and making its way towards the storeroom with its lethal contents.

Savouring his rejuvenated mood, Samson passed the school, the bright laughter of children spilling out of the classrooms and into the autumn air, lifting his spirits even further. But as he stepped off the kerb opposite the gates of the rugby club, the serenity of the morning was disrupted by the screech of brakes.

A van had come out of the small lane that ran alongside the rugby ground and he'd walked out in front of it.

Startled, he jumped back onto the pavement, his hand raised in apology to the driver, but with the sunshine bouncing off the windscreen, it was only as the vehicle pulled away in a snarl of exhaust that he noticed the red hair. Hannah Wilson, driving the mobile library. With the speed she was going at, there must have been a lot of books overdue somewhere.

Heart still thumping, Samson crossed the road.

*

It didn't take long for the fire to spread. Aided by the petrol, it scaled the walls, catching at the furnishings, devouring the carpet. When it found its way to the store-room, the precaution of padlocks and metal casing was made redundant by the neatly stacked piles of fireworks on the floor. The flames raced towards them.

He sensed there was something wrong the minute he turned onto the grounds. A weird light flickering behind the windows of the clubhouse. And carried on the wind, he thought he could detect the acrid smell of smoke. Bon-fire Night come early.

Samson started running, across the car park and down the path that led to the entrance. Kicking open the front door, he stepped right into hell.

Sheets of flame engulfing the walls, thick smoke, the snap and crack of glass . . . Samson staggered back. He slipped off his jacket, draped it over his head and pulled the neck of his jumper up to cover his face.

'Harry!' he called through the open door, the roar of the fire answering him. And then a staccato of explosions coming from somewhere towards the back.

The fireworks. Christ!

'Harry!' he yelled again, crouched low as he tried to peer down the hallway, eyes stinging in the dense smoke.

Another series of loud bangs from the far end of the building, a rocket screaming over his head and the fire beginning to creep across the ceiling. He didn't have much time.

Lungs searing with every intake of breath, he dropped

to his knees and began crawling forward, hands sweeping blindly ahead of him. He felt his eyebrows burning, his eyes streaming, could feel his faculties slowing as the fumes took hold, and he knew his search was futile. Then the whole world exploded in light.

The Godfather. Over two hundred quid's worth of pyrotechnics. As the flames licked across its fuse, it erupted in a shower of reds and blues, firing a hail of white flashes out into the hallway with the machine-gun staccato that had earned it the name, penetrating the thick smoke and allowing enough visibility for a stout leg to appear through the murk.

'Harry!' Coughing hard, senses reeling, Samson forced himself forward, reaching out to grasp the ankle of the body in front of him. Still prone on the ground, fireworks whizzing overhead, he pulled as hard as he could, dragging the unconscious auctioneer towards the doorway. Arms straining at the weight, he inched backwards. Nearly there. One more heave, then he was through the open door, dragging Harry after him.

Air. Sweet. Fresh. But still danger.

He staggered to his feet, vision fogged, hooked his hands under Harry's armpits and hoisted him up, the auctioneer slumping over him like a drunk leaning on a mate. He'd only managed a couple of steps away from the building when there was a blinding flash of light, and on a roar of sound, a staggering force knocked the two men to the ground.

17

The noise ripped through the town, windows rattled in the nearby school and a dark plume of smoke rose into the blue sky. It was enough to startle the people of Bruncliffe.

Standing idly in the kitchen while the kettle boiled, marvelling at how rapidly her good humour – which had originated from the unexpected treat of having Elaine Bullock staying over the night before – had evaporated under the curmudgeonly temperament of her tenant, Delilah was torn from her thoughts by the blast. She hared down the stairs and out onto the street, Troy Murgatroyd coming crashing out of the pub at the same time. Next door, Jo Whitfield was already on the steps of her salon, hands in gloves covered in hair dye.

'What was that?' asked the hairdresser.

'Sounded like an explosion,' Troy replied as the small road began to fill with people.

'Fireworks!' said someone further down by the antique shop. 'Someone's letting off fireworks.'

'That was more than a couple of rockets,' muttered Seth Thistlethwaite, who'd followed Troy out of the pub. 'That was serious.'

'Fireworks . . .' murmured Delilah, looking to the sky

where black clouds were blotting out the sun. 'Fireworks! The rugby club!'

She began running.

It seemed like the whole of Bruncliffe had descended on the rugby club. Delilah arrived, breathing hard, panic squeezing her chest, and had to squirm through a scrum of people gathered on the pavement.

'Samson,' she shouted, pushing past.

'Be careful, love! Don't go too close.' A well-meaning hand grabbed hold of her, but she shrugged it off and broke through to where a fire engine was already in place, hoses snaking away towards the clubhouse.

Or what had been the clubhouse. Flames were shooting out of the broken windows, part of the roof had already collapsed and fireworks were spiralling into the sky. On the grass, some distance from the inferno, two paramedics were preparing to lift a prone figure onto a stretcher.

'Samson!' She ran across the car park, past an ambulance with its back doors wide open, and staggered towards the man on the ground.

Harry Furness. An oxygen mask over his mouth. Blood gushing down his blackened face. Eyes closed. But his chest was rising and falling.

'Thank goodness,' she murmured. Then she looked over at the burning building. Samson. Where was Samson? She felt her knees weaken as she watched the firefighters battling the blaze, the wind whipping the flames. No one could still be in there and survive.

'Don't go collapsing on us, love.' One of the paramedics

was standing next to her, a firm hand under her arm. 'We've got our work cut out with these two buggers!'

'Two?' Delilah turned in confusion and the paramedic pointed back towards the ambulance.

She wheeled round and there, huddled in a blanket, was Samson O'Brien, perched between the open doors of the emergency vehicle.

'He's refusing to come back to hospital with us. But I tell you what – if it hadn't been for him, this one would be a goner.'

Delilah was already crossing the grass before the paramedic had stopped speaking. 'What happened?' she asked, taking in Samson's singed eyebrows, the cuts and grazes on his soot-covered face and arms.

He started coughing and winced, a hand going to his throat. She thought he wasn't going to be able to speak, but then a hoarse sound emerged and his words turned the chilly autumn day even colder.

'Attempted murder,' he rasped. 'That's what happened.'

'You should have gone to hospital,' said Delilah, watching Samson come down the stairs from the second floor, his hair damp, fresh clothes replacing the reeking, singed items he'd been wearing.

She'd tried to persuade him to join the unconscious Harry Furness in the ambulance, telling him he at least needed to get a check-up, but he'd stubbornly refused, walking back with her into town instead. In the five minutes it took to reach their building, it seemed like all of Bruncliffe came up to them, most already aware there had been an explosion at the rugby club; most already hailing Samson as a hero for saving Harry's life.

He'd shaken off the praise and quickened his step, his expression darkened by more than just the residue of the smoke-filled clubhouse. When Delilah opened the front door of their building and an anxious Tolpuddle came bursting down the hallway at them, barking at the top of his lungs in complaint at having been left alone, Samson had slipped past her and dropped to his knees, burying his face in the dog's ecstatic welcome.

Realising this was therapy for both man and dog, she left them there for a few moments, then gently pulled Tolpuddle aside.

'Come on,' she said to Samson, holding out a hand. 'You need a shower. You can use the one upstairs.'

He'd nodded, got to his feet mumbling something about having a towel and change of clothes with him because he'd been to the launderette that morning, and had gone upstairs, Tolpuddle shadowing him. Twenty minutes later, a change of outfit and a shower hadn't taken away the red-rimmed eyes, the hacking cough and the worry etched onto his cut and bruised face.

'I don't have time to go to hospital. We've got work to do.' He accepted the mug of tea she was holding out and followed her into her office, both of them taking seats before the computer.

'You're convinced it was deliberate then, the fire?' Delilah couldn't believe she was asking, when in her gut she already knew.

'Totally. Harry was lying on the floor in the hallway

when I got there. He should have had time to make it as far as the door, unless—'

'Unless he was already unconscious when the fire started. I saw the cut on his head. You think someone knocked him out and then set the building alight?'

'That's exactly what I think.'

'What if it's simply the case that he was careless hand-ling the fireworks? Then slipped, in his rush to escape the fire he'd caused?'

Samson stared at her and she bit her lip.

'Sorry. I just don't want to believe . . .'

'That we placed Harry in danger? Well, we did. Imagine how I feel.' Samson looked bleak. 'I was the one who twisted his arm into making up the numbers for Speedy Date night. If it hadn't been for that, I doubt any of this would have happened.'

'But it doesn't make sense,' said Delilah, staring at a list of client records on the screen. 'I made sure no one could contact Hannah or Sarah. So how—?'

'Hannah Wilson was there.' He said it almost reluc-tantly.

'Where?'

'At the rugby club. I saw her driving away as I arrived. She was in a hell of a hurry . . .'

'So what are you suggesting? That she set the fire?' Delilah couldn't keep the scepticism out of her voice.

Samson shrugged, a wave of fatigue washing over him. 'She was there. She's a suspect. In my line of work, that kind of coincidence usually means something.'

Hearing the lack of conviction in his argument, Delilah

persisted. 'But why? Hannah has no connection to Harry. Why would she single him out?'

It was the question he was asking himself. How had Harry Furness become a target, when Delilah had made sure that the two suspects were corralled behind a virtual cordon?

He shook his head, the throbbing behind his eyes intensified with the motion. 'I don't know. Is it possible Harry managed to get around your modifications somehow and contact her without you knowing?'

'Not a chance.' Despite her certainty, Delilah's fingers were flying over the keys, checking and double-checking her program. 'Look.' She pointed at the screen. 'You were the only one to get in touch with her. So it doesn't make sense that she's involved. Besides, you were happy to dismiss her as a suspect after the Speedy Date night.'

'I did warn you,' Samson said with a hint of exasperation, 'that when it comes to women, my judgement has been known to be flawed—'

He broke off, fragments of conversation, vague and shifting, tugging at his memory. Something about flawed judgement . . .

He pulled out his phone. The lawyer answered on the first ring.

'Matty?' Samson paced the office as he spoke. 'Yes, yes, I'm fine. Thanks. But I need your help. You said something the other day – something about Richard Hargreaves having poor taste in women . . . Yes, and you mentioned an exception . . .'

Delilah waited as Samson, voice rasping, conducted his

conversation with Matthew Thistlethwaite. When he finished the call, he stood staring down into the backyard.

'What is it?' she finally asked.

He turned to her, face haggard. 'We've been looking at the wrong people. We assumed Hannah Wilson and Sarah Mitchell were the only common link to your dead clients.'

'But they are. I've been through the records countless times and no one else dated all three men.'

'Dated them, no. Rejected them . . .' Samson reached out and clicked on one of the names on the computer, making a folder open onto the screen.

'*Lucy?*' Delilah stared at the man next to her. 'You think she had something to do with this? You have to be kidding!'

But Samson's expression was far from jovial.

'Goodness, what a morning!' Lucy Metcalfe untied the strings on her apron and slipped it over her head. Leaning against the counter, feeling as though she'd done a full day's work already, she looked out over her cafe, which was crammed full of customers.

'That's what tragedy does for you,' said Elaine, helping herself to a lemon-and-ginger scone while she manned the till. 'Brings everyone together for a cup of tea and a gossip.'

'You can say that again. I've never known the place so busy. I'll owe Harry more than just a cheese-and-onion tart when he gets out of hospital. Poor bloke . . .'

'Lucky bloke, is how I'd put it.'

'Don't! I can't bear to think what might have happened if Samson hadn't been there.'

'Haven't you heard?' Mrs Pettiford from the bank was waiting to pay. 'They're saying it was foul play.'

'What, the fire? I thought it was simply the fireworks that went up?' Elaine raised an eyebrow in disbelief, but Mrs Pettiford was undaunted.

'Apparently not. Mrs Hargreaves was in, paying in a cheque, and she said she'd heard from her nephew, Ian, that there's reason to believe the fire broke out in the kitchen, nowhere near the fireworks. And that an accelerant might have been used to start it.'

'Petrol?'

The bank clerk nodded. 'Mrs Hargreaves was in a right state about it. What with her suspecting her Richard was . . . you know. She was telling anyone who'd listen that Bruncliffe has a killer in its midst.'

Lucy shivered while Elaine continued to eat her scone.

'All seems a bit too dramatic for round here,' said Elaine. 'Ian Hargreaves, volunteer firefighter or not, should know better than to be spreading such tales. Sometimes I think the uniform goes to their heads.'

'Perhaps,' said Mrs Pettiford, taking her change and leaving a tip in the jar by the till. 'But there must be something in it when the police have decided to put a guard outside Harry Furness's ward. The minute he comes round, they're going to be questioning him.'

'Wow,' said Elaine, finally impressed. 'Someone might have tried to kill Harry? Why would anyone want to do that?'

Lucy shook her head. 'It doesn't make sense. Any of it.'

'And me being here covering your lunch hour doesn't

make sense, either, if you're going to stand around for the entire time,' said Elaine, looking pointedly at the clock on the wall.

'Okay! I'm off. Are you sure you're all right to do this for me?'

'For the tenth time, yes! And are you sure you're okay with me eating all these scones?'

Lucy laughed, threw her apron at her friend, picked up the cake box that was sitting by the till and, with her handbag over her shoulder, headed for the door.

'One o'clock,' Elaine shouted after her. 'Not a minute later. If I'm late getting to my real job, Titch will kill me.'

'I won't be late. I promise.'

It was to be a promise that Lucy Metcalfe would fail to keep.

'I can't believe you're suggesting Lucy is involved in any of this. What on earth did Matty say?'

'He said Richard Hargreaves had poor taste in women, with one exception. And that exception was Lucy.'

'So?' Delilah snapped. 'That doesn't prove anything. Did he say Richard dated her?'

'Not exactly. Richard contacted her through the website after October's Speedy Date night. But she sent him a firm *no*. Apparently he didn't take offence. He told Matty he'd always known she was out of his league, and he ended up going out with Hannah Wilson instead.'

Delilah threw up her arms in indignation. 'It still proves nothing.'

Samson wished he could share her conviction. And her loyalty. It would be so much easier to ignore this hunch of his. A hunch that was implicating someone he cared about in murder.

Lucy Metcalfe had rejected an advance from Richard Hargreaves and the man had ended up dead. Now Harry, having also been snubbed, was unconscious but lucky to be alive. Was it possible that Lucy was connected to the others, too?

It was preposterous. The widow of his best friend. Someone he'd known all his life. And the gentlest person you could ever meet.

But the inconsistencies were plain to see and, in cases like this, inconsistencies often led to breakthroughs. Samson wasn't inclined to ignore his growing concerns.

'Lucy lied,' he said. 'When we were in the pub last night for the darts match. She said she'd never received a date request. I didn't think anything of it at the time, but those papers . . .' He gestured at the desk.

'The papers you saw in my drawer when you broke in here that night?' Delilah's tone was even more caustic than usual, her affront at his accusation adding to her normal temper.

'Yes, those papers. You made lists of all the people who'd been contacted by Richard Hargreaves, Martin Foster and Tom Alderson.'

'And?'

'Lucy was on them. On all three lists, along with Hannah Wilson and Sarah Mitchell.'

'So? It doesn't mean she killed them.'

'But why would she lie?'

Delilah shrugged. 'Maybe you misheard her?'

'No. She clearly said she'd never had a follow-up after

either date night. So much so that Harry, being the kind-hearted soul he is, immediately sent her one. As a joke.' Samson began pacing the floor, thinking about the prostrate form of the auctioneer. Thinking about the fact that he'd almost abandoned him. If it hadn't been for that firework lighting up the place . . . He shuddered. 'Some joke it turned out to be.'

'Harry sent Lucy a date request? I didn't know that.'

'He and Ash thought it would make her laugh,' said Samson. 'She fired back with an outright *no*.'

Delilah clicked on the records for the last dating event, bringing up all of Lucy's interactions. There, clear as day, was Harry's request. And less than five minutes later, a brusque refusal.

She navigated back to the data for the October Speedy Date night. Three requests to Lucy, all of them rejected within minutes. All of them with the least tactful of the three reply options. And all three recipients were now dead.

'Okay,' she said, taking a deep breath. 'There's a connection, for sure. And it's weird the way she's replying so fast, almost taking no time to turn these men down. It also doesn't seem like Lucy to be so abrupt with them, either. But there's a hole in your theory.'

'What?'

'She had another follow-up after Tuesday night.'

'You mean other than Harry?' Samson made to approach the computer but his mobile began to ring. He turned to the window to answer the call. 'Hi, Danny.'

'Mr . . . Samson.' The constable's voice echoed in his

ear. 'Sorry, but I'm going to have to cancel our meeting. I'm still at the hospital.'

'Something wrong?'

'I hear you know all about it. Harry Furness. Sergeant Clayton has asked me to stand guard outside his ward.'

'Has he come round yet?'

'Not that I've heard. But the sergeant seems to think he might know something about how the fire started. Seems it could have been deliberate . . .'

Samson let the silence stretch down the line.

'Sounds like you might already have thought the same?' the constable urged.

'Yes,' said Samson, rubbing a hand over his face. 'I'm sure it was deliberate.'

'Can you tell me why you think that?'

'Harry was lying in the hallway when I got there. He was only a few yards from the front door, where the smoke was least dense, yet he was already unconscious. Somehow I don't think smoke inhalation was to blame. Plus, he was lying the wrong way for someone struggling to get out of a fire, with his feet pointing towards the exit. He wouldn't have been crawling in that position.'

'Anything else?' asked the constable.

'I'd get the doctors to have a close look at the cut on his head, too. Strikes me a flat floor wouldn't have made that mess, even if he'd fallen hard.'

'So you think he was targeted?'

'Yes.'

The blunt reply caused Danny to pause. 'Is this connected to your suspicions about Richard Hargreaves?'

'It could be. I'm sorry, but I can't tell you any more than that for now.'

'Keep me posted, then,' said the constable. Then he sighed loudly. 'What a day. A man run off the road by a stolen tractor and left for dead last night, who swears someone was trying to kill him, and now this.'

'Someone was run off the road?' Out of the corner of his eye, Samson saw Delilah glance towards him. He turned back to face her. 'Anyone we know?'

'That new estate agent from Taylor's. Stuart Lister. That's who I was interviewing this morning at the hospital. He'd gone out to meet a prospective tenant at that old farmhouse on Henside Road. When they didn't show, he headed home and was driving up the big hill before the Goat Lane turn at about nine o'clock, when a tractor came over the top and forced him into a wall. He's in a bad way, but he managed to talk. What's really weird is that he swears the driver of the tractor tried to smother him, after crashing into him. He reckons he's only alive because the Bruncliffe Harriers chose to take their evening run out by Fountains Fell.'

Samson wasn't listening. He was staring at the computer screen, where Lucy's data from the Speedy Date night was still showing. Staring at the name of the second date request she'd received.

'Christ!' he muttered.

'What is it?' The constable was alert on the other end of the phone.

'I think you might want to tell Sergeant Clayton to put a guard on Stuart's door, too.'

*

Two of them still alive. It was getting risky.

The first couple had been straightforward – a simple push at an opportune moment and accidents had been created. Fatal accidents.

But the farmer. That had taken more planning. The sheep had to be killed. The phone calls to the Parish Council made. And then the death itself.

And now . . .

Word was all over town that Harry Furness and Stuart Lister were both in hospital, although no one was suggesting there was any link. But it was only a matter of time before one or other of the men started talking.

There was no alternative. It had to be done. It's what he would have wanted.

She had to be stopped.

'Stuart Lister is in hospital?' Delilah was standing, the shock of the news having driven her to her feet.

'Someone tried to kill him last night. Ran him off the road with a tractor.'

Face grey, she put a hand out to support herself on the desk. 'Is he going to be okay?'

'Danny seems to think so. He's talking at least.'

She slumped back into her chair and gazed blindly at the computer screen, the names of the two men hospitalised in the last twenty-four hours staring back at her.

'We placed them in danger,' she said, voice small.

Samson sat next to her, a hand on her arm. 'What else could we have done? There wasn't enough evidence for the police to get involved. Whereas now . . .'

'Now there are two badly wounded men who got their

injuries as a result of our recklessness. And Lucy is somehow at the centre of it all. I just can't . . .' Delilah shook
her head, dazed by the day's revelations. Samson knew
how she felt.

Lucy Metcalfe. He'd experienced at first hand the
innate goodness of the woman. Never having a bad word
for anyone, she'd been the only one to welcome him back
to Bruncliffe, to treat him like a friend rather than a villain.
Even though she, of all people, had reason to see things
differently. His behaviour at the christening, his lack of
contact with his godson over the years, his absence from
her life when Ryan died . . . She should have been standing
at the door of her caravan with a shotgun, not throwing
her arms around him and offering forgiveness.

How could a woman of that calibre be involved in
murder?

But Samson had witnessed enough as a policeman to
know that the world of crime was never black and white.
And there, on the screen before him, was evidence that
Lucy Metcalfe had a direct connection with the latest
casualties amongst the Dales Dating Agency clients –
one attacked this morning and the other attacked last
night.

Last night . . .

He slapped his palm to his forehead, wincing as he
brushed one of the many grazes that now graced his face.

'Stuart was attacked around nine o'clock last night,' he
muttered. 'Lucy was with us in the pub until much later
than that.'

Delilah spun round. 'Of course!' Relief flooded across
her pale face. 'Which means she can't have—'

Samson shook his head. 'It's not that simple, Delilah. It only means there's at least another person involved. Someone who is aware of Lucy's dating responses.'

'But . . . why? I'm finding it difficult enough to believe that Lucy is killing people who ask her out. Why on earth would anyone be helping her?'

She was right. It just didn't make sense. He sighed, rubbing his aching throat, wanting nothing more than to crawl into his bed. Delilah's bed, as he now knew.

'Okay, so let's assume Lucy was telling the truth in the pub,' he said.

'About the date requests?'

'Exactly. Is it possible that she didn't know?'

Delilah looked sceptical. 'Not really. When a date request is received, a message is sent to the recipient immediately.'

'By email?'

'Email or text. They choose when they set up their account.'

'Would it be possible for someone to intercept those messages?'

A short bark of derisory laughter met his question. 'Only in Hollywood. Here in the real world, the short answer is no.'

'So, if Lucy was telling the truth and she didn't get those messages, why would that be?'

'A program malfunction. But I'd have seen that on her data. Or she changed her email address or phone number and forgot to update her account details. It happens sometimes. In Lucy's case, though, I can tell you she hasn't changed either in the last few years.'

'Can you humour me and check her account?'

She nodded, pulling up the relevant data with a few clicks of the mouse.

'Here,' she pointed at the screen. 'Lucy has set up her account so that she gets agency information through her email – notification of dating sessions, subscription payments and the like. But she gets her date requests sent via SMS.'

'Is that normal?'

'Totally. Most people want the immediacy of a text message when it comes to the important stuff, like whether or not they've been lucky on a date night.'

'And her contact details are all up to date?'

'Yes, that's her email and—' Delilah blinked. Leaned forward and then frowned.

'What?'

'That's not her mobile number.'

A fizz of adrenalin shot through Samson. 'You're sure?'

'Yes. Hers ends in 2001, the year Nathan was born. That's how she remembers it.'

'So whose . . . ?'

Delilah was already scrolling through her contacts on her mobile. She paused, then turned to him, face blanched, hand over her mouth. 'It's Nathan's.'

It was perfect. He'd love it.

Actually, she didn't know if he'd love it or not. Two months ago she would have been confident of her ability to please her son. But as the days had started to darken into winter, so Nathan had become more reclusive, and

Lucy Metcalfe had begun to feel like she was living with a stranger.

A brooding, sullen stranger who bore little resemblance to the carefree boy she'd brought into this world.

And she was hoping to change that with a cake?

She let the lid fall, swamped by an urge to swipe the box and its contents across the caravan.

'Sod it!' she muttered, brushing away the tears that were stinging her eyes. She had to get back to work. She tied a bow across the middle of the box and left it on the table along with a card, so he'd see it as soon as he came home. Then she gathered her coat and bag and stepped out of the door.

She didn't hear a thing. Just felt the hand across her mouth, the scratch on her neck, and then her legs gave way beneath her.

18

'Nathan?'

For a second Samson saw the young replica of Ryan standing in the doorway of the barn up at High Laithe, expression as sullen as the storm brewing in the distance. And more than anything, he wanted the suspicions that were forming to be wrong.

'Is there any chance you're mistaken?'

'None,' Delilah said, hand still trapped over her mouth as though stifling a scream. 'Nathan has been getting Lucy's date requests.'

'Could Lucy have slipped up entering the number?'

Delilah gave him a disbelieving look. 'And what? Nathan never thought to tell his mother of her mistake?' She shook her head.

'But how did he hack into her account?'

'Because Lucy, like a lot of people, used the same password for everything. I've told her time and time again that she needs to be more security conscious . . .' Her voice trailed off in despair.

'In that case, how come she didn't notice? Wouldn't she have got email notifications every time she got a date request?'

'Not necessarily.' She clicked the mouse and pointed at the screen. 'Look. Email notifications were switched off.

Probably Nathan covering his tracks. Lucy had no way of knowing what was going on.'

'But Nathan . . .' Samson felt sick.

'He was never happy about the date nights. He kicked up when he first heard Lucy was going. Said it was disloyal to his dad—'

'Wait a minute!' Samson started pacing the floor. 'Are we seriously suggesting Nathan killed three men and left two others for dead, because he didn't want his mother dating? Don't you think we're jumping to conclusions?' Then he turned to her, relief on his face. 'No . . . no, it can't be Nathan! He didn't even know his mother went to the last Speedy Date night. Lucy told me at the darts match how awful she was feeling because she'd kept it a secret from him.'

Samson's attempt to allay her fears faltered as Delilah bit her lip.

'He did know. He saw the list of entrants on my computer when he called in last week. I didn't say anything at the time – I never thought . . . oh God!' Tears flooded her eyes. 'He's just a child. How could he—?' A groan slipped from her.

'What?'

'Last night,' she whispered. 'Lucy went home to watch *Dirty Dancing*.'

'And?'

'She only did that because she had the caravan to herself. Nathan was out.'

It took him a moment. Then he saw the significance of what she'd said. Nathan, a typical farm boy, able to drive from an early age. He'd have had no trouble handling a tractor . . .

'He could have attacked Stuart Lister.' Samson's words triggered the tears that had been building.

'I shouldn't have suggested Lucy took part,' said Delilah, wiping the back of a hand over her wet cheeks. 'I thought it would do her good, get her back into life a bit. But it was too soon for Nathan. I should have seen that.'

'This could still all be an innocent mistake,' said Samson. 'Let's call Lucy. Find out where Nathan is, and we'll take it from there.'

Drying her eyes, Delilah reached for her mobile. After five rings Lucy's answering service kicked in. Delilah left a brief message and then tried the cafe. Lucy answered on the second ring. Only it wasn't Lucy at all.

'Elaine? I'm looking for Lucy. Is she there?' An explosion of muffled chatter came in response, triggering a look of alarm on Delilah's face.

'Okay. I'll let you know if I hear from her. Bye.' She hung up and took a deep breath and Samson realised she was struggling to control her panic.

'What is it? What's wrong?'

'That was Elaine. She said Lucy went home from the cafe over an hour ago. She was supposed to be back by now to relieve Elaine, but she hasn't returned. Elaine's been calling her. There's no response.'

Samson was already heading for the door. 'Keep trying Lucy's mobile,' he said, 'and try and find out where Nathan is.'

'And you?'

'I'm going up to High Laithe.'

Delilah was rising from the desk before he'd even finished speaking. 'I'm coming, too.'

'No!' He crossed the room to place both hands on her shoulders. 'Stay here, Dee. If there's trouble up there, you don't need to be part of it.'

She sank back onto her chair.

'And this time, I mean it. Stay.'

He strode out of the room and within minutes she heard the roar of the Royal Enfield tearing into the silence.

Something over her mouth, the texture rough on her lips like sandpaper. And under her cheek, a cold, hard surface against her skin. If it was her skin. She wasn't sure. Everything was so strange.

'I'm sorry.'

The voice coming from the end of her body, where the light was, the light that was dipping and swaying, expanding and contracting. But she couldn't see him, his outline distorted, bleeding into the background, the sound disembodied.

'You left me no choice. You have to see that?'

A flare of anger surging up through the hollowness of her mind. She tried to kick out, her limbs refusing to co-operate.

'All those men . . . It's not right. You know that. It's not what he would have wanted.'

He was fading, disappearing into the halo behind him.

'I'm sorry,' he said again.

Then the sound of a door slamming shut and footsteps over stones, overlaid by the smell. Something familiar. Something fearful. That was when she had a moment of lucidity. The moment when she realised she was about to die.

Nathan Metcalfe.

Samson held the image of the lad's face before him as he rode out of town. Those cheekbones, the same as Delilah's. The hair the same as his father's, a thatch of dark gold. The stature taken from his uncles – Delilah and Will the only two of the Metcalfe siblings to fail to reach above-average heights. And the temper?

He'd seen a flash of it that day at the caravan. Like Will's? Capable of blind rage?

But did that mean the boy was capable of murder?

As the houses of Back Street gave way to fields, Ellershaw Farm became visible up to his left and above it, out of sight, Lucy's caravan at High Laithe. Samson opened up the throttle and let the bike gather speed. Even though he had a terrible premonition that he was already too late.

'Nathan? He's not here, love.'

Delilah bit down hard on her impatience, her stomach acidic with tension and her hand shaking as she held the phone. 'I gathered that, Mum. But I've been trying his mobile and there's no answer. Do you know where he is? It's urgent.'

'Of course I know where he is. He's in Wales.'

'Wales?' Delilah felt a wave of relief. Then confusion. 'What's he doing in Wales?'

'Some outdoors adventure thingy for some award – Duke of York or something like that. Does that sound right?'

'How long's he been over there?'

In the background Delilah could hear her mother walking over to the calendar from the auction mart, an annually updated edition of which had been hanging on the kitchen wall for as long as she could remember.

'Lucy dropped him down to catch the school minibus two days ago. She's picking him up sometime this afternoon.'

'Have you heard from him? Has Lucy?'

'No, and we don't expect to, either. He said there'd be no mobile reception, so not to bother calling him. Reckon that'll be the biggest shock for him. He's used to being out in nature all on his own. But that blasted mobile – lately it's like it's attached to his hand. It'll do him good to be without for a few days.'

'Thanks, Mum. I've got to go.'

'Is everything okay, love? You sound worried.'

'Everything's fine,' said Delilah, adopting a more cheerful tone to varnish the lie. 'Give my love to Dad.'

'I will do, whenever he gets home. Don't know where he's got to this afternoon. Your brother's been looking for him, but—'

'Sorry, Mum, I really have to go.' Delilah cut across her mother's grumbling and hung up, a large sigh easing from her as she dropped her head into her hands.

Nathan was in the clear. He'd been on a camping trip with the school when both Stuart and Harry had been attacked.

With a snap, her head lifted and she was staring at the computer screen. If Nathan was somewhere out of mobile reception, how the hell had he rejected Harry's date request last night?

Entering her admin password, she accessed Samson's dating agency account and sent Lucy a date request.

Within seconds she received a response. An outright rejection.

'What the—?'

It took her a few moments to realise she was looking at the question all wrong. That really the puzzle was not how. But who.

Who was answering Nathan's phone?

With a sense of fear stealing along her nerves, she jumped to her feet. Samson. He was on his way to the caravan, but rather than confronting a teenage boy when he got there, it would be someone else. Something else.

She needed to get up there, but she didn't have a car.

She'd just have to take the more direct route.

Hurrying from the room, mobile clamped to her ear, she called Samson as she dashed down the stairs, the familiar sound of paws behind her telling her Tolpuddle was following.

No answer.

Stuffing her phone in her pocket, she bent and pulled on her trainers in the porch, the dog already beginning to wag his tail in anticipation.

'Not this time, Tolpuddle,' she said, blocking his path as she opened the door. 'You heard what Samson said. Stay here.'

He whined. A loud wail like a police siren, which she knew he could keep up for hours.

'Sod it!' She stood aside and let him past. 'We might as

well both break the rules. At least this way I can say it was your idea.'

He twisted his head to one side, regarding her with his ears cocked, and then they were both out of the back gate and running to help Samson. And Delilah Metcalfe didn't care who saw them doing it.

As he turned off the main road onto the track at High Laithe, he saw the van parked next to Lucy's static caravan, a large figure standing by its open doors. Rob Harrison. The stonemason glanced over his shoulder at the sound of the motorbike's approach. But there was no sign of Lucy's car. Samson pulled up a short distance from the van, leaving his helmet on the bike as he got off.

'Afternoon, Rob.'

'Samson.' The man tipped his head in greeting and leaned against the van, hands in pockets.

'Is Lucy around?'

'Nope. Just called up with some bathroom brochures that she asked for, but she's not in. Thought you might know where she is.'

Samson shook his head, concern gnawing at him. 'I don't. But I need to speak to her. Urgently. So if you see her . . .'

Rob nodded. 'Everything all right?'

'Not sure. I think Nathan might be in some trouble.'

'Nathan?' The stonemason straightened up, eyes narrowing. 'What kind of trouble?'

'I can't say.'

Rob stared at him. 'He's a good lad, like his father.

Whatever it is you think he's done, you must have it wrong.'

'I'm sure you're right,' said Samson with a smile, touched by the stonemason's faith in his friend's son. He nodded and turned to go.

The roar of a motorbike. She'd heard it arrive, sounds filtering through her befuddled mind with startling clarity. Then voices. Two of them. Both men. But the words, her brain couldn't cope with the words. Nor could she form any of her own. All she could do was lie there, eyes closed, breathing in that sickly smell with the damp of tears on her cheeks.

The wind – that living creature that blows up and down the Dales, swirling leaves in the autumn, turning the brightest of summer days chilly and tweaking at washing on lines – at the precise moment that Samson began to turn away, it chose to shift from its prevailing direction out of the south-west to due south.

Due south. Brushing over the caravan and straight towards Samson. Bringing with it a scent that he recognised – an odour he'd encountered that very morning. And, carrying across the short distance that separated the two men, the soft sound of a text being received.

It was enough to make Samson pause. To turn back. To inhale a lungful of the air and recognise the underlying taint. To see Rob Harrison glance down at his hand and the distinctive mobile he was now holding, a lion rampant on the back cover.

The smell was petrol; the mobile was Nathan's.

19

Less than a mile as the crow flies. But a bloody crow wouldn't have to run up the steps to the top of the Crag.

Chest burning, legs on fire, Delilah forced herself to pick up the speed as she cleared the rocky outcrop that towered over Bruncliffe and finally hit the open fells. If she'd looked back, she'd have seen the Lake District peaks, hazy in the distance; the stone-built houses of the town behind her with the river snaking between them; and the smoke still hanging in the air above the ruins of the rugby club.

But she didn't look back. She looked ahead, following the path uphill that she knew from years of training, concentrating as she sped across the distance between Bruncliffe and the caravan where her friend lived.

Alongside her, Tolpuddle kept pace, his grey body covering the uneven terrain in easy strides.

Less than a mile as the crow flies. They would be there in minutes.

The wind wasn't the only thing that had shifted.

As Rob Harrison raised his head, Samson O'Brien felt the change in atmosphere, an undercurrent of tension now shimmering between the two men.

'Is that Nathan's phone?' he asked, tone light, as though

they were having a relaxed conversation in the pub, while his brain turned cartwheels trying to work out the puzzling implications of this new piece of information.

Nathan's phone. Rob Harrison had access to Nathan's phone. Which meant he had access to Lucy's date requests. The loyal friend. The self-appointed protector. Perhaps Nathan wasn't the only one who didn't want Lucy dating. In which case . . .

He kept his focus on the stonemason, who seemed to be doing some re-evaluating of his own, attention flicking from the mobile in his hand to Samson with growing anger. All the while, the scent of petrol grew stronger.

Petrol. Lucy. She was in serious danger.

'What have you done with her, Rob?' Samson asked, beginning to circle slowly in the direction of the caravan.

The stonemason shook his head, so Samson tried again, edging nearer to the steps that led to Lucy's front door. 'If you've harmed her, Nathan will never forgive you.'

'You hypocrite!' Rob finally snarled, brandishing the mobile.

A date request was showing on the screen – from Samson to Lucy.

Whatever had prompted Delilah to send it, Samson didn't know. But it had handed him the edge. Because Rob Harrison was furious. And an enraged man is a lot easier to overcome than a rational one. Especially one as large as the stonemason.

Rob took a step towards him, fists clenched, shoulders tense. 'You're as bad as the rest of them,' he shouted. 'Making out you're concerned about Nathan while trying to date his mother behind his back. You're his godfather, for Christ's sake!'

His temper had brought him closer. Samson needed him closer still if he was to negate the difference in size between them.

'Where's the harm?' asked Samson. 'Lucy's young. And pretty. It's not like I'm asking her to marry me or anything.' He shrugged, as though Lucy's connection to his dead friend was of no account. 'Just looking for a bit of fun. Ryan would understand.'

It was the catalyst he'd wanted.

With a roar of rage, Rob attacked, and the detective had seconds to brace himself before eighteen stone of muscle and bone fell upon him.

Twisting slightly as the huge man lunged, Samson let the full impact land on his right side, hands grasping the man's jacket to continue the forward momentum, throwing the stonemason to the ground.

But the power behind the movement was too much and as the heavier man fell, the detective was pulled after him, the two of them collapsing onto the gravel close to the wooden steps of the caravan. Landing on top of the stonemason, Samson heard the air rush out of the man's lungs, but still Rob Harrison had the capacity to throw a powerful punch, catching the detective in the ribs. Rearing back in pain, Samson yielded too much space and two large hands were on his chest and thrusting him backwards, his head smacking into the side of the steps.

Dazed, he scrambled to his feet, a warm trickle of blood on his scalp. And a pungent smell on his clothes. Petrol. They'd been rolling around in petrol, the gravel dark where the liquid had been poured in a wide trail around the caravan.

He looked up, suddenly aware of the danger, only to see Rob Harrison standing opposite him, hemming him in between the caravan and the steps. He was holding a knife in his right hand, the blade ugly and serrated. Far more worryingly, in his left, he was holding a lit Zippo lighter.

An oblong of green in front of a stone barn. That's all Delilah saw of the caravan as she crested the fell above it, breath coming in short gasps, thighs trembling. Then she was hurtling downhill, concentrating only on the tussocky grass and the bits of limestone passing beneath her feet as she negotiated the tricky route which would take her to the road. Tolpuddle, as if sensing they were almost at their destination, started pulling ahead.

By the time Delilah ran across the tarmac, Tolpuddle was already racing down the track, towards the motor-bike, the van with its open doors. And the two men standing by the caravan, one of them holding a knife.

Delilah started sprinting.

'Don't be stupid, Rob. This isn't what Ryan would have wanted.'

Samson had both hands spread in the instinctive gesture of surrender, the metal side of the caravan against his back. He tried not to let the fumes from the petrol alarm him. Tried to concentrate only on the man opposite and the naked flame in his hand.

'At least let Lucy go.'

Rob's eyes flicked tellingly and Samson knew Lucy

must be inside the caravan, incapacitated in some way or she'd have been making a racket by now. The situation wasn't looking good. For either of them.

His only hope was to keep Rob occupied. To talk to him, in the chance of overpowering him.

'Please, Rob. For Ryan's sake.'

'Don't use his name!' the stonemason snapped, the lighter jerking dangerously in his hand. 'You abandoned him. And now you're back trying to steal his wife. You're scum, just like the others.' He spat on the ground at Samson's feet. 'Well, I took care of them. Like I'm going to take care of you.'

Samson fought the panic welling inside him. 'And Nathan?' he managed. 'Does he know what you're doing? That you're about to kill his mother?'

Confusion passed across Rob's face. He glanced at the caravan again and a blur of movement over his right shoulder caught Samson's eye.

Tolpuddle, racing down the track, Delilah following in his wake.

'Does Nathan know?' pressed Samson, trying to keep the stonemason's attention away from the fast-approaching dog.

'Leave him out of this,' shouted Rob, glare focused back on Samson. 'Nathan's a good kid. All he did was change the dating account to stop those men contacting his mother.'

'Then you need to let Lucy go,' said Samson. 'For Nathan's sake.'

The stonemason growled. 'I need to do no such thing.

Nathan's better off without her despoiling his father's memory.' He raised his left arm, the flame flickering in the wind. 'See you in hell, O'Brien.'

Samson flinched, waiting for the burst of fire that would be triggered by the dropped lighter. But a sharp bark cut through the air and Rob Harrison began turning to his right, leading with the knife as Tolpuddle hurtled towards him.

She saw the two men. Samson facing her. Rob Harrison the stonemason with his back to her, holding a knife in his right hand. And a lighter in his left. As she raced closer, the smell of petrol drifted across the space between them and terror clutched at her chest.

Tolpuddle was some way ahead and closing fast. When she heard his warning bark, she knew what was coming, the muscles in his haunches bunching as he prepared to leap. Then Rob Harrison was turning and the sun was glinting off the blade in his hand.

'Tolpuddle, no!' Delilah screamed.

But the dog was already committed, leaping at full stretch, front paws landing on the stonemason's right shoulder. The unexpected weight was enough to cause the man to lose his balance and he stumbled to his left, Samson lunging for the lighter. In a blur of motion, the dog and both men fell to the ground.

The lighter! Samson's hand closed around the thick wrist of Rob Harrison, trying to hold the flame away from the petrol-sodden gravel. But he was falling – him and the stonemason and the dog, a jumble of limbs as they hit the ground. He felt his already-sore ribs crunch against the hard surface, heard the dog yelp in pain, and he saw the fingers gripping the Zippo let go.

Then his head smacked into the ground and the lighter clattered out of sight.

It was a miracle, of sorts. The lighter tumbled from the stonemason's grasp, yellow flame still burning, and bounced on its bottom edge on the gravel, before landing on the concrete base under the caravan. It skittered across the smooth surface and was still alight as it came to rest against a pile of dead leaves that had been blown there by the autumn winds. It wouldn't be long before they began to smoulder.

The lighter. Where was it?

Shaking his head to clear his vision, Samson scanned the ground around him. No fire. The petrol still damp on the gravel. No lighter, either.

Heavy footsteps pulled his attention back to Rob Harrison, the stonemason up on his feet and running, cutting right between the caravan and the barn and heading towards the path that led up the fellside. Already veering after him was the much smaller figure of Delilah.

Head throbbing, his arm clamped to his side where his damaged ribs were making every breath painful, Samson struggled to pick himself up. 'Let him go, Delilah!' he called out as she approached. 'He's dangerous.'

She didn't even break stride. 'I'll be fine. Call the police and tell them to follow us, then see if Lucy's in there,' she yelled, pointing at the caravan. 'And check on Tolpuddle, too.'

'Delilah, no!' Samson shouted after her. Because the path they had taken led to only one place – Thursgill Force. If the stonemason ended up cornered, trapped between the waterfall at the end of the path and Delilah behind him, he wouldn't hesitate to confront her. He had too much to lose. But with a last worried glance at her dog, who had crawled towards the motorbike before collapsing, she was gone, chasing the huge silhouette of Rob Harrison up the hillside.

Grabbing his mobile out of his pocket, Samson started dialling as he staggered over to where Tolpuddle was lying with his eyes half-closed. He ran a hand along the dog's grey flank and got a soft whimper in response.

'Police and ambulance,' Samson said as the operator answered. 'High Laithe, the Metcalfe place.'

Then he noticed his hand. It was covered in blood. 'And a vet,' he said with urgency. 'We need a vet, too.'

If the operator thought it a strange request, she didn't say. Just took the necessary details and assured Samson that someone would be with him as soon as possible.

'You daft mutt,' said Samson, voice thickening with emotion as Tolpuddle whimpered again. 'I thought I told you to stay in the office.'

Then he turned back to the caravan. And that was when he saw the smoke curling out from underneath it. If Lucy really was in there, she was in trouble.

Smoke. Seeping up though the floor. Lucy could smell it quite clearly despite her muddled state. But there was nothing she could do. Her mind touched briefly on the awful prospect of fire. Of her lying there, unable to move. But then it spiralled away, Ryan calling her from beyond the space she was in.

'Lucy! Lucy! You need to get out!'

She smiled. Then she cried. Because there was no way she could join him when she couldn't move. And besides, she couldn't leave the cake. Not after the effort it took to bake it.

'Lucy! Lucy! You need to get out!'

Samson rattled the handle of the locked door, conscious of the acrid smoke rising up between the steps. He'd glanced under the caravan and it hadn't looked good. A small fire of leaves burning slowly but steadily, it had been enough to panic him. If the flames got as far as the petrol-soaked gravel, Lucy would be unreachable.

He pressed his face to the glass of the door once again, but Lucy was in the same position she'd been in when he'd raced over to the caravan moments before. She was lying prone on the floor, eyes closed, long hair draped across her face and a rag tied across her mouth.

'Come on, Lucy!' he shouted. 'You need to move!'

A leg twitched and he saw her eyelids flicker, but nothing more. Lucy was unable to help herself.

He needed to get in there. Samson ran back down the steps and assessed the caravan. Big windows at the front. He'd be able to get her out through one of those. But first he had to get them open.

A loud pop from beneath the caravan made him jump

and he heard the crackle of fire. It was catching hold. And there was a gas canister around the back.

He was running out of time. So was Lucy.

Delilah wasn't taking risks. She'd managed to gain ground on the stonemason as they cut across the open fell, his heavier muscle counting against him as the hillside rose steeply. But when they'd gone over the stile and into the copse that led to Thursgill Force, the path began to flatten out and Rob Harrison had started to pull away.

Ahead she could see his lumbering figure crashing through the trees, reckless in his headlong flight along a path strewn with rocks and roots, and only the width of a footfall. Behind him, Delilah was a lot more careful, aware of her running shoes slipping on the greasy limestone and of the abrupt drop to the right.

'One foot in front of the other,' she muttered, quoting her old coach Seth Thistlethwaite as she continued the chase. 'One foot in front of the other.'

There was no real rush after all. Because Delilah knew where the path ended. At the top of Thursgill Force, a waterfall that dropped thirty feet onto rocks below.

Rob Harrison was running into a dead end. She chose not to think about what might happen when he reached it.

'One foot in front of the other,' she said again as she kept up her pace.

Something to smash the double glazing.

Ignoring the slicing pain in his side every time he took a breath, Samson raced over to the stonemason's van, its back doors still wide open. Inside, a jerrycan lay discarded alongside some rope, a roll of gaffer tape and, thankfully, a toolbox. Choosing a robust mason's hammer from the array of tools, he sprinted back to the caravan, aware of the ever-denser swirls of smoke creeping out from under it.

Reaching the front windows, he pulled himself up onto the A-frame used for towing that jutted out beneath them. He balanced himself across it and then, concentrating on the middle of the three panes of glass, swung the hammer as hard as he could at the bottom right-hand corner.

The impact jarred his body, his ribs screaming in protest. But the glass remained intact. And the fire was growing in strength, the southerly wind breathing life into the flames and sending twists of grey curling up around his legs.

'Come on,' he grunted, tensing his body again in preparation. Spurred on by desperation and fear, he brought the hammer over his shoulder and crashing into the window.

The glass shattered, exploding into a thousand shards which rained down onto him, cutting into his face and hands. He barely noticed. Because at that moment a burning leaf blew out onto the gravel and the circle of petrol finally burst into flames.

20

In one swift movement Samson grasped the windowsill and pulled himself inside the caravan, jagged fragments of glass digging into his hands. He landed on the sofa where, what seemed like years ago, he'd sat with Lucy and had lunch.

Flames dancing high outside the windows now, he moved quickly past the table and into the small kitchen area where Lucy was lying on the floor. The floor that was already covered in spiralling smoke.

'Lucy!' He bent down in the cramped space and removed the filthy rag that had been used to gag her, but she didn't even turn her head. From her moving lips came a barely audible sound. Drugged. He didn't need his years of experience in the police to tell him that.

Slipping his hands under her armpits, he pulled her upright and her entire weight flopped against him. With her legs dragging uselessly behind, he hauled her across to the broken window. She weighed a heck of a sight less than Harry Furness.

But then he hadn't had to get Harry out of a window and across a cordon of fire.

Propping Lucy on the sofa, he crossed to the door and grabbed one of the coats hanging on a row of pegs, trying not to notice the thickening fog of smoke clinging to his legs. He draped the coat over her head and down her back. It would offer some protection. But as for him?

His clothes. They were already soaked in petrol. If he was going to brave the flames, he had no option but to take them off.

Fingers fumbling at the zip, he quickly removed his jacket and then his jeans, transferring his mobile and his keys to his shirt pocket. He looked at his trainers. And then at the flames licking at the edge of the caravan. No way was he going across them in bare feet. He'd take his chances.

Ready and terrified, he hoisted Lucy into his arms and she jolted awake.

'The cake!' she said, and he could feel her limbs straining to move.

'We're in a fire, Lucy. We have to get out.'

But she wriggled, making it difficult for him to hold her. 'The cake. Don't forget the cake.'

Tears in her eyes, she stared up at him.

'I won't forget. I promise,' he said. Then he looked out at the blaze he was going to have to get her through and his heart sank. There was no way he could manage to step through the window and onto the A-frame while carrying her. And even if he could, he'd then have to dive through the fire with her in his arms. It wasn't possible. Which meant the only option was to lower her out of the window. But how could he do that if she couldn't support herself? She'd fall into the flames.

With dread overwhelming him, he stepped up onto the couch.

*

Still out of sight, the waterfall could be heard thundering over the cliff, its noise getting louder and the path narrower as they approached the end. Rob Harrison had pulled further ahead, jumping and leaping over rocks and protruding tree roots, occasionally slipping and stumbling, but always managing to keep his balance.

Behind him, Delilah was going even more cautiously than before. The drop to the right was now terrifying, a sheer fall down into Thursgill Beck, the scattering of trees sparse enough to allow a body to tumble the entire way down to the bottom. She didn't fancy the chances of survival.

She also didn't fancy the confrontation that was inevitable when Rob Harrison realised he'd run out of path. Perhaps she could hold him long enough, keep him there until the police arrived?

Up ahead, the falling waters came into sight. In less than five minutes he would be there.

'One foot in front of the other,' she told herself as her courage began to fail.

He stood on the couch, teetering for a couple of seconds, staring at the flames below the window as he held Lucy in his arms.

'The cake,' she muttered, oblivious to their predicament. Samson wished he was as numb to the danger.

'I'll get the bloody cake when you're safe,' he said, and with that he took the first step out of the window and onto the A-frame.

'Samson!' A hoarse cry from the other side of the flames. Will Metcalfe was there, beating at the fire with his coat, Nathan at his side doing likewise, trying to smother the inferno. 'Throw her!'

Throw Lucy? With what he thought were broken ribs and while balanced half-in and half-out of a window?

'Throw her!' Will roared. 'I'll catch her.'

Samson glanced down at the woman in his arms. Could he do it? Get her across the fire?

'Hurry. It's almost at the gas canisters.' Will was beckoning, arms wide open, Nathan looking terrified beside him.

'The cake,' Lucy murmured again.

'You and your bloody cake,' said Samson with a swell of affection.

And he gathered every ounce of strength he had left and threw his best friend's wife from the shattered window. She twisted in the air, limbs flailing uselessly, and then Will was there, staggering back from the burning caravan as Lucy landed in his arms.

'Got her! Now jump!' shouted Will. 'Jump before the gas goes!'

Afterwards Samson couldn't explain why he did it. But he glanced back into the interior and saw the beautifully wrapped box on the table. Peaks Patisserie. And the card next to it.

The cake. Her damn cake.

He stepped back inside, tucked the card in his already bulging shirt pocket, lifted the cake in his hands and headed for the window. He got both legs out onto the A-frame, the flames scorching his bare flesh, and with a huge leap, flung himself across the fire.

He was in the air when the back end of the caravan exploded.

The sound ruptured the autumn afternoon. It could be heard down at Ellershaw Farm where Peggy and Ted Metcalfe were having a coffee, eyes avoiding each other as they sat in their customary strained silence. It rippled across the hills and made a muffled sound in the centre of Bruncliffe where Elaine Bullock was still working in Peaks Patisserie, worried about her friend and that uncharacteristic broken promise. For the police car and the ambulance that were speeding up the road to High Laithe, the noise was a trigger to drive faster. And for Delilah Metcalfe and the man she was chasing, it came as a whisper of wind and then a large bang, ricocheting through the trees from behind like a gunshot.

Rob Harrison reacted first, twisting round in surprise, face stricken. Then Delilah, grabbing hold of a tree trunk to steady herself as she turned to assess what had happened.

An explosion. The caravan. Had Lucy been in it? And Samson?

'No!' she wheeled back to face the stonemason, anger burning through her at all he had done.

But he wasn't there. Just the trees. And the rocks. And the narrow path. And behind it, the impressive fall of water cascading down into the gill.

She looked up the hillside, thinking he'd scrambled upwards, using the distraction to escape her. But no. Which left only one option.

Heart in mouth, she jogged forward to where she'd last seen him. Then she forced herself to look down.

Far below, on a large rock beside the narrow stream of water that was Thursgill Beck, she could see his body. It wasn't moving.

She turned away, legs shaking, and began running. In the distance were the dark shapes of men coming towards her. The police.

'One foot in front of the other,' she mumbled as she ran back along the path towards them, tears on her cheeks at the thought of what she might find when she reached High Laithe.

'You shouldn't have let her run after him!' Will prowled back and forth across the gravel, an eye on the men from the mountain rescue team who were setting out along the path that Delilah had taken in her pursuit of Rob Harrison. She'd yet to return.

Samson pulled the silver emergency blanket closer around his shoulders, a shiver of panic running the length of his spine at Will's words. 'I didn't have much choice,' he muttered. 'She's fairly stubborn.'

'If anything happens to her . . .'

If anything happens to her, thought Samson, Will's wrath would be nothing compared to his own self-reproach.

In the aftermath of the explosion, a police car had arrived as a dazed Samson was trying to pick himself up off the ground, an ambulance screeching to a halt just behind it. While the paramedics rushed to treat the barely conscious Lucy, a gabbled explanation of events from

Samson had sent the two policemen running towards Thursgill Force, one of them calling for reinforcements as he went. It wasn't long before another police car was on the scene, along with a fire engine and the local mountain rescue team.

A volunteer firefighter himself, Will had joined the attempts to get the blazing caravan under control, the flames a threat to the barn across the yard. Samson had overseen Lucy's transfer into the ambulance, calming a tearful Nathan as he took his place in the back with his mother, and had then waited with Tolpuddle until the vet arrived.

It was only now, with the fire contained and help for the injured – human and canine – on hand, that he allowed himself to think about Delilah.

He should have run after her. Ignored the pain in his ribs. But then, what would have happened to Lucy?

'Where the hell is she?' grunted Will, and Samson's guts twisted even tighter.

'Lucy! Lucy!' A loud cry came from the other side of the barn and Delilah appeared around the corner, running at full tilt, wild eyes fixed on the burning wreckage of what had been her sister-in-law's home. She turned desperately to the gaggle of people gathered around the emergency vehicles and spotted Will. 'Where is she?' she cried, rushing over. 'Where's Lucy?'

'It's okay, it's okay.' Will placed large hands on her shoulders and pulled her into a hug while Samson felt his legs finally give way. He slumped to the ground in relief, almost sitting on the box he'd saved from the caravan.

'Lucy's already gone to hospital,' explained Will to a

trembling Delilah. 'She's fine and Nathan's with her. But what about you? Are you okay?'

She nodded, bottom lip trapped between her teeth as he stood back to inspect her. 'I'm all right, Will. Honestly. But Rob—'

'Did the police get him? You should never have gone chasing after him. You could have been hurt—'

'He's dead.'

'Dead?' Will's expression changed from concerned to stunned.

'He must be dead after that . . .' Delilah shook her head as if trying to erase the memory. 'I was chasing him along the path above the beck and then we heard the explosion. He fell – at least, I think he fell. One moment he was there and then the next . . .' She shuddered. 'It was horrible, Will. The police are there and the mountain rescue are going to get his body.'

She took a deep breath to steady herself and spotted the grey shape by the motorbike, a man huddled over it.

'Tolpuddle?' Her hand went to her mouth.

'He's been stabbed, but Herriot's taking good care of him. He's going to be okay.'

'Thank God!' She staggered over to the dog, collapsing onto her knees beside him as the vet, James Ellison – but known to everyone in this Dales town as Herriot – finished tying a bandage.

'It's your turn for some attention, young man.'

Samson tore his gaze off Delilah to see a paramedic looking down at him. 'I'm okay.'

'Think I'm the best judge of that. You've got burns that

need treating.' He knelt down and began rubbing salve onto Samson's painful legs, as Will sat down beside them.

'Thank goodness she's safe,' the oldest Metcalfe muttered, his smoke-streaked face sagging with fatigue. Then he spotted the box next to Samson. 'Is that what you went back into the caravan for?'

Samson nodded, picking it up. 'It's a cake.'

'A cake? You went back into a burning caravan for a bloody cake?' Will was staring at him. 'What kind of a halfwit are you? You could have died!'

Samson shrugged, grinning as he held the precious box on his lap. He'd barely made it, in mid-lunge when the rear end of the caravan exploded, the propulsion of air catching him like a wave and depositing him beyond the reach of the flames. Even then, he'd been trying to protect the cake, landing badly as a result and possibly breaking a few more ribs. It had been insane.

'Ouch!' He winced as the paramedic applied ointment to a particularly badly burnt section of calf.

'No point in complaining when you decide to jump through a fire with no trousers on, lad,' came the brusque reply. Then the man squinted at him in recognition. 'Aren't you the bloke who was down at the rugby club this morning?'

'Yeah. That was me,' Samson muttered.

The man regarded him afresh. 'Two fires in one day? One a year's enough for most folk. You got a death wish or summat?'

'He's just a bloody halfwit, that's what it is.'

'I'm willing to put up with your abuse, Will,' said Samson with a smile. 'If it hadn't been for you and Nathan turning up, I don't think I'd have got Lucy out of there. Not in the state she was in.'

Will grimaced. 'Aye, that was a piece of luck all right. Nathan arrived back from his trip earlier than planned and I happened to be passing the school. I picked him up, intending to stop off at the farm first, but Nathan wanted to let his mother know she didn't need to go into town for him. He didn't have his phone with him and I couldn't get through to her on mine, so we drove up . . .' He shook his head at the thought of what might have been. 'Rob Harrison! I can't understand it.'

'I don't think any of us will be able to. He thought he was protecting Ryan's memory.'

'What, by killing a whole load of innocent folk and trying to kill a few more? And as for what he did to Lucy – he was supposed to be Ryan's mate. Some bloody mate when he drugs a man's wife and leaves her to die in a fire!' He scuffed the gravel with a foot, face troubled. 'What were those drugs? Could you tell? What with your background and all . . .'

'Hard to say for sure just from seeing her, but I'd put money on it being something like Ketamine.'

'Horse tranquilliser?' Will looked sceptical.

'It's not just for horses any more,' said Samson. 'I came across it a lot on raids down in London.'

'Where the hell would Rob Harrison have got hold of it, though?'

The paramedic gave Will a world-weary look. 'You'd be surprised how easy it is to get hold of drugs around here.'

'After today,' muttered Will, 'I don't think much

would surprise me about Bruncliffe. But will there be any lasting harm? Will Lucy be okay?'

'She'll be fine,' said Samson. 'It can't have been a large dose as she was already beginning to come round in the caravan, so she'll be a bit light-headed and probably queasy. Other than that, she'll be okay. Won't she?' He looked to the paramedic, who was already nodding his agreement.

The additional weight of a professional opinion seeming to pacify Will, a comfortable silence settled between the three men, allowing the voice of the vet to carry easily across the yard.

'Most of all, he needs rest and lots of love,' Herriot was saying to Delilah as they eased Tolpuddle into a van.

'Huh,' said the paramedic with a grin, wiping off his hands and standing up, satisfied that he'd done all he could for Samson. 'Don't go thinking I'm going to recommend the same for you.'

'What the hell would he need love for?' countered Will, a small spark of amusement in his eyes. 'He's got bloody cake!'

And Samson, verging on exhaustion, found himself laughing. And laughing. And laughing.

Delilah helped Herriot lift the inert Tolpuddle into the vet's van, her precious dog nuzzling at her hand as she held his head.

'I'll keep him overnight, if you don't mind,' said Herriot. 'Just to monitor his condition. But he should be good to come home tomorrow.'

'Thank you,' said Delilah, shaking the man's hand. 'You saved his life.'

The vet looked over his shoulder at the smouldering caravan, the firemen having brought the flames under control. And at the sombre faces of those waiting for the mountain rescue team to return from Thursgill Force after their unenviable task. 'Seems like quite a few people around here have been saving lives today,' he said. Then he ruffled the dog's ears. 'Tolpuddle among them.'

He closed the van door, a small whimper audible as it shut.

'He'll be fine,' Herriot said, noticing Delilah's anxious face. 'I promise. Now get yourself home. You need to rest, too.'

She waited for the van to pull out of sight before she turned, still not sure she could handle the overwhelming emotions that were swamping her.

Panic when she'd seen the burnt-out caravan. Relief when she'd heard Lucy was okay. Guilt at abandoning Tolpuddle. And then there was Samson.

Sitting there wrapped in an emergency blanket, clutching a Peaks Patisserie box for some unknown reason. She'd seen him as soon as she'd turned the corner by the barn and she'd felt joy. Pure joy. Amidst all of the other feelings, that rude burst of happiness, which was so inappropriate in the circumstances, had threatened to overcome her.

She'd hidden it by ignoring him. Focusing on the things she needed to. Now she watched him, laughing with Will and the paramedic, his bare legs protruding incongruously from the foil around him.

'Glad you're not too badly scathed, Samson,' she said lightly, as she approached the men.

'I don't know about that,' said the paramedic with a wink. 'He rescued someone out of a burning caravan wearing only his boxers. But he won't let me check any higher than his knees to see if anything else got singed!'

'It better not have done,' said Samson. 'I've got two dates tonight!'

And the men started laughing even harder.

Delilah sat down beside this man who'd been absent from her life for fourteen years, yet in the space of fourteen days had turned the town and her world upside down. She let the laughter wash over her.

21

As Friday dawned on Bruncliffe, news of the previous day's events had spread right across the town. The breakfast table at Fellside Court was alive with chatter, Eric Bradley bringing the residents up to speed over their porridge with the latest news from his grandson in the police station. In the marketplace Elaine Bullock was opening up Peaks Patisserie, marvelling at the way the world worked, having been simultaneously sacked and hired in the aftermath of yesterday's adventures. Her old boss, Titch Harrison, was in a state, given the involvement of his brother in such terrible deeds, and had closed his cafe indefinitely as a result; her new boss, Lucy Metcalfe, was lying in hospital overcoming the effects of smoke inhalation and being drugged. None of it sounded like a typical Bruncliffe day.

On Back Street, the Fleece – ideally located opposite the very offices at the heart of the whole thing – already had its door open. Inside, Troy Murgatroyd was wiping down the bar and calculating his profits from what would be another busy day as his pub filled with locals eager to catch up on events. He was also wondering if the team's top dart player would be in a fit condition to compete in the upcoming match, given the state of his ribs.

Meanwhile, up on the fells, as the sky grew lighter and the day began, Seth Thistlethwaite walked alone, knowing that this morning he probably wouldn't be granted a glimpse of his former star pupil striding in the distance, that familiar grey shape shadowing her. But there would be other days. Especially now her secret was out and everyone knew she was running again.

With all the excitement, no one in the town – not even the children gathering in the school playground, who were staring across at the burnt ruins of the rugby club – was complaining about the last-minute cancellation of the Bonfire Night celebrations. After all, there'd been plenty of fireworks in the end.

As Ida Capstick wheeled her bicycle into the backyard of the dating agency offices that Friday morning an hour later than normal, she was no less gripped by the revelations of the day before than the rest of Bruncliffe. She'd heard the news first from Mrs Pettiford in the bank in the afternoon, as dispatches began to filter back to the town. She'd been cleaning the glass partition that separated cashier from customer, grumbling about greasy handprints and people breathing too much, when Mrs Pettiford had come rushing over to inform her that there'd been a fire up at High Laithe, the Metcalfe place. And that Samson O'Brien had saved Lucy Metcalfe's life by leaping out of an inferno in his boxer shorts, while carrying her and a cake.

Mrs Pettiford seemed most flustered at the idea of Bruncliffe's black sheep in his boxers – making Ida mutter enigmatically that they should be thankful that at least he'd been wearing them – while Ida was much more interested in the last snippet of information. Why had he been carrying a cake? But Mrs Pettiford hadn't been able to shed any more light on that.

Then Ida had gone over to the estate agent's to do a quick bit of cleaning and heard from Julie, the receptionist, that one of their agents was in hospital, having been caught up in the dreadful events and nearly killed. And by the way, added Julie, did Ida know that Samson O'Brien had jumped from the top of a blazing caravan in his boxer shorts with Lucy Metcalfe and a cake in his arms? Again, the young lady was far more interested in the man's attire – or lack of it – than in the absurd presence of the cake. It was the same all over town. Everyone talking about Samson's heroics and his semi-nudity, and no one asking about the blasted cake.

By the time she'd got home to George, Ida had enough news to keep the pair of them up all night. And enough of a puzzle in her mind to keep her awake when she finally did get to bed.

It was no wonder then that she entered the offices the following morning with a sense of anticipation. She pushed open the back door, walked through the kitchen and was about to shout up a warning, just to prevent a recurrence of the previous morning's mishap, when she smelled the most delicious of smells.

Bacon. Drifting down the stairs.

'Morning, Ida!' Samson was standing on the landing above – fully dressed, thank goodness – with a spatula in hand. 'Fancy a bacon butty?'

She didn't reprimand him for dripping grease on the

carpet. She just opened her mouth and said the first thing that was on her mind.

'Why was tha carrying a cake?'

'It's true then? Tha went back in for a cake?'

'It's hard to explain,' said Samson, sensing Ida Capstick's disapproval as she sat opposite, eating her bacon butty. He'd already given her a first-hand account of yesterday's events but, out of all the madness that had happened, Ida was only interested in the cake.

'I'd say! Bloody daft, if tha asks me. Must've been something special, that cake.'

'I don't know,' said Samson, thinking of the box still on his desk downstairs. 'I haven't opened it.'

She took another bite of her sandwich, shaking her head in amazement, and then nodded towards the frying pan on the hob. 'So what's with the bacon? Can I expect this every morning?'

Samson grinned. 'No, so don't go getting used to it,' he said. 'It was a gift. I found it hanging on the back door when I got home last night.'

'Mrs Hargreaves?'

He nodded. Prior to leaving High Laithe the day before, he'd phoned Mrs Hargreaves to tell her what had happened and, once back in town, showered and changed, he'd walked over to the marketplace to see her, Delilah accompanying him. A subdued Mr Hargreaves had let them in and led them to a small office behind the shop where his wife was already sitting, a pot of tea on the table before her and a plate of biscuits next to it.

'Thanks for calling me,' she'd said, eyes red from crying. 'I'd hate to have heard that news over the counter.'

'It was definitely Rob Harrison?' asked her husband.

Samson nodded. 'No question.'

His words seemed to deflate the man. He lowered himself into a chair. 'It just doesn't make sense,' he muttered, staring at the floor.

Mrs Hargreaves reached across and took his hand. 'I doubt death ever does,' she said. 'But at least we know Richard didn't . . . that he wouldn't have done that to us.'

They'd stayed and talked for a while longer and then, as Samson made to leave, Mrs Hargreaves had got to her feet and reached across to a bookcase filled with folders and files. She'd taken an envelope from the middle shelf and held it out.

'Here,' she said with a small smile. 'You told me you'd find out who did it, and you did. So there's a bonus in there.'

But Samson backed away, both hands held up. 'No. I can't. Not with how things turned out.'

'You earned it,' she'd said, pushing it towards him again.

He'd shaken his head. 'Not this time. And besides, I still owe you for years of free meat.'

She tutted at him, putting the envelope on the table. 'You'll never last in business at this rate, lad,' she'd said, wiping a tear from her eye.

'I can live with that,' he'd replied. Then Delilah and he had ridden out to the Aldersons' farm in Gayle to talk to two more bereaved parents. They'd returned to the office to find the bacon hanging on the back door.

'Aye,' said Ida, finishing off her butty. 'I heard tha turned down good brass from the Hargreaveses, all right.'

'Does that make me more of a fool than for rescuing the cake?' he asked with a grin.

She flashed a dark look at him and he decided it probably wasn't the best time to tell her that the Hargreaveses weren't the only ones whose money he'd turned down. Nor was he in a rush to inform her that the Aldersons had pressurised him into taking the little grey Ferguson in lieu, and that the very same tractor was on its way to her brother George's already-cramped barn.

'Here,' said Ida, picking a large reusable shopping bag up off the floor and thrusting it at him. 'Seeing as tha's staying a while, this is for tha dirty laundry. Leave it with me and I'll sort it.'

He began to protest, but she quietened him with a glare.

'If tha thinks I'm letting thee mucky that bathroom with soggy underpants dripping all over the place, tha can think again.'

'I'll use the launderette—'

'Pah! Waste of bloody money. Tha'll fill this bag and be done with it.'

He took the bag. 'But I'll have to pay you,' he said. 'The same as a service wash.'

She glared at him again. 'No need,' she snapped. 'I've taken on cleaning at Fellside Court. Happen as Rick Procter will be paying me enough to cover a bit of washing on the side.' Then her gaze softened and a twinkle danced in her eyes. 'Happen as tha'd appreciate him paying to have tha underpants washed!'

Samson burst into laughter which, even when his broken ribs started screaming, he didn't regret for an instant.

When Delilah opened the door of her office building an hour and a half later, she thought she could detect a lingering trace of bacon beneath the sharp scent of pine floor polish. But Samson gave her no time to investigate further, turning her round and marching her back out of the door.

'We were supposed to be at the police station ten minutes ago,' he said as he hustled her towards the marketplace, walking as fast as his injuries would permit.

'I'm sure your new friend Gavin won't mind us being a bit late,' she teased.

He grinned, his face a patchwork of scratches and cuts. 'Sergeant Clayton to you. Want to bet on him having doughnuts for us?'

Delilah laughed. 'I'm still reeling from his about-face yesterday.'

'You and me both,' muttered Samson.

In the bleak atmosphere that had greeted the return of the mountain rescue team to High Laithe the day before, Rob Harrison's body carried on a covered stretcher between them, Samson had found himself standing next to Sergeant Clayton. The policeman, as shaken as those around him – many of whom were well acquainted with the stonemason, and so doubly stunned by his death and the revelations about what he'd done – had turned to Samson and offered him an apology. Swaddled in a foil blanket and staring at the smouldering remains of the caravan, Samson hadn't been in the best frame of mind to accept. But Delilah had taken pity on the shamefaced sergeant.

'I don't think anyone would have believed what Rob Harrison was up to,' she'd said. 'I mean, even we didn't really want to accept that someone was targeting the dating agency clients.'

The policeman had looked grateful. Then he'd invited them to come down to the police station to talk, managing to make it sound like a favour rather than a summons. Still, Samson was looking forward to it being over.

They crossed the marketplace, walked past Peaks Patisserie where a hassled Elaine was working hard inside, and turned the corner onto Church Street. Straight away it was clear that something momentous had happened in the town. For unlike the previous times Samson had been there, the old Victorian police station was buzzing.

Several official cars were parked outside, police in plain clothes were coming and going, and when Samson and Delilah entered the reception area, Sergeant Clayton emerged against a background of ringing phones, looking like a man used to sailing calm seas who'd suddenly found himself in the centre of a maelstrom.

'It's manic!' he said, escorting them into the back office. 'I'm understaffed for something of this magnitude. But at least I've got the two men back from the hospital, now that we know Harry Furness and Stuart Lister are no longer under threat.'

'How are they?' asked Samson as he copied Delilah in taking a seat before a desk piled with paperwork.

'Both are doing well. Stuart had an operation on his left leg yesterday, so he'll be in a while longer, but Harry should be released later today. He came round about an hour after all that commotion up at High Laithe and was able to shed a bit more light on the day's events.'

'In what way?'

'He identified Rob Harrison as the man who attacked him.'

'He actually saw Rob?'

Sergeant Clayton nodded. 'According to the statement he gave Constable Bradley, he went out into the entrance-way of the club and saw someone coming in. He thought it was you, but it wasn't. It was Rob. Then he was hit over the head and remembers nothing else.' The policeman looked grave. 'It shows how ruthless Rob Harrison was. He didn't care about being seen, because he didn't expect his victims to survive. Harry and Stuart were very lucky.'

'Or unlucky, depending on how you look at it,' said Delilah, feeling guilty all over again.

The door opened and Danny Bradley came in, carrying a tray of tea and a plate piled high with doughnuts. Delilah put a hand over her mouth to hide her smile.

'Thanks, Danny,' said Sergeant Clayton. 'You missed all the action while you were over at the hospital yesterday.'

'Action, Sarge?' asked Danny, face innocent.

'Turns out we had a murderer on the loose. Who'd have thought it? In Bruncliffe, of all places. You won't be wanting to leave us for the Met now, will you?'

Danny winked at Samson and Delilah from behind his boss's back.

'Tell you what, lad, pull up a chair and you can take the notes. Give you your first taste of a murder investigation.'

Sergeant Clayton extracted a notepad from the mountain of paper on the desk and passed it to the young constable with a pen. 'Right, then. Where's the best place to start?'

It took them over an hour. To explain about the Speedy Date nights. To describe how their suspicions had come about. To justify why they hadn't come forward earlier. And to outline their theories as to how the murders had been carried out. All the while, Danny Bradley made notes and Sergeant Clayton listened with growing astonishment.

'So you're telling me Rob Harrison was killing these men because they tried to date Lucy Metcalfe?' he finally asked, eyes wide with disbelief.

Delilah nodded.

'Bugger me! That'd put you off dating for a while. What was he – jealous or something?'

'I don't think it was that simple,' said Delilah. 'Rob served with Ryan out in Iraq and he'd been something of a mentor for him. Then he quit the army and, a couple of years later, Ryan gets killed in Afghanistan. I think Rob was left feeling responsible for looking after Lucy. And maybe even guilty that he'd survived and Ryan hadn't.'

'So when Lucy started getting attention from other men, he felt it was his place to stop it,' said the sergeant. 'Some twisted version of loyalty to Ryan.'

Delilah shrugged. 'Something like that. Although I doubt we'll ever know the whole truth of it.' She thought about the stricken look on the stonemason's face as the caravan had exploded. And the fact that he'd fallen to his death without so much as a scream.

'But you reckon it was premeditated enough that Harrison turned round the CCTV camera at the Old Station?'

'Worse than that. He killed a sheep to use as bait for Tom Alderson,' said Samson. 'And when I spoke to Bill Alderson yesterday, he told me Rob had worked on the farm repairing the stone wall next to the barn where the quad bike was kept.'

'What are you suggesting? That he checked out the bike while he was there?' The sergeant looked unconvinced. 'That'd be a hell of a coincidence. The wall falling down and him getting the call to fix it.'

Samson shook his head. 'Ask the Aldersons. You'll probably find that the wall fell down suddenly and Rob turned up just at the right moment.'

'You mean he knocked it down so he could work there?'

'So he could check out the bike. Like I said, the man was thorough, so I wouldn't put any of that past him.'

'He was thorough all right,' conceded Sergeant Clayton. 'We found a laptop in his van with a Hotmail account on it under the name of Dr Howson. That's how he set up the viewing that nearly cost Stuart Lister his life.'

'Then he claimed a shoulder injury to get him out of the darts match . . .'

'Which left him free to try to kill Stuart.' Delilah shuddered. 'Are you going to carry out a full investigation?'

The sergeant nodded. 'We're hoping to discover enough up at High Laithe and at Harrison's place to tie him to all of the deaths,' he said. 'We've already recovered a section of pipe with blood on it, which we think is the weapon that was used to knock Harry Furness out. Plus a roll of gaffer tape which could have been used to hold open the throttle on Tom's quad bike. Forensics are heading out to the Alderson farm to see if they can gather any fibres off the bike, so we can do a comparison.

'Then there's the empty jerrycan of petrol of course, which is pretty damning; and we found Lucy's car tucked out of sight behind the barn, so that might provide more evidence. I've also got men checking the stolen tractor that was used in the attack on Stuart Lister for fingerprints, in the hope Harrison got careless. But we don't have much to go on for the deaths of Richard Hargreaves or Martin Foster.'

'It's probably worth going over the CCTV footage from the Old Station again,' said Samson, glancing over at Constable Bradley with a discreet wink. 'You never know, something might turn up that points the finger of suspicion Rob's way.'

Danny cleared his throat. 'I'm happy to do that, Sarge,' he said, face completely straight.

'Good lad,' said his sergeant.

'And maybe you could try soil analysis in Martin Foster's case,' said Delilah. 'I'm sure Elaine Bullock will be able to tell you if there's any substance unique to Gordale Scar, where Martin was killed. If that could be matched to something on Rob Harrison's shoes . . .'

'Crikey, Delilah!' Sergeant Clayton raised his eyebrows in amusement. 'You want to watch it. O'Brien's turning you into a proper detective.'

Delilah blushed.

'But what I can't understand,' continued the sergeant,

'is how Harrison knew who'd tried to contact Lucy through the dating website.'

Delilah was about to speak when Samson interrupted. 'He used to sneak a look at Nathan's phone. Whenever the kid was around, which was a lot, Rob would make some excuse to borrow his mobile and he'd check the dating app.'

'You mean, this app that Nathan had rigged to stop his mother getting any date notifications? Harrison got the men's names off that?'

'Exactly.' Samson could feel the weight of Delilah's stare, but he didn't look at her. 'And he told me up at the caravan yesterday that when he heard the lad was going away for a few days and leaving the mobile behind, he seized the opportunity and stole it.'

'So he could monitor the app in Nathan's absence? Which is how Stuart Lister and Harry Furness were attacked.' Sergeant Clayton scratched his head while Delilah studied her nails, which she was suddenly fascinated by.

'Makes sense, I suppose,' said the sergeant, sitting back in his chair. 'Right, I think that'll do us for now. If we have any questions, we know where to find you.' And with a flourish, he pulled Samson's business card out of a drawer and placed it on his desk. 'Good to have you around, O'Brien,' he said, holding out a hand.

Samson smiled, shook hands and followed Delilah out of the station. She waited until they were across the road before accosting him.

'Why did you lie?' she asked, pausing on the corner of the marketplace.

'About what?'

She elbowed him and he groaned. 'Sorry, I forgot about your ribs,' she said. 'But you know what I mean. Why did you say Rob stole Nathan's phone?'

'Because, Delilah, that's what Rob told me.' He stared at her and then looked away. 'Nathan's fourteen. He's lost his dad. He's worried about his mother moving on, and losing the memory of his father. So he tries to stop it by changing her online dating account. And in his misery, he talks to the man who's always up at the caravan. The man who seems to understand his concerns. But that man takes the information and decides to go one step further, by killing the men trying to date Nathan's mother.' Samson shook his head. 'No one should have to carry the guilt for the actions of someone that deranged. Even if Nathan left his phone with Rob, it was done simply to prevent any contact with Lucy getting through. Not for the purposes it was used for.'

He looked back at Delilah. 'So, like I said. Rob told me he stole Nathan's phone from the caravan. And I defy anyone to prove that he didn't.'

Delilah held his gaze and then she smiled and slipped her arm carefully through his, mindful of his bandaged sides.

'Miss Metcalfe,' said Samson with a wicked grin, 'are you aware that you're linking arms with the black sheep of Bruncliffe? And in such a public place?'

She nodded, head held high. 'Yes, I am. And I defy anyone to say anything about it.'

He laughed and they walked back to the office, turning quite a few heads as they went.

*

By late morning they were still turning heads as they walked along the sterile corridors of the hospital. This time, however, it was Samson that was the cause, nurses staring as he passed, his face peppered with cuts and his gait stiffened by his broken ribs. Not all of the attention was from a purely clinical perspective, Delilah noted wryly, as yet another young member of staff flashed him a warm smile.

'Who knew the maimed look could be so appealing?' she remarked, subconsciously lengthening her stride.

Samson grinned, matching her step-for-step, despite the twinges in his side. 'It's not my fault if the female species is naturally attracted to men of action — Oof!' He doubled over as the box Delilah was carrying caught him in the stomach.

'You can carry your own cake, Mr Action Man,' she muttered with a dark look. 'And if you like all this medical attention, I can easily arrange for you to have that spare bed next to Stuart Lister.'

She gestured back in the direction of the side ward they had just left after visiting the hapless estate agent. Badly bruised and with his left leg in a cast following his operation, Stuart had looked even more delicate than normal. But he'd been in good spirits, and when Delilah had expressed regret for placing him inadvertently in harm's way, he'd brushed aside her apologies. Instead, to Samson's astonishment, he'd asked shyly if she could sign him up for the Christmas Speedy Date night.

Shaking his head at the foolhardiness of youth – and the quicksilver temper of the woman now stalking down the corridor ahead of him – Samson resumed walking.

When he turned a corner and heard loud laughter, Delilah waiting for him at an open door, he froze.

'They won't bite,' Delilah murmured, reading his thoughts.

'I'm not so sure,' he muttered. Holding the cake box in front of him like a shield, he stepped into the doorway.

The room was full of Metcalfes.

Lucy Metcalfe was propped up in bed, dark-blonde hair tied back, features pale and smudges of exhaustion under her eyes. But at least those eyes were clear and alert, free of the drugs Rob Harrison had given her the day before.

Gathered around the bed were her family. Nathan was sitting at the top end, looking every bit as pale as his mother; her parents were next to him; Peggy and Ted Metcalfe were sitting opposite; Will and Ash were standing behind them; and Harry Furness, dressed and ready to be discharged with only a white bandage around his head as proof of his ordeal, was perched on the foot of the bed, saying something that had them all laughing.

'My hero!' said Lucy, spotting Samson on the threshold, a huge smile lighting up her face.

'And he's brought the cake!' said Harry, making the room dissolve into laughter again.

'Morning, all,' said Samson, passing the box to Lucy, the card that he'd rescued on top of it. 'Good to see everyone in such fine spirits.'

'Morning, Samson,' said Lucy, pulling him down into a hug as he bent to greet her. 'Thank you,' she whispered, holding onto him fiercely. 'You saved my life. And you too, Delilah!'

Samson blushed, straightening up and stepping back to stand next to Harry. 'Not sure about that. Will and Nathan were there, too.'

'Aye, but they wouldn't have done it in such style,' said Harry, grinning. 'Underpants and no cape. You're a regular superhero now, lad!'

'He's already had the *Craven Herald* calling,' said Delilah, enjoying Samson's discomfort. 'And *Look North* have asked him to go on TV tonight.'

'Are you going to do it?' asked Ash.

Samson glowered at him. 'Not bloody likely.'

'It could be good for business,' said Harry, only half-joking.

'Good for business?' Samson laughed. 'I don't need the TV for that. My phone hasn't stopped ringing all morning. You'd be surprised how many people in Bruncliffe suddenly need a detective.'

'Especially one who looks so good in boxers,' said Delilah dryly.

Samson grinned. 'I can't help it if word's got round.'

'What about you, Delilah?' asked Lucy, concern clouding her face. 'Won't all this have an impact on the Dales Dating Agency?'

Delilah shrugged. 'It's too early to tell. Although that didn't stop Uncle Woolly from calling me from the bank this morning, anxious that another Bruncliffe enterprise might be about to meet its demise. Thankfully I was able to reassure him that the next Speedy Date night is almost full. I suppose if people don't like the connection to what happened, I'll start to get cancellations. But so far, there haven't been any. In fact I had two messages on my phone this morning from people wanting to join.'

Ash shook his head. 'As Seth would say, there's nowt so queer as folk!'

'Enough about business,' said Will, pointing at the soot-stained box on the bed, which was looking slightly crushed around the edges, its ribbon bedraggled and torn. 'What's so special about that cake?'

'Yeah,' said Samson, looking at Lucy. 'You were begging me not to forget it. Thought you weren't going to leave without it, at one point. Why was it so important?'

Lucy looked shamefaced. 'I don't know. I was out of my mind having all sorts of hallucinations, and in all of that delirium, it was the only lucid thought I had. Save the cake.' She shrugged, unsure how to tell them that, in her befuddled state, the cake had become synonymous with her son and she'd been paralysed with fear at the thought of abandoning it. 'Here,' she said, pushing the box towards Nathan. 'I made it for you coming home, love. To celebrate your Duke of Edinburgh Award adventure.'

Nathan glanced down at the box and then up at his mother, blinking away tears. Then he ripped off the paper, lifted the lid and they all craned forward.

'Damn!' said Samson. For he was staring down at something that had once resembled a cake – before it had been catapulted through the air and back to earth with a tremendous jolt. Now it was a squashed slab of green sponge with a blue streak in the middle, and cream oozing out of the side. But still, despite all the trauma, perched atop this misshapen creation was a perfect ridge tent, a small figure lying in it with his hands behind his head.

'It was supposed to be a tent by a mountain stream,' said Lucy, with a rueful smile. 'And that's you.'

'It's brilliant, Mum,' said Nathan, voice hoarse. 'Thanks.'

Lucy nodded and reached her hand out to her boy. 'And guess what,' she said, pulling him close and striving for a lighter note. 'Now we don't have the caravan, there are no more excuses for not getting the barn finished. With a bit of luck, you might have a proper bedroom by Christmas. But there'll be some rough living before that, as we'll be camping out in there to start with.'

'I don't mind where we live,' Nathan muttered. 'As long as you're okay.'

'I'll sort the barn out, Lucy,' said Ash. 'I've got a few favours I can call in and I'll work weekends on it. Will can help when he's free, can't you, big brother?' Will was already nodding in agreement. 'And Samson? You game to pitch in with some free labour?'

'Not totally free,' protested Lucy. 'I can pay. And I make a mean lunch!'

Samson grinned. 'You had me at lunch,' he said, choosing to ignore the frown that had darkened Will Metcalfe's brow.

'Talking of food,' said Ash. 'Anyone got something for cutting that cake? I'm starving.'

'Here.' Delilah passed her brother a knife and a pack of paper plates. 'Thought I might get a taste if I brought these.'

'Seeing as I risked my life for it, I reckon I deserve a bit more than a taste,' said Samson. 'In fact, make mine the biggest slice, Ash.'

'Seeing as Harry and I nearly died yesterday, I reckon *we* get the biggest slices,' countered Lucy.

But Harry was shaking his head. 'None for me,' he said, regret in his eyes. 'I'm watching my weight.'

'As of when?' asked Ash.

'As of a certain person paying him a visit yesterday evening,' said Delilah with a knowing wink, making Harry squirm.

'Who came to see you?' demanded Ash, and the auctioneer began to blush.

'Sarah Mitchell,' he said.

'What? From the Speedy Date night?' asked Samson. 'How did she know you were here?'

'Beats me.'

Delilah held back a smile. It hadn't taken much. In a small attempt to make amends for all the lives that had been manipulated and upset by the actions of Rob Harrison, she'd spent a bit of time on the dating agency website when she got back to the office the day before. As a result, Hannah Wilson – the flame-haired librarian who'd been briefly cast in the role of chief suspect, thanks in part to what had transpired to be an innocent trip to the school with the mobile library – would have received a flurry of date requests, all delivered a few days late with apologies for a glitch in the Dales Dating Agency app. Hopefully that would compensate for Samson cancelling their date.

Likewise, Delilah had accessed Sarah Mitchell's data from the last Speedy Date night and had been overjoyed to see there was a direct match: someone who'd tried to contact the ecologist was the one person she herself had singled out for a follow-up date.

Drawing back the strings on her bow, Delilah had played Cupid and made it happen. After breaking the news that Samson would not be able to make the planned rendezvous in the Coach and Horses, she'd given Sarah directions to the hospital instead. Judging by the smile spreading across Harry's ruddy face, he hadn't objected.

'She brought him an otter,' said Lucy, contributing to the red streak staining Harry's cheeks.

'An otter? A real one?' Samson glanced at the auction-eer in amazement.

'No, a bloody toy one. Honestly, this place,' Harry Furness moaned, pulling a cuddly otter out of his pocket to great mirth. 'You just can't keep a secret!'

Under the cover of the laughter, Will Metcalfe headed for the door.

'You off, Will?' asked Ash.

Will nodded. 'Work to do.' He paused and held out his hand to Samson. 'Thanks again,' he said brusquely. With a wave at the rest of the room, he left as the arguments over the cake resumed.

'Wow,' murmured Delilah so only Samson could hear. 'You've won him over. Wonders will never cease.'

'I wouldn't be so sure,' said Samson, aware of the hesi-tation in the older Metcalfe's farewell.

And he was right. For Will Metcalfe was walking along the hospital corridor thinking about Samson O'Brien. Thinking about the debt the Metcalfe family owed the man. But also thinking about his past. A past that Rick Procter had assured him was about to come back and haunt them all.

If there had been hesitation in that handshake, it was

because he didn't trust Samson O'Brien. Not for fourteen years. And not now.

It was gone lunchtime when Samson and Delilah left Lucy's ward. Flagging from the long morning and the pain in his ribs, Samson was glad that he'd caved in to Delilah's insistence that she drive them to the hospital, having borrowed her mother's car for the day. He was barely able to put one foot in front of the other, let alone ride his bike back to Bruncliffe.

'Do you want me to drop you in Hellifield?' Delilah asked as they walked down the corridor.

He was so tired he almost asked her why he'd want to go to Hellifield. Then he remembered. The subterfuge. 'Actually, the office would be better,' he said. 'I've got a bit of work to —'

'Samson!' A voice from behind made them turn and Nathan came running towards them.

'I'll wait by the main entrance,' said Delilah, guessing this would be a private conversation. She walked off, leaving Samson and her nephew in the corridor.

He was tall, Samson noticed, surprised to see that his godson was almost the same height as he was. In their two brief interactions – once up at the caravan, when Nathan had stormed off; and then yesterday, when his shocked face had been on the other side of the flames – Samson hadn't had a chance to have a good look at the lad. Now as Nathan glanced out from under his thick fair hair, Samson was struck again by the boy's likeness to his father.

'I wanted to thank you,' the lad said, eyes cast on the floor.

'I only did what anyone else would have,' said Samson. 'If Will had been there instead of me, he'd have got your mum out of the caravan just the same.'

Nathan nodded, then bit his lip. 'But he wouldn't have lied.'

'Lied?'

The lad stared at him. 'You lied. About how Rob knew who those men were. About him stealing my phone.'

'Ah. That.'

Nathan looked back down at the floor. 'I told Mum. About changing the account. She started crying, apologising for rushing things.' He gulped. 'I feel so bad. All those people – I only told Rob about it because he seemed to care. I didn't think he would . . .'

His shoulders heaved and Samson put out an arm and drew his godson towards him.

'It's okay, son,' he said as the lad broke down. 'No one can blame you for that. Rob Harrison was troubled. He was carrying a lot of guilt all of his own. And in the end, that's what made him do what he did. You had nothing to do with it. Okay?'

He felt the lad nod against his chest.

'As for your phone, Rob told me he stole it, so that's what happened. It's in a police report with my signature at the bottom. So if you go saying any different, I'll get in trouble. Understand?' He eased the boy back to see his face, the tracks of fresh tears on his cheeks.

'Thanks,' muttered Nathan, wiping his eyes with a sleeve. 'For everything.'

Samson thought about the fourteen years he'd been absent, the last two of them especially. 'I'm not much of a godfather, am I?' he said.

Nathan looked out from under his fringe, the beginnings of a smile tweaking his lips. 'You have your uses,' he said. 'All the girls at school want to know me, now they've heard about you in your boxers.'

Samson laughed and pulled Nathan back into a hug, not caring how much his ribs were hurting.

'Are you going to be okay riding back to Hellifield?' asked Delilah as she pulled up outside the offices and noticed Samson wincing in pain when he opened the passenger door.

'Hellifield? Oh . . . yes. I'll be fine. I'll take it easy.' He smiled at her, fingers crossed behind his back, before easing his legs onto the pavement and gently hauling himself out of the car. He'd already ascertained that Delilah was picking Tolpuddle up that afternoon and was heading straight home. With the office building to himself, Samson was planning nothing more strenuous than a mid-afternoon snooze.

'Okay. I'll see you Monday, then. Oh, and can you let me know how much I owe you for your sterling detective work?' She said it so breezily, but he caught the shadow of worry in her eyes at the mention of payment.

'I've been thinking about that,' he said, leaning on the car door. 'How about we simply add on another month to my tenancy and call it quits?'

She blinked, eyes flicking to the gold letters spanning the downstairs window. 'Are you sure?' she asked.

He nodded.

Lower lip trapped between her teeth, she looked back at the office again and then at Samson. 'Well, if that's all right with you . . .'

'More than all right. We can sort it out on Monday.'

'Thanks. Have a peaceful weekend.' She smiled brightly and he could sense the relief flooding through her. Then she paused, took a deep breath and leaned across the passenger seat, tone casual as she looked up at him on the pavement. 'Why don't you come to the farm for lunch on Sunday?' she asked. 'We're all gathering to celebrate Lucy's lucky escape. Even Craig and Chris are coming home. You'd be more than welcome.'

His reaction was instinctive. 'I'll see,' he said.

She gave a soft laugh, as though it was the reply she'd been expecting. 'So that's not a no?'

He grinned. 'It's not a no.' He closed the car door and watched her drive away.

He stood there for a while, thinking about Bruncliffe, the Metcalfes, Delilah, and how things had changed in the last fourteen days. He'd gone from being knocked out cold to being invited to Sunday lunch. And rather than being run out of town, judging by the number of calls coming in he was going to have enough work – and money – to last him the six months he planned on staying. As for that seventh month of rent he'd just negotiated – he had no intention of using it. He would be back in his adopted city by then.

Across the road, Seth Thistlethwaite was in the window of the Fleece, enjoying his lunchtime pint. The old man threw an arm up in greeting and Samson waved in response.

Was it really so bad being back? he wondered. Perhaps he shouldn't be in such a rush to return to London once everything was sorted, and instead should consider settling here. Take the time needed to get Twistleton Farm back and make Bruncliffe home again.

Slightly stunned by this unexpected rush of affection for his home town, he turned and entered the office building and his phone began to ring. When he saw the caller's name, his heart started thumping. It was the call he'd been waiting for.

'Boss?' he said, perching on the edge of his desk.

'Samson. There have been some developments.'

'And?'

'Sorry, son, but there's going to have to be an investigation. Things are going to get dirty. I won't be able to keep a lid on it.'

Samson clutched the mobile, knuckles white. 'Is there no other way?'

'I'm sorry. I've tried. We're going to have to let it run its course now. It'll be at least six months before we know the outcome.'

'What if I came back down? Tried to find proof—?'

'Don't be mad! You'd be putting yourself in danger again. Stay where you are. And keep a low profile. That way they won't find you. In the meantime, I'll keep doing all I can. We'll resolve this one way or the other.'

'If you're sure . . .'

'I'm sure. Take care.'

The line clicked dead before Samson had a chance to

thank him. He stared at the desk, the peeling lino, the red-flocked wallpaper and the pub beyond the window. And he cursed himself.

Who was he kidding? He couldn't make a life here. Not now, and not in the future. Because when his past caught up with him, the people who'd been making him welcome today would be queuing up to chase him out of Bruncliffe. So there was simply no point in trying.

Epilogue

'Delilah, sit down, child. Dinner is on the table.' Peggy Metcalfe's voice carried across the large room filled with people and brought her daughter's attention from the window.

'Coming, Mum.'

'Who you watching for anyway, Dee?' teased Ash. 'Father Christmas?'

Everyone laughed and Delilah pulled a face at him, to the delight of the kids.

Sunday lunch. It had been a tradition for as long as she could remember. All of them gathered around the big kitchen table, while Dad carved the beef and Ryan tried to steal an extra Yorkshire pudding. There were more of them now: Will's wife and kids, plus Lucy and Nathan. There was also one missing. But today, for the first time in two years, that absence didn't hang over them like a pall of black smoke. Instead, there was laughter. Even Will's mood lightened as he cracked jokes with his younger brothers.

It was perfect. And Samson would fit right in.

With a last look down the track, Delilah turned from the window and took her place at the far end of the table. He was late. If he was coming.

*

Chapman

Samson stood outside, clutching a bottle and a box of chocolates. He was nervous. Hesitant about getting this wrong. Anxious to get it right.

He took a step forward and stopped, the clink of china coming to him through the door. They'd already started. He was late. On the verge of turning round and heading home, he heard a burst of laughter.

'It'll be fine,' he chided himself. 'Just get yourself in there.'

He pushed open the door and walked in.

'Hope I'm not too late?' he said.

'Samson!' A hail of voices greeted him and he found himself being ushered to a chair.

Delilah heard it first. A vehicle pulling up. The snick of the latch on the outside door. Then the kitchen door was opening and she was smiling in anticipation. He'd made it.

'Hope I'm not too late?'

But as the man stepped into the room, Delilah felt the smile slip from her face.

'Rick!' Peggy Metcalfe was up out of her chair and offering her cheek. 'How lovely to see you!'

'I couldn't resist Will's invitation. Good food and great company – what's not to like?' said the property developer with easy charm, greeting everyone in the room as Peggy set a place next to Delilah.

'Not who you were expecting, sis?' asked Will quietly, his focus on her alone.

'I wasn't expecting anyone,' she muttered.

Will nodded. 'Best keep it that way. Less chance of being hurt a second time.'

Then Rick Procter was taking his seat next to her and she was left making small talk and trying not to show the disappointment that was swelling in her heart.

'So glad you could make it, son.' Joseph O'Brien leaned towards Samson and laid a hand on his knee. 'It means the world to me.'

Samson nodded. 'Sorry it took me so long,' he said, thinking of all the Sunday lunches his father had eaten alone. And as he sat there among the residents of Fellside Court and did his best to answer all their questions about the events of the last few weeks, Samson O'Brien tried not to think that, in six months' time, he would be missing from his father's table once more.

Acknowledgements

One of the many fascinating features of writing a novel is the research and where it takes you. Another amazing aspect is how willing people are to help you on that journey. For this, the first in a series of books set in the Dales, I had recourse to a wide variety of experts. All of them gave their time willingly and their advice freely. Hopefully I have used both wisely – if not, the blame lies entirely with me! Therefore, I owe the following a strong cup of Dales tea and a fat rascal:

Dr Matthew Townend for answering my questions about Dales place names and for sharing his passion for Viking Yorkshire; Ruth and Gary Cobb of Mosside Kennels, experts in all things Weimaraner who happily welcomed me in and introduced me to their beautiful 'girls'; David Carpenter and Curtis Parkyn, both involved in the world of the police and both generous with their time and knowledge; Elizabeth and Dave Booth who answered my naive questions about farming life and fed me wonderful cake too!; Isabel Price, my neighbour and friend, who encourages my interest in sheep and is always happy to share her experiences of life in the Dales; Dorothy and Alan Hemsworth, for introducing me to some fine Yorkshire writing and for the glimpse of a sunburnished crag that would inspire the name of Bruncliffe; Jane Marshall and Julia Murfin for odd questions about odd

Acknowledgements

things like ginnels and fell running . . . ; my ever-supportive family who have proven themselves to be stellar first-readers and superb sounding boards; the brilliant team at Pan Macmillan, especially Catherine for her enthusiasm for the Dales Detective and, most of all, Tolpuddle!; my agent, Oli, who threw an idea at me on a wet October day – yes, Oli, this is all your fault; and finally, to Mark and our much-missed Tomate, who sat by my side as I wrote this one – thanks both of you for keeping me balanced. Even if it doesn't always seem that way.